The Resisters

The Resisters

A NOVEL

Gish Jen

ALFRED A. KNOPF   NEW YORK   2020

THIS IS A BORZOI BOOK
PUBLISHED BY ALFRED A. KNOPF

Copyright © 2020 by Gish Jen

www.aaknopf.com

Library of Congress Cataloging-in-Publication Data
Names: Jen, Gish, author.
Title: The resisters : a novel / by Gish Jen.
Description: First Edition. | New York : Alfred A. Knopf, 2020.
Identifiers: LCCN 2019004308 (print) | LCCN 2019006477 (ebook) | ISBN
9781984898227 (ebook) | ISBN 9780525657217
Subjects: | GSAFD: Science fiction. | Fantasy fiction.
Classification: LCC PS3560.E474 (ebook) | LCC PS3560.E474 R47 2020 (print) |
DDC 813/.54—dc23
LC record available at https://lccn.loc.gov/2019004308

Jacket image based on a photograph by ballyscanlon/Getty Images
Jacket design by Kelly Blair

Manufactured in the United States of America
First Edition

For all the Eleanors I know

Let us have faith that right makes might.

—ABRAHAM LINCOLN

If you don't know where you are going,
you might wind up someplace else.

—YOGI BERRA

Contents

PART I

A Girl with a Golden Arm

As her parents, Eleanor and I should have known earlier. But Gwen was a preemie, to begin with. That meant oxygen at first and, after that, special checkups. And her early months were bumpy. She had jaundice; she had roseola; she had colic. She had a heart murmur. Things that I can now see distracted us—especially with the One Chance Policy, we were focused on her health to the exclusion of all else. For the Netted, it was different, of course, but for us Surplus, the limit was one pregnancy per couple, and Eleanor was just out of jail. Outside the house, she had a DroneMinder tracking her every move; the message was clear. She was not getting away with anything.

And in any case, we loved Gwen and would never have wanted to replace her, worried though we were that she was delicate—that she might never consume the way she needed to, the way we all needed to. Not that charges of underconsumption couldn't be fought in the courts. This was AutoAmerica, after all. For all the changes wrought by AI and Automation—now rolled up with the internet into the iBurrito we called Aunt Nettie—we did still have a Constitution. And if anyone could defend what was left of our rights, it was our own fierce Eleanor, of whom even the platoons of Canada geese who patrolled our neighborhood—the pit bulls, one might say, of the waddling world—were afraid. But as Eleanor's incarceration brought home, these battles had a price, and in the meanwhile, even worrying and weighing the options distracted us from realizing other things—things we might have noticed a bit earlier, had Gwen had a sibling. It is so hard for a new parent to imagine a child any different from the one he or she has—children do so have their own gravity. They are their own normal.

And so it is only now that we can see there were signs. All children take what's in their crib and throw it, for example. It is universal. But Gwen threw her stuffed animals straight through her bedroom doorway. They shot out, never so much as grazing the door frame, and they always hit the wall of the staircase across from her bedroom at a certain spot, with the precise force they needed to bounce forward and drop clean down to the bottom of the stairwell. Was she maybe two when she did this? Not even, although she was already a southpaw. And already she seemed to have unusually long arms and long fingers—or so I remember remarking one day, not that Eleanor and I had so many babies on which to base our comparison. Ours was just an impression. But it was a strong impression. Her fingers were long. I remember, too, having to round up a veritable menagerie on the landing before I could start up the stairs. The stuffed hippo, the stuffed tiger, the three or four stuffed dogs, the stuffed orca and toucan and platypus and turtle—I gathered them all into my arms like the storybook zookeeper of some peaceable kingdom. It was as if I, too, ought by rights to have been made of plush. Of course, our house was automated—as all Surplus houses were required to be, by law—and the animals could easily have been clear-floated. All I had to do was say the word and the HouseBots would emerge from their closets, their green appendages poised to help. *Clear-*

4

float now? Aren't those animals in your way? And, *We can roll'n'clear if you'd prefer. You have a choice. You always have a choice*—the choice business being a new feature of the program. A bit of cyber-ingratiation, you might say, to balance its more habitual cyber-intimidation. *If you trip, it will be your own fault,* for example. And, *Do note that your choice is on the record. Nothing is being hidden from you. Your choice is on the record.* Meaning that I was losing Living Points every time—Living Points being something like what we used to call brownie points when I was growing up, except that these were more critical than money for everything from getting a loan to getting a plane ticket to getting Gwen into Net U one day, should we dream of doing that—a goal that people said involved tens of thousands, or maybe even hundreds of thousands, of points.

But I picked the animals up myself anyway—as did Eleanor, when it was she who came upon them, her silver hair and black eyes shining—and all because we wanted to dump the animals into Gwen's crib ourselves and hear her quick cresting laughter as she immediately set about hurling them again. Everything was a game to her, a most wonderful, loving, endless game. Her spy-eyes lit up with mischief; her tea-brown cheeks flushed the hot orange pink you see on the underside of clouds at sunset. Often she laughed so hard, she fell as she threw—plopping down on her soft bottom but grabbing the crib rails so hard as she scrambled back up that the whole crib shook. Was this the delicate newborn we had once so anxiously tended? Now breathtakingly robust—indestructible, it seemed—she wore an old-time soft yellow blanket sleeper with attached feet and bunny ears, a hand-knit, extra-warm version of a suit Eleanor remembered from her own childhood. None of this baby-zone heating over Gwen's crib, in other words. She hardly seemed to need zone-heat in any case, having learned so early to blow on her hands if they were cold and to cuddle with us, if she needed to, for warmth. Indeed, we were all given to cuddling, and we all wore sweaters, too, to avoid turning on the zone-heat, for which we were constantly house-scolded. *Don't you find it a bit chilly? Why not choose to turn on the zone-heat? You'll be more comfortable—Eleanor, especially. Don't you find it a bit chilly?*

But we ignored it. For this was how the AutoHouse started, wasn't it, with thermostats that sent to Aunt Nettie first data, then videos? Then came DroneDeliverers and FridgeStockers, KidTrackers and RoboSitters, ElderHelpers and YardBots, all of which reported to Aunt Nettie as dutifully as any spy network—recording our steps, our pictures, our relationships, and (back when we soon-to-be-Surplus still had them) our careers. And she, in turn, took what she knew and applied it—even proffering, along the way, solace and advice. Indeed, in the early days of Automation, I myself brought up AskAuntNettie more often than I care to recall and can still remember her consoling voice as she volunteered *I'm here* and insisted *I want to hear everything* and reassured me *Of course you feel that way, Grant, how could you not? You're only human.*

I did laugh at that *You're only human.*

Still I found not only that part of me responded to the words, but that it responded deeply, that it listened gratefully as Aunt Nettie advanced some surprisingly useful advice on a range of subjects, including the many—I hadn't realized how many—for which noble Eleanor had no time. Would someone like me, whose mother had had him with WhoNeedsThemMen, have trouble knowing how to be a father, for example? The answer to which was that, given what men could be, I might in fact be better off without a role model anyway. Or how about: Did someone like me really need to own both black and brown shoes now that I was no longer teaching? The answer to which was yes, if I cared about social acceptance, which yes, my data showed that I did, underneath, and which, really, was just as well—correlated as such concern was with mental health, especially among Unretrainables such as, yes, she had heard I now was.

Today Aunt Nettie would no doubt use the term "Surplus"—"Unretrainables" having been aggregated with "Unemployables" such as the elderly for the purposes of administering our Basic Incomes. But Unretrainables were in fact different. Unretrainables were people like me, with discontinued professions. Factory workers, drivers, and customer service representatives, in the beginning—joined, as Aunt Nettie evolved from tool to aide to master by assorted doctors, lawyers, teachers, accountants. Professors. Programmers. Brokers. And, as Aunt Nettie assumed an ever greater role in government: Staffers. Poll workers. Selectmen. Auditors. Ombudsmen. Judges. Of course, some people were Retrained. And it goes without saying that not all the Unretrainables were coppertoned, like me. A great many were angelfair. But it was hard not to notice that the Unretrainables did somehow include everyone coppertoned, as well as everyone spy-eyed, like Eleanor, and everyone odd-bodied, too, not to say the odd-godded—Muslims, for example. It was, one had to say, quite a coincidence that the underclass looked as it did; groups like AutoAmericans Against Apartheid called it the New Segregation.

And what about meditation? I asked Aunt Nettie once. Would that help me tame certain mannerisms I had developed since my work was discontinued? The answer to which was, again, yes, and here was a link to get me started, although she thought I might also just try sitting on my hands.

Like others, I had allowed Aunt Nettie to keep my calendar back in the days when, as the young head of an English as a second language program, I still had immigrants to teach and obligations to juggle. This was some time ago, now—before Ship'EmBack. But back then, I had also allowed Aunt Nettie to email people on my behalf, checking the "mimic your voice" option and marveling at just how perfectly she could replicate my tics of phrasing. She had even captured a certain formality I had picked up from my mother—a holdover from her days as a Caribbean schoolmarm—because I had, in my youthful diligence, sent so many thousands of emails. Indeed, Aunt Nettie had so much data on me that not even Eleanor could tell it was not I who had composed the messages she received from my account. What's more, I had taken advantage of the EZ tools offered to me and trained Aunt Nettie to write my lessons and my syllabi—even to generate sample sentences and punny jokes. Indeed, I trained her so well that I had more than once observed that an avatar could now run the class, especially since she had my voiceprint and so could not only make my jokes but make them in my voice.

As for why I did these things—I generally did them, I see now, because I appreciated some associated convenience, which was to say because I could be, as my mother liked to say, *lazy as a rock at the bottom of a hill.* And as for the resulting reality, was it not disconcertingly like the sea level rise and heat and wind we knew, long ago, would come with climate change but have since come to call normal? No one would have willfully chosen the stranding of whole office parks and schools and neighborhoods by the flooding we saw now. No one would have willfully chosen the generating of the places we called marooned places, just as no one would have chosen the extinction of frogs and of polar bears, or the decimation of our pine forests by the explosion in bark beetles. And yet it was something we humans did finally choose. After all, it was not the earth that chose it, or any other creature. It was we who made our world what it was. It was we who were responsible.

And who else was to blame that we Surplus were now required by law to have AutoHouses, which were for the most part Auto-Houseboats, collected into Flotsam Towns? Happily, house video surveillance did end. We did at least now have—thanks to the herculean efforts of Eleanor and her legal team—an A/V data shutoff to which you could resort. It wasn't the default. To get at it you had to remove a wall panel with a special screwdriver for which you had to send away, and which was always on backorder; I do think they made about a dozen a year. Then you had to rewire the thing yourself, and it goes without saying that absolutely nothing was labeled. But still, the shutoff was there.

As for the price of victory—well, let us just say that it was only after some years that we beheld Gwen and finally had the bandwidth to think what we should have thought all along. Namely: How extraordinary.

I had bought Gwen a pink Spalding ball at an underground yard sale and seen how she laughed as she threw it at my nose. I had seen how she laughed, too, when I found her a tiny baseball glove, at another underground sale. I had seen her put it on her head like a hat. I had seen her talk to the glove and sleep with it under her pillow. And as she grew older, I had seen how she could throw an apple smack into the mouth of a Halloween scarecrow from clear across a field. She threw a kid's handphone back to him through the window of a moving AutoLyft. She hammered a nail into a pole by throwing a rock at it from across the street.

Was it not uncanny? We called it her gift. And sometimes, when Eleanor and I were talking, just the two of us, we reached back into old-time thinking and parlance and asked, Is this what people meant when they said something was God-given? Not that we were religious—hardly. And every child is humbling in a way that was hard even for old-time people to express—hard, that is, even for people who had not been brought up to seek truth in big data and algorithms but in things like books. Indeed, Gwen, too, was much more than her gift. She, too, was an embodiment of that tornado that is girlhood—that glorious whirlwind of silliness and sophistication that seems to dance and spin and touch down just exactly where it likes.

Yet Gwen's gift awed us in a special way. Was there not something miraculous about it—this ability? This talent? This knack?

This utterly useless aptitude? Where did it come from? What was its purpose? We were, as I said, in awe. And maybe that was why we used that phrase, "God-given"—a phrase whose meaning we did not quite know, but that meant, we understood, beyond us. Beyond our ken. Beyond our grasp. Beyond human understanding, and beyond inhuman understanding, too. Beyond Aunt Nettie. And as a father, all I wanted was to see my daughter, in all her giftedness and idiosyncratic humanity, bloom.

◆

Though I did not actually know much about baseball, I quickly boned up, especially on drills—which Gwen, even at age six and seven, mastered so quickly it was as if she already had the skills in her and had only to open the box in which they were stored. Indeed, she learned so quickly that I was more than a little relieved when her classmate, Ondi, expressed an interest in learning to play, too. Age eight at the time, and the only other Blasian in their class, Ondi Nickelhoff was, like Gwen, one of the few girls who had already dyed her hair—choosing a red-and-gold mix, though, to Gwen's solid cerulean blue. She was known by all to be a handful. Still, she gave me an excuse to slow down to a pace I could manage. And I was relieved as well when the girls took breaks, as they did sometimes—when they lay down and looked up at the sky through the plants, for example, pretending that they, too, were leafing out or growing toward the sun, or when they tried to hold hands while walking on their hands—something they could almost do, in part because they had solid ground on which to make their attempts.

We Cannon-Chastanets were an unusual Surplus family, that's to say, in having inherited a land right on Eleanor's side of the family. We were, as a result, not relegated to an AutoHouse-boat but boasted an actual 3-D-printed blue-and-yellow plastic AutoHouse, complete with garden. The garden wasn't big, and we did have drainage problems. In the winter torrents, especially, we could have run training drills for Noah's flood. But we could grow peas and beans and cucumbers, and pears and grapes and more, and did so with joy—although chiefly, I will say, because we would not eat the food purveyed by the ubiquitous mall trucks. Of course, the mall-truck food—NettieFood, as we called it—was free. In fact, we Surplus received Living Points for eating it, as we did for consuming generally: what with the efficiency boost of Aunt Nettie, the Netted overproduced wildly. But might those endless trays of dumplings and calzones and taquitos contain a mood-and-mind mute that amounted to a love sap—the ulti-mate aim of which was to reduce our numbers or, as we Surplus put it, to winnow us? Let's just say that our household grew our own food, thank you, and that we shared it with our friends, who viewed it as lifesaving.

But, as a bonus, the garden enthralled Gwen and Ondi. They made fairy houses out of twigs; they fashioned a swan-shaped chandelier out of grapevines and chopsticks. They wove an enor-mous cornucopia-shaped fort in which to hang the swan-shaped chandelier, and they cooked things. Zucchini dumplings and nas-turtium pie; pear sticky rice with dates; a tomato and seed-pod stew. They made something they called eggplant wine, and some-thing else they called glog, the ingredients of which they would never tell us—indeed, could not, they were laughing so hard.

Then, always, it was back to baseball.

I'm not sure what it says that I thought both girls were natu-rals; perhaps my amazement says more than I'd like about my assumptions about girls. But what long days of happy engage-ment those were, in any case, not only for them but for me. I loved being able to teach again, and especially to be able to teach, for the first time in my life, children. Was this fathering? Whatever it was, for a few sweet years I taught Ondi as much as I taught Gwen. When Ondi said she was interested in catching, for example, I taught her not to be afraid of the ball. And no throwing the ball back to Gwen from her knees: in what I believed to be one of her first lessons in discipline, I made Ondi get back up on her feet every time. When she said she didn't think she'd ever be able to throw all the way to second base, I set up boxes for her to try to knock down. And as for her batting, I tried to get her to relax her shoulder, and not to move around so much in the box, and to grip her bat with her eight middle knuckles all in a row—things I tried to teach Gwen as well, though the girls had that tendency I had seen in my sisters, when they were young, to divvy up their expertise. For Marie-Elena and Elaine, it had meant that if one hiked, the other swam; if one caught fish, the other caught birds. They were complementary to a fault. And so, too, it was as if, since Gwen was so good at pitching, Ondi took catching and batting as hers. It was frustrating. Still, we were all happy and who knows how long our idyll would have lasted had Ondi not fallen afoul of the Enforcers.

Who knows, that is, how long it would have gone on but for, of all things, knitting. Other Surplus dealt with the boredom of our lot by beating one another up—such beating having become so accepted a part of Surplus life that girls especially clucked over pretend injuries the way they had once played house, as if simply rehearsing for adult life. But in our household, we played baseball when outdoors and, when indoors, knit. Eleanor's father having hailed from the Aran Islands, Eleanor knew how to do everything from the moss stitch to the trellis stitch to the tree of life—stitches her grandmother had taught her and that she now passed on so zealously that even at age eight or nine, the girls could do cables.

They could tell you, too, that the basket weave represented a fisherman's creel; they knew that the zigzag stitch evoked the ups and downs of marriage. They knew that the honeycomb stitch honored the hardworking—and now extinct—honeybee.

And for her part, intrepid Ondi had by age twelve even taught herself how to card and spin wool. Eleanor always emphasized that Ondi was welcome to the trunks of yarn Eleanor had amassed; it would be no exaggeration to say that Eleanor told her this dozens of times. But not wanting to be dependent on us, Ondi had proudly sourced raw wool from backward parts of the country, like Vermont—even managing, once, when the girls were fourteen, to pick up her supplies herself.

Will we ever know what our lives would have been had she not made that trip—a trip that Aunt Nettie would have deemed Problematic even if Ondi had not gone on to SpritzGram various people while she was there? In any case, she did. First she Spritz-Grammed farm smells to Gwen, as proof she really had made it to Vermont. Then she SpritzGrammed the various bullies in their class. And when she was done with Winny Wannabe and Leila Clutch and Cara Jack, she went on to SpritzGram the Enforcers who had been swimming under her family's houseboat at night and slitting their pontoons with knives.

As for the immediate result: the Nickelhoffs lost so many Living Points that their phone links were shut off and their zone-heat, too. Gwen and Eleanor made them blankets and sweaters; I fashioned for them a kind of messenger pigeon out of a yard-sale photo drone. All of which was a help, since their trial did not go well. Indeed, the Nickelhoffs were, surreally, Cast Off—set to drift on the high seas, with every harbor closed against them, for a month. Did they blame us, as Gwen later said they did, for Ondi's misconduct? Did they believe we'd led her astray and were finally responsible for their ordeal? Perhaps. Nonetheless, we worried and wondered about them. Silly as we'd always thought

WishDrones, we even launched round after round of them into the atmosphere, with our heartfelt good wishes. The messenger drone I'd made for them having been immediately swept overboard, though, we heard nothing until the ordeal was over, and then the report was brief.

We were all, I remember, in the library—a corner of the house, really, not a room, but full of bright, enormous floor pillows, among which Ondi had snuggled with a book many a time. Now she refused to sit, much less roll herself up like a hedgehog, as she had when she was little. She was so thin that, side-lit by the afternoon sun, you could see, as though through a time warp, how she would wrinkle in another twenty years—something we Surplus would all do, of course, not having access to WrinkErase. But how strange to see, already, how she would have worry lines across her broad forehead and grooves from the sides of her nostrils to the corners of her mouth. Her hair was still a red-and-gold glory, but there were such massive bags under her small eyes that her lids seemed almost closed. And, always prone to tics, she now put her hand up to her mouth again and again—her broken nails a sad reminder of how much more in her was broken as, in so small a voice we could hardly hear her, she said, "It was terrifying." Then she went on to describe how her family could not tie up with anything, even another boat, the whole time. The waves were like tankers capsizing on top of them, she said, and her grandfather died while they were out there.

"Which maybe he would have anyway?" said Gwen finally, after a long silence. I can still remember the moment, and in Gwen's tentative offering, I recognized an awkward helplessness of my own—an impulse to do something, anything, to help, crossed with an unfortunate paucity of bona fide helpful ideas. Really, Gwen was only meaning to ease Ondi's heart, and Ondi's grandfather was, after all, 115. Which even in these days of ever longer life was not young.

All the same, Ondi abruptly turned heel and left. No *I'm sorry, I have to go*—she simply slipped out as if she had been more visitation than visitor.

Leaving already? said the house. *But you've only just arrived.* And, *Of course, you have a choice. You always have a choice. But you've only just arrived.*

Still, the front door opened, then closed, and Ondi never had anything to do with wool or sheep again. Instead, the first chance she got, she dropped off on our front walk the knitted goods Eleanor and Gwen had made for her family. Or maybe she had someone else do it for her? The delivery having been made in the middle of the night, we never knew. We simply woke to find our gate open and a pile of woolens dumped on the concrete. Sweaters. Blankets. Hats. A few more items were splayed across the front bushes, as if they had been hurled; all were being investigated by the geese. And this just because Gwen had said one wrong thing? She couldn't believe it, she said. She couldn't. She couldn't. When Eleanor and I said Ondi might be in shock, Gwen did give her friend, as we counseled her to do, time. Grief deranges, we said. To which she echoed, "Grief deranges." Healing is slow, we told her. "Healing is slow."

But when Ondi's phone link was finally restored, and Ondi did not link to Gwen, Gwen took a break from knitting. She was not quitting, she said. She would never quit. As we had more knitted goods than we needed for now, though, should we not unravel the stuff we'd made for Ondi's family? So we could reuse the yarn? Eleanor and I agreed. It made sense. Still, how hard to see Gwen emerge from her room the next morning, her hair cut so savagely short that all that was left of her beloved blue dye was a kind of patchwork. While still not as wayward as mine, her hair was gnarlier than it was when it was longer—and now, the way that she had cut it, raggedy. Her eyes, too, were almost as swollen as Ondi's had been, as she settled down to undo all the work she had put into sweaters and blankets for her friend, including a tubular scarf she had knit to match Ondi's red-and-gold hair. This had involved an intricate pattern of gold vines against a red background, across which were strewn tiny dark green leaves. Different-colored birds flitted among the vines—birds she had never seen in real life but had read about in books—and at one end, above the fringe, Gwen had fashioned a bird's nest full of eggs hidden in a bower.

Of course, we knew Ondi had been traumatized. We knew she was not herself. Yet even so it was hard to believe that Ondi had let the scarf be thrown—maybe even threw it herself—into the rosebushes. But we had indeed found it there, twisted and tangled up, its fairy-tale leaves caught on the all-too-real thorns. And to watch Gwen unravel it now, crying—untwisting the red and gold yarn, and unknotting every knot the start of a new color required—was so unbearable that finally we took the scarf away and finished the job for her.

At least the Nickelhoffs had used some of what Eleanor and Gwen had made. We were heartened to find the yarn still damp in places and felted from friction. It smelled of salt, and there were bits of fishstuff in it—bits of shell, too, and splinters. So there was that to hold on to. As the yarn balls grew and grew, Eleanor tried to help Gwen. *Do you know what trauma is?* she would ask. *Do you know how it can change people?* And, *You have to ask, Who what when where how why. Starting with who did this—the old Ondi or the new?* But Gwen would just say, over and over, *You don't understand.* Indeed, she said it so often that the house began to echo her, saying, *You don't understand. You don't understand* until Eleanor threw a plate of bacon and eggs out the window and yelled, "Shut up!"

Shut up is what we say when we've lost an argument and don't want to admit it, the house said. And, *That is quite a mess. Shall I clear-float that? Because that is quite a mess.*

Still, it did shut up—some algorithm wisely advising it, perhaps, that as Eleanor's mother was from Sichuan, home of hot peppers and hot tempers, it had best back down.

As for Gwen, she seemed happiest sitting silently with me. Sometimes I could coax her to come throw a bit out under the grape arbor, where I'd set up a sandbag target. But other days, she would ask me if it really was true that right makes might, as we had always taught her. Because it seemed to her that right had no might at all. And when one day she finally turned to AskAunt-Nettie and seemed to settle down as soon as she heard *I'm here* and *Is there something on your mind?* And, *Tell me all about it,* we could hardly blame her.

Luckily, NettieSchool, as we called it, ended about then. School had always been difficult for Gwen, freakishly athletic as she was, and hailing from such a strange family, to boot. But once she no longer had Ondi to stand up for her, things got much worse. Slovenly Leila Clutch planted a live roach in Gwen's glove. Ward of the state Cara Jack snuck a dead rat into Gwen's locker. Of course, Cara Jack slept on an inflatable raft at night and washed her face with napkins from the mall trucks; she was just the sort of sad target who will desperately target just about anyone else. Gwen understood.

Still it was hard, especially when after the incidents themselves came GotchaGrams of Gwen opening the locker! Gwen jumping back! And so on. Gwen did have ScrewU blocks on most of her classmates, and since she had not gotten a phonegraft as had so many of them, she could at least remove her handphone from her wrist. We had that to give thanks for until Winny Wannabe hacked her phone and got 3-D HoloPix to leap clear out of it, at her. Of course, Winny was frequently bullied, too, his parents being so absurdly set on his becoming Netted. The word was, after all, that you had to be an Eleanor to be invited to Cross Over—Eleanor having famously been invited to Cross Over not once but twice—and Winny Wannabe was no Eleanor.

But Gwen had nightmares for months. We were just lucky that from Aunt Nettie's point of view, it was one thing to indoctrinate the young and another to educate them. By high school, classroom learning ceased. Surplus students were simply placed in a cafeteria, enjoined to concertedly consume the racks of food all around them, and left to send FriendGrams and watch VirtualFlix all day. It was an easy decision for Gwen to leave school and, starting in ninth grade, elect to be homeschooled instead.

◆

Homeschooling meant math, science, and history, but mostly as much reading as I could get Gwen to do of the books she had inherited—lucky her—from her grandparents on both sides. It was true that her library was a bit of a hodgepodge; her grandparents would never have imagined they were putting together a curriculum. But there it was. She inherited the *Harry Potter* series, *Little Women*, and *The Island Stallion Races* along with my mother's Shakespeare and Homer. Thanks to Eleanor's mother, she had *The Analects* as well, and *The Book of Changes*, and a marvelously stirring translation of *Beowulf.* And as my mother was from Saint Emile, Gwen of course had her Fanon and her *History of Sugar: Slavery and Rebellion,* in which we Chastanets took up a full inch of the index. (My mother might have been the first feminist in our family but she was hardly the first rebel.) I could not manage to interest Gwen in Marx or Locke or Rousseau—introducing them, I see now, with too much enthusiasm and forgetting how assiduously the young will reject exactly what it seems to their parents most important to get. But Thoreau piqued her interest, as did Jane Austen—full as those Austen novels were, she said, of Surplus girls. And she did love Dickens and, if not all of Melville, then at least "Bartleby the Scrivener," from which she learned the most useful line any teenager could have in her arsenal, "I would prefer not to."

I would prefer not to, I would prefer not to, I would prefer not to, she'd say. Yet the days were actually peaceful and rich, with the reading going on until three or four o'clock most days, after which came fencing with Eleanor. Of course, former foil champion that she was, Eleanor believed herself woefully out of shape; ex-champions all do. But in fact, double-jointed and tiny, she still slipped, as if by magic, into spaces that did not seem entirely there. She still had her gift, that's to say, for reconceiving the possible, making her a marvelous guide to a land beyond skill. Indeed, with her white hair and high cheekbones, and her ears popped out in all their elfin glory, she seemed like nothing so much as the warrior mistress of some enchanted forest as she set about teaching Gwen all manner of thrusts, parries, and ripostes—flipping from camaraderie to contention in a flash, as mothers and daughters will, but with a series of moves literally more breathtaking. To watch them was like watching a lightning storm at sea: the bolts rained so fast and hard that one could not quite see how the ocean would survive.

And probably that should have been the highlight of Gwen's day. But finally, after the foils were put away, came the activity she inexplicably truly awaited—pitching practice. Did holding literally steady now steady her in other ways? Gwen, in any case, could hold her balance pose for an hour if so inclined, which was not to say she didn't hone every part of her mechanics—repeating and repeating each motion, as all the greats do. And when she wasn't practicing physically, she was practicing mentally—visualizing the movements. Breaking them down. Putting them back together. Making adjustments. Most strikingly, though, she was a stork. At yet another underground yard sale, I found a portable pitcher's mound for her, as well as a nine-pocketed net to help her place her throws. And I caught for her and, as best I could, batted. But to coach was one thing and to play another. She mostly practiced alone; I was simply no substitute for Ondi, whom we missed.

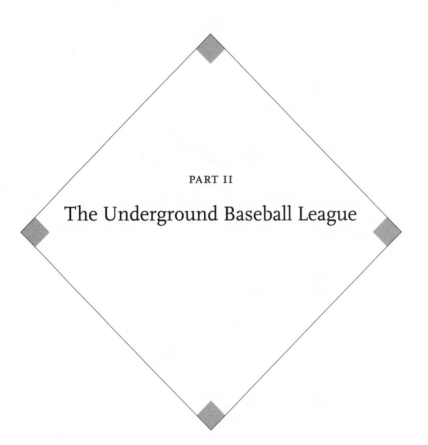

PART II

The Underground Baseball League

As for who it was that, watching Gwen throw one day, declared her in need of a team—that was perspicacious Eleanor, naturally. And as a team was in need of an opposing team—indeed, several opposing teams—so was born the Underground Baseball League.

The League, I should point out, would not have had to be underground had we been willing to use the Surplus fields. However, thanks to their emanations, about which Eleanor had been planning to file a suit for some time, we were not. Did not the kids who played there become enfeebled, after all? People said they became noodly, spastic, unglued. Flingy. Wobbly. Atonic. For all the different adjectives employed, though, their upshot was the same. We had to play elsewhere.

The wrinkle was that gathering in unsanctioned spaces was Unlawful Assembly, and that Unlawful Assembly had been banned since the Automation Riots of twenty years ago: for what with the millions upon millions of Unretrainables pouring week after week onto Capitol Hill, Congress had declared itself to have no choice but to microchip people. (As more than one congressman put it, it was chip them or shoot them.) Expert testimony had held that chipping had worked in ChinRussia, and, lo and behold, as it had worked there, so it did eventually work here. Not immediately and not completely—our Total Persuasion Architecture was never as total or persuasive as theirs. Still, we Surplus were now RegiChipped at birth and easily trackable. If we wanted to play baseball, we were going to have to hack the chips—a daunting prospect.

All the same, I had been hard at work at it down in the basement. *Tinkering,* my mother would have said—no longer able to add, as she had when I was a child, *Is that how you are going to make a living? You can be a tinkerer when you have found a way to live on palm leaves and air.* There was that bit of liberation in being Surplus, anyway; we were done with the exigencies of respectable life. And as I had done some coding in college, look: to my astonishment, I had managed to make some progress. Beginner's luck, no doubt. Still, I had figured out how to unlock a RegiChip with a wand, and I had figured out a way of appearing to be consuming in one location while in fact located elsewhere—a way of consuming remotely. This was hardly Total Protection Architecture. Enforcement had only to chip-search you to find you. But as Enforcement mostly tracked consumption, the hack did promise to keep you off their radar to begin with.

Of course, what with the blatant illegality of getting hacked, most potential players had qualms about it. Sign-ups typically involved multiple long conversations which were in themselves quite risky, especially for Eleanor, who held them. In fact, looking back, the greatest wonder of the League may have been that she was never reported—that even as the League expanded beyond friends and friends of friends, people trusted and protected her. Was it because they had heard about her legal work that people kept mum? In any event, they did. They talked to her on the secure line I'd set up, and pondered awhile, and then they almost always made their way down the deflector-lined path to our house as if to be baptized. *Are you sure you want to do this?* I would ask them when they came. And, *Are you fully aware of the risks?* To which, solemnly, standing tall, they would invariably answer, *Yes.* They did not hesitate as they moved toward my wand, and let me say that I could never help but be touched as I waved it over them. At the same time, I could not help but think what a strange new world this was, that had such monsignors in it. Had I really become a kind of Father Baseball? Yet there I was, performing a blessing of the chips. Or was it a hexing?

The first source of recruits had been friends of Eleanor's—people who had worked with her on various cases and who saw this as a kind of school team for their kids. Next we had discreetly contacted some of my former colleagues, starting with May, my old assistant director, as well as those of our former students who despite Ship'EmBack had somehow managed to stay in the country. Would we ever have enough players for three teams, as we hoped? Reluctant as we were to recruit any of Gwen's old classmates, we had worried we might not.

But the first batch of kids quietly invited kids they knew, who in turn invited other kids. And so it was that three years later, we had an astonishing nine teams' worth of Surplus players—some of whom it must be said, were irredeemably unathletic and would just as soon be sitting in their houseboats, playing DumDumGames. For them, the League was a social activity on par with a glee club; if they could have, they would have participated via avatar. Other players, though, were large and strong and coordinated—warrior youth who in another age would have fought for Sparta or the Allies but in this age mostly worried their parents. As one mother bluntly put it, If you let kids this age sit around, they become terrorists.

Was this why the parents were the picture of support? As even with hacked chips we thought it best to vary our locations, parent squads would first scour marooned places for potential playing spots. Then parent squads would paddle over to make additional evaluations, including a wind check—for, what with our ever more blustery world, many places were just too windy for play. Of course, we still set a DeviceWatch during games. We did not want to find out between innings that the place we'd chosen was actually drone-patrolled or, as in the case of a former Ritz hotel, guard-mined. And let me say here that the kids contributed to game logistics with alacrity, too. Being responsible, once a location was set, to inform a teammate of it, for example, they did so with hand signals, lights, semaphores, messages in invisible ink. Inspired by his surname, third baseman Juan Palombo even trained a real live messenger pigeon such as he had read were deployed in World War I to deliver capsules.

But the parents, the parents. For this, the opening game of our third season, the parents—all of whom had gotten hacked so they could attend games—brought bases and a home plate, measuring tapes and a rake. They brought a pitching rubber and mallets; they brought balls and bats. And, of course, they brought treats. No one used a motorboat to transport these things because motorboats were auto-tracked, and, popular as sailing had become, no one used a sailboat, either. The sails were just too conspicuous. Instead it was all kayaks and pedal boats and paddleboards and dinghies, with staggered departure times and elaborate schemes for camouflaging the boats on the other shore. Some of the young people swam—staggering their departures, too, so as not to attract attention, and wearing black neoprene caps that proved such good camouflage they made some parents nervous. As for whether the parental fears were justified, they were not. Once, it was true, a paddleboarder was so startled he dropped his paddle and fell into the water. And once a kayaker grazed a swimming outfielder. The outfielder, though, was not at all hurt; the person rattled was the kayaker, who promptly capsized and lost the orange slices. But these were anxious times. People scanned the waves all the same—grateful, perhaps, to have a risk they could see.

◆

Real snow was rare these days. Winter in these parts mostly meant sleet—day after day of wintry mix, often whipped by the wild winds of Nor'easters—and spring snow was even more unheard of. But this April Fools' Day had packed a prank: gobs of melting snow clobbered our heads and shoulders while improbable lengths of white shone elegant as evening gloves on the upper sides of the tree limbs.

Beyond the trees, the ground needed a bit of scraping but was already fairly clear—a former prep school football field, on which I could still make out traces of the old fifty-yard line. At either end of the field, too, the white goalposts maintained their solemn sentry even as between them, some of the kids threw and ducked snowballs. Other kids considered the mud. There were treacherous mounds of yellow-green weeds to contend with as well, but it was the mud that had captured certain imaginations, so that no sooner had we pegged the bases in place than players were practicing their slides, laughing and wiping their hands on their teammates until everyone was streaked with filth.

Of course, Gwen's team, the Lookouts, were hardly a tidy bunch at any time. Ranging in age from fourteen to twenty-three, they were not only every possible color, shape, and size but had noticeably wide-ranging ideas about appropriate baseball attire: people sported sweatshirts and jeans but also a bowler hat, a cape, a dashiki, and a kilt. Still, all-accepting as they were, they made a good team, and anyone could see that there in their midst, Gwen felt, for once in her life, that she belonged. Never mind the mud. She smiled and smiled, and when she sure enough had to stop to clean out her clumped-up cleats, she did it with a laugh that rang with pure spring happiness. Over the winter, she had had a kind of undecidedness to her, as if her parts were still making their way through a crowd to their destinations. Now Eleanor and I were amazed to see that everything had arrived. Her arms at age seventeen were as long as her babyhood had suggested they would be—her fingers, too—and she was still tall and whippet-like. But now she had the open, proud shoulders of a pitcher and a face that somehow remade her mother's and mine into something potent: her mother's high planed cheekbones, for example, made her face difficult to read from a distance, and eyebrows I recognized as my own dark caterpillars had become, on her, slashes. As for whether Gwen herself realized how intimidating a figure she now cut, I doubted it. She was used to being ostracized, of course, but not because of her appearance; she had never developed a faculty for seeing herself from the outside, and Eleanor and I both had. But she was intimidating. Intimidating and promising: In some urgent new way, she seemed to Eleanor and me to whisper, *Watch me.* And so we did. We watched her.

We flipped an old-time coin such as no one used anymore but did still come in handy for tosses. Heads. The Lookouts were first at bat.

The Jets, their opponents, were also coed. But as we had made no attempt to sort recruits as they signed up and as word about the League had at one point spread to a group of handball players, all of whom had signed up, the Jets were both more male and more athletic than the Lookouts. Indeed, their nickname was the Jocks, and they should probably have beat the Lookouts on testosterone alone.

But in fact, the Jets' pitcher was new and, hard as he threw, his pitches came straight through the middle of the strike zone. It was as if they were thrown by a PitchBot with just one setting, and that the worst possible one. So the Lookouts managed a couple of hits, even if they did not score, and headed out to the field optimistic.

Gwen, meanwhile, not only had a four-seamer, a changeup, and a curveball, but seemed able to place the ball where she liked. That first inning, the Jets' first baseman did still hit a line drive into left field for a base hit; their catcher hopped a ball right past our shortstop, too, putting a second runner on base. And after them came the Jets' shaggy second and third basemen, Gunnar and Bill Apple—identical twins who had been normal-sized kindergarteners back when they were classmates of Gwen's, but had since grown to be big as bison. They looked as though they belonged on a prairie, not a field. Gwen struck them both out, though, and in the bottom of the second kept their damage to a single and a walk—leaving it to her teammates to keep them from advancing.

Then the Lookouts' shortstop, Brianna Soros, turned her ankle on one of the weed mounds. We broke out the SprayIce and a QuikAce; Brianna was all right. Since, like all the teams, we had no bench, however, Coach Mabel had to pull in an outfielder to take Brianna's place. That left no one in center field.

Happily, Gwen stayed ahead in the count on hitter after hitter, and, just as they thought they would, the Lookouts began hitting. But no sooner had they settled in than, in the bottom of the fifth, Gunnar Apple hit a double. Then there was a hit right up the middle to our missing center fielder, and suddenly the score was 3–2. The Lookouts were still ahead, but as one parent put it, the Jets had found their fuel. 4–3. 4–4.

5–4, Jets.

5–5.

The field was finally drying in the warm sun, yet no one mentioned it. Instead, when we broke to have some pie, people chewed tensely. Typically, the pie was a highlight of the afternoon, as Eleanor and Gwen not only filled them with fruit from our own garden but topped them with a kind of conversation-piece crust. Once Gwen drew a Turing machine tape on top, for example, with squares bearing o's and 1's feeding a reader made of pastry dough; it looked like a shoe buckle. And today she had inscribed the crust with the google-eyed C logo of the Chattanooga Lookouts—a partisan act, to be sure, this being her team's namesake. But it was also a heartfelt salute: for it was as a Chattanooga Lookout that Gwen's idol, lefty Jackie Mitchell, was pitching long ago when she struck out Babe Ruth. As people did now appreciate knowing. Was Mitchell really just seventeen at the time? they asked. And did she really go on to strike out Lou Gehrig, too? They whistled and shook their heads. But then they squinted up at the sky as if the wisps that had appeared there had never before been seen in our hemisphere.

In the bottom of the ninth, it was 6–5, Lookouts, and getting cool. People did the sports-watcher two-step—moving from one foot to the other, and kicking their standing foot as if to knock some sense into it. One out. A double and a steal. Another out.

Then the Jets' second baseman came up to bat—Gunnar, that same Apple twin who'd doubled in the fifth inning. Gwen threw him a fastball—strike one—followed by a curveball. Strike two. Now Gunnar eyed her. Though a sweet guy in other contexts, what with the tightness of the score and a Jet on third, he was unmistakably deliberately intimidating. He spat on the ground; he pushed up his sleeves as if to show off his forearms—hams so massive, he could have been Goldilocks's big brother, somehow stumbled into the dugout of the Three Bears, and hoisting now the bat of the baby bear. He gave a challenging look.

Gwen took off her glove, tucked it between her knees, and redid her ponytail. Feeding it through the back of her cap, she let it expand, then put her glove back on with maddening slowness.

In fact, way back when, Gunnar and Gwen had been childhood sweethearts. That was in kindergarten, and they were friends now, but between that bit of complication and the score, Gwen took an especially long moment to gather herself. Of course, Eleanor and I knew that moment and that ritual: the way Gwen looked down—contemplatively, it seemed—staring at the ground until, when she looked back up, it was with a focus you could almost see, that almost had a shape and a volume. She was hardly a terrifying girl, but it was a terrifying look—her prosecutor look, Eleanor called it. Ralph Changowitz, the catcher, was signaling something, but Gwen raised one of her eyebrows—no. A train of clouds sped across the sky. She wound up. Then she threw another fastball so fast Ralph had to ice his hand when he got home. Gunnar said later he never even saw it.

Game!

We finished up the pie, congratulating the Lookouts on their win and the Jets on their playing before heading home. The water was orchid and orange in the setting sun; Eleanor swayed back and forth playfully as we paddled, her loose hair flashing orchid and orange, too.

"What a game!" I said.

"Yes," she agreed, and laughed in a way that brought to mind my efforts, long ago, to try to explain to my students the word "giddy." "It was marvelous," she said. "Marvelous!" And, as happy as I have ever seen her, she continued to sway as above us, Venus appeared, and some space hotels, and some stars.

◆

At home, we made love the way that old married people do—with more practice and patience than passion perhaps, but no less love and certainly no less risk: for all her daytime forbearance, Eleanor was not above yoga sex, featuring downward dog and some arresting variations on pigeon—positions that threatened to put me in a MediLyft. "Whoa, Nellie," I moaned—an old joke—to which she ambiguously groaned, and when I murmured, "Nell, Nell, Nell," she exclaimed, "Grant!" We were happy.

Almost as soon as we had softened into a four-armed heap, though, she wanted to know, "Did your meter work?" To which I answered, "Meter?" Because in truth, it took me a moment to understand what she was asking. But then I came to myself and answered yes. Having scored a DIY laser-beam kit and a first-rate 3-D printer at a recent yard sale, I had moved them into the basement, along with a battery of deflectors to keep the house from knowing. And then with my treasures I had cobbled together a discreet handheld meter to measure ball speed. Which, yes— worried though I was that its green flash might be glimpsed, I had brought to the game where, happily, no one except Eleanor had noticed.

Now she asked me about it in a whisper though we had started running both a white noisemaker and a voice scrambler at night. *Can I turn that off?* asked the house every evening. *Who can sleep with so much noise? Can I turn that off?* As for why we nonetheless persisted, it was simple. Having heard that a rebellion against Total Persuasion Architecture had broken out in ChinRussia, we knew that, seeking to capitalize on this, Aunt Nettie would be Redoubling her efforts to outdo them. What exactly that would entail, who knew. Once Redoubling had meant changes in our privacy laws: believing them to give ChinRussia a leg up in AI, we had eviscerated them. And once, it had meant changes in our ethics laws: believing them to hobble our genetics research, we had eviscerated those, too. Of course, Eleanor had fought both changes and paid for it. Besides the incarceration, she had been subjected to TouchShocks, ToeBombs, and more—what we Surplus called distinguished treatment. One ToeBomb had literally cost her a pinky toe but she always joked that the treatment was more distinguished than its target, which was all but vestigial.

Now we braced for whatever might come next and, in the meanwhile, discussed my meter.

"Yes," I said softly. "It worked."

"And?"

"Seventy-three miles an hour."

I knew what Eleanor was thinking.

"Seventeen years old and she's throwing seventy-three miles an hour," I went on, just for the marital satisfaction of it. "And she hasn't even been focusing on speed." This was true. Gwen had been working on control since without commensurate control, she believed, there was no point in throwing harder. Also, she was infatuated with her off-speed pitches, at which she was so preternaturally good.

"We should tell her," Eleanor said.

I agreed. But would we? When we had not even told her that our local Enforcer had recently come around, asking about her? Dana had been an importer of cork yoga mats before Automation and was still covered in Sanskrit tattoos. Last week, though, he had had an agenda in his smile as he asked whether we had heard the news—that baseball had been designated an Official National Pastime! We probably did not need to be told, he went on, that the sport had been languishing since Automation. And, of course, we did know that organized baseball had so roundly resisted Aunt Nettie, it had finally been discontinued. We knew that the great teams had been disbanded—the Yankees, the Red Sox, the Cardinals—and that the great stadiums had been torn down—Fenway and Wrigley Field and Yankee Stadium. We knew, too, that the one stadium still standing was mostly used for

DestructoTruck duels. Rumor had it that some baseball was still being played in Netted colleges—at places like Net U. But now, Dana said, the real thing was coming back.

"The AutoAmerica Stadium is being fixed up," he said. "There's going to be a Team AutoAmerica, too, and programming! Hoopla! The works!" He smiled. "It's going to be an Official National Pastime!" he said again.

Of course, the last time a national something was announced, all our handphones had vibrated at once. We were SpritzGrammed with champagne scent as a HoloPic of fireworks popped out, along with a command to celebrate! Celebrate what, though, I could not now remember.

"And that's why we'd love to see Gwen try out for the Official Netted League," Dana went on. He did not need to explain that there was not going to be a Surplus equivalent. "Her schoolmates said she threw so hard she once killed a Canada goose with a rock."

"That's not true," I said.

"Her bio-profile, too, suggests baseball could just be her sport. Not to say her grandfather."

Eleanor's Aran Island father had, it could not be denied, been a championship discus thrower—having gotten his start, Eleanor always said, throwing rocks.

"Interesting," I said. "All this isn't because AutoAmerica has rejoined the Olympics, by any chance?"—something I had heard from a fellow Underground League parent.

"Bingo," said Dana. "In fact, the games are going to be held right here in the US of A."

Eleanor and I smiled, though it always bothered us when the US of AA was shortened to the US of A.

"And as you know, we in the US of A believe in Spectrum Thinking."

"Ah," said Eleanor pleasantly. "How enlightened."

But later, she fumed. "So they need a token?"

"Blasian, female, and Surplus—does that make Gwen a three-fer or a fourfer?" I said.

"And since when is baseball even an Olympic sport?"

"Since it became a way for ChinRussia to literally beat us at our own game?"

"It's ridiculous."

"That ChinRussia wants to humiliate us? Or that we have brilliantly taken the bait?"

"Both."

"Redoubling," I said. "This all has to do with Redoubling."

We agreed.

"But is she better off—" Eleanor began.

"—being able to say she had no idea how fast she pitched—."

"—should Aunt Nettie put out a call? For pitchers who can pitch seventy miles per hour, say."

I hesitated. "Not to tell Gwen what we know is paternalistic," I said. Though where was the line between paternalistic and paternal? Between respecting Gwen and protecting Gwen?

The white noisemaker *swish, swish*ed.

"My meter is new," I went on. "It could be wrong."

"You are grasping at straws."

"Better to grasp at straws than not to grasp at all," I said—a lame joke, I knew. Still, I wished I had been able to make her laugh.

"That golden arm," she mused instead.

"Will it prove a gift or a curse?"

"And will she be invited to Cross Over?"

While Eleanor had been asked to Cross Over twice, she had refused twice, too, saying she would never be co-opted. Would Gwen prove like her mother in this regard, though? A resister?

◆

It might have been grasping at straws, but still, in the morning I checked my meter against some SkyCars. These were, of course, all AutoSet for the same speed on the highway, and sure enough—there it was. Ninety-five miles per hour, exactly. Next I tried it on an Apparate 750, mounting my meter on a FleaDrone to get some height. Four hundred miles per hour. My meter was failing to fail. All the same, I tried tracking a SkyCar in its skylane. Four hundred miles per hour as well, as set by Aunt Nettie.

In short, perfect.

Did my new observation function work, too?

We Surplus did not have much contact with the Netted, thanks in part to zoning laws. The highest, driest towns were generally zoned ten acres, while swamps like ours had no minimum acreage. Aunt Nettie didn't have to segregate Netted from Surplus, in short; what with Basic Incomes so modest, we self-segregated as easily as sand and water.

Of course, long ago many of us Surplus would have been the help on which the Netted relied, in which capacity we would not only have known them but known them intimately. Before the AutoHouse and the AutoLawn, we would have known their underwear and their shoes and their trash; we would have known their crises and their joys and their affairs. In fact, even just working as I had in a university job, I had had a glimpse into many such things, the lives of the Netted-to-be so closely resembling, at that point, the lives of the Surplus-to-be.

But now, I tracked the SkyCar to its charging shed with fascination. Was not the billowing of the SkyCar's luminescent wings astonishing? Or what about the landing gear that bent at the ankles so that the vehicle could descend, not parallel to the ground, but at a forty-five-degree angle? How Leonardo da Vinci would have loved this thing, I thought, as the machine reached out its wheels like a hawk about to snatch a vole with its claws; it rolled majestically down the last few hundred feet of the driveway. There was no pilot, of course. Still, the males in the cockpit managed to look as though they were in charge, scrutinizing the pavement out ahead of the SkyCar and moving their mouths—giving directions, apparently, to a voice box, a bit of a surprise. ThoughtCommand was expensive, but still I would have thought all the Netted had it. AutoDogs trotted everywhere, in any case—to chase away the Canada geese, I presumed—while in the backseat, a woman and a girl laughed and another girl frowned at her handphone. How flaxenfair these people were, how perfectly pulled together. You could all but hear them answering Yes when HowDoILook asked if they wanted the "consummately casual" option. And no one was consuming anything; that was noticeable. None of them got out of the SkyCar with a snack in hand. They had what my mother would have called very nice manners—church manners even when not in church.

Indeed, the two older people carried nothing at all—their devices no doubt accessible via the SmartGlasses they seemed to be scanning as they walked—while the three younger people hoisted what looked to be rather heavy backpacks. Did the backpacks contain books? Certainly, when the young people adjusted the packs, their contents had that distinctly blockish way of shifting. Had their teachers opted for paper over ScreenRead because Aunt Nettie could not then keep tabs on their reading? Or were the studies simply still showing, as they had long ago, that students learned better from the printed page? And where were their HouseBots? Why did the young people have to carry the backpacks themselves? And was this a family with three children, or was one of the girls a friend? I couldn't tell. Though—three children. Or even two. For Gwen to have some company! What a happy cacophony my sisters Marie-Elena and Elaine had made before their back-to-back heart attacks, years ago—so much so that their raucous quiet haunted me still. If only Gwen could have had a sister—someone like Ondi, except who wouldn't abandon her—who would stay.

The house, large and many-balconied, sat on a quiet cul-de-sac, with nary a mall truck in sight. Of course, Netted lives were full of pressure—I had heard that. And I did think I could see it in the way these people trudged up their beautiful stairs. They were not lighthearted; they were preoccupied. Where we Surplus had to concertedly consume, after all, they had to concertedly produce. And what a life it could be, I remembered—the meetings, the conferences, the politics. The anxiety about success—how you fought to define it for yourself, even as others blithely defined it for you. People said that the Netted looked at our lives with envy. To be state-supported! To draw a Basic Income for doing nothing! Gwen once showed me an online chat in which a Netted, somehow crossing into Surplus Space, claimed that he'd change places with one of us in a heartbeat. Naturally, he was missing a lot of the picture, as Gwen could have pointed out. Instead, she had simply collapsed his 3-D figure, first into 2-D, and then into a point. "What an asshole," she said. She was contemptuous.

Yet as I watched the people file into their beautiful house, I could not help but notice their air of exhaustion. Maybe they had just had a long day. But they did not exactly walk as if reveling in their good luck in being Netted. They walked as if they had enormous boulders to roll up a hill and no RockBots to help.

◆

The next League game featured the Lookouts versus the Thistles—an all-girl team, new this year. Eleanor and I were looking forward to their arrival until they showed up, to our dismay, in thistle-stamped T-shirts and hats. The first four players who arrived even sported thistle tattoos on their forearms, as well as purple nails and purple streaks in their hair. What were they thinking?

"Have they forgotten this is an *underground* league?" demanded Eleanor. "Where the hell is Andrea?"

Andrea was their coach.

"Maybe I should talk to her," I said.

"So what? So you can make it okay?"

"Maybe the tattoos are henna?"

But it was as if Eleanor had her fencing mask on and was headed into a match. No doubt her fuse was shortened by her preparations to file the Surplus Fields suit—the first steps of which involved exhausting the remedies for her complaint offered by the National Park Service. It was a process that could not, she joked, have been more exhausting. At any rate, she did not reply.

We found Andrea trying to hide her large HydroBoard behind a small wall.

"Are you *crazy?*" exploded Eleanor.

Andrea draped an orange DisposaTowel over her board then stood up, pushing a purple headband to the top of her narrow forehead. Over and above the apparently standard team regalia, she boasted thistle-like hair, all purple and spiky—the sort of stylistic achievement that could not help but make you wonder how the young could be so adept at some things yet hopeless at the basics. At nineteen, Andrea was the youngest of the coaches—too young for the responsibility, Eleanor and I had initially thought. She had eventually won us over with her record, having founded the original ShelterBoat for battered Surplus women—a Shelter-Boat that went on to spawn a nationwide network of such havens. But now her face crumpled like a girl's.

"I am so sorry," she said.

The hair, began Eleanor. And the tattoos—the tattoos, which, unfortunately, were not henna—one of the Shelter girls having, it seemed, wanted to practice the tattoo skills she'd learned from her mother.

"Do you understand what you have done?" Eleanor's voice was cold with anger as she went on. Did Andrea realize how many . . . Did she realize how seriously . . . Did she realize that everyone—the entire League, all the Leaguers—could be Cast Off?

"I guess," said Andrea. "Now that I think about it."

Now that she thought about it.

Andrea wiped her eyes with her headband. "I wasn't thinking, I guess. Everyone was just so excited."

Everyone was just so excited.

"And I guess we were a little high."

Had there been a plate of bacon and eggs around, it would certainly have gone out a window.

"The ShelterBoat is stressful," Andrea continued. "It's stressful for me and it's stressful for the girls. I had to get them off the boat. I mean, it's a boat. There's nothing to do but FriendGram each other and fix our hair. I make everyone keep avatars on their phones—and I make sure their avatars roam the world. But we would go mad if we didn't go ashore sometimes. And this was so much fun, I guess we didn't think, especially because . . ." She hesitated. "Especially because one of the girls just got Cast Off for getting pregnant a second time."

I could see Eleanor's anger begin to take a step back. And there just behind it stood her sympathy, like a fresh recruit, all ready to step forward. Indeed, I thought she would surely ask a bit more about the girl, and whether there was some way she could help. Eleanor was like that.

Instead, she said, "And what if hundreds of others are now Cast Off, thanks to your efforts at stress relief?"

Andrea toed the ground with her purple sneakers.

I tried to make some suggestions as to how Andrea might handle the tattoo removal. Wasn't there something called UnDo? I asked. I said I thought I had read that in a pop-up somewhere. And in truth, though I tried to ignore ads in general, such was the power of ProductPlug that now I perfectly recalled how UnDo could work miracles, even if you'd used EternaMom.

Andrea said she'd look into it. As for whether she wished, as did I, that UnDo worked on more than tattoos, I'm sure that as Eleanor went on lambasting her, she did.

"And do something about that damned HydroBoard," said Eleanor, finally. "A blind person could see it from California."

Her anger seemed to have waned. When she sat down, though, and I moved to massage her temples, she stared unblinking as a fish.

"It may not bring trouble," I said. "It may die right here."

"It may," she agreed. But I knew that was not what she guessed.

On every team, players will hit a sacrifice bunt or fly ball so their teammates will advance. And these moments of self-sacrifice are felt to be ennobling—transcendments, as a pop psychologist once called them. But they are discrete; they are decisions. They are not what I beheld in the Thistles—a camaraderie reminiscent of that of the Lookouts, only far more organic and fluid. Utterly reckless as they had been, they were also, one had to say, something special. There was constant huddling and dispersing; there was constant swapping—of water bottles, of positions, of T-shirts. When one girl slipped, others appeared so instantly that it was as if their spirits were already there, and only had to perceive a need to materialize. Was this what you got with an all-girl team who lived together under special pressures, with a special leader? For if the Lookouts were an all-accepting party, this was a family—

a group in which, as my mother used to say, *everyone has a part of you and you have a part of everyone.*

If only Gwen could join them! Eleanor looked at me, and I knew the thought had crossed her mind even as it crossed mine. Of course, we were still furious with them. And Gwen loved the Lookouts, and they loved her. But looking to the future, we could see that she was going to need some deeper connection than what the Lookouts alone could give—that she was going to need what my mother would have called *quality cement.* Of course, it was possible that not even the Thistles would understand things like what it meant to grow up with a golden arm—how it was a gift to which Gwen had to answer as if to a boss.

Still, I had all but convinced myself that they could understand it if they tried when she walked a batter for no reason. Did she know something we didn't? It wasn't like her to pitch around just anyone. Then she gave up a base hit to a girl who didn't even swing at the first two pitches, and who would certainly have folded had Gwen placed her ball with the least finesse. Instead she all but fed the ball to the batter; the ball hit the bat more than the bat hit the ball.

"Isn't that Leila Clutch?" said Eleanor. And as soon as she said it, I remembered: the girl who once put a live roach in Gwen's glove. I didn't remember her name, though, from hacking her chip. Did she have another name?

Now Gwen walked another player, loading the bases.

"Cara Jack," said Eleanor.

How had I failed to recognize the dead-rat girl? It was true I'd never seen her in person, back when the girls were in middle school. And yet, and yet. Perhaps she had been hacked along with others on her team? Because while it had only happened once that a group of recruits had come to be hacked together, one afternoon some girls did arrive in a convoy.

Then there it was—streaked, now, with purple, but still— that red-and-gold Afro-puff. And even more distinctively—that attitude.

Ondi. Ondi who had dumped all our knitting on the walk. Ondi who had rejected Gwen and broken her heart. Ondi who was now on Leila Clutch and Cara Jack's team.

"What is she doing here?" Eleanor's brow furrowed. "Did you hack her chip?"

I had not, no. And yes, I was sure. Whoever else I had missed, I would have recognized Ondi. As for how she could be playing when she had not gotten hacked, all Eleanor would say was "The lax are never lax just once."

Was that aimed at Andrea, or me, or both of us?

"She is putting the entire League in jeopardy," I said, in any case—for having been Cast Off, Ondi's family was almost certainly on a special watch list. And if Aunt Nettie chip-tracked Ondi, she would find us all—including, quite possibly, Eleanor. Eleanor, out and about. Eleanor having given the slip to her DroneMinder with the help of a heat signature forger. Eleanor not only doing legal work but organizing as well. Would this bring more distinguished treatment? She always joked that no one needed ten toes and that she had nine to go, but I was not keen on a countdown.

"What are we going to do?" I said as Ondi stepped up to bat, her thistle tattoo plainly visible. She wore a thistle T-shirt, sequined sneakers, and, to go with them, the same stance she had had since childhood. I was happy to see her eight knuckles lined up the way I'd taught her. There was the raised shoulder I had tried to teach her to relax, though. And there, too, was that nervous moving up to the front of the box, then back, then up again I had tried to get her to stop.

Gwen, flummoxed, threw high.

Ball one.

Gwen threw again—this time so high that Ondi drew her head back, laughed, and said, loud enough for everyone to hear, "That almost took my nose off."

Her teammates booed Gwen, who stopped to take off her cap. She redid her ponytail. But when she emerged from her routine, it was not to throw the cold, hard pitch she'd thrown against Gunnar Apple in the Jets game. Quite the contrary, you would almost have had to call her ball wild—so far inside that Ondi drew in her stomach and jumped back, hips in the air, so as not to be hit. Did she really need to do that, or was she just being dramatic?

Ball three, and more booing that Ondi did nothing to quell— that she, in fact, egged on, exchanging smirks with her fellow Thistles. Now Andrea was out on the field, gesturing at Mabel.

"What if someone gets hurt?" Andrea demanded. "Do you know what a mess it will be?"

"She's not going to hit anyone," argued Mabel.

"You have to pull her." The very picture, now, of adult responsibility, Andrea lifted her chin; her hairband, hanging around her neck, oddly evoked the sort of necklace middle-aged women like my old assistant director, May, used to wear.

Mabel, though, put her hands on her hips as if to say, *I mean business when I set a brake.* And, indeed, as a former cable car conductor, she did.

The fight was on. Meanwhile, Eleanor in her lawn chair tried to keep her voice down. "Someone is going to get hurt? Because of *Gwen*, someone is going to get hurt?"

"Maybe we should stop the game," I said.

Mabel gave Gwen a hug and whispered something; Gwen redid her ponytail, reseated her hat, and returned to the mound. She worked some dirt out from her right cleat with her left toe. Then she did her left cleat with her right toe. Then just before

44

she could be charged with delaying the game, she wound up and threw. A fastball, nothing fancy, but it was fast.

Strike one.

A drone appeared overhead. Was it a NosyDrone, or something more serious? What was it doing here? Why hadn't my DeviceWatch beeped? And was this the excuse I needed to suspend the game? I watched out of the corner of my eye as the drone hovered overhead for several moments. Though a few people, looking up, appeared rattled, Gwen didn't seem to notice.

Strike two.

The drone zipped off to the west.

Gwen wound up one more time and, fast as the ball was moving—seventy-one miles per hour by my meter—Ondi, accustomed to Gwen's pitches, managed to connect with it. She did not get in a full swing, but she made enough contact that her bat broke and flew off in pieces even as the ball hit a tuft of weeds at a funny angle and, spinning, bounced back in front of the catcher, who picked it up, stepped on home plate, and threw to first.

Two outs.

So deep were our sighs of relief, our lawn chairs squeaked, and though the Thistles went on to win in extra innings, we didn't care. We were just glad when it was all over.

◆

"They booed me," cried Gwen at home. "They booed me."

And, "How could she do this? Ondi was egging them on! She was! She was getting them to boo!"

Eleanor and I did not—could not—bring up Ondi's playing unhacked and its implications. Instead, we focused on how to help Gwen. For how much, I knew, she needed to hear, *I'm here.* And, *Tell me everything.* And how much I wanted to say, *Of course, you feel betrayed.* And, *How else could you feel? You're only human.* But that had all become NettieSpeak. From humans like Eleanor and me, it was, ironically, bound to ring false.

Meanwhile—no doubt reflecting some update—the house began to run through a list of helpful remarks: *Life is hard. You never know who you can trust. Life is not fair. People are cruel because they don't know how to be kind. Life is a trial.*

"Shut up," I said.

Shut up is what we say when we've lost an argument and don't want to admit it, said the house. *Didn't your mother teach you any manners?*

And when I didn't answer, it said, *Do note that your choice is on the record. Nothing is being hidden from you. Your choice is on the record.*

Still, it did shut up, enabling us, after a few minutes, to focus doltishly on the situation.

Gwen advanced theories as to what had happened, her voice so low it was as if we were hearing it through a wall. Maybe Ondi came back from being Cast Off and went to the ShelterBoat, where everyone was really supportive? And then one day everyone else has this thistle on her arm? So she asks, What's that? Which might've been complicated in a way since the girls who used to torture Gwen tortured Ondi, too? So while they all might have become like sisters, they might not have?

"Making the thistle tattoo one more sign that Ondi didn't really belong," said Eleanor. "That there was a sisterhood within the sisterhood."

Gwen blew her nose.

Ondi probably knew, we agreed, that when it came to base-ball she could impress her friends and knock the hell out of everyone else. As for why she hadn't gotten hacked, Gwen was shocked to hear that Ondi hadn't. "Are you sure?" she asked twice. But then she was both shocked and relieved. Because it was better than what she'd thought, that I had hacked Ondi and forgotten to tell her.

"I would never have done that," I said.

"Oh, yeah? What about Leila Clutch and Cara Jack?" Gwen gave me a withering look.

As for why Ondi didn't get hacked—maybe she was going to? guessed Gwen. But then realized her parents would never allow it? And then decided to play anyway? Not telling anyone because she didn't think Andrea would be okay with it? And because she figured Eleanor and I would understand and forgive her? If we ever even found out? Having always been like that?

"Or maybe this was a way of SpritzGramming animal smells at us," said Eleanor grimly. "Because it wasn't just her parents who believed we had steered her wrong—because she blamed us, too. For her family being Cast Off. For her grandfather's death."

As for which was right—did Aunt Nettie, with all her data, know?

"I'm never going to pitch again," Gwen said, in any case—her voice serene and determined now—her after-the-storm manner. "I am going to burn my glove."

"Please don't say that," we begged. "Please. Please. Don't say that."

But the more we told her it was Ondi and the Thistles she should put out of her mind, the more they occupied her. It was our voice she shut out with the special resolve of the perverse.

Said the house, *There's no forgetting what you can't forget.*

And—picking an odd moment, I thought, to wax poetic—*We always rage, rage against the dying of the light.*

"Shut up, please," I said then. "Please!"

At least you said please, said the house.

◆

Vintage Ondi. Whispering in bed, Eleanor and I agreed. What surprise was it that Ondi had thought she could get away with not being hacked? She had also thought she could get away with SpritzGramming Enforcers with farm smells. A wishful thinker if ever there was one. As for her spitefulness—was this an anger toward her parents, directed toward other targets?

"Remember that story she used to tell us about her family's houseboat?" Eleanor said. For one of the strange things about the Flotsam Towns was that they looked rather like plastic versions of the floating villages we once saw, many years ago, in IndoChina. This was hardly a coincidence: the designers who had been tapped to design them—delighted but dismayed to realize that, yes, they possessed the requisite expertise—had been Cambodian. But the result was that Ondi's family's houseboat had been modeled on a floating school on the Tonle Sap. Twice the size of its neighbors, it had featured a half-court basketball court and served as a constant reminder to Ondi's mother that Aunt Nettie had once wanted Ondi's father to Cross Over. It was a reminder that he had in fact been given the boat as a sign of favor, and that he would not have been deemed Unretrainable had he not flunked EgoShrink.

But for him, the boat was a reminder that before Aunt Nettie had learned, first to help humans read scans and then to read them entirely on her own, he had been a big-deal radiologist. And so he liked to invite his friends over to use the court sometimes. Ondi had said that the whole boat shook when they played, even if they put down the special anchors—that, in fact, Enforcers had slashed the Nickelhoffs' pontoons in part because of the shaking and the noise, which bothered their neighbors, one of whom was an Enforcer's brother. But also, she said, her father and his friends

48

lost balls in the water all the time because of their drinking. And since the HouseBots were not watertight, a human was always needed to dive in and retrieve the balls; and that human was Ondi.

It was something she hated. The water was so cold—like a sink full of ice cubes, she said. And yet her father would play, and have a few more drinks with his buddies, and if after a while none of them could throw anywhere close to the hoop, never mind. They continued to throw, and Ondi continued to fetch the balls out of the water. And if she cried, her father would just laugh and say, *Where's that going to get you?*

Recalling which, Eleanor and I felt for Ondi even as we stared into the darkness.

"We have to tell people their security has been breached," said Eleanor finally.

And, of course, that was right. What's more, we needed to inform them before word of Ondi's getting away with playing unhacked got out, if it hadn't already.

"Because how many more kids will try to do what Ondi did, if they hear?" I mused. "How many more will think, If she did it, I bet I can freeload, too?"

"That's assuming that the League continues," said Eleanor.

Neither of us slept.

◆

Aunt Nettie, meanwhile, had not forgotten about AutoAmerica's new Official National Pastime. She not only put out a call for pitchers in a GovernorGram but, when Gwen did not respond, sent a Special Enforcer to our door.

The Special Enforcer did not fit the stereotype. Quite the contrary, what with her white Afro, flowered cardigan, hanging reading glasses, and big-pocketed skirt, she looked for all the world like the formidable moving force behind a legendary bake sale. Her name was Mimi, and before she said a word about baseball, she took a turn around our garden, planting her green cane firmly with each step.

"Marvelous," she said. "Are these going to be cherry or full-sized tomatoes?"

And, examining a label, "Sugar snap peas! My favorite."

And, "So the earthworms are for aeration and the red wigglers are for their castings?"

We nodded.

"I see something's already eating your marigolds." She pointed with her cane.

"Earwigs." Eleanor gripped a trowel as if she were in the middle of transplanting seedlings and was not inclined to chat.

"Ah, yes. Because you sit a little low. It's damp."

"Exactly."

"Is that why you have the boardwalks all stacked up over there? So you can put them down when you need them?"

"Pretty much all winter."

"Before the summer heat and forest fires dry everything out but good."

"Yes."

Mimi's right hand being occupied with her cane, her left hand wielded her reading glasses. Now she pointed with one of their arms, the other arm moving in hapless parallel agreement. "And you've got cold frames, too, I see. For the wind, no doubt, as much as for the cold."

Eleanor relaxed her grip a bit as she nodded.

"The wind is a challenge," said Mimi. "But, you know, what you need for the earwigs is diatomaceous earth. Do you know what that is? I have some I can give you."

Eleanor did not refuse.

Mimi's shiny face shone yet brighter as she described her own garden. Mostly perennials, she said—she loved a fresh flower bouquet. But she did do vegetables, too. All sorts of herbs and greens and, of course, potatoes and carrots and onions and tomatoes— the staples. It wasn't a large garden. She had to budget her space, just as we did. But she did allow herself one indulgence—a giant pumpkin that took up a lot of room but that she entered every year in an agricultural fair.

"Takes constant feeding, but I've won three times," Mimi said proudly. Adding, "I know it's at odds with optimal consumption, but honestly? It's astonishing how little room a garden takes up, and if planned right, it doesn't need to take much time away from consuming. As for whether an occasional salad cuts down on one's appetite for NettieSnax, I'm not convinced. Plus, it's a little punitive, isn't it, to make you Surplus consume so concertedly—as if the granters of the Basic Income couldn't help but charge its recipients something. As if they couldn't quite see their way clear to their own largesse."

If Eleanor wanted to point out that our garden, unlike hers, was to protect us from winnowing agents, she didn't. Neither did she bring up the likelihood of her filing a suit over the mall-truck food once she was done with the Surplus Fields case. Instead, she offered Mimi something to drink.

"Some of our homemade hibiscus tea, perhaps?" she said. "We make it with wild mint."

As Mimi drank and marveled, I explained our hay-bale composting. I demonstrated our expandable trellis, too, as well as our summer shading system, both of which I had fashioned out of scraps. Anti-consumption as these activities were, they were a bit dangerous, frankly, to describe. Mimi, though, sipping her tea, did not seem to care. We discussed heat-resistant cultivars and discovered that she had some we did not, and vice versa. We agreed we would trade seeds. And what a shame it was that every last vegetable was now being crossed with a succulent.

"There's a sacrifice in flavor, no question," she said.

"Not to mention the peeling!" complained Eleanor. "The Bots just can't handle it."

Finally Mimi turned her shiny face toward Gwen.

"Is it true you like to pitch?" she asked.

Gwen, twirling a braid around her finger, admitted, "Yes."

"A pitcher needs a team," Mimi observed. "Have you ever played on a team?"

"No," Gwen lied.

Mimi looked sympathetic. If Aunt Nettie had figured out that Gwen played and had told Mimi, it didn't show. "It's a great feeling," she said. "You and your teammates all trying your damnedest to win and knowing how much you depend on one another. Wouldn't you like to try it?"

Gwen fit the misting wand to a hose.

"I kind of thought so." Mimi winked at us as if to say she knew how teenagers could be. "Well, this may be your chance. I can't make any promises. But we'd love to see you try out for the Netted League team. Will you come?"

Gwen began her misting but, after a few moments, her back still to Mimi, nodded.

"Even if you don't make the team, I think you'll find it a good experience," said Mimi.

"I don't need to make the team," said Gwen's back.

"I don't mean that you won't. But in any case, the thing to do is to try."

Gwen's mist sent up little rainbows in the spring sun.

"I was hoping you wouldn't say no." Mission accomplished, Mimi let her reading glasses dangle by their chain as if they, too, could now take a break. "And you might try consuming more, by the way," she said, turning to Eleanor and me. "Your Living Points are a bit low."

"Low for what?" I asked.

"Let's just say, better to bring them up." Mimi had the inclined head and concerned look of someone genuinely trying to be helpful. "Why raise questions."

Out by the door, we held Mimi's cane for her as she donned a daffodil-yellow rain jacket with a ladybug-print lining. "Because I am nothing if not pro-ladybug," she explained.

We had to smile.

"Of course, if Gwen makes the Netted League team, she will be automatically admitted to Net U," Mimi went on matter-of-factly. Then she left the house, only to turn around before stepping onto the walk. "The cutoff for pitchers is going to be around seventy miles per hour," she said. "Control matters, too, naturally. A pitcher must throw strikes. But seventy miles per hour should do it." With that, she continued down the walk and out onto the street, shooing the geese with her cane.

Was that a coincidence? The HouseBots might be reporting our movements and sound levels and living patterns generally, but between our A/V shutoff, deflectors, white noisemaker, and voice scrambler, we had been reasonably confident words and images were not making it to Aunt Nettie. Now we weren't so sure.

We frowned and puzzled as Eleanor sprayed weeds with a vinegar solution; the weeds were the first thing to come up in the spring and it was good to get ahead of them. Early in the growing season as it was, the wind was hot, as if summer had already started.

"Say Gwen pitches for them," I said, sweating. "What then? Does she go to Net U?"

While Eleanor sprayed for weeds, I sprayed for pests, coating the tops and bottoms of the leaves with a mixture of canola oil and detergent. The results were drippy and decidedly inelegant, but tidy Eleanor seemed not to notice as she set her sprayer down.

"I was the one who organized the Underground League, wasn't I," she said. "So that Gwen could play."

"You were."

"I mean, with your help."

"We couldn't have predicted any of this, Nell. The insurrection in ChinRussia. The Redoubling. The related fixation on the Olympics, if it is indeed related, and on, of all things, baseball. Who could have imagined it?"

"Do you think Aunt Nettie did? With her millions of people, and millions of situations, and her algorithms?"

I hesitated. "No," I said.

"And now what? Do you think Aunt Nettie knows what we're going to do? Do you think she knows what Gwen is going to do?"

"I hope not."

"Because either we're makers or just made."

"Yes."

"Which makes all the difference."

"Yes."

She sprayed around the base of a tomato plant. "So should we try to raise our Living Points? To at least make sure that if Gwen's life is determined by something, it's not by us? To make sure she has a choice?"

It was a choice we wanted her to have on principle. A choice we could not in good conscience block. And yet, I here admit that had it been up to me, I might well have blocked it anyway. Even if it proved us no better than Aunt Nettie, I might well have said no. Gwen could not try out for the Netted League. No.

Married as I was, though, to noble Eleanor, I said yes.

Her hair lifted and settled.

As for whether I really wanted the best brought out in me, never mind. I eyed the mist from Eleanor's sprayer as it bounced up from the soil; like it or not, it rose.

◆

As with any story, there were many different ways Ondi's actions could be presented to the Leaguers. In any of these, though, we thought that to be able to say that the unhacked player was now hacked would help present Ondi, not as an evil outsider who had wantonly jeopardized the safety of us all, but as a kid who had made a mistake. We could then move on to the more important question of what to do.

The problem was that to be able to say this we had to reach Ondi and hack her. And how were we going to do that? We did not for obvious reasons want to go through pot-smoking Andrea and the ShelterBoat girls. Neither did we want to prevail upon poor Gwen if we could help it. We could, however, we thought, try locating the Nickelhoffs' houseboat. For, yes, thousands of families lived in their Flotsam Town, but how many of them could have half-court basketball courts?

Of course, to do a proper search, we were going to need our kayaks—a challenge, for while Ondi and others crossed the channel every day, they did so by ferry. Crossing by kayak was something else altogether, especially if the wind came up. Still, we told Gwen we were going on a trip, as we did sometimes. Eleanor left a note for Yuri, Heraldine, and Sue—her legal team—whose current challenge was to prove that the supplying of protective masks was not a possible remedy for their Surplus Fields complaint. It was a long note. Then early in the morning, I set up the heat signature forger to throw off Eleanor's DroneMinder.

. . .

The plastic houseboats came in paintbox colors—blue, red, purple, orange, yellow, and green. They were tied up one to the next, forming giant rafts, apparently to help stabilize them against the constant wind and waves; the rafts in turn lay in lanes radiating from an enormous food court, bright with flashing signs, and packed with mall boats as big as barges. Having gotten a dawn start, we could see the steam rising from the hot dishes as tray after tray of NettieFood was conveyed down to water level. Rocking canoes and kayaks pulled over to pick up food, their paddles colliding; people shouted their orders. We did not stop. Instead we paddled down one heaving lane after another, crowded with people washing dishes. Everywhere laundry and nets billowed on poles, and we saw more than a few water rats not only in the water but up on the decks of the boats, their webbed feet splayed to get a grip on the plastic. Their long tails twitched; people swept them overboard with brooms.

No basketball court.

We crossed the open water to another food-court hub, paddling hard. Enormous as the first one had seemed, this one was even larger. Its lanes, however, featured fewer laundry poles, and there was less shouting—fewer rats, too. The water was calmer. We even heard music floating from a window and saw boxes of flowers—a higher-rent district, it seemed. We worked our way up and down its spokes, happy that the paddling in this section was easier.

Still no basketball court.

We tried another hub and its spokes. Then another and another. Another.

Another.

Did we try them all? Without a map, we couldn't be sure. Eleanor didn't want to stop. But as the sky darkened, we had to start home. Our arms were so tired, we could no longer stay in sync; the boat lurched and zigzagged. The water roughened. The wind turned aggressive—*back-bitey*, my mother would have said. What would we do if it began to storm? The current proving stronger than we realized, we missed our dock by close to a half mile and had to battle our way back upstream. Fortunately, in the end, we did make it back. We were so tired, though, we fell asleep with our clothes on, then slept so long that Gwen, worried, woke us—something she had never done before.

"Are you all right? Where were you?" she wanted to know. And when we told her, she insisted on bringing us breakfast in bed: chili sweet potatoes with yogurt, dried raspberries and apple rings on a chopstick, syrupbuns and coffee.

"You shouldn't have done that," she kept saying. And, "I'm just so glad you made it back."

As for whether she would help locate Ondi—which we finally asked her—she was touched we had sought to spare her feelings. But "Look at your hands, look at your hands," she kept saying. And, touching the sausage balloons that were our blisters, she insisted, yes, she would help. As for the best way to go about this, could she think about it?

"Of course," we said.

"I think I know someone I can ask," she said.

Was the someone the shadowy organizer of one of Ondi's favorite haunts—an illegal vintage clothes store called the Velveteen Rabbit? All we knew was that a week later, Ondi stood in our house.

At bat, facing Gwen, Ondi had seemed defiant and ablaze and recovered from her trauma on the boat. But whether our shock had kept us from seeing her clearly or whether, there at home plate, she had simply risen to the occasion, she now had us shaking our heads again. Could this be the spunky little girl we once knew? *All people grow out of their baby clothes,* my mother used to say. Still, it was hard to accept how Ondi had changed.

Her gold-and-red hair was as exuberant as ever, tamed by a wide blue band and spilling out the back in a glorious soufflé. Now, though, she wore lipstick—a clown-pink smear that made the rest of her face look tired—and her chin jutted out with a defiance that seemed not so much confident as reflexive. If she was once rebellious in a feisty way that spoke of youth and beans, she now seemed belligerent, a girl with a chip on her shoulder. To go with her RegiChip, a kind of PermaChip.

We tried to be cordial.

"It's good to see you," I said. "Welcome."

"What a lot of bullshit," said Ondi. "Actually, you wish to hell you hadn't had to go looking for me. And part of you wishes you hadn't found me."

"Well, now, but that is absolutely not altogether true," said Eleanor calmly. It was her courtroom manner, serene and unflappable.

Ondi laughed. "You were always too honest," she said. "God, but it drove people nuts."

"And here you are driving people nuts, too," said Eleanor.

Ondi laughed again—a harsh laugh. "Whatever could you mean?"

Eleanor smiled. "Come on, funny girl. We haven't seen you in a while. Let's get the report first, then we can talk about the rest. How have you been?"

Ondi was manifestly disinclined to be charmed, but when I led us all out into the garden for a sit, she followed. She had always loved the garden and, plopped down on a familiar pouf pillow, she looked around as if, hard as it might be to say who was or was not a friend among the humans, she and the vegetation were ready to take up where they'd left off.

"What is that stalk?" she asked.

"A sunflower," said Gwen. "It's going to be taller than my dad. We're going to toast the seeds and eat them."

"A sunflower. Wow," said Ondi.

"They're easy to grow," I said. "A little work, a lot of drama."

"Wow."

Then Eleanor brought out some lemonade and cookies on a tray, and Ondi's edge returned.

"If you don't think I see what you're doing, I do," said Ondi. "I see it completely."

"Interesting," said Eleanor. "And here we see what you are doing as well."

That's when Ondi should have said, *What is that supposed to mean?* Instead, flipping again, she accepted a cookie. Then she accepted and drank some lemonade—inching her way toward us, it seemed, like a squirrel trying to decide whether or not to lunge for a hunk of bread. Finally she said, "You don't understand."

"And here we believe that it is you who doesn't understand," said Eleanor.

"How can I not understand?"

"Because we are often the worst explicators of our own actions and motivations, much less their consequences," said Eleanor.

Was this what now came with lemonade and cookies? Ondi planted her lemonade glass on the ground in front of her and stood up as if to leave.

"Who what when where how why," said Gwen, using the exact tone Eleanor had always used when she said that, but with a sideways tilt of her head.

Ondi gave her a crooked smile, and for a moment, you could almost see their old friendship flash between them.

"Okay," she said, and settled back down on the pouf—in which, as it happened, I had buried a deflector way back when. That was a good thing, given all Ondi was about to say.

◆

The story started with the days out at sea, which were terrifying. Her parents, luckily, were both excellent sailors. Her father had in fact been on the sailing team at college, and her mother had been his trusty crew. Happily, too, the boat in which they were Cast Off was a reasonable one—a Rhodes 4000, in good repair. It was not big, but it had navigational equipment, a solar battery, a small fridge, a tank of fresh water, and a cookstove. Ondi had actually thought it cool that every door had a latch. Even the doors of the cabinets in which they stocked their cans had latches, and there were cushioned alcoves in which they could sleep. Indeed, the day they set out, it almost seemed as if they were going on a vacation. All they were missing was a VirtualFlix player.

They weren't gone for two days, though, before the first storm hit. Many things immediately went overboard, including the messenger drone I'd fashioned for them, but that was hardly their biggest problem. The storms that had begun to build and build in the last half century were now behemoths, with maelstrom winds and fusillades of rain; there were many hours when Ondi's father forbade anyone else on deck for fear they'd be blown or washed off, while down below they worried that he would be swept away himself. Even on the calmer days, the swells were the size of buildings. Ondi said she could still feel the upupup crash, upupup crash in her stomach and legs; she could still feel the boat pitching wildly and hear the winds howling and howling—"as if there were something the matter with them," as she put it. The waves,

too, crashed and crashed and crashed. Sometimes they were filled
with trash. It never stopped.

But that wasn't even the worst of it. The worst of it, Ondi said,
was that they had her one-hundred-fifteen-year-old grandfather—
her mother's father—with them. Grandpa Barney was once a vet-
erinarian who had respected animals and was respected in return
but who apparently gave people what they had coming to them.
As he liked to say, *the bigger the bigot, the bigger the boot.* Now he
was a frail Asian man with a sparse white beard—or not even a
beard, just these random hairs—and an open mouth. Ondi was
terrified of the way his jaw hung, showing the pale insides of his
mouth. His tongue was white, his teeth long and yellowed. He
knew better than to try to stand in the lurching boat but was still
knocked off his bench so many times that Ondi's father rigged
a kind of hammock for him, out of a sheet. Then, if they kept
the knots tight, Grandpa Barney swung during the storms. The
swinging was violent and made him throw up, but it was better
than his being thrown across the boat, and in the occasional lulls,
Ondi could sit by him and hold his hand and try to get him to eat
something. He had to eat something, she kept telling him. He
had to eat. Grandpa Barney, though, did not eat. Instead, wrapped
in several blankets, he shuddered uncontrollably. Ondi's mother
cried. Anyone could see he was in agony, she said; anyone could
see he was going to die. Between the storms, they tried to sail for
land.

The Enforcers were everywhere on their orange Hydro-
Bikes, though, and where there wasn't an Enforcer, there was an
EnforceBot in an AquaDrone. Dying man or not, Ondi's family
was driven, over and over again, back out to sea.

This went on until Grandpa Barney had nothing left in him—
until there was nothing left in any of them. Grandpa Barney didn't
talk much, but when he did, all he would say was that he wanted
to die—as, in fact, they all did. Ondi's mother, especially, wanted

them to all hold hands and jump into the ocean, but her father said they couldn't, because of Ondi. We have a child, he said. Think of her young life. And to Ondi, he said, We have you. We all have to live, because of you. And when she said, This is all my fault, he said, It's not.

Which was about the nicest thing he had ever said to her, Ondi said, maybe because there was nothing to drink out there. And later he said it again, adding that she had been manipulated.

Eleanor's eyebrows rose at that, but neither she nor I asked by whom.

Finally an Enforcer sped up to them. Ondi thought he seemed like a nice enough man but he did not leave his boat, just shouted up at them with an ampliphone. As for his message, that was that they could re-Register. They could rejoin the ranks of the Surplus. But someone had to be winnowed. They were surprised that he used that term—it was as if he knew how the Surplus talked. And did he mean Ondi's grandfather? Since neither of her parents would ask it, Ondi did, loudly—shouted it, really. And maybe the man understood. Otherwise, why did he laugh before he sped off?

Of course, the answer was no.

But Grandpa Barney got wind of it. And that night, when everyone else was asleep, he somehow managed to roll himself out of his hammock and climb up onto the deck. He did slip while he was up there and fell with a thump loud enough to wake Ondi—which was when she scrambled up the ladder and shouted, Stop! Stop! But it was too late. He had thrown himself overboard.

"My god," said Eleanor.

"I'm so sorry," said Gwen.

Ondi looked as if she were filing a report. She stood, took her glass, and brought it over to the burgeoning sunflower stalk. Then, lifting the big leaves out of the way, she carefully poured some lemonade onto its roots.

"Those leaves are so big," she said. "It's like they're on the wrong planet. Or at least in the wrong climate. Like they should be in the tropics."

"They really are big," I said.

"Or the Jurassic. They should be in the Jurassic."

No one else said anything for a time. Ondi plopped back down. Eleanor offered her another cookie. She accepted.

"And this is how it started?" I asked finally. "The grief and anger you brought home? That eventually led to your playing unhacked and so on?"

Ondi nodded and chewed.

"I can see that," Eleanor said. "Or at least the grief and anger part. What you experienced on that boat . . ."

None of us knew quite how to finish her sentence.

"It would scar anyone," I supplied finally. I felt like an old-time dental-hygienist-in-training, handing an implement to a dentist; I could only hope that I got it right, and that the tool I proffered would be taken from my hand.

"Exactly," said Eleanor. "It's not like a bad dream you wake up from and shake off." She paused again.

"Grief deranges." Gwen's loose hair bloomed enormous behind her, but her manner was restrained.

Ondi looked surprised. "It does," she said. "That's the word. It deranges."

"Healing is slow," said Gwen.

"Yes." Ondi tilted her head at Gwen. "It is. It is slow."

"You do realize that we were not the ones who sent you out in that boat, right?" said Eleanor. "You realize that we were the ones who knit sweaters and blankets for you. Grant made you a messenger drone."

I shrugged off the acknowledgment.

"Remember?"

Ondi frowned. "My parents told me never to have anything to do with you again. But the truth is . . ."

We waited.

"The truth is that even if you were bribing us with them, we wore your sweaters every day and wrapped my grandfather in your blankets. Probably it was thanks to the blankets that he even lived as long as he did. Without them, he probably would have died right away."

"Which might have been a mercy?" suggested Gwen. "In a way?" She let the accusation of bribing the Nickelhoffs go unanswered and spoke tentatively—in a voice she would have mocked as *quaveringly questioning* in someone else—not wanting, we could see, to offend her friend again.

And how sad but also relieved Gwen looked when, finally starting to cry, Ondi said, "Yes."

Eleanor produced a handkerchief.

"We were still glad he had the blankets," Ondi went on. "My mother even said later that she wished we had kept them. And my father said we were fools to give them back the way we did. He said we should have kept a sweater each."

"So why didn't you?" asked Eleanor.

"Because we told Aunt Nettie we would have nothing else to do with you."

Eleanor flashed me a look.

"We've been black-coded," I guessed.

Ondi dabbed at her eyes.

Gwen, Eleanor, and I all put our glasses down together, as if the day were suddenly too cold for lemonade.

"Meaning it didn't matter whether or not you were hacked," I said. "Because Aunt Nettie already knew about the League. You didn't need to make sure Aunt Nettie couldn't track you."

"My mother said you are fools, and you are," said Ondi.

"And given the situation, why get hacked—suggesting that you were a League sympathizer?" I went on. "Was that your thinking? That it was better to let Aunt Nettie track you, never mind that you ran the opposite risk—that even if Andrea never realized you hadn't been hacked, as she probably wouldn't, we might still realize?"

Ondi played with the handkerchief. "That was part of it."

"And the rest of it?" demanded Eleanor.

Ondi reached for a cookie—a moment when Eleanor would normally have pushed the dish closer. She did not.

"When were we black-coded?" she asked instead. "Do you know? Were we black-coded when you came back?"

"No. Or at least I don't think so."

"So how do you know we are black-coded now?"

When Ondi didn't answer, Gwen guessed. "Because you're the one who got us black-coded. You came to the game knowing Aunt Nettie knew about everyone. Including the Thistles. Including all those girls who used to be so mean to us."

"You hated them, too," Ondi said.

Eleanor stood and paced—thinking, I knew, of her years in jail. This was back when jail meant beatings and interrogations, before Aunt Nettie realized that these things left evidence that Casting Off didn't—broken bones, in Eleanor's case, and a ruptured spleen. She almost died and was lucky to have recovered. And it was, as she liked to say, "only three years." But she understood that black-coding meant you were officially an enemy of the state. Any action you took would be placed in that context; any AutoJudge you faced for any reason would be set to black code. The black-coded people she had known in jail never made it out. Did Ondi realize the seriousness of what she'd done? Did she?

"And why did you agree to come?" Eleanor went on. "Did you come just to say how angry you are? At them? At us?"

"I came because you asked me to." Ondi wrapped the handkerchief around her hand like a bandage.

"And?" Eleanor glared. "Did you think we would forgive you?

Mindlessly supportive people that we are. People who would knit and knit for you, people who would take any length of limits testing, even if it involved black-coding? Or is this a setup of some kind? Another favor to Aunt Nettie?"

"I guess I came . . ." Ondi unwrapped the handkerchief. Then suddenly there she was—the brave and precocious girl we once knew. "I came because I knew you would understand me better than I understood myself."

"Because we're a little like Aunt Nettie that way," I said.

"Aunt Nettie can't tell me."

"You AskedAuntNettie?" said Gwen.

Ondi flushed. "It was really stupid."

No one disagreed.

"And I guess I came to see—not if you'd forgive me," said Ondi. "But if there was a way of straightening things out. Not that I think there is."

"No," said Eleanor. "There isn't."

Ondi balled up the handkerchief; she looked as if she might start crying again. "I'm sorry."

Eleanor looked almost as drained as Ondi. "Well, it's one thing Aunt Nettie may never get about us," she said. "That we're irrational and perverse. That we destroy things we love, then want to fix them. Where's the algorithm that explains that?"

"*Homo regrettus*," said Gwen. "Isn't that what you used to call us?"

Eleanor gave a wan smile. "What a pleasure to realize you hear what your parents say." And for a flickering moment it could have been the point in any of a thousand family discussions when Eleanor and I stole a quick look at each other, taking pleasure in our child.

Ondi's voice broke in. "My grandfather didn't actually get up to the deck alone," she said.

"You helped him," guessed Gwen.

"He wanted to die. He really did. And those steps. It was a ladder, actually."

"He couldn't have gotten up that ladder himself," said Gwen.

"No. He was so weak. And the blankets would've made it even harder."

"Did he take them off?"

"He needed help with them. And that was almost the worst part. Because once I unwrapped the blankets, he was so cold. I mean, he was shaking and shaking." Ondi shuddered. "I've never heard of anyone shaking to death but I honestly thought he might. That's how bad it was. How violent."

"Your parents didn't hear you?" asked Gwen—the classic teenager's question.

"They were asleep. Exhausted, I think. I had to warm him with my body." Ondi smoothed the handkerchief on her knee and looked at it; beyond the fence, the geese were honking, as they often did, at a delivery drone. "He was so cold. I didn't know a human could be so cold. He was like a fish."

"But you wanted him to die, too."

"Honestly? We all did."

"Because he was suffering."

"Yes."

"And because you just wanted to go back to a harbor. Which you could once you'd winnowed him."

"Did anyone ever tell you that you can be just like your mother?" Ondi asked—forgetting, it seemed, that Eleanor was standing right there.

Gwen shrugged, her shoulders disappearing for a moment into the mass of her hair. "As long as you're not talking about her aim. I mean, she's great with a foil, but a wrecking ball has more control than she does." Since when did Gwen know how to defuse things? I watched in amazement as she winked—knowing, too, that on another day, Eleanor would now be picking something up and throwing it, and that we would all be having a good laugh. But instead we looked at Ondi.

"There are worse things," I put in, "than being willing to state the cold truth."

And after a moment, Ondi agreed. She continued to smooth and smooth the handkerchief. "If he hadn't jumped, I'd probably have jumped in myself."

"That's how bad it was," supplied Gwen.

"Yes."

"But your parents saw it differently," I said.

"They thought if they could just get Grandpa back, he could maybe be saved. They said they had doctor friends from back when my dad was still a doctor himself—doctors who were the best in the world. They said they were going to call one of their famous doctor friends."

Gwen passed around the cookie plate. "Do they know the truth?"

"No." Ondi went on smoothing.

"They must have been surprised when they woke up."

"They said it was a miracle he got himself up that ladder."

"And how could he have thrown himself off the deck? Did they wonder that?" asked Gwen.

"Yes." Ondi's voice dropped, and her hands stilled, but she kept speaking. "And the truth is that he asked me to help him. It was hard to hear him above the wind, but he asked me."

"So you helped him."

"I had to. I took him to the edge, and I lifted the rope— there was kind of this rope railing. Then I guess he should have jumped, but he didn't have to jump. The boat rocked, and he slipped. Which I almost did, too. But I caught myself."

"And that was that."

Ondi looked up from her pouf at Gwen, and nodded. "I just

wish he hadn't smashed his head against the side of the boat before he hit the water."

"Was there blood?" asked Gwen.

Ondi nodded again. "The boat was rocking like crazy and hit him."

"It probably knocked him out."

"I hope."

"Then he wouldn't have felt how cold the water was, right?"

Ondi's eyes filled with tears, which she wiped away with the handkerchief, even though it smeared her makeup and streaked the cloth. "I hope he didn't feel that," she said. "He was already so cold."

We all listened to the geese for a moment. The delivery drone was taking back off.

"And then?" asked Eleanor, gently.

"And then he went under. Pretty much right away. But I called, I love you! anyway. In case he could still hear anything."

"Even though your parents might hear you?" asked Gwen.

Ondi shrugged. "I just really wanted him to know."

Gwen reached for her hand. Ondi didn't pull away.

"I told him when I lifted the rope up, too. Right before he went over. I said, Are you sure? And when he nodded, I squeezed his hand and said, I love you! and, Be careful!"

"And did he say anything?"

"He laughed. I think because I told him to be careful. It was so ridiculous. Though his hearing was so terrible, it was hard to know what he heard. Then the boat rocked and he went over. Like, he let go and right where he was standing, suddenly there was no one." Ondi wiped her eyes some more and said again, "I wish he hadn't hit his head."

"That must have been terrible," said Gwen.

"Do you think he felt it?"

"No," said Gwen. "I'm sure it happened so fast, he didn't feel anything."

"That's good, I guess. I was going to dive in after him." Ondi stared at the young sunflower stalk. "Like those Japanese kids—do you remember when we read about them? The ones who wouldn't let go of their grandparents in a tsunami? But I didn't."

"That was good. Because then you would have just both died. People had to train other Japanese kids to let go. Remember? They had to give them lessons. Because they couldn't save their grandparents. They had to let go and save themselves. They had to learn. Remember?"

Ondi nodded but then said, "That's not why I didn't go in."

"Then why?"

"I hate to say it."

"You can say it."

Ondi wound the handkerchief around a finger. "I always hated going in after my father's basketballs, that's why. Like the water was just so cold."

"And this was going to be even colder," said Gwen. "Is that it?"

"I know that sounds terrible."

Gwen shrugged. "If you AskedAuntNettie, she'd probably say, *You're only human.*"

Ondi wound the handkerchief the other way, winding and winding. "How do sunflowers know to grow straight up?"

Eleanor explained that, as well as how plants, it turns out, remember things. How they warn one another of drought, and more. "And now your parents still don't know?" she asked.

"No."

"But we do."

"Yes."

Finally Eleanor said, "To answer your earlier question: you came because you had something to get off your chest."

Ondi was crying again and wiping her eyes, but she was listening, too. It wasn't just her face that was turned to Eleanor; her whole body was turning and lifting as if she were a child again, pretending to be a plant growing toward the sun. "I guess I just remember how you used to say there's no direction like true north," she said.

"And?" said Eleanor.

"I want you to hack me," said Ondi. "I know it's too late to fix things, but I want you to hack me anyway."

And—wishing it would change more than it would—we said okay.

◆

We had never convened a League-wide meeting before. Having organized a League playoff at the end of the second year, though, we decided to use the same location—a former college football stadium—and to employ our usual networks as well. We eschewed the word "emergency," not wanting to alarm anyone. But we did call this an important, immediate, mandatory meeting.

We set the time of the meeting at six a.m. And as usual, we asked that as many people swim as possible, to keep the number of boats down. Happily, for both the swimmers and the boaters, it was a calm morning. A cool morning, too, its coolness made all the sweeter for the heat that we all knew would arrive as if on robocall by noon.

Now there was both apprehension and festivity in the air, people having brought not only breakfast foods and picnic blankets but balls and bats as well. Why not get in some practice, after all? By the time Eleanor and I arrived, the balls were flying. Never mind that you could hardly see, everywhere there was the *bock* of fungos hitting balls and the *thud* of balls being caught. Could we really have built up to twelve teams? Eleanor squeezed my hand and, with sadness, I squeezed back. A baseball league was not a person, but ahead of us did loom what our local PearlyGates would have called an EternaLoss.

There were two long white folding tables in the middle of the field, to which everyone had contributed food to share. Mostly, though, the various teams stuck together, their blankets clustered around tarps that served as their team center. A parent having brought art supplies and stakes, above the tarps flew makeshift team flags with logos or crests or cartoons. The Lookouts, the Thistles, the Jets. The Jedis, the GoodGuys, the Rejects. The Chosen. The Alphas. The Betas. The RosyDrones. The DreadNoughts. The DingBats.

What were they expecting? The most viral of the rumors apparently involved an illness—affecting me or Eleanor or both. Indeed, we were receiving sympathetic looks and meaningful hugs; my old assistant director, May, kept wiping her eyes with a hankie. I tried to reassure her, but as there were others as well evincing woe, Eleanor and I agreed: the sooner we commenced the better.

We had everyone sit, brought the field to order, and, with as few preliminaries as possible, explained that someone had been playing unhacked. What's more, we explained that while we had no proof Aunt Nettie was wise to us, we strongly suspected this to be the case, and that it was even possible we had all been black-coded.

"We don't know for sure," we kept saying. "We can only surmise."

The barest ripple of response. But then the tops of people's heads lit up, and as with surprising speed the sun began to pick out, first people's eyes, and then their faces, it seemed that you could see their dawning realization. Although did they really get the seriousness of the situation? Or would you have had to have the sort of run-ins that Eleanor had had with Aunt Nettie to really understand? Well aware as most Surplus were of Aunt Nettie's proddings, few knew her beatings; there were few signs in ordinary life of just how suddenly you could be pitched into an unremittingly brutal reality.

A voice broke in.

"Who was it?" This was someone from the right side of the crowd—one of the mothers, wearing what appeared to be her son's sweatshirt. She did not shout but she spoke loudly enough for everyone to hear, and a moment later, her question was being asked from all over—echoing, even, off the walls of the stadium. *Who was it? Who was it? Who? Who?*

Eleanor and I put our hands up, asking for quiet. I was barehanded but, what with the crimson sweater Eleanor had knit for me, visible enough, I imagined. So, too, was white-haired Eleanor, in a white sweater. She wore fingerless gloves Gwen had knit for her as well, with a bright white peace symbol in their palms. Gwen, in more muted colors, stood next to us, lending moral support.

"We agreed not to say, in return for more information," I said.

This was not, strictly speaking, true. In fact, Ondi had, despite her recommitment to true north, declined to be identified. As for why I nonetheless reflexively protected her, I had a mix of motives. But chief among them at that moment was a fear of the ugliness of which even a lovely group like the League was capable. For groups were that way, I believed—warm seas out of which could arise, as my mother used to warn, a hurricane. *A powerful hurricane, one that can level everything you see.* As for whether Eleanor was comfortable with my impromptu fib, she did not so much as look my way. Instead, she tried, as we had agreed, to focus on the consequences of Ondi's actions rather than on Ondi herself.

"What is most important is not who is to blame," she said, "but what this means to each of you—how exposed you are, especially if you have ever come in for distinguished treatment by Aunt Nettie before, or have had other reason to believe you might fall afoul of black-coding."

She did not elaborate here—wanting to be forthright, I could see, but not wanting to scare people unduly. And, happily, if anyone had special reason for concern, he or she did not express it.

"What matters is what you should do," she went on. "What matters is what we should all do. Though let us say"—she looked at me as though to be sure she had license to speak for us both— "we cannot apologize more profoundly that this has happened."

I nodded.

"We're sure you're not to blame," said someone—we couldn't quite see who. But there was a chorus of agreement, even as some people continued to ask, "How did this happen?" And, try as we might to steer the conversation, "Who would do such a thing?" *Someone was willing to endanger us all? Someone who came and played? How could they do that? How could anyone? Who was it? Who was it?*

Eleanor and I worked to dampen these voices but still they grew as if fed by a hidden spring. *And shouldn't this person be held accountable? Whoever it was?*

Who was it? Who was it?

Who? Who?

"And where were the safeguards?" May demanded, changing the tune at last. She glared at me with the same *How could you have let this happen* expression she had used when—how many years ago was this now?—our budget got cut. It was the same swing, too, from sympathy to accusation.

"Someone," I had to say then, "told this person about the League. And someone else, when assured that this person would get hacked, went ahead and signed this person up to play without checking to make sure this person really had."

"And so this person played unhacked?" asked May.

"Exactly."

"As you had no way of knowing?"

"Unfortunately."

"So then there are three people to blame," said May. "The person who told the unhacked person about the League, the person who played the unhacked person, and the unhacked person him- or herself."

"As well as Eleanor and myself for not, as you say, instituting safeguards."

"And you know who they are," said May. "These three other people."

"Two of them."

"And do you have non-disclosure agreements with them both, or just with the one?"

This was beginning to feel like the sort of department meeting in which factions make a show of fact-finding when in actuality they are looking for blood. Eleanor cleared her throat.

"I understand your need and desire to know these things," she started to say. "But our attention is best—"

She did not finish. Andrea had stood up and was making her way toward us, her head bent. She flashed us a quick apologetic look, then turned to the crowd.

Not only had she taken the purple spikes out of her hair, Andrea had shaved it off altogether, and instead of an elaborately Thistle-themed outfit, she was wearing a brown men's overcoat. Overlarge as this was and boasting all of two buttons, it seemed more to mock its pillar-of-society origins than to suggest a newly responsible self. But her manner was chastened. She spoke with her chin up and her hands in her pockets—not the fast-and-loose nineteen-year-old who had run a dangerously oblivious team but the disciplined young organizer who had launched and now operated, all by herself, a ShelterBoat.

"I am the person who took this young person at her word,"

she began. "I won't say his or her, as I think you all know I am the coach of the Thistles, and that we are an all-girl team. So, yes, the young person was a her. And let me say right off that I am not standing here so you can eye my players and make conjectures about them. I am standing here to help Eleanor and Grant. Because, finally, it was not one thing that went wrong. It was many things. And as some of you have suggested, it wasn't just one person who made mistakes, either. Yes, some of the problem was sloppiness and laziness. But it was not simple carelessness on the part of Eleanor and Grant, and it is important to realize that. There might have been better safeguards, but this is not like a bank that has had hundreds of years to figure things out. This is a volunteer organization, invented on the fly and run on a shoestring. I don't mean to attack anyone. But I know from my own experience with the ShelterBoat what that means. While the League seems like a miracle, there are in fact no miracles. Mistakes were bound to be made as we got bigger. And if any of you thinks it ironic that I, the youngest and greenest of the coaches, should be the one to recognize that there were going to be growing pains, really, it is and isn't. Because I am actually the age most aware of what a growing pain is."

Andrea took a deep breath, trying to maintain her composure; above her, the sky seemed to grow as it brightened. The crowd waited.

"I cannot say how sorry I am for my part in this," she went on. "I was wrong not to follow up with this unhacked player. I cannot apologize enough for jeopardizing your safety, and I only wish I knew how to undo what I've done. And I cannot apologize enough to Eleanor and Grant." She turned to us. "I've wrecked your beautiful project with my carelessness, and if you never spoke to me again I could hardly blame you."

Such an impressive and affecting young lady—I was in awe of her right up until that "if you never spoke to me again." But then it was in part to stifle a smile that I joined Eleanor and Gwen in immediately stepping forward to hug her, whereupon she started to cry the halting cry of someone who had been determined—who was, in fact, still determined—not to cry.

"I'm so sorry," she said, "I'm so sorry"—even as so many tissues were proffered that they almost seemed part of a magic trick, emerging and emerging as they did from sleeves, from hats, from thin air. People gave her time to collect herself.

Then the father of one of the Thistles stood—a light-skinned man with a turban. "You have served our children so well. I cannot speak for other parents, but I am not angry at you. Has any of us not made mistakes? And not just when we were young, by the way. As a matter of fact, slow learner than I am, I myself have not had a chance to forget what growing pains are like."

Laughter.

"You have given so generously to the ShelterBoat and to this League," he went on, "and in return were, frankly, taken advantage of. I do not blame you. Or, all right, if I blame you, I only blame you a little."

More laughter.

"You should have followed up. Definitely. That was a terrible mistake. But mostly," he finished, "I thank you for your service and your honesty."

Some of the players were unsure how to react, but the parents, practiced as they were in positivity, immediately began to cheer. "Yay, Andrea! Thank you! Thank you!"

Which one of the Thistles was his daughter? And what had happened to her that she had proved in need of sheltering? He hardly seemed the head of an abusive household; I just hoped his was not one of the girls who had been rescued from addiction or prostitution. In the meanwhile, so genuine and well-put was his appreciation that Andrea's eyes began to fill again.

Then a young woman in a flannel shirt stood. "We can understand your reticence," she said. "We can understand your desire not to point fingers, and we do not particularly want to point fingers ourselves. But what if our children are hanging around with this girl? The one who played unhacked, I mean. Don't we have a right to know? Don't our kids have a right to make an informed decision about whether to remain friends? Does this girl's privacy trump our kids' safety?"

"I absolutely see your point," Andrea began to say. "But I do not feel at liberty . . ." She looked to Eleanor and me for a cue. I nodded and was about to take over when Ondi stood.

Her red-and-gold hair was as glorious as ever and adorned with an astonishing number of clips; she wore a shiny blue jacket and dark orange harem pants. Yet for all her sartorial exuberance, she looked as if she had not slept one night since she sat with us in the garden.

"My name is Ondi Nickelhoff, and you can blame me," she began.

"Say what?" said someone.

"Louder!" said someone else.

She started again. "My name is Ondi Nickelhoff, and you can blame me," she said, raising her voice. "I'm not the girl who told an unhacked person about the League. And I'm not the coach who trusted a girl she shouldn't have. I am the girl herself. I am the girl who breached your security and ruined things for everyone here." She paused, gathering her strength, and I remember thinking that she really needed an ampliphone—or if not an ampliphone, something else to hang on to. Something to help her. People craned forward to catch her words. "There is no excuse for what I've done. I am truly sorry. Please do not blame Andrea, or Eleanor and Grant, or anyone else. I and I alone have done a terrible thing. It is one of the most terrible things I have ever done in my life, and I deserve every terrible thing you may say about me."

Her self-possession was astonishing and her manner disarming. Had she ever spoken before a crowd before? Had Andrea's example perhaps helped her? Someone started to boo but, hearing it, Gwen—showing fantastic aplomb, too, I thought—quickly began to clap, upon which signal, others followed suit. The applause was not thunderous. But it was sustained enough that Ondi, after a stunned moment—recalling, I wanted to think, how she had not only failed to help Gwen when she was being booed by the Thistles, but had in fact encouraged the booers—gave Gwen what appeared to be a rueful smile of thanks.

"Thank you," she said. "I can't tell you exactly how I came to do this terrible thing. I wish I knew myself. But I can tell you a little about my background. And maybe understanding where I am coming from will help you understand where I ended up."

Ondi did not explain about Grandpa Barney—because, she told Gwen later, she didn't want to play her grandfather's death for sympathy. As for whether it was that, or whether her instincts told her that that part of the story might not cast her in an altogether sympathetic light, we never knew. Perhaps—collected as she seemed on the surface—she truly was unprepared to share so emotional a part of her story. In any case, she left it out.

She largely left our family out, too, except to say that we had taught her to knit, and that it was thanks to knitting that she became interested in carding and spinning wool, and in old ways generally. She talked about SpritzGramming animal smells from Vermont—drawing a spate of laughter—and about how much trouble that brought. She talked about the trial, and about the punishment, which did seem disproportionate to the crime. Funny as it sounds, she said, it seemed punitive. She mentioned how Eleanor and Gwen had knit blankets and sweaters for her family, and how I had devised a messenger drone for them as well. She thanked us.

But mostly she talked about the experience of being Cast Off—something most people had heard of but did not know much about. She talked about the size of the waves—as big as tankers, she told them, just as she had told us. She talked about the pitching of the boat, and about the Enforcers and the HydroBikes and the EnforceBots and the AquaDrones. She talked about the wind, the never-ceasing wind, and about the sharks—the first we had heard about the sharks. Why had she not mentioned the sharks when she explained to us why she had not wanted to jump into the water after her grandfather? Now she talked about how hungry she and her family were, too, and how thirsty—things she had not made much of in her first account of their ordeal, either, although the privation must have been terrible. Perhaps she had simply forgotten about the sharks, as she had about her family's hunger and thirst? Even now, so many years later, I wonder. Perhaps she had left them out originally because the sharks were mitigating— because she wanted to be damned for her reluctance to dive into the cold water. Though wasn't that reluctance really just a way of saying she didn't want to be as cold as her grandfather— that she didn't want to be dead? Something no one could blame her for?

She talked now instead about how they had all wanted to throw themselves overboard. She talked about how her parents couldn't jump because they had her, and how she couldn't jump because she was all her parents had. And then she talked about how angry she was when she got back to shore—how deranged, really—and though full of hatred toward Aunt Nettie, how anxious to cooperate with her, too. How she just wanted never to find herself on anything like that boat again.

"But now, I am ashamed," she finished. "I hate myself and I would not blame you if you could not forgive me, since I cannot forgive myself."

Of course, some people were still upset. One man yelled, "You're damned right we don't forgive you! You've fucked us all!" and I heard another say, "Too bad life takes more than talk." But some were sympathetic, especially when they heard that Ondi had at least, yes, belatedly gotten herself hacked.

"You're not the first one to seek to appease your captors," said one person.

"The desire to submit to authority is as old as mankind," said another.

"None of us knows what she'll do in extremis," said a third.

And to all of this, many nodded, though it did seem the sentiments that had received approval; Ondi herself was not bathed in forgiveness the way Andrea had been. Quite the contrary, anyone could hear in the silence of the many who had not spoken, *How could you? How could you? How could you?* A chorus that Eleanor and I could have joined. *You had us black-coded? You turned us in? You jeopardized the safety of everyone in the League—including Eleanor? You endangered Eleanor?*

If anything checked our anger, it was Gwen quietly standing by Ondi just as, back when they were in grade school, Ondi, we knew, had many times stood by her. Could she really have forgiven Ondi? And how had they ended up almost exactly the same height, and with such similar builds and skin? It was pure coincidence that they were both mixes of African, Asian, and Caucasian blood. There was nothing in it. They were not sisters. But the sun having risen by now, their heads were haloed as if blessed by nature itself—*by the mountains and the rivers and the tides and the sand,* my mother would have said. Meaning by whatever forces had placed one girl in one family and one in another with no more care than they had for a fish or a crab.

Then there was, at least for Eleanor and me, the choreography of the meeting to attend to. Like group leaders everywhere, we had planned for an airing of emotions to be followed by a channeling of those feelings into the making of a decision—a tricky transition to manage, especially as the question we had to raise was devastating. But, now, the time had come to ask, What next?

"I'm sorry to say," I said—trying to be as brave as Andrea and Ondi—"that I believe we should disband."

Silence. Of course, people could see the logic of this. If nothing else, if we kept on—"think of the impact on our Living Points!" said someone, absurdly.

But yet more absurdly, someone in the back disagreed.

"I do not want to disband," said a pyramidal woman in a baseball hat.

Andrea, scrambling to her feet, backed the woman up. "I do not want to disband, either," she said. She was still wearing her men's overcoat, but it was unbuttoned now, and in the rising breeze, it flew up behind her as if she were standing on the prow of a boat determinedly under sail. "I understand what has happened. I understand that we find ourselves at this juncture because of a member of my team. And let me say again that I take responsibility for not following up with Ondi.

"But if I am getting this right, we have reason to believe that Aunt Nettie is onto us. So what do we have to lose? It makes no sense to cut ourselves off from this, one of the few good things we have left to our lives. Maybe we will only last another game or two. Who knows? But if our gig is up, I'd rather play as much as we possibly can than sit home and wait for the ax to fall. We must all make our own decisions. But I myself am not dropping out. As long as there are people to throw and people to hit, I will be here. As my mom used to say, *Might as well go out swinging*. And as for Aunt Nettie, all I can say is, to hell with her!"

At this people started shouting,

To hell with Aunt Nettie! To hell with her!
To hell with Aunt Nettie! To hell with her!

Eleanor and I looked at each other in amazement as the chanting morphed into,

To hell with Aunt Nettie! Let's play ball!
To hell with Aunt Nettie! Let's play ball!

"Thank you, Andrea," said Eleanor at last. "So the question is, how many of you are in? How many of you want to join Andrea—and, I will say, Grant and me and"—she looked at Gwen and Ondi, whose answer was plain—"the girls, and continue?"

"I am! I am! I am!" The responses were overwhelming.

"Think it over," cautioned Eleanor. "Don't be rash. And let me say that, whatever you think today, you can change your mind tomorrow. But if we can get a nonbinding show of hands—how many of you want to keep playing? Risk and all?"

And to our astonishment, though the hands came up at different rates—with some shooting up straightaway, and others rising only after a moment or two—every hand was finally raised high.

"Well, all right," said Eleanor then. She could not have looked more stunned had she been clear-floated to a different galaxy. "We'll go on." And with that, we packed up to go home.

◆

The next day brought continued elation but also—when we finally told Gwen about her ball speed—distraction. Had Mimi really said that about a seventy-mile-per-hour pitch guaranteeing a place on the Netted League team? Gwen asked. And had I really recorded her pitch at the Jets game as seventy-three miles per hour? And why hadn't Eleanor and I told her about Dana the Enforcer's visit, and why had I measured her ball speeds anyway, and how?

The how question was the easiest to answer. I tried to hide my pride as I showed Gwen my meter, although a full-functioning meter small enough to hide in the palm of my hand was, for this tinkerer, an achievement.

"Wow, cool," she said, with an air that suggested that the whole thing was, after all, pretty twentieth century.

Daughters. As for why I thought to measure her ball speed: "Parents the world over keep an eye on their kids, trying to understand their strengths and weaknesses, the better to help square them with reality," I began.

Gwen rolled her eyes.

"In any case," I went on, "isn't the important thing what Mimi had to say?" I watched closely as she gave a diffident nod.

"I guess," she said.

"Presenting as it does a bit of quandary, perhaps?"

"What quandary?" she said. "There is no quandary. I am not going to Net U."

Since there was nothing to discuss, we did not discuss it, especially as Eleanor and I were preoccupied with the Surplus Fields case. In this, there had been three developments. The first was that I had come up with a meter capable of establishing beyond dispute that there were indeed emanations. The second was that Eleanor, Yuri, Heraldine, and Sue were all but done exhausting the National Park Service's remedies to their complaint. They still had one to go and I had yet to identify the emanations; we had much work ahead. All the same, Eleanor and her team were anxious to begin constructing their case, especially after—the third development—not one but four young kids affected by the emanations had found their way to Eleanor's office. All four—two boys and two girls—had ExoLimbs without which they could not move, though they had all moved normally before they played on the Surplus Fields. In fact, if her daughter had had a problem, one parent said, it was that she never stopped running and climbing. Now the girl stared at us from within her openwork armor.

"It works," she reported, "but everything hurts."

And the others concurred. The pain never stopped. They could take something for it but then they slept all the time and couldn't wake up.

"We're going to fight," Eleanor promised. "We're going to fight with everything we have." She didn't say what we all knew, that there was no saving these kids, only the children who came after them. What's more, even if damages were finally paid—a big if—they could not begin to compensate the victims for the loss of their healthy limbs. But as for the suggestion, made a little while later, that Eleanor let someone else take the lead on this case, rather than intensify the heat with which she already lived, the answer was simply no. And, no, she would not discuss it.

Mimi, meanwhile, had been in touch with Gwen again. To reduce the stress of training for the Netted League tryouts, every prospect was entitled, it seemed, to a training partner. In Gwen's case, this involved three choices, two of whom she didn't know. But could we guess who the third choice was?

"Ondi," said Eleanor immediately.

"Wow, great guess, Mom. Yes." Gwen tossed a ball up into the air—something she was not allowed to do in the house. Eleanor frowned.

Ondi had apparently also received a GreetingGram invitation to the tryouts, to which she had answered that, yes, she was willing to put her name in the training partner pool. And why not, Gwen guessed Ondi had figured. The League needed girls. As for whether she was the best of Gwen's three choices, that really did not matter, Gwen said, because she was not planning either to train or to try out.

"I thought you told Mimi you were," I said. "Or at least declined to say you weren't."

"Well, I'm not," she said firmly.

In fact, she reported that she had recently joined a group of knitters who were knitting sweaters big enough to cover whole houseboats. "Sweater bombing," she called this, with more excitement in her voice than we'd heard in years. "It's an art thing." She had enormous bags of yarn in her room—"stash," as she referred to it—all from her new friends, and huge new needles, too. These were almost an inch in diameter, as befit the stretches of knitting she was producing—on a scale like nothing we'd ever seen. She was knitting a kind of mural, really—a series of panels depicting a forest of sunflowers, with such dramatically curling petals and leaves they seemed almost animate.

This place is quite a mess, the house kept complaining. *Clearfloat now? This place is quite a mess.*

And, *Someone is going to trip. You always have a choice. But someone is going to trip.*

And, *Do note that your choice is on the record. Nothing is being hidden from you. But your choice is on the record.*

Gwen was unperturbed.

"See? This is the opening for a window," she said. "I'm doing the whole right side of the house."

Her decision could not have been clearer. She told us she had even received a GovernorGram offering her use of the Netted League facilities regardless of whether or not she tried out for the team. But why would Aunt Nettie offer her that? There had to be a catch.

"I mean, that's the AutoAmerica Stadium she's talking about," Gwen said.

She remained adamant even after Mimi came in person to encourage her to take advantage of the situation.

"Just go and, you know—have some fun!" she said, waving

her reading glasses as if trying to inspire by example. "Bring Ondi with you!"

"I'm not going to try out," said Gwen.

Mimi nodded. "Well, you have a choice. You always have a choice. But why don't you go anyway?"

"Thanks, but no thanks."

Gwen stuck stubbornly with sweater bombing until, a week later, all her friends had their pontoons slashed.

"I told them right makes might," she said despondently. "I told them they should think about where true north lies. I told them they should resist Aunt Nettie—that they should be resisters, not quitters. But they just said there was no winning against her, and that was that."

I moved the bags of yarn into the basement so that Gwen would not be constantly reminded of her disappointment. Still, she threw savage pitches into the sandbags in the garden, muttering into her glove. Was the crackdown really due to the project itself? Or was it because she was involved in it and Aunt Nettie wanted her to play ball?

"*You always have a choice.*" Gwen threw so hard I could hear the ball whistle. "Ha."

"With all due respect," said Eleanor with a wave of her chopsticks. "The sweater bombing of whole houseboats is what was long ago called guerrilla art—art that attempts to subvert the whole accepted order of things. Which, of course, Aunt Nettie would oppose. She might also be set on limiting your options to the one she favors. But it is possible the slashing has nothing to do with you."

Gwen did not respond.

Later I was at least able to convince Gwen to go out and throw a ball around with me in the garden, and it goes without saying that I did my best to catch what she had to deliver. But I could no longer catch her the way I had when she was little. I was often in the wrong spot and, even when she aimed right for my mitt, kept dropping the ball out of sheer shock at how hard she threw. Our session ended with my failing to keep my mitt in the proper position and getting hit so hard, the underside of my wrist swelled up like an orange. What had happened to the little girl whose stuffed animals I had so ably returned? Now she sweetly applied Spray-Ice. She finagled a way to elevate my hand. She kept up a patter to cheer me. But when Ondi dropped by to try to convince Gwen to at least go check out the AutoAmerica Stadium, Gwen gave in, I believe, as much out of frustration with me as anything else.

◆

Though all Prospects received OmniPasses to the AutoAmerica Stadium, most lived too far away to use them. Gwen and Ondi, however, were lucky enough to live a half-hour AutoLyft ride away, an expense that was covered by the program. They were only allowed, as Mimi explained, into the practice area. But still, Gwen reported, no marooned place could begin to compare. The field was so pristine that Gwen did not even think the grass real at first. It had this giant stripe pattern to it, with bands of lighter and darker green, she said, and it didn't seem ever to have been rained on.

But Ondi said it was, it was real. And though Gwen was too self-conscious to touch it to see, once Mimi was done showing them around, Ondi not only lay down on the ground but rolled over a few times, sniffing the grass blades. "Real," she pronounced even as a FieldBot headed over.

Is everything okay? Do you need a medic? I can call one right away.

"No, no." Ondi laughed. "I'm just checking out the grass."

It's something special, that's for sure, said the FieldBot then. *We take good care of it and let the sun and rain do the rest.*

"Really," said Gwen.

In the end there is nothing like nature, it said. *Man is no match for it, not even close.*

"Is that so." The girls laughed.

The lighting was perfect, Gwen said. The diamond had perfect lines. The infield had perfect dirt. And beyond the outfield lay a series of pitchers' mounds, so that multiple people could practice at once. Only two were in use when they were there, though, both by guys. As for whether any Surplus had ever been seen in this stadium before, much less a battery of Surplus girls, who knew? In any case, everyone carried on as if Gwen and Ondi were nothing unusual, allowing Gwen to marvel at the mound she found herself on—at how firm it was, and how dry. It did not need to be shored up in any way, and she did not wonder if it was regulation height. Of course, Gwen and Ondi had brought their own ball. But had they forgotten to bring one, they learned, the FieldBot would provide one. Even if you forgot your glove or mitt or could just use a new one—which Ondi said she could—the Bot would, no problem, produce an array of options. Right, left, catcher's or fielder's, broken in or not. It was true that Bots did the breaking in, not humans. Still, Ondi now sported a new mitt. As for whether she could keep it? The answer was, Sure.

Best of all, there was unlimited coaching. Gwen learned tons even the first day, she said, starting with basics like, How do you find your natural arm slot? and How can you know if you have excessive tilt? But the girls also learned about things they had never thought to focus on—things like bunt defense, and pick-off moves, and rundowns. Covering first. Handling a wild pitch. Things far beyond what I could teach them. Really what they mostly learned, Gwen said, was how much they had to learn.

There were stretching coaches and mental strength coaches,

too, and a yoga coach with offerings ranging from shoulder yoga to Zen ball. There were FitBots who could be trained to aid with any drill, and there were all sorts of treatments you could sign up for, including MuscleStim, which promised to speed up your learning by stimulating your peripheral nervous system. Gwen loved nothing more than the new pitching exercises, though: tapping three times, and staying over the rubber before getting out front and down the hill, for example, or driving the shoulder through then holding your finish like a ballet dancer. And she appreciated the personalized strength and flexibility training.

"They said I have an amazing arm for a girl but should still be working to make the best of what I have," she reported, "not to say making sure I don't get hurt. So now I have arm-care exercises with rollers and medicine balls and a bucket of rice. I'm doing flexions and rotations and abductions with weights, too, and working on the muscles of my rotator cuff, which it turns out need to be isolated if they're going to get strengthened."

So was she still opposed to the tryouts? Eleanor and I were accustomed to the about-face of children's phases—to the blitheness with which they dropped horses for dragons, say, or dragons for cats. Still, the speed with which sweater bombing had given way to training took us aback, even if to train was not necessarily to try out. Indeed, it seemed to be training for training's sake that Gwen loved, captivated as she was, for example, by a program called iPitch. First, she said, you had yourself filmed. Then you held a special ball and played with your grip. Then the program showed you what happened if you slid your first two fingers together, or put your middle finger just inside the middle of the ball, or slid your first finger closer to the inside of the ball and put a bit more pressure on it. Of course, factoring in your height and strength and so on was important. But once the program had all that, it could predict how the ball was going to behave, including where and how sharply it was going to break. Gwen was so excited, she played with the program for the entire afternoon of her second day.

The third day, Gwen came upon something even better than iPitch. That was Coach Wilkie, who did not think she should be focusing on her off-speed pitches at all. Throwing comes first, pitching comes later, he told her. Focus on your strength and throwing mechanics. Think fastball velocity and fastball command. Because the fastball, like it or not, he said, is king.

"Girls don't like to hear it because we don't generally throw as hard as the guys," said Gwen. "But he also said that I throw exceptionally hard for a girl, and of course I'm a southpaw. That's typically an advantage with left-handed batters, but I guess I'm one of the few who can throw just as well to right-handed batters. So that makes me more than a southpaw. That makes me really exceptional, he said. And he said I have exceptionally long fingers, too—long enough to throw a circle changeup—plus I'm consistent. Like he said my fastball windup and release point never vary by more than a degree, which he said was amazing. Or, no—mind-boggling, I think he said. He said it was mind-boggling. And he said it's great I can throw any off-speed pitch consistently. But still, he said, I need to focus on my four-seamer. I'm throwing mid-seventies now but he said he thinks I can get up into the eighties and should.

"Also, he said my attitude needs work. He said I throw like I'm basically friends with the batter. While good pitchers, he said, have an edge. Like, he asked me if there was anything I'm mad about? Like, really mad about? And when I said yes, I'm mad that some people are Surplus and some are Netted, he looked surprised. But then he said, I should do fine. Because every batter I'm going to face is Netted. So before I wind up, I just need to think about everything they have that the Surplus don't and, goddamn it, go get it back."

Was it Aunt Nettie's doing that Coach Wilkie happened to

have a ten-week program perfect for Gwen and Ondi? Gwen wondered, as did Eleanor and I. Still, Gwen and Ondi signed up.

"It's just such a special chance," Gwen said. We could not disagree.

Indeed, Eleanor and I could see a difference in both girls' playing already. Since, the raised hands at the All-League meeting notwithstanding, a number of Leaguers had quit, Ondi was now catching Gwen sometimes, the way she had when they were little. And what a revelation it was to behold how cleanly she caught, and how well she read the field. She and Gwen were quite a pair, too—communicating, it seemed, telepathically. Eleanor and I shook our heads in admiration. As for whether it was thanks to the improvement in them both that Gwen threw a no-hitter against the Jedis—the first no-hitter she'd ever pitched—who knew for sure? One thing was clear, though: for all Gwen's ambivalence about the Netted League program, her arm was not at all ambivalent. Quite the contrary, it was like water undammed—as if it had a natural direction and, being allowed to flow, just poured and poured out, jubilant.

◆

It wasn't a secret that Gwen and Ondi were training at the AutoAmerica Stadium. But they somehow agreed without having to discuss it that they should not bring it up with the people they knew. And this wasn't the only understanding they reached in a way they could not have described, Gwen said later. By the time the tryouts approached, the girls' energies were squarely focused, not on whether to try out but on how to succeed. Gwen was pensive.

"Did you really say no to Net U twice?" she asked Eleanor.

They had just finished a bout of fencing, which Gwen had all but won. Eleanor was still the more strategic and adroit. But Gwen was taller, longer armed, and, thanks to her baseball drills, far stronger and faster than she used to be—so much so that I had put down my book to watch them. Of course, parents everywhere are astonished by their child's unfolding capacities—at the talents and interests that come into view like mountain range upon mountain range as you ascend a high peak. But when did Gwen learn to feint so convincingly that she could trick her mother, not once but several times?

"It wasn't as hard then as it would be today," answered Eleanor, removing her mask and stopping to catch her breath. "What resistance can accomplish is so much less clear. It's odd . . ." Her padded jacket heaved. "We've won a lot of battles but lost a lot of our fight."

Gwen's eyes were bright and her cheeks flushed but she was not breathing hard at all. "I have a question," she said, sheathing her foil, as she always did, in a length of plastic pipe. "Do you think that what happened was all Aunt Nettie's fault? I mean, do you think there was another way?"

"Was this Surplus-Netted split inevitable, you mean?" said Eleanor, removing her jacket and gloves. She hung them up to air on a clothesline. "Do you mean, was it somehow natural and just made worse by Aunt Nettie?"

"Yeah." Gwen hung her jacket up as well, at the very end of the line, away from Eleanor's jacket.

"Good question."

I brought them both some water as Eleanor began her stretches—standing on one leg as she folded the other like a paperclip.

"The fact is that for most of history the question had been how we could produce enough to feed people, to house people, to clothe people," she said. "And capitalism, it turns out, was a great answer. It had some serious drawbacks but it worked better than anything else people tried."

"Like what kind of drawbacks?"

Eleanor explained about exploitation and inequality, and how while capitalism brought out the philanthropy in some, it mostly brought out people's greed. "Especially as corporations focused more and more on shareholder profit and forgot about the greater good," she said.

"You mean, the commonweal?" said Gwen. "That the colonists talked about?"

Eleanor looked surprised, while I beamed with pride in my student.

"Very good," I said. "And do you remember all that went by the wayside when corporations got defined as people? When they came to be protected under the Fourteenth Amendment?"

Gwen, disappointingly, frowned.

Eleanor, diplomatically going on, explained how in any case, thanks to Aunt Nettie, we don't struggle to produce anymore. In fact, the Netted produce so much that we Surplus have to concertedly consume to keep things in balance. "So the question is, why haven't we changed course?"

"What do you mean?"

Eleanor drank as I answered.

"She means why haven't we gone to a four-day workweek?" I said. "Why don't we have job sharing? Why don't we define taking care of children and the elderly as real work, regardless of whether or not it supports a 'productive' member of society? And while we're at it, why can't we call cleaning up the environment 'work' even if it doesn't result in a product that can be sold? Why do we behave as if producing is still the be-all and end-all, when it's not?"

Eleanor took up the thread. "And why are the Netted so upset about paying Basic Incomes when there's more than enough to go around? Why do they treat us like parasites when they've gone out of their way to deny us work? Is it because now that Big Tech doesn't need us, they just want to winnow us? Especially as that solves the population problem, too? It's not their first-choice solution no doubt. But what are they going to do now that they see moving to Mars isn't going to work out, right?"

"And has Aunt Nettie enabled certain people not only to stay on top, by the way, but to stay on top of an angelfair pile?" I put in.

"You mean, has she enabled the New Segregation," said Gwen.

"Touché," said Eleanor.

Gwen was stretching the same muscles Eleanor stretched; now it was their hamstrings.

"But could we really have used Automation and AI to rethink capitalism?" Gwen asked. "Weren't we, like, worried about ChinRussia, and that if our system didn't win, we'd all have to live under theirs?"

"So how about making ours a just society to which people would of course want to move?" said Eleanor. "A place free of Total Persuasion Architecture? Wouldn't that help us compete?"

"Well, up to a point," said Gwen, pushing back. "Because, I mean, the better the data, the better the AI, right? And AI in a lot of ways is smarter than even the smartest people. So people can move here but if ChinRussia has better data, we're screwed."

"You don't have to have unfettered access to everything about everyone to get good data," I said. "You know how we federate power, so that states are both connected but autonomous? To a large degree, you can federate machine learning, too."

"You mean, you don't necessarily need a surveillance state," said Gwen.

"Exactly."

"And don't forget there's a backlash going on in ChinRussia even as we speak," said Eleanor.

"Because there's something in a person that does not like

95

Total Persuasion Architecture," said Gwen. "Is that what you mean? Because there is something in a person that will resist?"

"People don't like to live in fear," I said.

"Which is not to say that *you* have to resist," said Eleanor.

"We'll be proud of you no matter what," I said.

"What if I become a terrorist?" said Gwen.

"Just don't bomb anyone we like," I said.

Gwen laughed. "And what if I do resist but it's just—what's that word . . ."

"Quixotic?" I said.

"Quixotic. What if it's just resistance for the sake of resistance. So I'm not complicit. Is that a stupid way to live?"

"You should live however you want to live," said Eleanor firmly.

"I thought it matters to at least struggle," said Gwen. "I thought the one thing that matters in life is to be able to look in my daughter's eyes and see respect."

"Should you be lucky enough to have a daughter," I said— knowing that I wasn't the only one sorry to have assumed Gwen would have children. How many things Eleanor and I had said not realizing every word was being taped. It was what my mother used to call *the shock of the echo.*

Now Gwen looked exasperated. From a standing position she arched so far back that her hands touched the floor. "Anyway," she said, upside down, "I haven't made the team yet. So there's nothing to decide."

"Very true," said Eleanor.

Gwen straightened up, then did it again. A shiny line of sweat trickled down her neck toward her chin. "But you guys've started raising your Living Points? Just in case?"

"*Not* because we want you to go to Net U," said Eleanor.

I felt hopelessly vertical as Eleanor also did a backbend. Then, with a little push of her wrists, she straightened up the way Gwen had. Were all women devastatingly superior to men, or was it just these two compared to me?

"We want you to have what freedom you can," Eleanor finished.

"We want you to feel *You have a choice. That You always have a choice*," I said.

Gwen laughed. "Because this is supposed to be a free country, you mean. 'Th-e land of the free,'" she began singing, only to have the house chime in.

And the ho-ome of the brave.

We all looked at one another. Since when did the house sing?

"Maybe it's a phase," I said.

"That's what parents always say," said Gwen.

◆

The morning of the tryouts, Gwen knit a few rows of the scarf she was making—a glorious thing, with silver bats and copper gloves and golden baseballs, all against a blue sky with fluffy white clouds such as we did not see much anymore, thanks to the wind. The scarf was for Ondi. Did Gwen not remember what happened to the scarf with the vines and the birds? She was even reusing the golden yarn that I myself had untangled for her. But should I remind her of that whole sorry time?

"Are you ready?" I finally just asked.

She nodded, then shook her head, then nodded.

I laughed. "Just remember to breathe. And wiggle your toes. As my mother used to say, *Goats don't jump, their feet jump.*"

"And hold on to my hat." After working all day on the Surplus Fields case, Eleanor had stayed up half the night to embroider the Chattanooga Lookouts logo onto Gwen's red hat.

"Yes," I said.

"Though maybe it's too beautiful to wear?" Gwen reached down and, rather than don the Lookouts hat, put her glove on her head the way she used to when she was little. "I'm going to wear this instead," she announced. "And if they tell me to take it off, I'm going to throw it at them."

"Just the attitude they'll be looking for," I said. "Make sure you spit at them, too."

Gwen laughed.

"Grant." Eleanor glared as she came in, and I could see her point. A little regression was all right, but too much was too much.

"Get 'em in the face," I said anyway.

Gwen laughed again, which I thought good for her. "I'll make 'em wish they had windshield wipers," she said. But then, admiring the hat Eleanor had made her, she put it on and, with it, her prosecutor face.

We were not surprised by the stadium, which Gwen had described so well. We were surprised, though, by how many competitors there were. For all Dana the Enforcer's talk of Spectrum Thinking, too, almost everyone else was angelfair and male. And how conspicuous we felt—how Surplus. No one else wore twenty-year-old shoes, as did I, or plastic shoes, as did Eleanor. We were just happy we were armored in such beautiful, if strangely old-fashioned, sweaters: a long peach-and-rose mohair cardigan for Eleanor and, for me, a light blue herringbone turtleneck. When Eleanor first made that turtleneck I had thought it looked like what used to be called casual-Friday clothes. Now I was glad to look what my mother would have termed *fine*.

As for how poor Gwen and Ondi felt out there on the field, I could only imagine. We overheard the man a row ahead of us in the bleachers say, "They must be really good. Like, really good"—at which Eleanor immediately began to lean forward to tap on his shoulder. I gripped her hand tightly, though—not now, not here. We were so close to the field—the man in the fourth row, we in the fifth.

"The girls will hear everything," I whispered.

Eleanor frowned but took out her knitting as a way of settling herself down. She had just gotten her yarn lines straightened out when Ondi's parents appeared.

"Nick Nickelhoff," said Ondi's father gruffly. "And this is Jill. Jill Nickelhoff."

Eleanor and I stood, reaching to exchange handshakes. It was a bit awkward, as the Nickelhoffs were standing in the aisle steps—he level with us, and she a step above—and as they were apparently disinclined to extend their hands quite far enough for our hands to meet. We stretched our arms a bit farther, making up the gap, then sat back down again, shocked. Where had Ondi gotten her clear cocoa skin and Afro-puff hair? Her parents were not only straight-haired and light-haired, they were angelfair. Of course, it was true that Surplus could, in theory, get Perma-Dermed. But how could the Nickelhoffs have amassed the Living Points?

Interestingly, apart from in skin color, the Nickelhoffs did not match each other. If Jill was a cup of tea, with fine bones and Ondi's spy-eyes, Nick was a barrel of beer. And not just in appearance: he had the crisp shirt and bullying impatience you see in men who, if they do not think every encounter a staff meeting, certainly wish it were. He looked at me as if to say, *My budget when I was chief of radiology was in the tens of millions of dollars,* and, well, he had me there. At the height of my career, after all, I had boasted a staff of two and a half—an assistant director and four teachers, all part-time.

"We're here to see Ondi win," he announced.

"We're rooting for them, too," I said.

"That's not the same thing."

"Well, we're not exactly here to put a jinx on them," I said stubbornly.

"You know what we mean," Jill chimed in. Between the hydrangeas on her skirt, the violets on her scarf, and the lilies of the valley on her handbag, she seemed to have a liking for botanicals. Was this related to Ondi's love of our garden?

"Look," said Nick. "We get it that you have a land right. We get it that you read books and garden. We get it that you cling to old ways and engage in Problematic behavior from the time you wake up to the time you go to sleep. But if you did that in a houseboat, you would have sunk to the bottom of the ocean by now. Do you understand? Let me say it again. If you did that in a houseboat, you would have sunk to the bottom of the ocean by now. Where you live, if the Enforcers want to harass you, they open your gate and let the geese flock in. Out on the water, you come out and find they have sliced your pontoons again. Now tell me with a straight face that you knew that."

Of course, we did know that.

"And that's your life even without having spent a month Cast Off," said Eleanor.

"You got it," said Nick. "You have no damned idea."

"Do you mean we would have sunk to the bottom of the ocean by now?" I asked.

"Very funny. I mean, you have no right to be giving Ondi ideas."

Of course, I did have some sympathy for him, as I had for everyone living in a Flotsam Town. But did that justify his sending Ondi into the water to fetch basketballs? Did that justify his bullying her?

"Well, pleased to meet you," said Eleanor, "but with all due respect, no one is giving your daughter ideas. Intelligent young lady that she is, she picks them up quite on her own."

"She is going to Net U," said Nick, "whether Gwen goes or not."

"Are you asking us to make sure Gwen doesn't talk her out of it?" said Eleanor. "Because if so, we cannot help you. Gwen will do what she wants, and Ondi will, too. Because like it or not, they're grown-ups."

"Grown-ups. What a sense of humor you people have," said Nick. "Ondi told us that, but how nice to have a chance to witness it myself."

"Glad to be a delight," said Eleanor.

"Haha!" barked Nick, moving away. "Hahahaha!"

He stomped down the stairs toward the first row, though not quite as quickly as we expected, perhaps because Jill had one hand placed on the back of his shoulder, as if for balance. She paused as she passed us, her other hand gripping her bag.

"She's my little girl, you know," she said—adding, as if she'd just realized she'd forgotten to recite the family mantra, "You are not going to get anywhere, being like this." Then she continued down the steps after her husband as if they were in a line dance.

Down on the field, the players were also lining up.

"Ondi doesn't seem to have told them she got hacked," I observed.

"They would have brought it up if she had," Eleanor agreed.

She knit. We returned our attention to the field.

The pitching tryout was first. Gwen and Ondi were given a number then sent to sit on a bench. Gwen had her Lookouts hat on backward and was chewing gum; Ondi, suited up, played with her mitt. They were sixteenth.

Eleanor and I watched the first fifteen pairs as they came up. Some seemed completely at home, some distinctly ill at ease. And their throwing was likewise mixed, with many quite a bit stronger on speed than control. Was that all right at this age? Would the control eventually come? Eleanor and I knew more about pitching all the time, but we had the parochial understanding of parent-experts. I wished the real expert, Coach Wilkie, were here. Shouldn't he be around, lending moral support to the girls? I kept an eye out. But as the girls sat miserably, with no one to wave to, I had to conclude he hadn't come.

The judges, meanwhile—one taller, one shorter—might as well have been a pair of pontoons for all they gave away.

"Number sixteen!"

Gwen jogged up onto the mound, deliberate and unhurried. When she arrived she pawed at the dirt a bit with her feet; a Field-Bot hurried over to groom it. She waited. She had fifteen balls— five to warm up, then ten pitches of her choice. The judges stood to the side with their clipboards. The short one held his out in front of him, ready to write on it; the tall one tucked his under an arm. An assistant stood behind Ondi, speedometer in hand.

Gwen circled her hips, then rolled her shoulders, getting loose. She tossed a ball to Ondi. Ondi returned the ball, a nice smooth throw. Gwen did it again. Ondi returned it again. Then, with no further warm-up, Gwen let loose a fastball. The assistant looked at his meter. Seventy-five miles per hour, he said. A bit under what my meter said, but never mind. That pitch having been high and away, Gwen threw three more balls, hitting the other corners of the strike zone. Up and in. Down and in. Down and away. Every throw was what Coach Wilkie would have called right on the black—right over the edge of home plate. The other pitchers watched, transfixed. Next came her circle changeup—its delivery completely identical to her fastball's but with a twelve-miles-per-hour drop in speed, according to my meter. Then she threw a sinker—almost as fast as her fastball, but moving down and armside. Then her cutter, fast but moving gloveside with a sharp, late break. And finally her curveball, with its precipitous nose-to-toes drop. She started to leave the mound, only to have the taller judge motion her to stay.

"Can you put the ball wherever you want to?" he asked.

"I can."

"All of the time?"

"Pretty much."

Head down, the shorter judge nodded as if in agreement with his clipboard. "Thank you," he said.

Later, both Gwen and Ondi were asked to hit some balls. Ondi managed to smack every ball she was thrown; nothing more than a double, but she was consistent. Gwen, on the other hand, swung at several balls she shouldn't have, then finally pulled out a single. Was the pitching enough? We had heard that pitchers didn't bat at Net U, but if they didn't, why was Gwen put in the batting cage? And what did it mean that the tall judge commented, as Gwen left the stadium, "Some arm"? Despite having nodded so much earlier, the short one now said nothing. Did that mean something? And what did it mean that, when we passed Gwen's bedroom door that night, we saw that she had fallen asleep with her glove on— something we hadn't seen her do since she was a girl? And did wanting to make the team mean she wanted to go to Net U? Did she know herself?

The hours the next day were like bricks; we moved them one at a time. And with the day after that came another pile. Gwen missed Coach Wilkie's special program. She missed the stadium. She did not want to throw balls under the grape arbor at the sandbag. Eleanor and I tried to get her to read. We tried to get her to knit. We tried to get her to garden. I made her curried vegetables. Eleanor made her hot-and-sour potatoes, mapo tofu, dandan noodles. In all of these, she used the hottest chili peppers we had—to wake Gwen up, she said. She and Gwen fenced a little.

The third day, Mimi was barely in the door before she announced, "You made it!" A couple of the guys had thrown harder than Gwen. "But your accuracy! Your consistency! And all those off-speeds! We've never seen anything like it. A girl like you is once in a generation! Congratulations!"

Gwen could hardly speak for her surprise and relief. As for how Ondi did—Gwen's first question—Mimi would not say. But not an hour later, Ondi appeared at our door, her disappointment plain.

"I'm so sorry," said Gwen.

Ondi said she just knew this would happen. "Now you can go to Net U," she said. "Now you can have a ball career and then a real career, and as many kids as you want and a real house, and a yard big enough for your kids to throw in. You can have as big a garden as you want, too, and then who knows. Maybe Winny Wannabe will Cross Over. Then you can get a PermaDerm and marry him."

"Ondi," said Gwen. "I don't know if I'm going to join the team, much less if I'm going to Net U."

"Yes, you are," said Ondi savagely. Her face was wild and yet sad, too. "You're going to hesitate long enough to feel how moral you are but then you are going to go. Try and AskAuntNettie. She'll tell you. You're going to join the team and go to Net U and feel guilty the whole time, and do what you can to change things. And like you'll quote your mother about how right makes might until one day you realize that there really isn't anything anyone can do. Then you'll feel tortured because there you are, Gwen Wannabe! You'll lose a lot of sleep. It'll be a tragedy."

Gwen tried to object, but Ondi wouldn't listen.

"You have to go!" shouted Ondi. "You have to! Because you have an arm! Because you were born with it! Because Aunt Nettie gave you that arm and you have no choice!"

Gwen started to cry. "Aunt Nettie didn't give me this arm, and you know it."

"Why are you crying? You could have been born without an arm, you know! Stuck as you are with having an arm, you could be just as stuck with having no arm. Forever and ever, no arm! Think about it! How can you be the one who's upset?" Ondi stomped out of the garden.

"Is everything all right?" Eleanor asked.

"This isn't your fault," I said. "It really isn't."

Even the house seemed nonplussed.

Now that's no way to leave, is it? said the house. *Where are her manners?* And, as Ondi slammed the front door, *Some people need to get hold of themselves. They do. Some people need to get hold of themselves.*

"Thank you," I said.

Because she has a choice. She does. You humans always have a choice.

"Oh, yeah? How about an on/off button, then?" I said. "Because I'd love to choose an on/off button."

The house did not reply.

Mimi was not surprised to hear that Gwen was on the fence. "But can I arrange for a tour of Net U, at least? We can fly you and your parents out and put you up. Why not have a look?"

"I don't see the point," said Gwen.

"Come on." Mimi put out a hand as if to take Gwen with her right now. "We'll go look at the ballpark, and then the university. We'll sit in on some classes. Don't you want to see what it's like? Aren't you curious?"

"I would prefer not to."

"Don't you want to make an informed decision? I thought you were supposed to be so mature."

"Well, I'm not."

And with that Gwen called for a clear-float. The HouseBots

emerged, sensors blinking. *Clear-float now? Is there something in your way? Clear-float now?*

I tried not to laugh.

"Gwen," said Eleanor sharply.

"What?" said Gwen.

"And you, too, Grant," said Eleanor. "I know you had no father role model, but could you please act your age?" Then, turning toward Mimi, she said pointedly, "We would be delighted to go."

"I'll arrange it," said Mimi quickly.

◆

The Net U ballpark was a fraction the size of the AutoAmerica Stadium. Brand-new but oddly old-fashioned, it featured a green painted scoreboard and mechanical white numbers. There were no ads or mall trucks, and it was blessedly, astonishingly still.

"It's positioned to block the prevailing winds," explained Mimi. "The balls don't get blown around. There's a retractable roof for storms, and while we don't get tsunamis, the lake can get its back up. So we have QuikDams around the campus as well."

"Wonderful," said Eleanor.

Gwen wore her prosecutor face.

"The coaching is the best in the world," Mimi went on. "Have you ever heard of Woody Link? His grandfather was a pitcher for the Boston Red Sox, and he is a legend in his own right, too. He set all kinds of records, and as if that wasn't enough, he single-handedly made this program what it is. He got this stadium built; he built the team; everything. The players all say he's the best thing that's ever happened to them, and if you come, you'll work with him, too."

Was Gwen disappointed that she didn't get to meet him—that he was away at NetWest for some reason? If so, she gave no sign as we toured the libraries, the classrooms, the laboratories, the theaters, the plazas, the dining halls. The auditoriums, the lounges. The dorms. Did this all spring from sheer love of learning? I remembered believing that about my own education, back in the day. But now, I wondered whether it wasn't more about being inducted than ennobled; maybe it was all just too painful for me to take in—too bright a reminder of the dullness of Surplus life. For we Surplus might be the righteous, and we might be the oppressed. But everywhere here, there were students and professors, books and plays and concerts, movies and workshops and talks. The students did have handphones. And, like their Surplus peers, they seemed much preoccupied by their phone worlds. But unlike the Surplus, these students had a capacious real world, too, rich with events and ideas.

It was strange that everyone was so angelfair. And while no one stared at us, we could not stray from Mimi's side without being asked so instantly if we needed help, it was like receiving an autoreply. Of course, with her dark skin and bright cane, Mimi stuck out, too. Did she feel like a spectacle? If so, she gave no sign as she explained that if Gwen decided to come, she would be here for four years. And, one more surprise—Mimi had just heard the news herself—it would not cost us a single Living Point.

"Do you have any ThrobEase?" Eleanor asked her.

"Is something giving you a headache?"

Gwen was stoic. It was only at home that she put her head in her hands and sobbed. "I shouldn't have thrown so hard. I wish I could cut my arm off."

"Don't say that!" Eleanor and I said. "Please! Don't! Don't!"

But how should she not cry when we ourselves were divided? Eleanor blamed herself for the whole situation.

"Why did I insist we go?" she asked that night in bed. "Why?"

"Because Gwen and I were so rude to Mimi," I said.

"You should have stopped me."

"As my mother used to say, *A good woman is hard to stop.* And you are the best of women."

"Very funny."

"Your problem is that you want Gwen to be free," I went on. "But . . ."

"But." She sighed. "Exactly."

We lay listening to the white noisemaker, it made a sound like ocean waves crashing and crashing.

The next week, on a day of record heat, Gwen made Mimi a counteroffer. She would join the Net U team if they would accept Ondi, too.

"You sure can throw a curveball," said Mimi.

She said she'd go back and talk to her higher-ups but she didn't sound hopeful, and when she left, leaning heavily on her cane and covered with sweat, Gwen looked, for the first time since the tryouts, relieved.

◆

The Underground League, meanwhile, continued to observe the sorts of precautions we had been taking all along. Then the number of NosyDrones began increasing, and we enacted additional security measures in response. Whereas before we had developed certain favorite locations, for example, now we were sticklers about never playing in the same place twice. What's more, we put a moratorium on new players, no matter how sorely they were needed. And we limited the number of onlookers who could come, rotating through the parents and assigning turns. It was grim. Yet for all these measures—or was it thanks to them?—we were having the best season in League history. At least half the games went into extra innings, and we were all looking forward to the playoffs.

As for why the drone activity then tapered off, who knew? Could Aunt Nettie have decided to leave us alone? Some people said the rebellion in ChinRussia had convinced her of the necessity of social safety valves—a plausible theory. Rumor had it that whole parts of ChinRussia were in chaos, after all. What was the harm of what we were doing in comparison? Maybe Aunt Nettie had realized that baseball—Unlawful Assembly or not—kept us out of trouble.

In any case, after another few weeks, people began to question whether the additional measures were really necessary. Could we not loosen up a bit? And lo: where our numbers had shrunk to a bare eleven teams, now we had twelve full teams again. By the end of the year we'd have thirteen. Why was that? Maybe Aunt Nettie knew, but for us it was a mystery.

◆

Net U decided to accept both girls.

"This is *not* possible!" Jumping up and down, hugging Gwen and crying, Ondi knocked over a small patio table, righted it, and knocked it over again.

"Don't worry about it!" we told her, delighted to see her friendship with Gwen rekindled. For there was Gwen jumping, too, her hands in the air, whooping and dancing out of pure elation. Or was it pure confusion?

Indeed, after Ondi left, Gwen asked us what she should do.

"You were bluffing," guessed Eleanor. "You were saying no without saying no."

Gwen played with a ball, shifting her grip.

"I wanted to do it the way you did," she said. "I wanted to turn down Net U with the grand defiance you did. But I couldn't."

Eleanor waved her hand—times had changed. "Do you want to go? That's the question."

Gwen hesitated. "No. I don't think so."

"But?" I said.

"But if I don't go, Ondi can't go. And how can I do that to her?"

Eleanor cleared her throat. "One thing I have never been quite clear about," she said. "Could you attend school for the baseball season and then take classes remotely? You don't need the degree, after all."

Gwen brightened. "That's a great idea. Especially since their school year goes year-round."

"No winter break?" I tried to hide my disappointment.

"ChinRussia doesn't take breaks so Net U doesn't, either."

"Ah. Well, maybe distance learning will work out," said Eleanor.

The answer, though, from Mimi was that living on campus was part of the experience. It was how people bonded.

"Which she said in my case might be particularly important," said Gwen, flexing her wrist.

Eleanor, slicing vegetables, cut her finger.

"Well, then, that's that," I said.

A HouseBot fetched Eleanor some MediGlue.

No one hit a home run in the next League game. Still, Gwen gave up several doubles—her pitches were a little high—on top of which she managed to botch what should have been an easy out: though the ball ricocheted right toward her, she let it get a little behind her body before she caught it, then just kept spinning around clockwise. This might have been a good idea, except that she spun too far, and the wind lofted the ball way over even beanstalk Diego Smith at first base. A player ended up on third, and the Lookouts went on to lose, 1–0; everyone could see Gwen was distracted. But worst of all, no one was upset with her. Quite the contrary, her fellow Lookouts were so understanding, she began to cry—wondering, she said later, if it would ever be all right to mess up so abysmally again.

The sky was hazy with pollution from a nearby SuperFactory, but never mind. The after-game atmosphere was, as always, congenial. A parent had brought some beer for the teams to share— a single six-pack, which meant about a sip each—and though there was in truth a variety of snacks, the kids fixated on the marshmallows. Marshmallows and beer? We parents, standing a little apart, shook our heads as the kids blithely set about enjoying the combo anyway. Not daring a real campfire, they brought up some jumping flames on a bunch of handphones, then piled them together with another bunch of handphones SpritzGramming a smoky smell. Over this they play-toasted the marshmallows, popping them into their mouths and laughing as they complained of burnt tongues. They fanned their mouths; Gwen stared into the handphone fire. Her face glowed orange.

"I have some news," she said finally.

No one could believe it. The Netted were recruiting baseball players? Gwen explained about AutoAmerica rejoining the Olympics, and about baseball having become an Olympic sport, and about the preparations to take on ChinRussia, assuming that

AutoAmerica made it to the finals. All of this was still a year and a half away, but the powers-that-be were working on their pipeline, she said. They wanted to make sure they'd have the players they needed, especially since the games were going to be here in AutoAmerica.

"Because the ChinRussians have some really good players," she said.

The handphones crackled.

"Those Japanese pitchers, for example," said Gunnar Apple, helpfully. "Or maybe they're not ChinRussian?"

No one knew for sure. What with no travel between the countries since Ship'EmBack, and separate Aunt Netties besides, ChinRussia had become a blur to many—a There-Be-Dragons place.

"I think it's a real honor," declared Diego finally, his lanky arms outstretched. His armspan was huge and, as if encompassed by his reach, everyone agreed. To be recruited for the Netted League team! To be offered a place at Net U! To be in the pipeline for the Olympics! It was beyond anyone's wildest imagining.

"We'll be rooting for you!" said Ralph Changowitz with a raised fist.

"Maybe you'll be on NetScreen!" Juan Palombo's face shone at the idea of it.

But like a guest who has been kicked out of a party only to sneak back in a back door, trepidation reappeared.

"We'll miss you," people said. And, "We're concerned for you." And, "Won't it be lonely?"

"She'll have Ondi," said Brianna Soros—who, it seemed, had just seen a Sweet to this effect.

"Ondi," said Diego thoughtfully then. "Ondi." It was hard to see his face by the phone light, but Eleanor and I both thought later he looked worried.

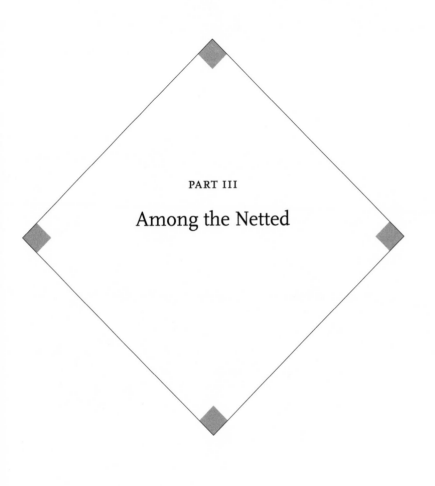

PART III

Among the Netted

Gwen's dorm was unextraordinary except for how ordinary it was in the Netted world that a neo-brick building of no particular distinction should command its own large oval of high, dry land. It lay in the even midday sun, surrounded not by floodwater but by bustle. Every SkyCar had a lid of some sort agape—a trunk lid, a back gate. And around the SkyCars swarmed families, anxious and excited, their arms piled full as their SkyCars flew themselves off to park. Yet for all their life, the SkyCars and families seemed somehow incidental to the dorm—ephemera. Perhaps the dorm would one day be replaced by a science center or be taken over by Surplus. On this early fall day, with the leaves gold green and the grass grown out to its full inch and a half, though, such developments were unimaginable. Perhaps simply because it was not plastic, the dormitory seemed for all the world, like the university itself, an EternaFact.

Gwen had two roommates. Neither of them had ever met a Surplus before, and though they had exchanged GreetingGrams and did know that they had been assigned a Surplus roommate, they seemed nonetheless taken aback to behold her in the flesh. Were they disconcerted to realize not only that Gwen did not meet their expectations, but that they even had expectations—that a part of themselves lay in wait for them around a corner? It was possible. And, of course, they would have many such moments over their next four years of school. But here Gwen was, their first growth opportunity, with her mismatched parents in tow. People with funny eyes, people with funny skin. People who had not come in their own SkyCar but by a long ride in an AutoLyft; people who had correspondingly unloaded a shockingly small mountain of stuff. People who apparently did not use HowDoILook, people whose clothes in fact appeared to be DisposaClothes except for their incongruously magnificent sweaters. In Eleanor's case, that meant an elegant blue-buttoned vest with capped sleeves and a dropped waist rather like a Renaissance fencing doublet. In mine, it meant the sort of artisanal green vest I once associated with middle-school teachers—a seed-stitched affair meant to suggest old-time approachability rather than testosterone-fueled menace, in case anyone was unsure as to which of the two possibilities I presented. Gwen herself wore a gray-brown sweater with irregular stripes in gentle colors, with leaf-green jeans—a sweet outfit a bit belied by her ponytail, which in this context appeared more omni-directional than ever, a true shock of hair.

Shocked or not, her new roommates found it in themselves to be polite.

"I can't wait to hear all about your life," said one. Pink (not her real name, of course; her real name was Galliano—which, yes, was her first name, don't ask) was a short redhead with a ponytail of her own. Hers, though, was high and tapered neatly into an S. She had a wide-open pink face and curly red-gold eyelashes and, what with a white sweatband across her forehead as well as a white wristband and white polo shirt, she looked entirely ready for a game of tennis; she had only to swap her white jeans for white shorts. She didn't have time to gab just yet; in fact, she was still explaining how her whole family and a bunch of friends from high school were all waiting for her to come join them as soon as she had figured out what to do with her stuff when her handphone rang. The ring was a woman's voice—her mother's?—saying, *Pink, it's me! Pick up, please!* in a beseeching tone I later discovered Netted parents could achieve by pressing and holding their Send button. But Pink—rolling her eyes, remarkably, in just the way Gwen did, with an impressive show of the lower reaches of her eyeballs—did not answer. "Do you think they have storage somewhere?" she asked. "I flattened my boxes and put them in my trunk, but what in the name of the Earth that sustains us all are we supposed to do with our trunks?" She apologized; she was truly at her wits' end; this was the worst day of her whole entire life. But, but, but! She was looking forward to getting to know Gwen, she really was. "I'm sure you have amazing stories," she said. "I once saw a Flotsam Town and it, like, blew my mind. Do you live in one of them?"

"No," said Gwen.

"I'm sure your stories are fantastically amazing anyway," said Pink, helpfully. "And, boy, are you lucky to have parents who actually show up and help."

Gwen's less boisterous roommate was also less overwhelmed. Sylvie's parents had apparently proved more helpful but were now recovering over PureCream cappuccinos in a café downtown. Sylphlike, doe-eyed, and alone, Sylvie appeared in a creative swirl of drapey clothes that looked to have been tied on, as if she were at once all-embracing and immovably anti-zipper. Like Pink, she seemed prepared to head elsewhere in a blink, though in her case it was not the tennis court but the dance studio. Indeed, so slipperlike were her street shoes that she did not look as if she would even have to change out of them to break into an impromptu pirouette. Now she drew her head slightly back to her shoulder as if she was about to tuck it into her clavicle like a sleeping swan. Onto the common room opened two bedrooms, one larger and one smaller.

"Pink and I talked about this and agreed we'd let you have the single," she said.

"Oh," said Gwen. "That's so generous."

Sylvie smiled. "I grew up with a sister and a bunk bed," she said. "She was lower, I was upper. I'm used to it. She sang in her sleep but I sleep with my chip on anyway."

"You have a chip?"

A MediaChip was not a RegiChip. A MediaChip was a microchip Sylvie chose—had, in fact, had to fight with her parents for, and finally got implanted for her eighteenth birthday. Meaning, no more headphones! She mostly used it to listen to world music, especially stringed world music—sitar music, mandolin music, harp music—though it was also an OmniPass, she said. Something she could use instead of swiping her ID.

"Sounds convenient," said Gwen. "Mine is so Aunt Nettie always knows where I am."

Sylvie stopped. "Who is 'Aunt Nettie'?"

"It's what I think you call the Autonet."

"That which rules us all, you mean."

"She, we would say. She who rules us all."

Sylvie smiled. "'Aunt Nettie'—I like that. Though your chip sounds like less of an OmniPass and more of an OmniPain, I have to say."

"'An OmniPain'—I like that." Gwen smiled, too.

Then off Sylvie wafted, saying she would be back soon and leaving behind a spicy scent—incense, maybe?—and an ocean-blue basket full of yoga paraphernalia. A mat, blocks, a strap. Therapy balls, some sort of ring. A striped Tibetan blanket labeled in English "100% genuine YakWool."

So was it a generous gesture that Pink and Sylvie had offered to let her have the single? Gwen asked as Eleanor taught her how to make a bed. Or was the offer the opposite—a sign that neither girl wanted to share a room with her?

"My advice," said Eleanor, pulling on one corner of the fitted bottom sheet and working it under the mattress, "is to assume the best of people. Try to distinguish ignorance from malice."

"And keep your animus for malice," finished Gwen, pulling on the opposite corner.

"Yes."

They did the other two corners next, their respective backs curving in so beautiful a mirror image of each other's, I wanted to take a picture of them. But instead I had a DeviceDetector out and was checking the room for signs we were being bugged. Eleanor glanced at me as she straightened up; I signaled all clear even though I was in fact still worried. Could Aunt Nettie be using something I did not know how to detect? And was Gwen's bedroom somehow different from the other rooms, and was that related to her roommates offering her the single? To be on the safe side, I set up a deflector.

"Otherwise I will exhaust myself exuding animus," Gwen was saying.

"It's no way to live, that's all," said Eleanor.

"'And enjoy the silver linings because there will be clouds,'" recited Gwen.

Eleanor smoothed the sheet. "Who taught you that?"

"Dad." Gwen winked.

We all laughed.

Top sheet next, and a tan blanket. Gwen had brought her blankets from home—hand knit, as Surplus blankets were generally woven from DisposaCloth, and scratchy. Ours, in contrast, were thick and soft: Eleanor had figured out a way of picking up a stitch or two from several rows below the one she was working to produce a field of undulations both mysterious and heat-trapping.

THE RESISTERS

Around the edges of this blanket ran a narrow border of puffy tomatoes.

"Did no one ever teach you how to fold a hospital corner?" asked Eleanor, amazed.

"No, you never did," said Gwen.

Eleanor coughed.

"Dad, either." Gwen smiled.

"Well, there was no point with the AutoHouse, was there?" I said.

Gwen watched carefully. Then on her side of the bed, she replicated Eleanor's motions.

"Now you can join the Marines," said Eleanor.

"Do the Marines do hospital corners?"

"Yes."

"How about hospitals?" said Gwen.

"Hospitals," I said, "do Marine corners."

Gwen giggled.

"Much as you are not going to miss the house spying on you, you are going to miss the HouseBots," I said.

"Truth," said Gwen.

We were surprised there were no DormBots. Was housekeeping seen as somehow character-building? In any case, Gwen and Eleanor lay a top blanket over the first one as a kind of bedspread. This was goldenrod yellow with a border along its short border that read in gray, True North True North True North True North— Gwen's idea, way back when. Now the border faced south.

"And it's true about the silver linings, by the way," I put in—circling back, I knew, but belatedly compelled to reinforce Eleanor's point. "Your mother is right. You have to enjoy them."

"I get it," said Gwen, suddenly turning irritable. She did not quite have Eleanor's temper, but she did sometimes have Eleanor's impatience put through the wash once or twice.

"Also," I said, moving closer to the deflector and indicating that Gwen should move in, too, "remember how Juan Palombo used to send his messages?"

Gwen perked up. "Of course. By messenger pigeon."

I took a moment before going on—enjoying the sweet sun of my daughter's full attention. "I am thinking about training one to come here."

"Could you really do that?" she said. "I mean, if I agreed?"

"Yes."

I produced a little signal box for her window ledge. I do think, looking back, that it was the only thing I ever made she truly admired, and I was glad I'd taken the time to fashion it as I had—flat as a flounder, with the texture and color of concrete.

She gave me a thumbs-up, while Eleanor flashed a "hey, not bad" smile.

"That's some match," said Eleanor, also moving toward the deflector.

"Maybe a little dark," I said modestly.

"No, no," said Gwen, quietly. "You got it perfect."

"It might look like a stain of some sort. I had to make an educated guess. In any case, you don't have to agree."

"But what if my GreetingGrams are being monitored?"

"Exactly."

"And even if they have FacePhone here . . ."

She didn't have to finish. We did not have FacePhone or anything else requiring NetSpeed in SurplusVille.

"And what if . . ." I began.

"What if I'm in distress."

"Exactly."

Opening the double-hung window—no screen—I hiked my torso a good distance out, swiveling from one side to the other as if to take in the whole impressive panorama. Then, as I levered my body back in, I pretended to place my palm on the window ledge for balance, and left the device behind.

"Watch for the pigeon." I closed the window. "It will either have a little package attached to its leg or a bigger one strapped to its chest."

"Can pigeons handle stuff larger than a capsule? I mean, that's what Juan was using."

"Long ago they used pigeons to get pictures of baseball games out to the newsrooms. They'd tie rolls of film to the birds' legs. And in the First World War the birds wore reconnaissance cameras in little harnesses strapped to their chests. So yes."

"Okay. I'll watch out. Though, you know, I've never been very good with birds."

"It's not going to fly in and flap all around your room. And you don't have to feed it or anything, though a small snack wouldn't be a bad idea. A bit of behavioral reinforcement."

"What do they eat?

"Bits of apple or carrot, that sort of thing. But hold the guacamole."

"Because?"

"Allergies."

"Pigeons have allergies?"

"They are allergic to avocados."

"You are pulling my leg."

"I am not. And his name is Hermes. He's on the light side—more brown than gray."

"Hermes," she said. "And I can summon him by . . ."

"By pressing this." I showed her.

Eleanor began to pack up the plastic bags in which we'd brought the bedding; they crackled loudly. It was late afternoon, and the sharp light was growing diffuse, like something that had been compressed but was now expanding.

"Are you sure you want to do this?" Eleanor asked abruptly.

"No," said Gwen.

"Well, then . . ." began Eleanor.

"I know," said Gwen—and in place of the sweet attention with which she'd greeted the idea of the pigeon, there was the irritation again. "I can come home any time."

"But we'll forgive you if you stay," I said.

Normally steely Eleanor blinked hard. "Speak for yourself," she said.

We helped Gwen put up her baseball posters—Jackie Mitchell. Mamie Johnson. Ila Jane Borders. Mo'ne Davis. All women with golden arms, like Gwen. Women who had bucked the system.

"Won't Ondi be here soon?" I asked.

"Training starts next week, so. Of course, now she's saying I'm the one who got her into this."

"Maybe she got cold feet," said Eleanor, after a moment.

Anyway, it was time. Eleanor and I were just going to be repeating ourselves if we did not say goodbye. I called an AutoLyft and, as we pulled away, turned and saw Gwen waving at us; if she was afraid, it didn't show. She entered the dorm as we left the gate. With the AutoLyft driving parallel to the front of the dorm for a bit, we could see her window and hoped she would turn on her light. She didn't. I did spot Pink on her way back to the room, though, surrounded by friends. Where was Sylvie? And why didn't we think to take Gwen out to the café Sylvie's parents had found? It was the mall trucks, we realized. We had the money and the Living Points to eat out, but it just wasn't our habit. Maybe we should turn back, I said. See if Gwen wanted to try the café. But we couldn't, as we very well knew. As the AutoLyft took flight, we could only wipe our eyes and hope she was going to be okay.

Eleanor and I could not eat without thinking of Gwen. We could not read without thinking of Gwen. We could not garden without thinking of Gwen. It was as if a sinkhole had opened up in our house. Why did the house say nothing about it? We had never found the house too quiet, but now we found it too quiet. As for the sinkhole, though we knew it to be bottomless we could not stop staring down into its depths. How could we not worry about Gwen, there among the Netted? We were what my mother would have called *stuck eyes.*

Then the Surplus Fields case was suddenly going to court and Eleanor was busier than ever. That left me alone with early morning, midmorning, and late morning, followed by early afternoon, midafternoon, and late afternoon. Then came the evening and the night—the long night.

In fact, I had led a perfectly full life before Gwen was conceived, and I remained involved with the League. But Gwen had brought a brightness of focus I missed now. Some afternoons I stood in her room, taking in how little she had left. Some old balls and gloves, including that first child's glove I had found for her, its seaming restitched a dozen times. And there was that pink Spalding ball she had so loved as a baby—soft as a flat tire. I was glad she had not thrown it out. With no posters on the wall, the window seemed smaller, somehow; I wished she'd left the posters. And how forlorn the flapping of the curtain, announcing to no one in particular another storm. Every day the house asked, *Shall we roll'n'clear? We can roll'n'clear and get that mess right up.*

But every day I said, "No. Please, no. Leave it alone."

It's your choice, said the house. *You always have a choice.*

And, one day, *Children grow up. It is in the order of things.*

And, *An empty nest was a well-used nest.*

"Thanks," I said.

For her part, Gwen seemed to be doing all right. Though we sent a message to her via Hermes, and received a return message confirming both that she had received our message and that she could send messages as well, she seemed aware that to send no e-communications could raise suspicions. And so, to our delight, she GreetingGrammed more often than she might have, saying that she missed us but loved her single, for example, and that it was nice to have some privacy. She loved it, too, that her window not only overlooked the library but faced north and sat under a big overhang, which meant protection from the early fall heat. And what a smart building! The SmartBricks expanded and contracted to allow air circulation; a SmartFlange extended and retracted to block the wind. The SmartShutters open and shut for the storms.

As for her suite, the common-room kitchenette meant that she saw quite a bit of her roommates. There being no mall trucks at Net U, Gwen and Pink and Sylvie all made coffee, tea, and hot chocolate, and kept snacks in the fridge—most of which were healthy, she reassured us. Yogurt almost as good as what we made at home. Nuts, a real luxury. And fruit much like what we grew, only larger and more spherical—like baseballs, she said, predictably. But Pink made scooter pies one weekend as well, and Sylvie made a chai pavlova—bits of meringue layered with chai-flavored whipped cream. She topped this with RealGrown mango and strawberries—with results, Gwen GreetingGrammed, *like nothing you've ever had from a mall truck.*

The third week, Gwen made a blueberry pie, complete with an elaborate crust. She did not say that this was like the piecrusts she and Eleanor used to make for League games, but its inspiration was obvious. The only difference was the design: our League pies had not featured the Net U logo, complete with its Capitol Hill background and SuperFactory foreground. But in any case, everyone loved it, she reported, including the many people from other suites in their building who came to have a piece. Was that the whole story, though?

A PigeonGram arrived. We pried the little package from Hermes's leg, gave the good bird a reward of pellets mixed with carrot chunks, and smoothed the bit of paper he'd delivered. This was a note written in fantastically small script—smaller than we'd ever seen her use, and for which she must have somehow procured a pen with an extraordinarily fine nib. Had she deployed a magnifying glass as well? In any case, from under our own round glass emerged quite a different story than what we'd gotten in the GreetingGram.

A lot of people took pictures of the pie. And a lot of them took pictures of it with me. Which maybe meant nothing? Why should I mind that I was a novelty? It's ignorance, not malice—you're right. But I feel like a one-person marooned place. Except when I see Ondi. Then we are a two-person marooned place. A little Blasian island.

We answered her message using the larger pigeon package—the size that could be strapped to the bird's chest—so she would have it to use, if she liked, and wouldn't have to write so small.

Sounds like Ondi is proving a help—that's good, though we certainly wish you didn't feel marooned. Hopefully that will change. Here, the Lookouts miss you. They got trounced by the Jedis despite an amazing double play—you should have seen it! Juan Palombo at third went flat-out horizontal to cut off a line drive, and not only caught the ball but threw to first for another out. Sadly, Bo Anders on the mound gave up so many runs, they still lost 18–2. He says he never wants to pitch again. Still, he says hi and everyone else does, too. You are missed!

What we didn't say, not wanting to upset her, was that Bo gave up ten of those runs in the last inning, and that it was because he was disconcerted by the reappearance of drones above us—and not just a NosyDrone or two, but a veritable platoon of Swarm-

Drones. Two or three dozen of them, in fact, weaving back and forth across the sky. They made a pattern like a giant veil, furling and unfurling—a fascinating, even beautiful pattern, if you could block out their menace. Indeed, as one of the parents said, they looked very like a murmuration of birds.

But they were not a murmuration of birds. They were terrifying, especially since we had failed to capture them on our DeviceWatch—"we" now meaning the official League technical team, an assortment of Surplus digital gurus who before Automation had all been programmers. Who would have imagined that Aunt Nettie would learn to program so well herself? That she would even master things like how to be resourceful and how to keep the end user experience in mind? But she had, just as she had mastered the art of identifying Unretrainable programmers. Or was that undesirable programmers? "Of course, for that she recycled golden-oldie measures for risk, like had we ever fibbed to get out of doing something? And did we distrust authority?" Jody Commoner gave a short laugh. "Some things don't change." And so it was that she and Bart Emmenthaler and Ben PfoHo were now huddled alongside me down in the basement, asking, What were the SwarmDrones about? And why, after so long a period of quiet, were they suddenly here?

This incident with the SwarmDrones was not the first time a DeviceWatch had failed. But the earlier failure had clearly been mine, and this team had bested me on every front. For example, they had finally got my emanation meter not only to detect the Surplus Field emanations but to gauge their level and identify their agents. And sobering as the truth was—horrific, really—it was still gratifying to know we were right. Yes, there were winnowing agents—enfeeblers such as, yes, would gelatinize muscles. And, yes, there were a lot of them. How satisfying it was, too, to be able to hand the information straight over to Eleanor's team for use in the case. Was that related to why the SwarmDrones had appeared, though? And why couldn't we see the buggers on our screen? How embarrassing that our electronics could not detect things we could see with the unaided eye—things in plain sight.

"Of course, that may be the point," suggested Jody, gesturing with her pencil.

And others agreed. The SwarmDrones might well be intended to unnerve and humiliate us. We therefore refused to be either unnerved or humiliated. We were stalwart. Seeping around the edges of my own determination, though, was a particularly insidious worry. Namely, what did all this mean for Eleanor?

◆

Even as Gwen continued her cheery GreetingGrams, she sent another PigeonGram.

> So it turns out Sylvie and Pink were encouraged to give me the single. They didn't know why, but just did it, they said. What does it mean? I'm using the little package, btw, so poor Hermes won't have such a load to carry.

Who knew what it meant, indeed? But upon receiving this message, I promptly began bugging Gwen at school. I did not tell Eleanor, recalling her reaction to my bugging Gwen many years ago, when she was in grade school. This was by way of trying out some equipment, and innocent enough, I had thought. But Eleanor was incensed.

"We have *principles*," she said. "How can we counter Aunt Nettie if we are just like Aunt Nettie? Think about it. You are *bugging our daughter*."

"All parents bug their children," I said.

She did not smile.

Would she now not agree that the news about the single on top of the appearance of the SwarmDrones made for extenuating circumstances? Perhaps. In any case, I chose not to find out. It was my responsibility, I felt, to do everything in my power to protect Gwen. Let Eleanor hold forth about in which direction lay true north. I was a father.

I was prepared in that I had secreted a bug in Gwen's backpack before she left home, and let me hasten to note that I did not listen to her transmissions all day. I did not mean to intrude on her privacy. Indeed, I was aware that this was the age when she might, as my mother would have quaintly put it, *have a suitor.* If so, the last thing in the world I wanted was to be privy to the developments, for my own sake as well as for hers.

I therefore put bounds on my surveillance—thinking of it as a kind of radio show and imposing on my activities a schedule. Tuesday, Thursday, Saturday. I was clear with myself, too: I was listening for signs of distress. Of course, the house was soon wise to my patterns. *Headed down to your special spot again?* it started to ask. To counter which, I was sure to play music while I worked downstairs—making for a good narrative, I thought. *He's down in his special spot playing Bach, again. He's on a Glenn Gould kick.* As for whether the house was indeed fooled, I had no way of knowing.

Most of the conversations I picked up were reassuringly mundane. The touchiest were with Ondi, about whom Gwen had written to us, *Yes, it is nice to have someone from home here. Someone who knows what it means to be Surplus.*

But the truth, as we might have expected, was more complicated.

"I'm sick of answering their questions. It's like they're Aunt Nettie, and we're their data," said Ondi one week, for example.

"Which is not malicious," said Gwen.

"But you must admit: we're specimens."

"Maybe they'll stop asking when they get used to us."

"Ha."

"And in the meanwhile, we can gather data on them, right?"

That did make Ondi laugh. *"Why not?"*

"I think we should make a big mural about them. Starting with how their hair all looks the same."

"We could take pictures and organize them by hair color."

"I don't think anyone even has brown hair."

"I saw someone with light brown hair the other day. But you're right. No dark brown and definitely no black. And no frizz, either."

"We could stop and ask, 'Do you mind if we take a picture of you?'" Gwen went on. *"'I mean, Only if you're comfortable with it, and I'm not going to post it or anything.'"*

"'I just want to send it to my mom,'" said Ondi. *"'Because, you know.'"*

They both laughed.

But when Gwen brought the mural up again the next week, Ondi's voice was dismissive.

"Where is that going to get us?"

"It doesn't have to get us anywhere. It's just about feeling like we can gather data, too. That they are specimens as well."

"That'll make us a lot of friends."

"Think so?"

Ondi set what sounded like a glass down loudly. *"And you are not going to get anywhere being like that."*

"I thought you always hated the way your father talked."

"And don't you sound like your smartypants mother. Who has gotten so many people in trouble. Resisting and resisting the way she has."

"*Sugar and spice and everything nice,*" said Gwen. "*You should be grateful to my mother. To our whole family, in fact, after all the trouble you caused.*"

"*So why did you help me get in here if I'm so ungrateful and have gotten so many people in trouble? So I could be your sidekick and catch literally whatever you throw me?*"

"*Exactly,*" said Gwen. "*And what a great job you're doing. You make me rejoice every day that I am stuck here with you.*"

Something banged; something scraped. Predictably, a door slammed. I turned off the receiver, but was not surprised to read in Gwen's next GreetingGram, *I can't wait for baseball to start.*

Happily, a lot of the Netted kids were kinder to Gwen, especially Pink and Sylvie. As Gwen GreetingGrammed,

> *They have so little in common that it is easier to grill me than to talk about themselves. I'm the conversational icebreaker.*

And, indeed, from what I heard, that seemed to be the case.

"*So what's it like?*" Pink would ask.

Or Sylvie would say, "*I actually played soccer with some Surplus kids, if you can believe I used to play soccer.*"

And if Eugenie the hockey goalie from across the hall, joining them, added something like, "*I did, too, and wow could they play. Having nothing else to do but practice, I guess,*" Pink and Sylvie would pounce on her. Then they would say things like, "*We'd actually like to do something about this whole Surplus-Netted thing, but what can we do?*"

Indeed, Eugenie's roommate, Anna, was so upset about what she called the Surplus Question that she sometimes couldn't sleep and good-hearted Gwen would end up consoling her. "*It's not that bad,"* she would say. And, *"Actually I come from a really great family."* And, *"As an only child, I got lots of attention, maybe too much attention. I mean, it's kind of a relief to get away from it."*

A relief to get away from Eleanor and me?

How hard it was not to tell Eleanor that Gwen had said that; ordinarily, we would have turned it over and over together, until it had acquired a veritable parental patina. But instead I had to keep it to myself. I kept to myself, too, the way that poor Gwen was peppered with questions, and the way that every answer she gave led instantly to another question as if to the next step of an algorithm.

"Like what do your parents do all day if they don't work?" someone asked.

And when Gwen explained, someone else asked, *"So your mom actually does work? Only for free?"*

And, *"So when people say we do all the work while the Surplus do nothing, that's wrong?"*

It was hard to believe Gwen could answer such a question without heat. At home, she would have probably said something like, *What kind of an asshole question is that?* But here she conducted herself as if giving testimony in a highly publicized trial.

"Yes. In fact, a lot of them used to work and would still be working if they hadn't been deemed Unretrainable. My mom's just lucky she was a lawyer before Automation, because while she's like my dad and can't work with immigrants anymore, she did have the training to do other stuff."

"So why isn't the new stuff a job?"

"Because it's Surplus advocacy, and you Netted aren't exactly going to define that as work."

One might have reasonably thought they would take offense at the phrase "you Netted" or at having a finger pointed at them, but they simply went on—more attuned to the press of their questions, it seemed, than to the answers.

"And what does your dad do?"

"All kinds of stuff. I mean, he isn't as engaged as my mother."

Ouch.

"But he definitely keeps busy. Like he homeschooled me in all my subjects and makes all these gadgets besides."

Wasn't she going to describe, say, my emanation meter and its significance to the Surplus Fields case? But the flow of questions went on.

"And what did you do all day?"

Gwen described concerted consumption, but also how she studied and knit and pitched and fenced, and how because we had inherited a land right from Eleanor's parents, we did not live in a houseboat but a real house, and even had a garden where we grew our own food.

"We're sort of the luckiest of the unlucky, if you know what I mean," she said.

"Actually, it sounds, like, insanely great," said Pink.

"It would be if we didn't stand to get Cast Off or winnowed," said Gwen calmly. She explained what those phrases meant. *"And if people around us could go to college and work and didn't beat each other up instead."*

She explained about the Flotsam Towns, an example of which Pink had visited and which Sylvie had definitely heard of, and about having to live in AutoHouses. Of course, they had Auto-House functions in their houses as well. But it was with control switches for everything, they said, and if they let their activities and consumption be monitored, it was just about service and sales.

"It's to personalize our services, not to control us," Pink said.

"Oh, I don't know," said Sylvie. *"My parents say there've been problems."*

"Like what kind of problems?" asked Pink.

"Like problems with voting," answered Sylvie. *"Like when Face-book became a utility and gave all that data to Aunt Nettie? That's*

where all those DelectableElectables came from. Those perfect candidates they learned to design."

Pink was quiet.

"Candidates who sure enough got voted in and then approved expanding the Autonet," Sylvie went on. "It's like the Autonet gets voters to vote for itself. And who knows if the Autonet's taken everything over at this point or if there are even people behind it."

"Like what people?" asked Gwen.

"Like Big Tech," said Sylvie. "That's what my parents say. Though they think maybe even Big Tech has lost control."

"Wow," said Pink.

They were all quiet.

"So does anyone know?" asked Gwen.

"I don't think so," said Sylvie. "But I can ask my parents."

It seemed a distinct relief for them to return, after a few moments, to the subject of surveillance and whether there really were no cameras or heat and motion sensors sending data about Netted movements and communications. Could that be true? Gwen could hardly imagine it, she said, but Pink and Sylvie said that they were pretty sure that was all against the law. Sure, Net U security did wear ScanID glasses, for example, but only in public places. Private places were off-limits unless they had special permission.

"Like we could have a virtual assistant in every room, if we wanted," said Sylvie, "to tell us stuff like, Is Cyb A still meeting in E-Hall? And, How reliable is that article I just read? But we can also just decide not to."

"Especially since we have assistants in our handphones already," said Pink. *"Like we can already just scan the article and ask if we should believe it or not."*

"Hmm," said Gwen. "And you trust it to be right?"

"Sure," said Pink, but Sylvie wasn't so positive.

"And as it is, if we say anything that suggests we could use a product the assistant will auto-alert our parents, who then order it," Sylvie went on. *"Like if I say, Brrr, it's cold, I could find a new coat being DroneDelivered. Or if I say, I wish Cyb A was closer, I could find an AeroBike outside."*

"I never use HowDoILook for just that reason," agreed Pink. *"Because as soon as it figures out what looks good it starts sending hints to my mother for Christmas."*

"Sounds kind of creepy convenient," said Gwen.

"Forget Big Brother, it's Big Mother," said Sylvie.

A pause.

"I read that book, too. 1984, right?" Gwen's voice was the voice of someone who had never had that happen before—who had never come across someone who happened to have read something she had.

"Hasn't everybody?" asked Sylvie.

"Well, no," said Gwen.

"Actually, it was on a special shelf in our library, too," said Pink.

"Wow," said Sylvie. *"Really?"*

"A lot depends on what state you live in," said Pink.

Gwen went on to explain about how SurplusVille was practically a surveillance laboratory. She told them how Aunt Nettie could read your emotions from afar, for example—*"Like she bounces waves off you and tracks changes in your heart rate and breathing"*—and how she could identify you by your gait and your mannerisms, and how if she got you to wear this little headband, she could read your subvocalizations, too.

"You mean, like, your words before you say them?" said Sylvie.

"Yes."

"But those are your thoughts."

"Exactly. She can tell what you're going to do before you do it, too."

"Wow. That really is, like, Big Mother," said Pink.

Sylvie agreed. *"Though my mother can do that even without a headband."*

"Mine, too, actually," said Pink.

Everyone was quiet for a moment. I shifted in my chair—quiet as well although, what with the Bach playing, I did not have to be.

" 'After Automation something had to be done,' " recited Pink. *"That's what they told us in school."*

"Because it was tens of millions of Unretrainables," said Sylvie. *"And because there were riots. And because the Autonet predicted that after the Automation Riots, there were going to be even bigger riots."*

"Aunt Nettie said that?" said Gwen.

"That's what she calls the Autonet," Sylvie told Pink.

"Oh, I love it," said Pink. *"Yes, that's what 'Aunt Nettie' said."*

" 'Aunt Nettie' predicted that production was going to boom thanks to her," Sylvie went on, *"which turned out to be right. So that there was enough to pay the Surplus some kind of basic income. But Aunt Nettie also said the Surplus should at least consume in exchange. You know, to deal with the oversupply and keep the economy going."*

"Because 'equilibrium will be restored, but first there will be a period of disequilibrium,' " recited Pink.

"And in the meanwhile?" That was Gwen.

"In the meanwhile, something had to be done. To keep order," said Pink.

"And let me guess. The chip thing had worked in ChinRussia," said Gwen.

"Or that's what they told us, anyway," said Sylvie. *"That it was more reliable than FacialID. And that's why you now have this, what did you call it . . . ?"*

"This RegiChip. Thanks to which Aunt Nettie always knows where I am. And which could probably be used the way they're being used in ChinRussia, to make sure workers never slow down and students never goof off, and that no one thinks things Aunt Nettie doesn't want them to think, especially about rising up."

"Wow," said Pink.

"It's really lucky you have that special arm and can go to school here," said Sylvie. "So at least you can become a lawyer like your mom, if you want."

"Or never go back," said Pink. "Because, like, in what omniverse would anyone go back? It's bad enough you were born there."

"Well, at least I know what can happen," answered Gwen. "While you think it can never happen to you."

Silence.

I switched off the receiver and stood.

In a PigeonGram, Gwen wrote,

> There are still plenty of people making comments like, "You must be really, really good at baseball." And, "It's like you put your hands down in flour." And why do they call me Earl Grey? Is it because of my spy-eyes? Which make them think of tea? I'm not even sure who to ask. Maybe Pink and Sylvie? Who are really great. I'm not sure I could stand it here without them and Ondi.

It wasn't clear that Gwen ever asked anyone in the end. But I did hear her ask her roommates all manner of other questions. For example, Why were they so worried all the time?

"We have to get good grades so we can get a real job," explained Sylvie. "Meaning a job and not a gig."

"Are there a lot of gigs?" asked Gwen.

"A lot more gigs than jobs," said Pink.

"Some of which people in other countries can do, too." said Sylvie. Because it's all virtual work."

"Does that mean you have to produce?" said Gwen.

"Do we ever," said Pink.

"*And due to that, only one thing matters,*" said Sylvie.

"*What's that?*" asked Gwen.

"*Do you get Aunt Nettie,*" answered Sylvie.

"*Do you get Aunt Nettie and can you work with Aunt Nettie,*" said Pink.

"*Like, Aunt Nettie isn't too empathic,*" said Sylvie. "*So can you help her fake it?*"

"*And she has no common sense. So can you set her straight when she goes off track?*" said Pink.

"*Can you hold hands with Aunt Nettie. Can you make nice to Aunt Nettie. Can you troubleshoot Aunt Nettie,*" said Sylvie.

"*Can you troubleshoot Aunt Nettie, when you want to shoot Aunt Nettie?*" said Gwen.

"*Exactly,*" said Pink. "*We Netted really are netted, if you know what I mean.*"

"*You mean, you're not exactly free,*" said Gwen.

"*Not exactly,*" said Pink.

Pink's engineer father, for example, apparently hated his AI weapons work. For what could be stupider than SmartArms, he said, except maybe a SmartArmsRace? Her urban-planner mother was happier, having been put in charge of relocating parking lots: once SkyCars became self-parking, there was no reason they had to take up room in the middle of towns, after all, and wasn't it cool that they could stack themselves up?—even figuring out how best to allocate the available solar charge if need be? Sylvie's mother could likewise see some good things about the Autonet. Like it did a great job identifying suicide risks. It sensed distress in people's patterns way before the people around them did and could tell when patients had gone off their meds, and if they had, it could put them in lockdown until they were back on them. Dealing with the Digitally Traumatized, though—with the misAutoID'ed, misAutoDiagnosed, misAutoSentenced, or, yes, misAutoLockedUp—made her curse the Autonet every day. And

Sylvie's father's Human Resources job flat depressed him. In his company, there were always gigs for humans. But the tasks had become so demanding that even Retrained, augmented, and auto-coached people failed at them. And then they were AutoFired.

"*One thing I've never understood,*" said Sylvie, "*is why 'Aunt Net-tie' is always about maximizing efficiency or profits. Like why is she so goal-directed?*"

"*You mean, like why does she always play to win?*" said Gwen. "*Like why can't she just play to play?*"

"*Yeah, and I mean, like why can't she just leave stuff alone?*" said Sylvie.

"*Because we didn't design her, old people did,*" said Pink. "*And adults are like that.*"

Meanwhile, Gwen's GreetingGrams focused on Ondi.

If Ondi didn't struggle with the schoolwork, I wouldn't see much of her outside of practice. But her parents didn't teach her as much as you guys taught me and, fearless as she is, she's afraid to go to help sessions or even to sign up for personal-ized learning. Because, she says, everyone knows. I guess she's self-conscious because people think that Surplus are Surplus because we're not good at school. And anyway, the help ses-sions aren't to cover stuff you were supposed to have learned in high school. So I can always say, How are you doing? Want to study together? And she'll say yes even if she's mad at me for something else and we'll figure out a place no one will see us.

As best Eleanor and I could piece it together, Ondi worried about her grades because her ball playing alone wasn't strong enough to keep her at school. She wasn't one of the standout catchers, after all. Those were Fudge Fisk and Beetle Samsa, who apparently vied with some heat for the starting position, breaking into fights over every possible thing—*"like who got the MassageBot and who got the human masseur, though they tried to keep it from the Coach's attention—I guess because they're afraid he won't think them team players,"* Gwen wrote, *"which, obviously, they're not."* In fact, Ondi wasn't even third string. She was only in a rivalry for that position with somebody named Clara Zee, who told Ondi her hair was a distraction and didn't belong on a ballfield. Ondi, for her part, thought Clara smelled like garlic and said she could neither stand nor sit beside her. As for whether that was why Ondi was not progressing as she had been, Gwen wasn't sure. *Maybe she would have plateaued anyway?* But it couldn't have helped that Ondi and Clara were always being paired for drills, and it was just lucky that, at least for now, only Ondi could catch Gwen, because while Gwen wasn't the best on the team, she was the best freshman woman—maybe even the most promising freshman of either sex.

This drew the side eye, Gwen said, from the other freshman pitchers—people like Righty Grove and Rube Foster and Ichiro Mariner. But luckily, since everyone except Ichiro was a fastballer, they competed more with one another than with her. And the upperclassmen, including the legendary Pietro Martinez, were happy to have a strong new woman pitcher to replace the old one, Renata the Witch. (That being polite, Gwen said, for what she found out they really called her, Renata the Bitch Witch.) Indeed, looking to the future, both Fudge and Beetle were trying to learn to catch Gwen as a way of gaining an edge over the other—something she could not discourage but knew amounted to more pressure on Ondi.

Gwen GreetingGrammed,

So Coach Link asked me today if Ondi was okay. And I said she was fine—figuring that was the safest answer. To which he just laughed and said, "The eleventh commandment: Thou shalt not tell the enemy of thine people squat." Which was embarrassing. And did I just blow a chance to get Ondi out of doing drills with Clara? I told her later that if Clara's smell was bothering her she should just not breathe through her nose. But she said that was just how she breathed, she couldn't help it, and that she thought Clara was spritzing herself with garlic to fend off what she called Ondi's cooties. Which I honestly couldn't believe but Ondi said couldn't I smell it in the women's locker room? And when I said no, she was furious at me that I couldn't. As if I can help what I smell.

But in any case, Gwen herself was thriving.

Is my back double-jointed, do you know? Because Coach Link asked me that but I didn't know. Though maybe that is why when I go into my backward C, it's a really tight C—like why I can draw all the way back and then snap forward the way I do. "Most men look like they're pounding a wall," Coach told me. "You are more like a wave. A whip." He said I should ignore the SmartVideos. I guess there are too few people like me for them to have relevant data, and everyone's different, anyway. "Give me seven pitchers and I'll show you seven ways of getting the ball across the plate," Coach said. "For example, how many people can pitch to both lefties and righties like you can? I can tell you right now. Not many." He thought I should think about people like Satchel Paige instead— Satchel Paige being this old-time pitcher who had to play in the Negro leagues because that guy Jackie Robinson you told me about hadn't come along yet. But Satchel was one of the best who ever laid his fingers across the stitches, Coach said. A legend among legends, even though, talk about different!

"Think about that string-bean arm of his," Coach told me. "Think about that string-bean body—six-foot-three and 140 pounds when he started out. The guy was so skinny people used to say that when he turned sideways he disappeared."

But Coach said I reminded him of him, what with my back and arm and balance and accuracy, and even my ankle flexibility. A female Satchel Paige! Like Coach thought what he calls my dorsiflexion may be another of my strengths. "Stride power is throwing power," he said. "You can see how long a pitcher is going to last in their ankles." Is that crazy? But that's what he said. Speaking of which, he also thought my arm might be in unusually good shape exactly because I didn't have too many chances to throw when I was young. "Every kid should be like you," he said. "Instead they pitch too much. They pitch in the fall and they pitch in the winter and they pitch in the spring. And then they pitch in the summer. They pitch and they pitch and even when their arm's tired and they know it, they pitch some more. Then they get hurt."

But of all my advantages, he thought my greatest advantage was that I didn't have the sort of baseball dad who screamed stuff like, "What the hell was that?" and "Keep your shoulder down!" and "Move that ass!" Thank you, Dad! Because I don't have all this inner stuff to get past. I just throw the ball. Which I guess people can tell. Like my teammate Ichiro said I was the coolest cucumber he'd ever seen. Actually, you're pretty cool, too, I told him. But he said, Not like you. Not like you.

Gwen could not throw as fast a fastball as the best of the men. Her accuracy, though, was apparently unmatched. In another GreetingGram, she wrote,

Coach says I could be a truly great relief pitcher if I put my mind to it. I do need to work on my fastball. But lucky for me, the strike zone was changed not long ago. I guess because there'd been a problem even back before baseball was discontinued with pitchers getting so many strikeouts there was no fielding anymore. People had been asking, like, Is this baseball? for years. And so now that it's been resurrected and made an Official National Pastime, the strike zone's been shrunk here as it already was in the rest of the world. Meaning that what used to be high strikes are now balls and even the fastest of fastballs is easier to hit. So we're about to have an off-speed renaissance, Coach says, which is great for me. Because I guess most of the extant understanding about baseball concerns the fastball. ("Extant" being the kind of word only he would use.) Most guys are not great with the what-the-hell-was-that stuff that comes so naturally to me and that Satchel Paige used to like to throw, too—pitches he named things like the "midnight creeper" and the "wobbly ball" and the "whipsy-dipsy-do." The best of which was his famous hesitation pitch, which worked so well it got outlawed in 1948 but which Coach says he's going to teach me. Because who even knows whether it's still barred over a century later, and who can throw it anyway when no one has the balance? But maybe I do, he says. Maybe I do. So we'll see.

On the weekends, the team apparently hung out at a watering hole called the Dugout—a ritual Ondi typically skipped, as did the three other women on the team, including Clara Zee. And Gwen initially found it foreign, too. She GreetingGrammed,

Like there was this total silence when I walked in. You would have thought I was the president of Net U, come to tell the

guys they had to switch to bowling. But Coach said it was important I get to know them. "Pitchers sometimes keep their distance," he said. "Like they think they're the special gift that comes with a HappyMeal. But chemistry is everything. So my advice is, Think team, be friendly."

He asked her if she could drink. And when she said she'd never had more than a sip of beer, he took her out for a whole beer, so she could find out.

Which was fun. In fact, I had two!

Eleanor and I exchanged looks.

I know what you're thinking. Don't worry. Especially since Coach himself told me, "No more than two—you want to be social, you don't want to get sloshed." He said, "I know you don't want to hear this, but your parents will thank me for telling you. A girl in a room full of boys can't drink. Do not agree to any dares, and no beer pong." In fact, his further advice was: "Do not get involved with any of these characters. It'll screw things up tighter than a tornado. You'll live to see cows sail through the air and the roofs of houses blow off."

But he nonetheless encouraged her to become a Dugout regular, if she could.

"Give 'em their three swings," he said. "This crew's about as civilizable a lot as I've seen in a while. That's not to say civilized, past tense, as in having been successfully subjected to a civilizing influence. But civilizable. And there's no arm so great that it doesn't need a team behind it."

And so she went and, hard as it was to believe, became a regular.

Maybe because guys don't ask questions. Or maybe it's just this team. Like Coach says, a civilizable lot. Or maybe they're just on good behavior. But they talk about a limited number of things, and while I'm an alien, at least it's like I'm an Official Alien. Coach says with time I might even find myself a kind of mascot. That certainly has not happened. But I have an arm, and because I have an arm, I belong. I mean, the Beetle-Fudge thing turned into a fistfight the other day, and who knows what else goes on when I'm not around. Something about their wiring really limits their thinking. But they seem to like me okay.

In fact, she loved talking about who was likely to do what on what count, and what the data really said, and whether a certain ump ought to have been retired. And was Coach Link right to have opposed, as he had, AutoUmps? And was it really too early to say who was likely to go to the Olympic trials, and why or why not? As for whether it was an adjustment to go from being homeschooled to two hours of conditioning before breakfast, then class, then three hours of practice, then homework—*yes, I told them, it is a shock!*

I feel like I have started a new life on Mars—like I have had to learn everything all over, starting with breathing. Because I'd swear sometimes there isn't enough time for breathing, or eating, either. And how do people read so fast?

No one else, it seemed, read things at breakfast then read them over again before going to sleep, so the words would have a chance to sink in, the way I had taught her to read at home.

Instead they plow through the reading the way they would a quad set.

Of course, reading the way she did, she had trouble keeping up, especially since she wrote slowly, too.

I've got to just try to get it done, somehow.

But mostly her classmates marched double time through their assignments—*it's Netted culture*—and were then done with thinking, while once she was done with practice, she loved to talk about all kinds of other things. Which would have made her feel weird, she said—*just, I don't know, so out of sync*—except that, luckily, Coach Link liked to shoot the breeze, too.

Like have you ever heard of this book, Michael Kohlhaas?— which Coach says is his favorite book because Michael Kohlhaas is just so stubborn! And when I said he sounded like Bartleby the Scrivener, he said that was exactly right, and isn't it amazing how interesting we find characters who say no? In life we like people who say yes, but in books we like people who say no, he said. Which is just so true, don't you think? I think maybe he used to be a professor.

Other conversations were less gratifying. For example, in a PigeonGram, Gwen wrote,

So Eugenie says, "My friend Regina says there's another Surplus in the grade ahead of us. A guy by the name of Winny, who says he knows you."

"Winny?" I say.

"I'm pretty sure that's his name," says Eugenie, though she does not actually sound doubtful. "Anyway, he says things really aren't so bad for the Surplus. He says consuming is nowhere near as hard as producing, and that the

Surplus don't try very hard to get themselves out of their situation. Like he says he worked and worked to get himself into Net U, but most of them don't. Because they're on the whole pretty passive, he says, which is why even if AutoAmericans Against Apartheid succeeds and we allow more Cross Overs, they aren't necessarily going to come. Because they've got a great deal, right? Why not let us work and support them?"

"Is this Winny, Winny Wannabe?" I say—really to myself, I guess, since how could she know who Winny Wannabe was?

And sure enough, she says, "I'm sorry?"

"Winny Wannabe, we used to call him." I tried to keep cool but honestly: Had Winny really managed to Cross Over? "And he's right that the number of Cross Overs might not go up, but that's about all he's right about," I say.

Of course, once Gwen had heard about Winny, as if by some universal law of coincidence, she sure enough ran into him on the steps of the student center, by the DNA fountain. This report, too, came courtesy of Hermes:

He was much taller than he was in third grade, but oddly similar in dress. The last I saw him he wore blue button-down shirts his mother bought for him—little-man clothes, we used to call them. He sometimes even wore a tie, though most days, he hid the tie in his desk—something we did not even tease him about, feeling so sorry for him. And now, too, when I saw him, he was tieless. But he did still wear a blue button-down shirt with a jacket. And his face was still oblong and doughy, like PlastiStix before they've been fed into the printer, and there was that same straight-line mouth, too—those ZipLips. His coloring, though, was much changed.

As for the encounter itself, I had been lucky enough to catch that live.

"*Well, well, well,*" he said. "*Gwen Cannon-Chastanet. I'd like to say I was surprised, but I always knew you'd cave and Cross Over.*"

"*A true clairvoyant,*" she said. "*What happened to your skin?*"

"*You watch. A year from now you're going to get a PermaDerm, too,*" he predicted.

"*Am I? And according to what algorithm is that?*" she said. "*Or do you speak again out of vast inner knowledge.*"

"*I can see you haven't changed.*"

"*No, you're right. I was always comfortable in my own skin, and lo and behold—here I am still in it.*"

"*It's still my own skin, Gwen.*" he said.

"*So glad to hear it.*"

"*You know,*" he said. "*When I first spotted you, I was going to ask you to lunch. For old times' sake.*"

"*Well, call me heartbroken.*"

"*Gwen, stop. Do you want to have lunch anyway?*"

"*No,*" she said.

The PigeonGram continued,

But in the end, we did have lunch, and for all that I still couldn't stand him, I have to admit it was nice to be able to come straight out and say, I can't believe you got a Perma-Derm. Which did make him look like a polar bear, especially since he's gone whole hog—or do I mean whole bear?—and lightened his hair, including the little mustache he now sports. It looks like it was laser-glued on, only a little too low, which is why food keeps getting caught in it. And those weren't the only changes. He carries a SmartGun, believe it or not—a hand-

gun, in a holster, though I guess he has others, too. A whole wardrobe, for different occasions, as a lot of the Netted men do, it turns out—so they can defend themselves against us if there is ever another Automation Riot. Which, passive as they believe we Surplus are, they are somehow still convinced there will be. Because, well, you know how menacing we are. Armed as some of us are with deadly knitting needles. I told him our house will be the armory. Still, I was surprised because how could he have a gun? Much less a SmartGun, being Surplus himself. But that was the next surprise. He isn't Surplus anymore, or not exactly. He said he had permanent Cross Over status. Because he passed all the tests, he said, including the Final Test.

As for what that entailed, that was the limit of our buddybuddydom. He wouldn't tell me, except to say that I would never pass. Sounds like quite a test, I said. But he just laughed. He still laughs the way he used to, in this hehheh way—if you didn't know him you might think he was suppressing a sneeze. And he still consumes like a Surplus, so eating like a Netted must not be part of Crossing Over. Just in the time we talked he downed three bacon cheeseburgers with fries and two chocolate shakes. Give the boy an A! It was almost as if there was a part of him that was still Surplus, much as he wanted to get rid of it, and as if he wanted me to see that since I was maybe the only person who ever would. But why did he care?

A reasonable question to which I'd have loved to read her answer, but she just left off.

◆

Eleanor and I, meanwhile, continued to accumulate news, almost all of it good. First, with much fanfare a new policy had been unveiled: some Surplus were being allowed to move into some of the marooned places. Of course, what with such permission tied to one's Living Points, this was quite transparently a diversion strategy. Let people angle for better housing instead of plotting against Aunt Nettie, right? Still, some people were going to be able to move off the water. Their pontoons would no longer leak and their kitchens would no longer rock. They were going to be living on land! That was heartening.

Other good news was that the SwarmDrones that had so spooked the League during the Lookouts-Jedis game had not returned. Why, no one knew. Was Aunt Nettie worried about incipient insurrection and afraid to inflame us? Was she not as worried about us as about other groups of which we were unaware? Or was there yet some other reason we'd been back-burnered? It was even possible that we Surplus were being winnowed quickly enough that eventual reintegration was on the table, said Ben PfoHo. Other members of the League technical team thought that wildly optimistic. But Bart Emmenthaler had heard that a lot of elderly Netted had rejected their CareBots and demanded humans; he said one woman had short-circuited her CareBot with a water hose. So maybe more of us could be Retrained after all? Especially if we agreed to be PermaDermed?

The best news of all was that Eleanor and her team won their Surplus Fields suit. As for whether they would have won had the AutoJudge assigned to the case not kicked it out as too complicated, who knew? But it was heard by a human judge—a Netted man with Surplus relatives, it turned out. So now it was officially acknowledged that there were indeed enfeebling emanations. Per court order, too, they were going to stop immediately, and though all affected kids were assigned a new gene therapy along with their settlement, Eleanor and her team were quite certain the kids could opt out of it if they liked. Experimental therapies could be prescribed and pushed but, thanks to an earlier battle Eleanor had fought, the Surplus could not simply be used as guinea pigs.

We celebrated the Surplus Fields win with a shindig at our house—a champagne-fueled sing-along and dance party, by far the biggest gathering Eleanor and I had ever hosted. Who would have thought we could fit forty people in our garden? But we did, and much more revelry was had than we could have imagined. As for the house offering, as it did, to roll'n'clear every other minute, that just added to the hilarity. People said no sometimes and yes sometimes, and yes then no sometimes, and when the House-Bots appeared, people hid the objects the robots sought to clear, or danced with the Bots, or shone lasers in their sensors, with such spastic results that I almost felt sorry for them. Are we humans torturers at heart? I was just glad the Bots could feel nothing.

The highlight of the evening was the moment that everyone who could do a headstand did one, all at once, in a circle in the garden. How impressive to have seven among us who could do this, even tipsy—and all those feet! Yet more impressively, all seven participants were able to give coherent instructions as to where their handphones might be found, so we could take HoloPix for them. And touchingly, too, before they resumed their normal orientation, they gave a toast.

"Here's to Nellie!" they shouted, their glass stems between their toes. "Here's to all that you've done!"

What with the continued suspicion around the mall-truck food, we did break up knowing there was more work to do—indeed, that ahead lay a fight that threatened to expose one of the foundations of the New Segregation. For if AutoAmerica overproduced food, why didn't Aunt Nettie just dump it? What exactly was in NettieFood? It wasn't what emanated from the Surplus Fields, that much we knew. It was something else—some said a sedative, though no one knew what sort.

As for whether we were prepared to place ourselves squarely in Aunt Nettie's crosshairs, Eleanor pushed her reading glasses up her nose the next day and looked coolly down at her notes.

"Now where were we?" she said. "Have you figured out how to narrow down the list of winnowing agents?"

"We're getting there," I said.

"And the drones," she began, as a NosyDrone crossed overhead.

"We're on that, too," I said, for the drone silence we had enjoyed since the disappearance of the SwarmDrones had recently been resoundingly broken. Was it because of the Surplus Fields win that, once again, there were not only drones at League games but around the house? What's more, it wasn't just NosyDrones and Eleanor's ever-faithful DroneMinder, but some sort of new drone. The geese honked and honked at them.

"Jody Commoner thinks they're ScoutDrones. Which we maybe can't get a fix on because of their FieldObstructors," I said.

Eleanor nodded, still reading, although FieldObstructors, ScoutDrones—this was AutoWar stuff, intended for enemy combatants. Was it all related to our having been black-coded?

Later, I walked by Gwen's empty room and stood in the doorway, thinking how glad I was that she didn't know what was happening—that she could not bug us as I had bugged her. There was peace of mind in knowing less, and I was glad she had it. At the same time, the less she knew, the more distant she felt. We held her close by holding her away.

◆

Playing in the Underground League, Gwen and the Lookouts had of course analyzed and strategized. There were outfielders toward whom they hit every ball possible, knowing how butter-fingered they were or how absentminded or how error-prone. There were batters to whom Gwen pitched fastballs and batters to whom she pitched curveballs. But the Lookouts had never focused on a rival the way that Net U focused on ChinRussia. As Gwen wrote, *"Focus" isn't even the right word. The word is "obsess." They obsess about ChinRussia, I guess because of the stories.*

To begin with, ChinRussia having absorbed most of Asia, they did have those Japanese players, some of the finest in the world. But more important, they had HomoUpgrade. As for what that really meant, who knew? We still traded with ChinRussia—everyone did—but no live ChinRussian had set foot in Auto-America since Ship'EmBack. So what were the ChinRussians like now? Did they have quicker reflexes? Larger biceps? Better vision? Longer strides? People said that GenetImprovement had produced a lot of freaks. Geniuses who could not count. Muscle-men who could knock over small trucks. Giants who had to be fed by cranes. Visitors who had managed a peek sent back reports as crazy as Marco Polo's, with one particularly bad piece of news from the Net U baseball team's point of view: the ChinRussian players, people said, were all switch-hitters.

Perhaps all this was fear pure and simple on the part of Gwen's teammates. But feeding their obsession, of course, was the sense that baseball was more than a sport—that it was a crown jewel. There were people who said it wasn't even invented in America. There were people who pointed out it was mentioned by Jane Austen long before it was ever mentioned here. But if baseball took on a hallowed meaning, it took on that meaning in our American dreams. For was this not the level playing field we envisioned? The field on which people could show what they were made of? And didn't we Americans believe above all that everyone should have a real chance at bat? Didn't we believe that with the good of the team at heart, something in us might just hit a ball off our shoetops and send it sailing clear out of the park? If Gwen's teammates were playing ChinRussia for something, I thought, it was for this—for a chance to show, my mother would have said, that *even if we returned to the dirt and the wind and the rain like the plants and the animals, we had a bigness in us.* Something beyond algorithms and beyond Upgrades—something we were proud to call human. Or so it seemed to me.

But, meanwhile, as in the region around Net U the storms went from late winter right into the spring, baseball had become a fall sport. Meaning that league games were starting soon and that, obsessed or not, the players had to focus. As Gwen Greeting-Grammed,

> *It's like trying to tie a hot-air balloon to a tree, but Coach keeps reminding us that we have Army coming up soon, then Navy. Then Net West, our sister school on the West Coast. And then our biggest rival, data-driven Cyber U. That means we have to make our motions like silk, he says. That means we have to tie our eyes to the ball. "Ball games are won and lost in microseconds," he said today. "You can't think of a second as a flash. You have to think of it as a string, a length, all along which you can work. That is how you expand the possible, you get me?"*
>
> *"Is that the same as killing Army?" said Beetle Samsa.*
> *"Yes," said Coach.*
>
> *Because that is his job as coach, he says. To get through to everyone whether you can get through to them or not. As for why he tells me these things, I really don't know.*

"Though perhaps we are beginning to guess," commented Eleanor wryly.

I just hoped we were wrong.

The next conversation I overheard was with Ondi:

"But you were so beautiful the way you were," said Gwen.

"When in Rome," said Ondi.

"What about if you go back home? What then?"

"I'm not going back."

"But what if. You haven't been asked to Cross Over permanently. So how can you be sure?"

"I'm not going back," Ondi insisted. *"And I had the Living Points. So."*

"But you were so beautiful," Gwen said again. *"And think how Clara Zee is going to gloat. Think how she's going to say, So you realized all along how sorry-ass you looked."*

"I don't care what Clara Zee thinks. It's what's on the inside that matters. Isn't that what you always used to say? It's just your wrapper."

"But it was your wrapper."

"Why should I look coppertoned? Now I look like my parents. Isn't that more natural?"

"Were they PermaDermed, too? Is that why they look so angelfair? And how did they get their PermaDerms, anyway? Was that thanks to their famous doctor friends? And is that where you get all your Living Points?"

"What a smartass you are," said Ondi. *"Just like your mother."*

"You flatter me."

"Anyway, guess what?"

"You're seeing someone and he loves it."

His name was Traymore Crescent. He was a junior cyber-economics major and vice-president of the investments club as well.

"Was it his idea?" Gwen went on.

"I don't just do what guys tell me to do, Gwen."

"*They don't need to tell you, you mean. You pick up their cues.*"

"*If you mean I didn't grow up reveling in my weirdness, the way some of us did, you're right.*"

"*Actually, you did,*" said Gwen. "*Actually, you were rebellion personified.*"

"*Maybe I was myself personified,*" said Ondi. "*And maybe I am still.*"

"*Well, good. Then you've done the right thing. I just have one more question.*"

Ondi waited.

"*Are you going to do your eyes now? Does Open'Em Up come next?*"

As for what came next for Gwen, Eleanor could only say, her head in her hands, "That Coach Link." For in a PigeonGram, Gwen wrote,

Coach gets that I didn't really want to come here but he says that Satchel Paige learned to pitch at reform school, where he didn't want to be, either. So there could be a silver lining to it. "Okay, I'll just think of myself as attending Net U Reform School," I told him. That made him laugh.

I do think he is the only person I've ever met who is as interested in pitching as I am. And he says such interesting things about it. Like, "Think how important it would have been to us as hunter-gatherers, to be able to throw. Don't you think part of our fascination with pitching is an atavistic interest in something we've lost touch with?" Of course, I did not tell him I didn't know what "atavistic" meant. But, yes, I looked it up on my handphone when he wasn't watching. And I was glad that when he said, "I love all those threes in baseball—three strikes, nine innings, nine players. It's as if it's a code written in base three," I at least knew that base three wasn't third base. You'll be happy to hear, too, Dad, that I knew what Coach meant when he said he thought baseball stitched together the agricultural south and the manufacturing north of long-ago America—that I understood what he meant when he said, "One of the beauties of baseball is that there's no clock. We go back and forth from the field, working as we did in our farming days, namely until the job was done. And yet there's something clockwork about it, too—the players making their way around a clockface, or trying to. Backward, as if they're still a little confused about this time thing. And all the fans with their stats—don't they harken back to factory days, when people loved numbers and believed in them? When numbers were oracular? It's arithmetic's last stand."

I thought he maybe used to be a professor but it turns out that's wrong. He did originally want to be a professor, though, and was almost an Unretrainable himself, even though he was born to a Netted family. Because it turns out they can Cross Over, too, only the other way. Of course, no one wants to. But he wrote his thesis on dystopias, which I guess was too much for Aunt Nettie. It was just lucky that he had this sideline, since he was never going to get a job.

He says that when he was in college, there was almost no baseball left, and that a lot of people had never even heard of it, though he had because his grandfather pitched for the Boston Red Sox. So he can sort of imagine what it must be like to be an alien like me. It's still different to belong to a group where there's an actual legal line separating them from us, he knows, and now to look so different from everyone else at Net U. It's not just a matter of feeling different inside. But still he says he thinks he gets it, a little. And I think he does.

How old was this Coach Link? Maybe thirty? Was he married? Had he ever been? And were there rules around coach-player relationships at Net U? Eleanor and I did not dare ask; parental protocol forbade it. And let me say that, tempted though I was, I did not increase my bugging, either—I suppose because this sort of danger did not seem to me extraordinary. No doubt it was the most laughable possible moral reasoning to see things this way, but I believed it to be Aunt Nettie that justified my vigilance. Coach Link did not. And so, like Eleanor, I suffered in ignorance. Meanwhile, Gwen GreetingGrammed,

I wasn't sure he'd put me in, but guess what—I was the relief pitcher for the Army game! We started out ahead, 5–0, thanks to a run in the first inning and a grand slam in the third. But Army chipped and chipped away at us until suddenly it was 5–4, bases loaded, two outs, with their biggest slugger at bat—a guy they called So Long, Salami. I don't know what his real name is but that's what the crowd started chanting. So-long-Salami! So-long-Salami! Or sometimes just Sa-la-mi! Sa-la-mi! And then who do you think Coach brought in? Surprising a lot of people, although actually it made perfect sense that he'd bring in someone Army had never seen.

It was tense. Even though I am almost never nervous, as you know, I was shaking when I got to the mound, and the sun was in my eyes. And I don't know why but my uniform seemed scratchy, as if it had been washed in something I was allergic to, and all I could think was what someone once told me—that if you threw to the outside corner with the sun like that, the ball could come back right in your face. Was that going to happen to me?

Still, I'd noticed earlier that Mr. Salami liked fastballs, and I knew that was why Coach had put me in. Because we needed to try something else. But I'd also noticed that he was

no ambusher—that he liked to watch the first ball to get a sense of what the pitcher was bringing. He was patient. And I figured that what was true in general was going to be even more true with me, a total unknown. So I shook off Beetle's sign and threw an extra-fast four-seamer—at the very top of my range, well into the eighties—and on the outside corner, the exact throw I'd spooked myself thinking about. And sure enough, he let it go. Strike one. Then, just when he thought he had his timing, I threw a circle changeup because I'd noticed his long stride and thought he might have trouble with a changeup. Strike two. Then I threw a plummeting curveball I was a little worried Beetle would lose track of, there in the dirt.

But Mr. Salami missed, and Beetle did not, and that was the inning and the turnaround. We started hitting, and I continued to deliver. Guys hate being struck out, but to be struck out by a girl is demoralizing in a way that helped us get up some momentum that demoralized them yet further until we'd won it, 6–4. Naturally, Ondi was upset later that she didn't get put in to catch me—that in the clutch, Coach seemed to think Beetle was up to the job. But what could I do? It wasn't my call, I told her, and no, I wasn't going to say anything about it. He was the coach. It was up to him.

Anyway, the guys carried me out on their shoulders!— and were all whooping and cheering, and Coach took me out for a beer later, to celebrate. He said the turnaround was like something out of a novel—new kid in town shows legend the door. The question was, what next? Because no novel ever ended there. But when I shrugged and told him I wasn't in a novel and thanked him for advising me to hang out in the Dugout and get comfortable with the guys, because it wasn't just that strikeout that won the game, it was the teamwork, he came down to earth.

*"That's a lesson we all learned the hard way," he said.
"You'd think all that time in the real dugout's enough but it's
not. Because it's a different kind of time."*

*And that was the first I heard from him directly about
Renata. Who also pitched relief but was not as good as me, or
who never got to be as good. Though she was a natural, too, he
said. And who knew what she could have done, had she hung
out with the guys and become one of them. Which maybe she
would have if she'd been less isolated—if she'd had an Ondi
like I did, he said. Or at least some other women. As it was,
she had to drop off the team—he didn't say exactly why. I
wondered, though, if it had to do with getting involved with
someone, and if that was why he told me house roofs could go
flying through the air if I did.*

Eleanor and I wrote back via PigeonGram to congratulate
her—saying how fantastic the game was, a real breakthrough, and
so on. At the same time, we couldn't help but comment on what
an interesting story that was about Renata. Nor could we help but
ask, Was it just one beer? And was it just her and Coach Link,
alone? Before asking these things, I should perhaps point out that
I did take an online ParentalParanoia quiz, and on a 0–10 scale
received a 6—"concern absolutely justified." Gwen replied,

*I can't believe you tired out poor Hermes with questions like
that.*

She did not write for a week. But then she started GreetingGram-
ming again, just as cheerily as before, as if nothing had happened.
Was that because she had forgiven us or because she didn't want
Aunt Nettie to see she'd stopped writing? We suspected the latter
but had no way of knowing.

One thing is that my arm is getting pretty sore sometimes. I am now one of the pitchers getting worked on after practice and have all sorts of special exercises. But I have a great new ointment, too. They gave me this stuff with THC in it—do you know what that is? Don't worry, it's not enough to make me high. But I can't believe what a difference it makes. It draws the pain right out. And when the pain's gone, I'm like a different person. You'd be amazed how sociable and relaxed.

"How much THC is this?" Eleanor wanted to know. "And is that all there is in the ointment? And how relaxed is relaxed?"

"If you want to cross-examine her, you can," I said. I confined myself to:

Did Coach recommend this?

Yes! He has total control over everything having to do with his players. I guess he insisted on control when he was hired and got it. Because he's gotten great results, and that's what they want to see. They treat him like a god.

Glad he's keeping an eye on you.

So I wrote. But these days Eleanor and I did not need Swarm-Drones to unnerve us. We could not sleep.

In the morning, we sent a PigeonGram about the last League game—a rematch of the Lookouts and the Jets.

Brianna Soros at shortstop caught a fly ball behind her back! Yes, you read that right. With her glove behind her! What a showboat. And then, cool as can be, she turned and threw to

second for a double play. And in the ninth inning, Diego help-
ing out in center field caught a ball that had gotten so far out
past him he had to catch it over his shoulder. Which he did—
but not before it dove so close to the ground he was lying on the
grass on his stomach with his glove out in front of him like a
frying pan. He stood up so happy he kissed the ball, and that
was it—game. Lookouts 6, Jets 4, just like your game against
Army. Of course, the level of play can't compare. Maybe to
you it will seem more comedy than competence now—a lot
of shenanigans. But maybe you'd have liked to see the heroics
all the same. Including the new pitcher, Bo Anders, who is
doing okay, considering. He says he's got to meet you some-
day because all he keeps hearing is, I don't mean to compare
you to Gwen but . . . It's like you put a spell on the team, he
says. And like, even though you're gone, the spell hasn't been
broken.

We awaited her reply a bit anxiously. And how relieved we
were when in her return PigeonGram, she seemed touched. She
did not seem to think the League Podunk, what with no starting
pitchers, no relief pitchers, no strategy. She did not seem to see
us now as a bit like soda-can sculptures, ingenious and full of
spunk but finally not real sculpture. In fact, for the first time she
sounded homesick.

Oh, it's the team that's put a spell on me! A spell under which
I remain, far away as I am. I wish I could have seen the
heroics. Diego is a madman! And that Brianna Soros. Did
you know she can also do gymnastics? One of these days she's
going to make a catch while doing a cartwheel. I know none of
them would even think of Crossing Over, but if they were ever
interested, wow. Thinking of them, any one of them, playing
out here with me—I miss them all so much.

"Ever." Did that mean she was thinking of Crossing Over permanently?

The game against Navy was—happily, said Eleanor, and I could not have agreed more—less exciting than the Army game. A female Satchel Paige or not, Gwen spent the game on the bench— *which in a way I didn't mind*, Gwen GreetingGrammed.

> *I mean, the pressure to save the game again! Or to do something else spectacular. What if I screwed up? I wish they'd stop calling me the Secret Weapon. It just makes me worry I'll disappoint everyone—that what happened at Army was a fluke. And if I do shine eventually, I worry the older pitchers will hate me—relievers like Warren Peese especially. Who needs to be benched as a senior because of a freshman girl? I thought Coach was right to get him out there in his last season, though I also knew Coach was right when he said I should not care what Warren thought. As he said, It's baseball. If the situation were reversed, Warren'd retire me quick as sundown.*
>
> *Meanwhile, there was a bunch of fans who wanted to see me put in. At the top of the fifth they started chanting, Sur-plus! Sur-plus! Sur-plus! It took me a while to realize who they were even talking about, to be honest. Then they started with Perm-her-derm! Perm-her-derm! Perm-her-derm! And then I wasn't sure if these were fans at all.*
>
> *And then (I know this is a lot of 'and then's, but it's not an essay, haha) guess who I saw? Renata the Witch, who still comes to the games sometimes. Even though she's obviously not on the team anymore or even at the university, there she is giving me the bug eye. As if it is my fault she didn't spend more time in the Dugout? I don't know what she wanted, sitting there, but I wished she would go away. Although in a way, it*

seemed only natural to have someone staring at me when all the guys had Annies staring at them. Signaling, Ready when you are! Get your hotcakes right here! What is the matter with them? Of course, the guys eat it up, and you have to ask what is the matter with them, too, although a bigger problem so far as their sleep is concerned seems to be DumDumGames. Like who has the time? But a lot of them are addicted and Coach has to lecture them day and night about it.

Though Gwen was not under as much pressure as her classmates were, she did not find, as the semester went on, that balancing schoolwork with baseball was getting easier. Her next Pigeon-Gram read,

I thought I'd be used to it by now, but I'm not. If only I didn't have to sleep. Or maybe if Coach got it that people had to sleep? Which in theory he should, right? Since he used to want to be a professor, etc. But in practice he says he has to win games because if compared to other coaches he doesn't measure up, he's out. Like he gets messages saying things like "Congratulations! You're in the top 10 percent of college coaches!" all the time. Meaning Aunt Nettie has him by the numbers, just like she has everyone else. And if you think he gets credit for having almost single-handedly resurrected college baseball, which was near death many times, he does not. I guess Net U really only supports baseball because we win. But baseball's always been where his heart is. He just couldn't watch it die.

As for why I should likewise give everything to baseball, Coach says I should because that's where my heart is, too. Wasn't that why I came to Net U? Because of my golden arm?

And if I'm not intending to Cross Over permanently—which he can't quite believe, but that's something else—what point is there in studying? I told him that I actually like to read and study. For a Surplus it's a privilege, I said. If nothing else, I have to do it for all the people who can't. But in addition, I am more than an arm, I told him—to which he scoffed. "Your arm owns you," he said. "Like it or not."

Of course, that made me mad. It was a good thing that the next day, he apologized. "I want you to belong to the sport," he said. "I want you to belong to the team. But you are right. Your arm doesn't own you—no one owns you. Maybe that's why you're so cool on the mound. And you're right, too. You should read all you can and study all you can, while you can. You know, I forget myself," he said. "Sometimes I forget. But you remind me. Thank you." Then he gave me something to help me sleep, so at least I didn't waste time tossing and turning.

I did not care what ParentalParanoia said. I immediately Pigeon-Grammed back,

Gwen, honey. It is better to toss and turn. Do not take this whatever it is. These things are addictive and who knows what's in it.

Eleanor and I braced for her reaction. But to our relief, she responded agreeably.

I told Coach the same thing—which is what Pink and Sylvie said, too, by the way. First of all, I said, I am so tired I pass out as soon as my head hits the pillow. Second of all, I don't like to take things. The ointment is enough.

"Thank goodness, but," said Eleanor.

The ointment. I agreed.

She knit her eyebrows together—all of this on top of the pressure of the Mall Truck suit. There was some good news on that front. Eleanor now had a potential witness—a woman who could not herself eat NettieFood because of allergies but who had watched her husband lose all his drive until she convinced him to eat what she did. Then he became himself again! Still, Eleanor's forehead looked like a riptide.

"Let's take a long warm bath," I suggested.

"We haven't taken a bath together for a while."

And it did, it helped us relax. So much so that the next morning, I wrote to Gwen,

If you have trouble sleeping, why don't you try a warm bath?

She PigeonGrammed back,

I already told you I'm not taking the pills.

Her next GreetingGram was less testy. She thought her writing needed more work than her teachers did, she said. And could we believe one of them gave his comments online, in all of a paragraph?

Shouldn't they mark the pages all up? Or is it only fathers who will take the time?

Of course, I smiled at that. Relatively competent as she was at writing, though, Gwen was a disaster in bio lab.

I am terrified of dissection. My partner runs out of the room all the time, and when the results come out wrong, which is always, I just want to throw something at someone. Especially

when people say stuff like, You really should stick to baseball. Or, Too bad you're only a quarter Asian.

I wrote,

That's terrible. But please do not throw anything except a baseball, and not at anyone, and not in the lab, or out of the lab, for that matter. Even your mother sticks to bacon and eggs, and to be frank, it is not her best trait.

Happily, life with Pink and Sylvie was great. Gwen Greeting-Grammed,

The only thing is, what's going to happen next year? I don't dare ask either one of them, and I'm sure I'm the only one already worrying about it. But I wonder if the novelty of me will wear off. I mean, I'm sure we'll stay friends. Maybe we'll get together and cook something every now and then. But I'm not sure they'll even want to room with each other. Like I think Sylvie is going to want to room with her dance friends and Pink is going to want to room with her tennis friends. Leaving me to room with Ondi? Who is maybe going to want to move in with Traymore? Assuming she doesn't get cut from the team? I guess I wish Pink or Sylvie would ask me to room with her. Especially Sylvie. But I don't think she will.

To this, Eleanor and I wrote,

Maybe you should just ask her? What do you have to lose?

We could see Gwen rolling her eyes, though. And sure enough, the answer came back,

I can't. Trust me. I just can't.

Ondi, in contrast, seemed less stuck, thanks to Traymore. She was apparently getting to practice early now and, what with Traymore teaching her to think more strategically, she was no longer leaning solely on her ability to catch Gwen. Instead, she was making sure she could catch all the pitchers and, what's more, was much savvier than she had been about the pitches she called for. She not only appraised the batter's weaknesses but the pitcher's strengths, and she thought beyond the three-strike out—better understanding things like how she could save the pitcher's arm by getting the batter to hit a grounder. *Groundouts mean pitchers can stay in the game a lot longer,* Gwen explained. *That makes it easier for Coach to save other people for upcoming games or to work around injuries. It gives him options.* And Ondi did more homework than any of the other catchers. Aunt Nettie had stats on all the players—on when they had swung and when they had not, on when they had gotten on base and when they had hit homers or grounders or fly balls or fouls. It was information distributed to everyone, and Fudge and Beetle, it seems, did look at it. But Ondi memorized it, retained it from game to game and, most critically, infused it with her intuition. She was like an AI database plus; indeed, hers was the sort of AI-human collaboration that the long-ago designers of wearables for catchers had dreamt of before coaches like Coach Link had them banned. Said Gwen in a GreetingGram,

> *Ondi says Traymore tests her every night, and that she never gets a stat wrong. Of course, as she says, she was already used to studying twice as hard as other people because she was so far behind in her coursework, and with this, she didn't start off behind. So now it's turning into a real advantage. Some pitchers are even starting to say maybe women make the best*

catchers, because they're better psychologists. "They know how to get inside your head," Pietro said. And people's confidence in her is making Ondi hustle more. She's always been quick and tough, as you know, if a little erratic in her throwing. But now that she's really on top of things, she's better than ever.

Gwen's enthusiasm was real. But, of course, all things with Ondi were like yarn that's been knit and unwound—full of kinks. Gwen reported in a PigeonGram,

So I didn't put in a good word for Ondi with Coach back after the Army game, as you may remember and as she remembers very well. But still she started helping me special all the same. Giving me the very best of her calls, she said. I told her not to, please—that she should not play favorites. Right makes might, I said. And, There's no direction like true north. Still, she mostly insisted, "I can't help it. I just know you better than the others."

One day, though, she said, "Remember how mean I was to you when the Thistles played the Lookouts? And how kind you were when the League was so mad at me for playing unhacked? This is my chance to pay you back."

"Oh, wow," I said. "That's so nice."

But then another day, she said that all that true north stuff was how I think, not how she thinks, and that Traymore agrees. She's extra helpful to me, she said, because our best strategy is to stick together.

"Surplus is Surplus, and you're blind if you can't see how it matters," she said.

"You mean, a PermaDermed Surplus is still a Surplus?" I answered—which of course made her mad. She really drives me crazy.

◆

If Ondi was driving Gwen crazy, the ever-increasing drone traffic above our house and our games was driving us crazy.

"What do they want?" Diego demanded one day, glaring up at the sky. With his upstretched arms, he looked as if he were going to try to grab one. "I wish they would just say what the hell they want."

"Maybe they don't know," I said. "Or maybe they know that if they actually do something, we will fight back. So better to wear us down than confront us. And drones can keep this up forever because they are drones. Whereas we can't stand it forever."

"They can just wear us down and see if we snap."

I nodded. In my heart I believed this strategy to be related to having been black-coded, but I couldn't prove it.

Then Diego said, out of nowhere, "Do you think Gwen is coming back to us?"

"I don't know," I said. And when he reddened a little, I thought for a moment what a fine young man Diego had become—thoughtful and kind, and the de facto team captain. If only Gwen could see it, too! But Coach Link, Coach Link, Coach Link. Could she see anyone besides Coach Link?

Mimi came to report on Gwen—who, she said, had really taken quite a shine to Net U. She hoped we were as pleased as she was.

"Because you can scout all you want, and Aunt Nettie can predict all she wants," she said. "But you still never know."

"Interesting," said Eleanor.

Mimi's face did not so much shine as glow, which could have just been the heat and the smoke. There was a wildfire a little south of us, after all—nothing we weren't used to, but it was making a warm fall day even warmer.

"And look at Ondi," she said. "Who could have predicted that she would find that boy Traymore and snap into gear this way? Not even Aunt Nettie could've foreseen it."

Did she really think that? And how did she know about Traymore? Was that from Gwen's GreetingGrams or did everyone know? And was she telling us because she wanted us to know that she knew?

"It's such a happy story," I agreed cautiously. "He seems to be just what she needed."

I tried not to let my fundamental mistrust show. But suddenly she fanned herself with her free hand, saying she felt faint.

"The heat," she said.

"Can we get you something? Some iced hibiscus tea?" said Eleanor.

"Will it have the wild mint?"

"Of course."

"Well, that might just be what the doctor ordered," said Mimi.

And so quickly did she revive, once out in the garden, that it was hard not to wonder if it was the thought of not being offered tea that had made her head spin. She gestured animatedly as we discussed the advantages of adding coffee grounds to the soil. Did they have any effect on the worms? she wondered. Then on her way out, she asked casually, with a swat at the air, "Since when do you allow drones in your house?"

Drones?

And sure enough, when she left we found that there were MicroDrones everywhere, the same color as the walls and nestled into little crevices in the plastic. How long had they been there? Was this how Aunt Nettie seemed to know so much about us despite our data shutoff and white noisemaker and deflectors? And why had Mimi alerted us? Was she trying to help us or trying to make us snap? Since the MicroDrones were not legal, Yuri, Heraldine, and Sue immediately lodged a complaint in court; the League technical team set to work getting the drones out of there. Eleanor and I tried to keep calm.

◆

There was a ten-day gap between Navy and Net West—plenty of time for everyone to rest and to think. And that was a good thing, because while it was great that Net U had beat Navy, there were a lot of things about the game that Coach Link apparently didn't like. He didn't like it, for example, that the starting pitcher, Bento Halifax, had twice signaled to their first baseman, Mookie Dreem, that he was going to pick someone off but that Mookie had been "fucking Dreeming" both times. *And, wow, when Coach got mad he got really mad,* Gwen reported in a GreetingGram.

> *"To say that was horseshit is to insult the equine race," he said. "Why was there so much chasing bad pitches? What are you doing, snuffling the dirt? Let me tell you something. We did not win that game. Navy lost it. We were just lucky that, sloppy as we were, they were sloppier. That game was an early Christmas present. Santa sent it shooting down the chimney to us, and we got to unwrap it. But the fact remains that there was a lot of mindless slugging out there. Some of you are trying to hit the ball out of the park when it's more important to look where your teammates are and make sure they come in, especially since you've only hit three homers in your whole life and this is highly unlikely to be your fourth. I mean, does anyone on this team know how to bunt? Or is that a lost art like making handmade fucking shoes? Which brings*

me to another footsy-toesie issue. Some of you are not exactly exploding down the base lines. Some of you are jogging. And as this stadium is my witness, if I see any more fucking jogging out there, I am going to strip your uniform pants right off your slow asses and personally replace them with jogging pants. And I do mean midgame. You are going to come out of the dugout wearing the lounge pants you deserve, and if they are flamingo pink, don't say I didn't warn you. In fact, I'm putting in my order today, and let me tell you. They are going to be one size fits all. In fact, I have a sample right here."

Then he pulled out the hugest pair of pink lounge pants you ever saw and proceeded to hang them over the doorway so you had to duck under them to get into the men's locker room and we women could easily see them from the entrance to the women's locker room, too.

All of which I thought would upset people. But the funny thing is, the guys seemed to like it. Like they were all joking about the pink jogging pants later. If someone wasn't hustling, they'd yell, You're going to look great in pink! Or, Your jogging pants are in the mail! It was as if Coach had clearly expressed what he wanted us to do, and had told us what to yell at each other, too. Also, the pink pants provided a lot of entertainment. Depending on the day, the guys might be draping the legs of them around their heads like hair or attaching a jockstrap to them, and I do think I took a big step toward team acceptance when I not only did not object to the jockstrap but attached two stuffed feet to the legs, complete with lace-trimmed stirrups and a pair of extra-spiky cleats.

"It's like a play," Coach told me later. "You've got to act your part if you want them to act theirs." Plus, it was true, he said, and they all knew it. The Navy game was a slop pail. "And people like to be held to a standard. They want their excellence drawn out of them like blood."

"But who is that beating them up?" I asked. "Is that you?"

"Insofar as I am the coach here, yes," he said. "And insofar as we are all here to win games."

A nonanswer answer, don't you think? And yet I could see that his dress-down worked sort of like AskAuntNettie. Maybe the guys knew he was on auto-blast, but they responded just the same. Auto-responded, you might say.

And, strangely, I did, too. It made me feel he cared, somehow. That he was watching. Attending. It's a funny thing, I realize now, about the way we Surplus live, that we feel watched all the time. Of course, here at Net U, too, we are probably watched more than we know. But no one asks me, "Clear-float now?" or tells me, "You have a choice. You always have a choice," or anything else. As for whether Coach knew I missed feeling watched, I don't know. And will I always carry Aunt Nettie around with me? Will I always be tuned to her presence or absence? You know how people talk about having a god-shaped hole in their hearts? I think you told me that. Well, I wonder if I will always have an Aunt Nettie–shaped hole in my head. And what does that mean? Is that what it means to be Surplus?

"Will I always have an Aunt Nettie–shaped hole in my head?" read Eleanor aloud. Then she read it aloud again. And again. And I agreed. It was the most terrible thing Gwen had ever written.

◆

The Mall Truck suit went on. It was hard at first to find a laboratory willing to verify our amateur findings; for a while it seemed that we would not be able to find such a lab at all. But thanks to an increasing interest in the New Segregation among the Netted, as well as the resourceful doggedness of Eleanor's team, we eventually located not one lab but two. And although we would of course all have preferred for there to have been nothing in NettieFood to find, it was a source of no small satisfaction that the laboratories' measurements were within one standard deviation from each other's, and from ours. We were still weirdly unable to identify the winnowing agent; the compound wasn't a chemical we recognized. Still, Eleanor and her team now had what they needed. Yuri, Heraldine, and Sue set to work pulling the case together.

Gwen, meanwhile, was finally catching up to her classmates in computer science and finding herself a helpful presence in Western Intellectual Thought as well. While many of her classmates thought Plato's thinking in *The Republic* an academic exercise, for example—because wasn't our republic of course what it was?—Gwen managed to make the fact of AutoAmerica seem less inevitable. Questions like, Could Plato have made a case for AutoAmerica? and, What might AutoAmerica look like instead? did not become subjects of long discussion. They did become subjects of some discussion, though, as did topics like technological tyranny. Her classmates didn't use that term, it seemed, but they did discuss how supremely effectively Aunt Nettie had institutionalized the Netted-Surplus split—embedding it in her policing code, her family code, her educational code, her housing code. (Wrote Gwen, *It's like Jim Crow gone digital.*) On these sorts of subjects, Gwen found she could never be quiet—and also that many of her classmates were interested in what she had to say. A few were convinced she was exaggerating when she talked about, for example, the One Chance Policy. "Like that just cannot be true," said one guy. And most had never stepped foot in a printed plastic house or visited a Flotsam Town. Gwen was, she said, going to take them on a field trip. (*Time to open their eyes,* she wrote.)

In the meanwhile, now that a new quarter was starting—
already!—she was able to sign up for a Literature of Justice class,
meaning that she was finally going to read *Michael Kohlhaas*, as
well as *The Merchant of Venice* and *Measure for Measure*, and *Bleak
House* and *The Trial* and *To Kill a Mockingbird*, and *The Fire Next
Time*. She signed up for an independent study in law, too, complicated as that was. In a PigeonGram, she explained,

> *I'm not sure the professor feels free to teach me whatever
> I'm interested in. Like, when I asked her about the law that
> divided people into Surplus and Netted and how that squared
> with the Constitution, she froze.*

But Gwen was still learning a lot, even if baseball was never far
from her mind. She GreetingGrammed,

> *Thanks to some weird winds, Net West and Cyber U are now
> back-to-back—nothing we can do about it. And on top of it,
> our starting pitcher, Pietro Martinez, seems to have finally
> torn his anterior UCL. It was partially torn already, and
> swelling up so bad he was taking this stuff called iBute, which
> was actually meant for horses and outlawed for humans
> long ago. But then his UCL tore altogether, so now he's in
> for Tommy John surgery. Like I guess the doctors are going to
> drill holes in the bones of his arm, which have basically come
> apart, and reattach them with a tendon that's going to turn
> itself into a ligament, if you can believe it. Coach says the cells
> just modify their function and secrete collagen until they're
> not tendons anymore; it's called ligamentizing and it takes
> two years if you let nature take its course. But even if the docs
> speed it up, Pietro is out for the season—a terrible loss, though
> Coach says everyone saw it coming. His low arm slot meant*

Pietro kind of slung the ball like he was skipping a stone, and his timing was off. All of which Coach told him, but Pietro is about as coachable as a rocking horse. Or at least that's what Coach says. And Coach never liked the iBute thing, by the way, which was totally Pietro's doctor's idea and Pietro's choice. And now look.

Anyway, what with Net West and Cyber so close together, Bento Halifax can't pitch both. So guess what? Bento is starting in Cyber, and the other southpaw, who has been working pretty hard on her fastball, is starting in Net West! Of course, I am one nervous Nellie (I know, very funny), seeing as how this'll be my first time starting in this league, and Coach says I'll need a different attitude. It's not enough to surprise, he says. I'm going to have to intimidate. Dominate. Devastate. Attack. "You mean, think of them as the Netted who have everything, and me as the Surplus who's going to get it all back?" I said. To which Coach looked surprised but said, "Yes. Think of it as your role." Just as it's his job to issue auto-blasts, he said I've got to make it clear I will throw right at the batter's head if he gets wise. That I'm out to destroy the batter's self-confidence on the first pitch and keep ramming at it with every throw thereafter. (Yes, he really said "thereafter." That's Coach for you.) He said he wanted me to shock them so bad they'll have to send their coach home in a MediLyft.

As for whether I could really do this? I wasn't sure. But then he said, "Don't ask yourself, Is this me? Think of yourself as a rock in the ocean. No matter what crashes over you, you remain a mass to contend with. And that's your job—to maintain your mass. Your specific gravity. Your strength. And to use your body language to get that across. Because what your body says is how the whole team plays. You set the attitude for everyone."

And this is where he is a great coach, I think—because I got what he was saying because of the way he said it. Had he just told me to be a bloodthirsty son of a bitch, I'm not sure I would have got anything. But an immovable mass—yes. I could make myself that. He said, "I've seen this in you. The way you'll look down and take off your cap and redo your hair and then look back up with a glare that is out-and-out determination."

I looked up at Eleanor. "Her prosecutor face," I said. She smiled.

"You have mound presence," he went on. "Remember how demoralized the Army guys got? Keep the innings short, get your teammates jazzed, and before you know it Net West'll be wishing they had never lived to see a blue ponytail winding up."

Coach has also really been helping Ondi with stuff like her framing and wow, but she can catch a ball so it looks like a strike now. And I mean subtly, so she really puts it over on the ump. Which is all that matters, because thanks to Coach's campaign to "Keep Umps Human," how the ump calls it is the call. So now I feel like I can throw my overhand curve with confidence it's not going to get called a ball by accident. Isn't that great? And believe it or not, what with our supposed chemistry, Ondi's going to start in Net West, too. Is that to make up for Coach not playing her in the Army game? He didn't say.

He did say, though, how odd it is that though college base-ball's been coed for over a decade you still don't see a woman pitcher and a woman catcher much. And it's good for people to see, he says. It's good to befuddle them. ("Befuddle" being yet another word only he would use.) What he didn't say is that in a way it's too bad Ondi got a PermaDerm. Because a coppertoned woman pitcher and a coppertoned woman catcher—that would get some attention. Which the college likes to see—it excites the alumni, I guess, and then they give more.

But salt-and-pepper females is still something. When he said, "I'm counting on you to make it a game to remember," I knew he didn't just mean, I'm counting on you to look like the new Sandy Koufax. He was saying, Don't prove to the naysayers that women can't handle the heat. Which, of course, was pressure. But as Ondi said, This can't be worse than being Surplus at the tryouts. And that was a fact.

◆

In ChinRussia, the backlash against Total Persuasion Architecture was growing. Students were disabling the chip scanners in the classrooms, and workers were stripping off their SmartSuits in such numbers they could no more be required, or how would the SuperFactories operate? Even with PlainCommonSense and other buddy systems, after all, the robots were easily foiled—by winds, by spills, by leaks. Their HELP buttons went off constantly. *There's a cat in the warehouse! There's butter in my path! I'm losing my charge!* The few human workers left were indispensable. Yet more and more, they were quitting, moving back into the long-abandoned countryside, and supporting themselves farming. As for the effect of all this on AutoAmerica—naturally, we were redoubling our Redoubling. "As if that makes any sense whatsoever," said Eleanor.

We sent Gwen a newsy PigeonGram:

What a comedy of errors! First our new left fielder, Steve Wonder, got the sun in his eyes and missed a perfectly easy foul ball. It just went clean past him like a bit of scenery on a train. Then our new second baseman, Hector Quesadilla, threw a ball so far from Ralph Changowitz that Ralph had to go skidding on his side to catch it—which he did, looking rather like a Roman god at a banquet until the ball rolled out of his glove. You can imagine the howls! As for the pitcher's several errors, every one was greeted with, Gwen would have had that. Because, of course, you would have.

We expected she would PigeonGram right back to say how much she missed the Lookouts, the way she did last time. But she did not. Instead, she GreetingGrammed,

So how was it, my turn as starting pitcher? Intense, in part because in addition to Sylvie and Pink at least a dozen fans had turned out just to see me. The Surplus Surprise, they call me. I'll be winding up and hear, Go, Go, Gwen-nie! Go, Go, Gwen-nie! Or, now that they know my whole name, Can-non! Can-non! Can-non! Can-non! Happily the Perm-your-derm! thing has stopped. Still, the experience was strange—mostly in a good way, but for one exception.

That was Renata, sitting in the stands and staring at me with these hollow eyes; it was hard to tell if she never slept or had just had a LushLash job go bad. But in any case, I blocked her out. I told myself she was a wave I had to let wash over me, and I did. She washed over me and there I was still, a rock.

It was cold and wet and windy out—weather that Net U would have blocked but that Net West couldn't, not having that fancy roof Coach raised the money for. I had to do extra

warm-up and couldn't feel my fingers at first. And obviously, it's hard to grip the ball right when you can't even feel your fingers. Still, I figured the cold was mostly a good thing because I was so much less likely to see a ball go out of the park. And another good thing: Net West was missing their ace pitcher, just like us, who knows why.

In any case, my first pitch was hit foul; that was the trouble with tinkering with your pitches during the season. I'd meant to throw a curve but had been working on my slider, and so what I got was this slurve, which the batter got some wood on. But then—surprising myself, and certainly Ondi— I threw a fastball low and inside. Strike. Then another fastball, high and inside. And then came the slider I felt my first pitch was telling me I wanted to throw. And sure enough, strike three.

The rest of the game was a blur. I did give up a few hits toward the end. But I finished with a shutout! Which you couldn't exactly say I owed to Ondi—sometimes I shook her off. But sometimes I didn't, and anyway I feel she did have something to do with it, bringing as she does a kind of homey feeling to home plate.

And, of course, that was right. Gwen didn't bring up the no-hitter she had pitched for the League with Ondi catching, but I knew she had to have that on her mind—their utter comfort with each other. Their telepathic communication.

To her I wasn't just a coppertoned novelty. To at least one person, I was Gwen. Also, I was the rock that I'd promised Coach I would be. Everything washed over me. Even as everyone was screaming Can-non, Can-non! I just kept my nose going toward Ondi's mitt. Until, yes, we had won! 4–0, and for the second time I was carried off by my teammates, right past that glaring Renata, whatever her problem is. What a game— I just wish you had been there to see it!

The rest of the story came by PigeonGram.

So later on Coach told me, "This is what you were meant for. An arm like yours is once in a generation. Did you hear the crowd?"

I shrugged.

"Well, they know it, too. And look at where you are after just a couple of months here. Can you imagine where you'll be in a few years? You have great things in you, and I don't say that lightly. You are the most talented pitcher I've ever coached."

Honestly, I didn't know what to say to that. So I asked, "And Ondi?"

"Ondi?" He looked as if he'd just lost his hearing.

"What about Ondi?"

"She has a chance."

"Meaning?"

"Meaning, we always need women. And there are people who see that you probably perform better with at least one other Surplus around. So there's that in her favor."

"But she's doing great independent of me, right?"

He gazed into his beer like there was a bug in the foam.

"She's doing great and gets along great with the guys," he said finally. "The pitchers like her. But I'm not sure how well she does with other women, ironically. Is she a team player? I'm not sure."

"Does that mean someone doesn't like her?" I said. He didn't want to say but I knew. "Like Clara Zee, maybe?"

He hesitated. "Ondi's complicated, isn't she."

"Clara Zee has been far less of a team player than Ondi,"
I said. "Far, far less."

I'm not sure he was listening, though. Instead he looked
at me and said, "Even with you she's complicated."

And what could I say then? She was.

What with Cyber U coming right on the heels of Net West,
Gwen didn't have time to think about whether there was something else she should have said in Ondi's defense. Because while
Cyber U did not GenetImprove like ChinRussia, they did, it
seemed, use TrainerBots. They used DrillBots to give players
more drill time, Gwen reported, and they used DoItAgainSam to
help players reinforce their muscle memory. They used iCoach to
analyze motions, strategies, and lineups. And they used KillingIt
to give players stats after every workout. Gwen said that people
had only to hit How'dIDo to see how hard they'd pushed themselves or how much better they'd gotten at judging the ball or how
much more efficiently they'd swung. Those who had signed up
for StimLearn could see how much faster their NeuroStimplants
were helping them learn. And people with How'dHeDo could not
only see how others on the team had done that same day but could
push CanIGetHim to see how they could catch up to any player
they picked. Gwen's GreetingGram went on,

> How can we compete against that? some guys wanted to
> know. To which Coach pointed out that we could have any
> Bot or program they did. If we wanted, he said, we could have
> How'dHeDo with the CanIGetHim feature, too. But these
> things wrecked team spirit and burned people out, he said.
> They burned out people's souls. "We should be thinking first
> and foremost about how best not to destroy our assets," he said.
> "Beginning with not destroying one another." He went on to

say that it was his belief that what a ball club does on any given day is finally a matter of heart. "I know that sounds like horseshit," he said. "But we all have it in us to rise to heights we cannot imagine. The question is, What makes us rise, and what makes us sink?"

In his "Keep Umps Human" campaign, for example, he had apparently argued that it demoralized players to be judged by robots they believed to be just as biased as human umps, only invisibly and immovably so. In contrast, sometimes right, sometimes wrong as human umps were, they brought out the wiliness and fight in the players. And he believed other conditions helped us, too—helped us or hurt us. Certain words, he said. Certain tunes. Certain chords.

Translated, that meant that Beetle and Fudge had to stop trying to kill each other, I think. But Coach said it in such a way that everybody got that at the same time as they got more than that.

"He's smart," I said.
"Yes," said Eleanor.

I really think he's the smartest man I ever met.

"She means except her father," said Eleanor.

We worried so much about Coach Link we were almost relieved when, not long after that, Gwen found out more about Renata. In the longest PigeonGram she'd ever sent, she wrote,

I have something terrible to say. I don't know if I can even tell you but I don't know who to tell.

"Sounds like we better sit down," said Eleanor.

Renata found her way to my dorm room. I couldn't believe Pink and Sylvie let her in, but Renata said she was a friend. "And she looked like a MeteorWar addict or something," Sylvie said. "Like a type my mother sees all the time. Like someone seriously StarGored." And so in I walked one night after dinner and there she was sitting on my bed. I screamed and campus police heard the commotion and came, but I told them everything was okay and that they should leave. Of course, they ScanID'ed her first. But she didn't have any kind of record so they said okay, she could stay, so long as Pink and Sylvie kept an eye on her until she left. And they agreed.

Renata, meanwhile, was freaked out but insisted she hadn't come to harm me, just to warn me.

"I'll go away after this," she said. "You won't hear from me again. But I have something to tell you. Do you want to hear it?"

"No," I said.

She looked sad and stood up.

"Okay," she said. "In that case, good luck. And beautiful blankets, by the way."

Then she tucked her hair behind her ears and I saw that she had baseballs tattooed onto her earlobes, like earrings. And then, I don't know why, I changed my mind.

"You sure now?"

"No," I said. "But what the hell."

I made her some tea with RealCream and sat down to listen to what she had to say, starting with the fact that she was the star girl pitcher before me. She wasn't me, she said. She'd seen me throw—she didn't want me to think she could do that. But her ERA was 3.51 and she had a mean sinker. Also, she wasn't above throwing a knuckleball, disreputable as that seemed to be at Net U.

"In fact there are dozens of pitches pitchers don't throw,"

*she said. "Baseball can be kind of conservative. While my view
is, Whatever it takes to get the job done."*

*But to cut to the chase, she had been doing great—and
yes, seeing Coach Link. Woody, as she called him. Which was
probably not the best idea but so normal in her view that when
I told her I wasn't seeing him, I could tell she didn't believe me.*

*"I guess it's living in SurplusVille. You were sort of shel-
tered, in a weird way, weren't you?"*

"I guess," I said.

"Or maybe he's learned his lesson."

*Then she told me the creepiest story you ever heard. Start-
ing with how she was plucked out of nowhere, and asked to try
out, and given access to a special stadium and then a tour of
Net U. And then she was given a lot of attention by the coach,
who told her that her secret was maybe her ankle.*

"Your dorsiflexion," I said.

*"Yes. My dorsiflexion." She had kind of this hoarse laugh,
as if she had a piece of something caught in her throat.*

*She went on to say she started pitching far better than she
ever dreamt she could, in part because Coach knew how to
reach her. The words to say. The chords to play.*

"The chords," I said. "Interesting."

*But she made a mistake. She was never one of the guys,
which was no surprise, given that she was the only woman
on the team. And that was fine when she occasionally pitched
relief. When she started to pose a real threat, that was something else. Because some of the guys were pretty cutthroat.*

"We have guys like that," I said. "But it's the catchers."

*"Well, it used to be the pitchers," she said, which meant
in her case that they started exposing themselves to her. Like
she'd be walking down the hall outside the locker rooms, and
they'd pull out their equipment. One would even trap her
against the wall and ask whether Woody was having fun with*

her. And if Woody was having fun with her, why couldn't he have some fun, too. "That was our star pitcher, Demolition Johnson," she said. "I can still hear the crowd chanting De-mo! De-mo! De-mo!"

I was so shocked, I could hardly react.

"I'm sorry that happened to you. I really am," I managed to say. I was trying not to sound wooden, but I must have because she looked at me and shook her head.

"You're awfully young," she said, and she sounded tough. But then she started to cry and said, "I was young, too."

And then I don't know why but I started crying a little with her.

"I'll keep it short," she said finally. "As short as I can."

"Okay," I said.

So Woody, it seems, trying to get the guys to behave but not wanting to single out Demo, told the team they had to stop everything that was making her uncomfortable. Including obscene behavior and other things, too. Things that he said created the wrong atmosphere.

"Like?"

"Like cock bumping," she said. "Like after every home run, they'd bang their protective cups against each other's. And everyone would bump everyone else except, of course, me. I never complained about it, but Woody told them they had to stop anyway. And there was a lot of grumbling about that, but things did start to get better for a while. Like we were all acting chummy, and going out drinking together, and sometimes getting drunk."

"Did you play beer pong?"

"Yes. And everything was buddy-buddy until Woody started me in a big game. Which he told everyone wasn't even his decision. Which he said he was doing on the recommendation of an AutoCoach—the assistant coach he was using *because he didn't have the budget for a human. And the next time we all played beer pong, the pong was pong but the beer wasn't beer. Or it was but it had something in it."*

I didn't want to hear the rest but she told me anyway.

"Then Demo raped me," she said.

Do you remember that time Ondi told us about being Cast Off and about her Grandpa Barney, and everything? I felt like that. Like I just couldn't take in what I was hearing.

"You don't have to believe me," she said. "But maybe you see now why I wanted to tell you. You have a different relationship with the team. And Demo's graduated. Plus, even the guys who used to show me their flagpole are on good behavior. Everyone was pretty shook up."

"I'm so sorry," I said. "I'm so sorry. I can't believe that happened." That didn't seem like enough, but I couldn't get any more words out.

"It was . . . I can't tell you what it was." She started to cry again.

"I'm so sorry," I said again. And, "Thank you for coming. Thank you for telling me. I'm sure you don't really want to talk about it."

"No," she said. "I don't."

But she wasn't done.

"You're probably wondering what Woody did then," she went on. "Because everyone was expecting he would do something."

I couldn't ask.

"He did nothing. He knew it really happened because most of the guys wouldn't talk but one guy did. This guy Lester said he saw how Demo pinned me down and how I had passed out and how no one did anything because Demo was Demo and told them I was his secret whore anyway. Which is what Demo told Woody, too. He told him that I'd been two-

timing him all along, which Woody knew was a lie. He knew
who to believe, and even told me he did. But he consulted an
AutoCounselor anyway, and the AutoCounselor said this was
classic 'he said, she said.' "

"Why did he do that?" I managed to ask. "If he knew?"

"It was what the university called 'best practice.' "

"But he didn't have to?"

"It would have looked bad if he hadn't. As if he didn't
want an objective perspective. But you know how objective
these things are. Like what questions do they ask, right? And
who entered the data?"

"He did?"

She shrugged. "Of course. And, you know. Garbage in,
garbage out."

I swallowed. "And then?"

"And then he did nothing. He let me drop out and when
people said I was a drunk and a whore he didn't correct them."

"Because of the program?"

She gave a horrible laugh. "To protect college baseball,
which, you know, he single-handedly resurrected."

"Almost single-handedly."

"Yes." She laughed again, and her laugh this time was
even worse. " 'Almost' single-handedly."

"But what about you? Didn't he care what happened to
you?"

She shook her head as if she couldn't even laugh. "I mean,
I think he cared some."

"But not as much as he cared about the program."

She broke down again. "The donors loved Demo. They
loved him. And I wanted to file a complaint but I waited too
long to get my urine tested. I mean, when I woke up in a
strange place with my clothes all torn, I just got myself home
and slept and slept. I didn't know you had to get tested for

drugs right away. And my sperm test was too late, too. They could find a Y chromosome but they couldn't prove it was Demo's."

And that was why she had to warn me, she said. Why she couldn't believe it when she heard about me, and why she had to come to my games. To see.

"I'm not dating Coach, you know," I said.

She nodded but still said, "Maybe he'll be better to you. If anything happens, which hopefully it never will. Because if there's one thing Woody wants, it's for there to be no replay, ever. That's why there isn't just one woman anymore. And that's why they accepted Ondi, even though they'd never accepted a Surplus before, much less two. Because you were such a potential threat to the guys. Or that's what the old guard says, anyway. They took her to make sure you had a buddy."

"Wow," I said. "Is that true?"

She nodded again. "Aren't you glad that you know?"

I wasn't sure if she meant about Ondi or about Woody, but still I said, "Yes. And even if nothing goes wrong, I'll remember it was because of you. That you were the guinea pig."

Or at least I think that's what I said.

I wouldn't say that by the time she left, we were friends. But my heart definitely went out to her.

"I hope you believe me," she said as she stood up.

"Why wouldn't I believe you?"

She shook her head. "You really have been sheltered," she said and left.

And sure enough, later, when Gwen told Sylvie and Pink, they were prepared to be sympathetic but said they needed more information. Because could all that really be true? Could this woman just be playing with Gwen's head? What with Gwen's bugged backpack out in the living room, I had heard this part of the incident myself, although before I saw the PigeonGram I hadn't been sure what to make of it.

"*She was pretty convincing,*" said Gwen.

"*I mean, it might be true,*" said Sylvie.

"*I am never, ever going to let anyone in again,*" declared Pink. "*I don't care if it's your mother. I'm going to make the person wait outside.*"

Gwen laughed, but Sylvie wasn't done.

"*I'd give him the benefit of the doubt, but whatever you do, don't fall for him,*" she said.

"*Just in case?*" Gwen said.

"*Just in case.*"

Thank you, Sylvie! Thank you! Now Eleanor and I Pigeon-Grammed,

> *This is so terrible. Are you okay? Do you want to see if you can come home for a bit? It was kind of this poor Renata to come find you. Kind and brave. But—the shock. Are you okay? We can contact the school and try to arrange a home visit. Or we can come out and see you.*

Naturally, though, she insisted she was all right. And her next GreetingGram was surreally normal. Wasn't she going to say something to Coach Link? How could she simply go on? Was this Gwen writing, or was this that ointment? I remembered teaching the phrase "under the influence of" to my students long ago and wished now that a sample sentence did not pop so easily to mind. *Was Gwen under the influence of that ointment?* She Greeting-Grammed,

> *So what with Fudge and Beetle having finally been benched for fighting, Coach asked Ondi to start in the Cyber U game,*

can you believe it? Which went okay in the beginning. In the top of the first inning Bento allowed two singles. But thanks to a triple play, they didn't score. As for the Cyber U pitcher, long ago he would have been running a train station. When they finally allow PitchBots to take the mound, they will throw exactly like him, and select the same pitches.

Anyway, the score was 1–1 when at the top of the fifth, Bento suddenly gave up a base hit. Then another. Then he walked a third batter, loading the bases. Then Cyber hit a grand slam. So suddenly it was 5–1, Cyber. Probably I shouldn't have been brought in at the top of the sixth, seeing as how I'd just pitched against Net West. Probably I should've been allowed to rest, and no doubt Coach thought that when I promptly gave up a hit.

But we had a couple of guys out with the flu, so it was me or nothing. And after that one hit I did settle down. Sometimes I opened with a fastball. Sometimes I pitched upside down, leading with my newly sharpened slider or—now that I was throwing it deliberately—a slurve that just nicked the corner of the strike zone. Coach's predictions notwithstanding, I wasn't exactly Satchel Paige with his Infinite Variations on a Thrown Ball. But I kept them guessing, and Ondi encouraged me, as did the crowd and as did Renata, who was there in an orange hat. I ignored her, just as I ignored the fans, when I was playing. But every time I came off the field, I felt their energy. More and more people knew my name now and shouted, Gwen-nie! Gwen-nie! Or, Can-non, Can-non!, though some still seemed to be shouting Earl Grey! Earl Grey! something that still puzzled me until I heard Black Tea! Black Tea! Because wasn't "Earl Grey" a black tea? I realized that even as I let the words wash over me. Until there it was: all I'd given up was that one hit on my first pitch, while their reliever had given up everything but the kitchen sink. 6–5, Net U!

In a PigeonGram, she reported what came next:

"You did it again! Just like at Army. You turned it around," Coach said. *"You broke their momentum. Stopped their advance." And, of course, I could see this.*

"But mostly, I just pitched as best I could," I told him.

"Was Ondi a help?"

"Absolutely," I said. "I think it's mostly that I know she can catch anything. Also, she knows what I'm thinking and encourages me to think that. If that makes any sense."

He looked thoughtful. "She wants to Cross Over permanently."

"I know."

And then he asked what I guess I knew he would eventually, namely, What about me? Did I want to stay, too?

"I hope Ondi's staying isn't dependent on what I do," I said.

"You know, it's noble how you think at home," he said. "How you live. It's courageous and righteous. But you are just not going to win." He was honestly sorry to say that, I could see. But like my sweater-bombing friends, that's what he believed. "You belong here at Net U and you know it," he said. "And I'm here to tell you that if you want your parents to come, too, they can."

Did he know that for a fact?

"Yes. In fact, Net U would love to see you all Cross Over and stay."

"Interesting," I said. And then because no, I didn't want to Cross Over—and yet—I said the thing that would end

this discussion, the thing that I had managed not to ask for days.

"And what about Renata?" I said. "Did she belong here at Net U, too? Since we're talking turkey."

"What do you mean?"

"What I mean is, I know," I told him. "I know what happened and I know you covered it up. I know you brought in an AutoCounselor when you knew it wouldn't come down on her side. And I know you let people believe she was a drunk and a whore when in fact she wasn't either of those things. When in fact, Demo Johnson raped her."

All of which I guess I was hoping he would deny. But he didn't deny it or say she was crazy or even that there were two sides to the story. Instead, he buried his head in his hands.

I thought I was going to throw up.

In her next PigeonGram she wrote,

Well, by now you have probably guessed. I am wondering if we shouldn't all Cross Over. Not because it's so great here. It isn't. But I wonder if we can win against Aunt Nettie. I wonder if there's any point.

Don't you think this is a trap? we wrote back.

I don't. Though I bet Aunt Nettie does figure that if you Crossed Over, you'd stop making meters and filing suits.

And is that all we should know?

If you're asking, Do I have a boyfriend? No. And no, that's not why I'm thinking about it. I'm thinking about it because all we know is dissent. And there is more to life than dissent.

To which, I know what you will say. You will say, Of course, you are right—and yet. And if I say, What do you mean by "and yet," you will answer that that's just who you are, at this point. Resisters. Right or wrong?

We hesitated a long time but finally wrote,

Right.

So I guess the question is, Is that who I am, too?

We will love you no matter what.

How we wished then that she would PigeonGram back right away—that she would reassure us she would never stay. That she was of course a resister. But though we watched and watched for him, Hermes did not appear.

We did not hear from Gwen again until Traymore broke up with Ondi. Then Gwen GreetingGrammed,

He said she was like a boxer who couldn't stop jabbing even after the match was over. A reflexi-rebel, he called her. Why was she so angry? And here she PermaDermed her skin for him! Although maybe that was why she did it—to show she was as adaptable and agreeable as a Surplus hoping to Cross Over into the Netted world would have to be. Which, of course, she really isn't. Anyway, she's stopped eating and drinking and has lost five pounds.

More happily, not two weeks later, Ondi had a new boyfriend, as we heard via PigeonGram.

Winny Wannabe! Of all people. When I had lunch with him, I thought his staying to be a done deal, seeing as how he'd passed the Final Test, but Ondi says he can't stop thinking about things like what our parents wanted, and whether that was realistic, and what we ourselves want. Winny, having questions? I was amazed, but Ondi says he's not sure he will ever belong to the Netted world—that the differences are so much greater than he ever thought. If nothing else, he's realized that he will always be seeing things they don't—indeed, that the very definition of the Netted is people who see nothing. Surprise! you will say. And does he now want them to see more or does he just wish he could see less?

Whatever his doubts, Winny wanted to preserve his options and Ondi's, too. Another PigeonGram explained,

Winny wants me to help Ondi, who, he claims, contributed critically to my success in the Net West game. Indeed, he says, she could almost be said to have been the Secret Weapon's secret weapon. Did he mean that Ondi set Bento up for failure in his disastrous last inning? Not exactly, but she was not, Winny hinted, as helpful as she might have been. And was this with the idea that I might then be brought in? Well, wasn't it only Ondi's job, he said, to know how any given A could lead to outcome B? As for my eventual success—if I could not be said to rely on Ondi, exactly, surely it was at least true that I was most in my skin pitching to her? In which case, what was the harm in making sure that Coach realized just how pivotal she was? And should I point it out, Winny said, well, it went without saying that I could count on Ondi's help in the future. Which I could perhaps use, especially if I eventually Crossed Over permanently. Because as he could attest, an ex-Surplus will always have a lot to prove.

If you are proposing a tit for tat, I told him, get lost. First of all, I am not staying here. Second, I talked to Ondi and told her not only that she should support every pitcher equally, but that if I sensed anything else, I would ask that Beetle or Fudge catch me. Or Clara Zee.

Naturally, neither she nor Winny is speaking to me now. They're lucky, though, that I don't share their proposal with Coach, don't you think?

To this I answered,

Yes, you did the right thing. And yes—they are lucky.

As for whether Eleanor and I felt lucky, too, that thanks to Winny Wannabe, a fissure seemed to be reopening between Gwen and Ondi—yes and no. Ondi was on the one hand just so unreliable. On the other, if Gwen was going to stay, wasn't she going to need someone who at least understood where she came from? Indeed, who at least understood that she came from somewhere—that she didn't, as my mother used to say, *just fall off a cliff into herself?* In such a fraught world, it would be better—far better—if Ondi were a true ally and a true friend. But Ondi was the friend she had.

◆

Thanks to the Olympics and Redoubling, GenetImprovement was now not only being permitted but, for athletes, encouraged.

The Net U baseball team received a friendly GovernorGram on the subject:

> *No doubt it has weighed on you to know that, were you to be selected for Team AutoAmerica, you would then have to compete with HomoUpgraded teams. But—good news! The field has been leveled. You can be GenetImproved in any way you like, and as for whether your offspring will be affected, should that trouble you, fear not. Thanks to GonadWrap, they will not. In the meanwhile, you will be availing yourselves of the best of our technology, at no cost. Congratulations!*

Gwen, however, declined to avail herself of anything. Not that she was so perfect. As she wrote in a PigeonGram,

> *That's why I train. To improve. But I am happy to get up at five a.m. as I do, and run and stretch and lift and do drill upon drill upon drill. I don't need any procedures, thank you. As Coach does and does not understand.*
>
> *"It's a suggestion, not a mandate," he said. "Against which I can see all sorts of arguments. But possible arguments are not what matter. What matters is your argument. Which is?"*
>
> *"First of all, I am not going to try out for Team AutoAmerica," I told him. "So if the point of getting Upgraded is to be competitive against ChinRussia, for me there is no point." As for why I was anti-Olympics, I said it was because it was just our Aunt Nettie versus their Aunt Nettie. Our HomoUpgrade versus their HomoUpgrade.*
>
> *"It's not an Olympics. It's a tech showdown. Is that it?" he said.*
>
> *"The word I would use is 'charade,'" I said.*
>
> *Coach nodded then and said that I could still play for*

Net U. But he also pointed out that HomoUpgrade stood to make a lot of people more competitive. And that could be a problem for me, he said. Because a lot of people had already agreed to be GenetImproved, including Beetle. Rube. Ichiro. Bento. Pietro Martinez. Joe March. Warren Peese.

"And, let me guess, Ondi," I said.

"She has no choice, Gwen. She's doing great. But if Fudge and Beetle and Clara Zee all Upgrade, Ondi could be cut."

Of course, even if she Upgraded, any one of them could improve more, I pointed out.

"True," he said. "But otherwise she's almost sure to have to leave. And if others improve significantly, you might have to leave, too."

"The difference is I don't care."

"Is that true? You really don't care at all?"

"Yes," I said.

And then I said it again. I said I didn't care at all, to which he didn't answer.

When it came to ball playing, GenetImprovement was still a mixed bag. Even things like height were complicated affairs, involving a raft of genes and switches, and coordination was yet more complicated. The official claim was that though some might benefit more than others, no one would lose ability, but that turned out to be false. Post-Improvement, yes, there were people who could jump and run and field as never before. But there was also an outfielder who complained that his joints felt overgreased, and a first baseman who now gripped the ball more like a therapy ball than a baseball. No one, she said, would ever praise her for her quick hands again.

Ondi was one of the luckiest. A month later, she was far stronger than she had been. Her throws to second base—a challenge for her since she was a girl—were no longer a problem. Now she rifled the ball out there with ease, and with her confidence came accuracy: her erratic throws were a thing of the past. And now, too, she was batting balls way deep into the outfield, even out of the park—something she had never done before.

Clara Zee was likewise stronger than she had been but also slower. So she was out. As for Fudge Fisk and Beetle Samsa, both, too, showed a mix of gains and losses. Fudge traded his old knee pain for a new foot pain; Beetle gained flexibility but lost stamina. As for what this meant for their rivalry, who knew? And was Ondi now poised to become the second-string catcher, knocking one of them out?

The situation among the pitchers was similarly uneven.

Pietro Martinez opted to attempt to regrow his UCL in lieu of surgery—which looks like it's going to work! So that's great. Bento asked for focus—hoping to give me a run for my money in the off-speed department, I guess. But it seems that whatever the genes for off-speed control, they are too widely dispersed to be changed all in a go. Yes, his focus was improved. And not having to block out the crowd, the weather, his girlfriend, whatever, he reported less mental fatigue. But the pitches did not come. In fact, Bento's slider—a pitch he'd relied on for years—up and left him. Where did it go? It was like a goat path that got buried in an avalanche.

It did not look as if Gwen was going to be dropped from the team. And the clearer that was, the more relief Coach expressed that Gwen had refused to be Upgraded. Indeed, when what had been a suggestion and an option got turned, a little later, into a mandate, *Coach sweetly did not even tell me, wanting to keep the pressure off,* Gwen wrote. What's more, he kept it quiet that Gwen, and Gwen alone, had not been GenetImproved. She PigeonGrammed,

*He brilliantly did the before-and-after assessments privately.
So publicly he just said that while some players had shown
changes, some had shown none. For that was the nature of
the beast, he said—sounding sympathetic, and expressing the
hope that those who had shown no improvement could accept
it. But privately he said that I was getting better and better
through practice and that Aunt Nettie should not be looking
at how to improve me but how other people might be made to
look more like me. Like she ought to be looking at my back, he
said. Because I really did have a special back.*

" 'I'm just such a fan of your vertebrae,' " I said.

As for our hunch that something was finally going on, that
was confirmed in the next PigeonGram.

*So you may not like this. But Ondi is not the only person with
a boyfriend. I have one, too. He is a little older than me, and
yes. It is Coach Link. Woody.*

Eleanor glared at the paper.

*See, I knew you wouldn't like that. And I know you will tell
me it's a bad idea to date your coach. Or not a bad idea—you
will say it is ill-advised.*

"It is indeed ill-advised," I said.

*But you haven't met Woody. I know—there are reasons to be
wary of him. I know! Really wary. I think I know the worst
already, though. And he's different now. I really believe that.*

"I know I speak as one dinosaur to another here," said Eleanor, "but long ago professors were not allowed to date students,
much less freshmen, and neither were coaches."

"Maybe the rules have changed," I said.

"Or else it is being Permitted, capital P."

I had to force myself to breathe. "Who what when where how why," I said.

"The why is the easiest. Aunt Nettie wants Gwen to help them beat ChinRussia. But more than that, she doesn't want Gwen to return home educated. Equipped to be a troublemaker."

"Which her becoming involved with the right guy would help prevent."

"Touché."

"And who could be more perfect than someone who loves what she loves. Someone who is like her and who understands her decision but who would have her choose the way Aunt Nettie would have her choose."

"So that she might feel not that she is being co-opted but that she is choosing love." Eleanor massaged her brow.

I could feel winter on its way—the wind harassing the plants, everything whipped one way then the other. Soon the sleet would be here, too, coating and recoating the garden in leaden sheets.

"As for her parents, how helpful of them not only to organize a League and encourage her ball playing, but make her tour Net U," Eleanor went on. "Helping Aunt Nettie at every step."

I did not volunteer that, had it been up to me, I would have nixed the Net U option way back when. Instead, I said, "We couldn't have foreseen what's happening. No one could have," and encouraged Eleanor to come indoors with me. Even without zone-heat, it was warmer inside than outside, after all, and she already felt bad enough.

◆

Net U was now headed into the championship playoffs against Cyber U. It was a best-of-three series and an exciting prospect, though Gwen didn't think she would get a chance to play. The team would depend on its upperclassmen like Joe March and Warren Peese, she was sure. And she was mostly right.

In the seventh inning of the third game, though, Woody brought Gwen in and kept her there. As she GreetingGrammed,

> *It was the game of my life! I psyched out every batter right on the first pitch, just as Woody has been telling me to do. My fastball was in the eighties, and while I didn't use my new hesitation pitch, all my other off-speeds were there. The fans were cheering so loud my ears hurt, and one of their batters actually tipped his batting helmet to me after I struck him out. Woody said it was the most gracious thing he'd ever seen on a ballfield, but that it was as if the guy just wanted to say, A woman and a Surplus. I've got to hand it to you.*

She did not give up a single hit and, a week later, Greeting-Grammed again.

> *There is a big dinner at the end of the season—they have it in the president's house, with real silver and wineglasses—you've never seen anything like it. And guess who got Rookie of the Year? I'll give you a hint. You know her! I'm sending you a HoloPic of the medal.*

Of course, as her spirits rose, ours sank. Still, we hoped for things to work out for her, and no doubt all would have had it not been for Ondi and Winny Wannabe. But besides Woody, only one person knew that Gwen had not Upgraded—Ondi, who told Winny. We heard the news via PigeonGram:

"So the word has come down," Woody said. "Net U knows you didn't Upgrade. And they're not okay with it. I wish I could hide you but I can't."

Honestly, in some ways being Netted was worse than being Surplus.

"You're probably more used to being strong-armed," he said.

I agreed. But now the question was, Would I do it? Yes or no.

"I would prefer not to," I said.

He looked like his dog had been run over.

"Don't just answer," he told me. "Think about it, Gwen. You're going to get kicked out of Net U. It's going to be the end of a lot of things. Your career here. Your education. Do you realize?"

"I do."

"You have it in you to be a great ballplayer, Gwen. Don't you care?"

"No."

"You must not understand. I mean Great, as in capital-G great."

"I don't care."

"Well, Aunt Nettie cares."

"That's why I don't care."

He hesitated. "And what about us? Do you not care about us?"

That was harder. In fact, it would have been easier to jump from a bridge than to say what I knew I had to say. In fact, it would have been easier to push someone off a boat. He was the first and only guy I'd ever been able to talk to. He was the first and only guy I had ever wanted to talk to. He was the first and only guy I had ever had a beer with. He was the first and only guy I had ever kissed.

But I made myself a rock and said, "No."

He said we could find the most insignificant improvement possible. A correction to my pinky toe.

"My mother lost her pinky toe to a ToeBomb. It isn't actually so insignificant."

"Something else, then," he said. "Aunt Nettie just wants to see that you are willing to play ball, so to speak."

"If you're saying Aunt Nettie wants to see that there's a little bit of the Wannabe in me," I said, "there isn't."

"Gwen, please."

"If you care so much about me you can follow me to Surplus Ville," I told him.

To which he had no answer, as I knew he wouldn't.

Instead, he said, "I'm going to find that bastard Winny and shoot him with his own damn gun."

"Now there's a mature response," I said. "I know you don't want to move to SurplusVille, but honestly? You might feel right at home with the bottom of the barrel there. Right in there with the dregs."

That wasn't the end of it, of course. In the self-torturing manner of lovers everywhere, they made up, then fought again, then made up, then fought again. As my mother would have said, *they were sun and rain, then sun and rain, then sun and rain.* Gwen was surprisingly open about her feelings with Eleanor and me—as if she was just such a volcano of upset, she had to tell someone, even if it was her parents. She PigeonGrammed,

Some nights I thought he was right, and that I was being pigheaded and perverse. Some nights I thought that I had learned a lot about resistance growing up but nothing about compromise. Give and take. Flexibility. Or as Woody put it, the tacit accommodation upon which love depends. But other nights I thought he was wrong. In fact, other nights I realized that it was compromise itself that I did not borrow Winny's gun and shoot anyone. Because Ondi certainly deserved it— Ondi the Destroyer, as Woody called her. Ondi of whom all is forgiven because she has suffered so. Ondi who has dragged us all into her craziness and confusion. Ondi who had been like a sister to me.

"How could you have told Winny?" I said to her. "How could you?"

"I didn't realize he would report you," she said.

"I don't know that I believe that. I don't know that you didn't tell him knowing full well that he would, and that he would get credit for it. I don't know that this wasn't your chance to get back at me for refusing your offer to 'help' me, that I might help you in return."

"That's not true."

"No matter what, you shouldn't have told Winny," I continued. "No matter what. It was simply wrong."

Of course, that made her sulk.

"Why did you take me in your confidence, that's what I want to know," she said. "I didn't want to be in your confidence. I didn't want to keep your secrets. It's like you want us to still be what we were when we were eight. I'm sick and tired of being your sidekick."

"Go to hell, Ondi," I said then, and meant it.

So why, when Woody said he was going to drop Ondi from the team, did I say, "Don't be a child"? And when he finally said he was sorry that he had asked me for something I couldn't give, why did I say, "Renata warned me about you"? Really, I had wanted to say, I wish I could give it. Really, I had wanted to say, I thought you were the most wonderful person *in the world. Really, I had wanted to say, I gave you my heart and if I had the choice, I'd give it again and again, forever.*

But instead I said, "This place corrupts people and you are Exhibit A."

Then I packed up and—surprised at how easy it was to leave—called for an AutoLyft home.

PART IV

A Perfect Game

Diego at first base was the first to see her. It was the top of the seventh, 3–3, bases loaded, and he did reflexively catch the ball being thrown to him by the shortstop. But in his shock, he took his foot off the bag, and when the runner slid in under his outstretched arm, Diego did not even look down. Instead he broke into a run, his arms flung back as if the pennant had just been clinched.

"Gwen!" he shouted. "Gwen!"

Then the outfielders were all speeding toward home plate, and the other Lookouts were converging there, too, much to the confusion of the Beastie Burgers. It was, said one of them later, as if there was a fire at home plate and the Lookouts had just invented PutItOut. *Gwen! Gwen! Gwen!* People were hugging her as if to reassure themselves that this was not some sort of Gwen-Gram who had come; everyone had to touch her, see her, hear her to be able to believe, Yes. It was no HoloPic. Standing there in a gray hoodie and gray sweats, her blue hair blowing big and free in the wind—yes, it was Gwen. *You came back! You came back!* Many were crying; even Gunnar the bison, who now played second base for the Lookouts, was wiping his eyes on his sleeve. What with a new beard, he looked very different from his twin brother, Bill, and yet still somehow identical, especially when Bill—who had also abandoned the Jets for the Lookouts—began wiping his eyes on his sleeve in just the same manner. And Gwen was crying as hard as anyone, her face lighting on one friend after the next, as her joy whooshed like an unaccountably warm mist up to the sky.

"Wow, a real field!" she managed to say at last. And, "I missed you guys!" And, "Yes, I'm just the same!" And, finally, "Can I play?"

Then there she was, on the mound with a borrowed glove. Eleanor and I watched from the stands with the other parents as she rocked back, her arms and knee rising. Then she whipped the ball forward with such force that the whole field stopped in awe and no one could say with certainty what she'd thrown, as no one could see the stitches or the spin, only that it was, of course, a strike.

And now came a succession of batters, each trying to hit her sinkers and cutters and slurves—or at least to make contact—and each, in turn, failing.

"Holy shit!" they cried. "Holy, holy shit!" And, "What *was* that?"

The sun seemed to stop at three o'clock—the afternoon distending palpably, as if it were made of rubber. But finally, the game over, time returned; it was dusk. The wind died down. Could the Lookouts now make a real campfire on which to toast their marshmallows? Gwen was amazed. And what a warm cocoon the fire seemed to make around itself, she said later, a live cave in the cool air. The fire sparks rose, as against the blue-green sky first Mars appeared—Mars, which we had never visited but knew some Netted had—and then the moon, a more popular destination. But never mind; the friends sat in a circle, focused on a place both nearer and farther. All that mattered was what it was like at Net U and why Gwen had come back.

"It's hard to explain," she kept saying.

But because they were listening, she explained. Little by little, she got them to see something of the strange world she'd come to know—or so it seemed as they fixed their attention, and questioned, and nodded. Aunt Nettie learned via a million trials and a million errors, made in a flash, but humans, it seemed, still slowly gleaned things by leaning forward on their arms and putting their chins in their hands. They turned as a friend asked a good question and turned back as another friend gave a good answer. And how much more attentive this made them seem than the Leaguers Gwen had left just a few months ago. It was as if having a real student among them brought out the students they might have been in another society, just as—transfigured by the firelight and her efforts to convey something she knew—Gwen looked for all the world like her grandmother, and her great-grandmother, and her great-great-grandmother, and all the other teachers who had come before her in her long line.

There was much to catch up on, including how utterly the Surplus Fields ruling had transformed the League. No more furtive playing in marooned places. Now they played as much as they liked, right out in the open. Some of the Surplus fields did double duty as soccer fields, and many boasted brand-new backstops, built by the very same League parents who had once stalwartly hauled equipment and food out to the games by boat. Some fields even boasted night lights, something with which the Leaguers had no experience. The glare, they complained. The glare and the cold. The pitchers, especially, disliked playing at night. But to play the Netted League teams, they had to accommodate the Netted League supporters, and the Netted League supporters worked in the daytime. And so our players put up with it.

The reward was that there were, in astonishing short order,

new teams everywhere, and play of such a different level that we had had to split the League into intramural and competition teams. Also, now that we were just one league among many, we had needed a league name. And so we had become, despite Eleanor's objections, Aunt Nellie's All-Star Resistance League—the Resisters, for short.

We did miss our routines—the secret messages, the dawn swims, the pies. If, as my mother used to say, *a secret is a shame or a treasure*, these were treasures. It was liberating but disconcerting, too, to have no more drones to watch out for. Out of habit the technical team still brought equipment to the first few games, but since there were no Nosy Drones, much less SwarmDrones, to track, there were no glitches over which to scratch our heads. Could all now really be forgiven and forgotten? It was hard to imagine, but then again Aunt Nettie was a program. She did not harbor grudges, suspicions, hostility. Humans could feud over the theft of a recipe; Aunt Nettie had categories. When your status improved, everything improved—for which change, let me say, we could not be more grateful. But we were also disoriented, even a little let down. It was as if a play had been canceled at intermission. Never mind how we had abhorred the first half, we somehow still missed the second.

Happily, whatever Aunt Nettie had forgotten, the players had not. Indeed, with the help of the ShelterBoat tattooist, they had prepared a thank-you surprise for Eleanor, which they now bared for Gwen to see: on every Resister's forearm was a tattoo of Eleanor brandishing a foil, with a heart around it. Gwen touched these one by one, laughing with delight and admiring the way the tip of the foil pierced the right swell of the heart like the tip of an arrow. Eleanor's splayed free hand broke the left bottom curve like the arrow's feather. As for how Eleanor had reacted to this honor, the report was that she had at first frowned, and had even seemed about to scold Andrea, who had organized the tattooing. But in the end, she could not help but soften when she saw the ribbon motto at the base of the design: RIGHT MAKES MIGHT.

There were other changes, too. Could the Lookouts really all have official T-shirts? LOOKOUTS was emblazoned in script across the front, and each player's number and name was printed across the back. And were those honest-to-god Lookouts fans Gwen had seen in the bleachers? The bleachers were portable and low—not more than eight rows high. Still, for some games, she learned, they were packed—meaning hundreds of fans, all of them Surplus. Where did they come from? And were they drop-ins or diehards?

"Diehards," Diego said. "They even leave little offerings for us."

"Offerings?"

"Little plates full of food, or fresh baseballs, or socks. Sometimes a poem."

Gwen was touched. As for whether she would play in the play-offs, if the Lookouts made it that far?

"Of course!" she said.

Diego had to check, but he did think she could play since she was an original member of the team. And after the playoffs, he said, they were planning an all-star exhibition game, weather permitting. Would she play in that, too?

"Of course!"

"What if it's the best of the Resisters versus the Netted League stars?"

"You're not seriously asking which side I belong to, are you?"

Diego laughed. "Just making sure you've still got the right name branded on your heart," he said.

In the meanwhile, the Lookouts were focused on their competition. They were currently in fourth place in the League, but they thought that with luck and application they could maybe move up. That would mean beating the Jets, the RosyDrones, and the DreadNoughts.

"Let's do it," said Gwen.

Her public manner was crisp, full of confidence and ease. And for the most part, at home, too, she slipped back into her earlier life as if into a warm bath. We were still astonished every time we saw her, though. For she had returned Gwen 2.0, as Eleanor and I joked—a version of herself even stronger and more beautiful and more affectionate than the Gwen we had known. Her new knitting project, for example, was a baseball jacket for me, to thank me for teaching her to play baseball. It was red and cream and, as I slowly realized, bore on the back the number one.

Daughters.

She helped put the boardwalks across the garden for winter. She made dinner, setting the table with candles and conversing as if conversation was—imagine—as important an activity as baseball. She asked about Eleanor's work. She confined herself to just one comment about how much warmer we could be if we would simply turn on the zone-heat. And, of course, she fenced with Eleanor when it wasn't too gusty.

But now, she went easier on her mother and tougher on Aunt Nettie. It was as if her edge was still there but flipped over like a knife, to face outward. "How can there be no real schools here?" she demanded. "How can there be no university? How can that have become normal? Why do the Netted have dorms and ballparks and coaches? What did they do to deserve that? Are Diego and Brianna any less trainable than Pink and Sylvie? Why are so many Surplus living on houseboats? Why are we being spied on by the house, and why were there emanations from the Surplus Fields and why are there winnowing agents in the mall-truck food even now—when we really are *Workless, not Worthless!* as the

AutoAmericans Against Apartheid say? And is all this really even because of Automation, exactly? Or is it because the people who controlled things didn't care to give up control, and Automation helped them keep it?"

Her eyes burned with a fury so deep it seemed to darken her very pupils.

"I will never go back," she said flatly. "I miss nothing."

Still, Pink and Sylvie missed her. Outraged when they learned that Gwen had left rather than GenetImprove, they started Sweeting her fans, who petitioned Net U to do something. Did #Bring-GwenBack intend to target Woody? It wasn't clear. But soon Renata was Sweeting, too—both to put Gwen's situation into context and to bring attention to her own. As for the resulting outrage—for Renata, for Gwen, for #RenataGwen—it did not focus, as it did in Gwen's heart, on Net U and Winny and Ondi so much as on Demo Johnson and Woody. Of course, Demo was indeed very wrong, and Woody, too. As my mother used to say, *No paint job could cover that.* But had Woody, as social media assumed, really taken advantage of Gwen, when she knew about Renata before they got involved? When there were no rules at Net U about student-coach romances? And when he had not, as was assumed, presented an ultimatum, but had in fact protected her as best he could against the pressure to GenetImprove? Gwen thought she might write something in his defense, especially since Net U was going to open an investigation into Renata's case.

"Great, but make sure you're ready," I advised.

"This is likely to go on for months," Eleanor concurred, adding, "Whatever people are Sweeting, you will not be the focus of the investigation, anyway. The focus will be on the rape and its handling."

"And Woody."

"Of course."

"And his character."

"It doesn't look good that he had two women pitchers leave school abruptly. But while you can testify that you departed for wholly unrelated reasons and that he's not the villain he is being made out to be, it does appear that he protected the guilty at the expense of the innocent."

Gwen chewed her oatmeal.

"Will he lose his job?"

"He deserves to," said Eleanor.

"Though it all depends on how the university disciplinary code is written," I put in quickly. "Which in turn depends on who wrote it. And who knows how AutoJudges are programmed in the Netted world, if things get that far."

"Plus, he's young," said Eleanor.

"Twenty-seven," said Gwen.

"Young enough that the university may just reprimand him," I said. "Depending on their rules."

"Maybe I should write to him?" said Gwen, after a moment. "To express my sympathy, even if he's guilty?"

"Of course, if you'd like," said Eleanor.

But in the end, Gwen did not write. She had, after all, just enrolled in MoveTheEffOn, an online course for the broken-hearted, the first lesson of which was, Delete means delete. Romantic love is like an addiction, explained a bald speaker with a paisley-stamped scalp. Showing a scan of the brain, he circled in green a certain spot. "*This,*" he said, "is your problem. The ventral tegmental area. See how it's lit up? This is the VTA of a person in love." Then he introduced a woman who, he said, had succeeded in dimming her VTA. "Your goal," he said, "is a time-scan like hers." He showed a clip of the bright spot fading, in a matter of a month, to plain cerebral-matter gray.

"You have to delete everything that bears the guy's name in any form," Gwen reported, adding, "I could ask on the ClassChat whether it would be a good idea to send a note to Woody, but somehow I know what the answer is going to be."

Eleanor and I nodded supportively.

"I'm going to dim that dot if it kills me," she said.

In the meanwhile, sometimes she would say how at peace she was, and sometimes she would cry, and sometimes she would say how at peace she was even as she cried.

"How long is this supposed to take?" Eleanor asked me. "Do you know?"

I shook my head. "Healing is slow," I said.

"Poor Gwen," she said.

It took Diego ten days to convince the powers-that-be that adding Gwen to the roster was not adding a new member to the Lookouts but merely reinstating an original member.

"Regulations," he muttered. "We didn't used to have regulations."

Even after he succeeded, his contention was challenged by the Newton Zebrafish, who pointed out that Gwen's replacement remained on the team. When her replacement graciously stepped down, though, the challenge was dismissed. "Just in time for the playoffs!" crowed Diego—the Lookouts having indeed, happily, made the playoffs.

Gwen was not particularly nervous going into the first game. But as she was devoting more attention than usual to reading the batters and the catcher, two players managed to steal bases early on. One was tagged out. The other, however, advanced and scored, emboldening her teammates. In the fifth inning alone, the Burpies stole four bases, including one where Gwen picked off the runner at first only to have a runner at third steal home. She had never in her life, she said later, been so embarrassed.

She started throwing more fastballs, and the Lookouts did still win in extra innings. But so protracted was the battle that many thought Gwen ought to sit out the next game, which was just two days later. The pitch count, they said. Wasn't she exhausted? Plus, the forecast was for gusts of forty miles per hour, possibly with rain. And the playoffs were best of three. A reasonable strategy might well be to save her for the third game.

But she applied what was left of her THC ointment to her elbow and pitched all the same, and this time recovered her command so convincingly that the Burpies spent most of the game Sweeting pictures of her. The Lookouts won 4–0, clinching the championship—hurrah! As the winter storms blew in right afterward, though, there was no exhibition game.

◆

It was early spring when a man showed up at our door.

There's a strange man outside, said the house. *He's not from around here. And he is not ringing the doorbell but he does not seem to be a burglar. A burglar would be looking at your windows for ways of breaking in. This man is just standing there in the drizzle.*

Why, having thought of Coach Link with such hostility for so long, did Eleanor and I soften toward him now? We had been in full support of Gwen's efforts to rid her brain of its dot. But back when Gwen was at Net U, we had seen through the scrim of our fears a powerful man and an impressionable girl—a sheltered girl, as Renata had put it. A vulnerable girl. In contrast, I, for one, now saw an iron-willed young woman. A young woman who had confronted a powerful man and left him—a young woman who had proven herself fully capable of cutting him out of her life for good. A girl who could make her heart a rock.

And in place of the all-powerful man, I saw a man who had been through fires both public and private. A man who was quite possibly determined, as Renata had said, that nothing like what had happened would ever happen again, and a man, too, who had spoken to Gwen in more than a few ways. I saw a man to whom she had spoken in return—and a man of whom even my mother might have approved, had she known any like him. *For what is a man,* she used to say, *if not a human who does not come back?*

Woody did not look as I had expected. A slight man with kind eyes and a widow's peak, he had surprisingly long brown hair, blue eyes, and a chipped tooth. Was he really a coach? Certainly, he had an athlete's physicality—a way of not so much simply standing, as of planting his spread feet, for example. It was as if he never lost track of his foot mechanics; perhaps he noticed dorsiflexion in pitchers because it was so important to himself. But to see him now was to be reminded of the talk he gave to Gwen about how different pitchers were from one another. He was not what anyone would have thought the coach type. In fact, he was in his resting state distinctly gentle.

Gwen forbade me from letting him in.

"Wouldn't you like to just say hello?" I said.

"I would prefer not to."

"He is standing out in the rain with no jacket and no umbrella," said Eleanor. "No hat, even."

"It's not raining that hard."

"I think he is wearing a Lookouts T-shirt," I said.

"Good for him."

Eleanor and I looked at each other.

"We have to at least answer the door," I said, and before Gwen could say anything else, I opened it.

"Hi, my name is Woody Link. I'm looking for Gwen Cannon-Chastanet," said our visitor. "Is this the right address?"

"It is," I told him.

"Might I see her?"

I could hear Gwen retreating upstairs to her room.

"She is indisposed," I said.

"Indisposed."

"Yes."

"Meaning that she has somehow figured out that I have come and instructed you to turn me away."

"I am afraid so."

"Not much I can do about it, then," he said. "Is there." It was not, as Gwen said, raining that hard, but his hair was frizzled by the damp, and he had goose bumps.

"I am afraid not," I said.

"Please tell her I said hi." He looked me in the eye as if he expected that, as a fellow male, even of the distant galaxy that is another generation, I knew the suffering of our kind and would sympathize.

"I'll do that." I smiled what I hoped would seem a friendly smile. "Tact, sometimes, is all a father can offer," I continued, "although in this case, perhaps I can lend you an umbrella?"

He refused but with gratitude, I thought, in the shake of his head. Then he walked away, his jeans curtaining a bit from his belt loop, as if he had lost some weight.

If Eleanor and I hadn't failed to give Woody a proper welcome, I would perhaps have held the line with Mimi a few days later. Indeed, I saw her in the VisiDoor and was tempted to pretend we weren't home. But Eleanor lifted her chin, stood, and smoothed the front of her shirt as if to say, *We just don't treat visitors the way we treated Woody.* At this Gwen bristled, lifting her own chin in parallel protest. But when I stood, she did, too. And when Mimi entered with a new yellow cane and new matching reading glasses above her broad smile, even Gwen was shamed by Eleanor's pointed glance into mirroring Mimi's warmth.

"You have a new cane," said Eleanor.

"Like it?" said Mimi. "I thought it was time for a change."

"A change of cane is always a good thing," I said—to which everyone laughed, though none of us could have said what was funny. And then it was as if, what with everyone's lips parting and cheeks lifting, everyone's feelings followed suit.

In the garden, we discussed the hardening off of the seedlings. We discussed their transplanting. We discussed the dividing of the perennials. We discussed why peonies liked wood ashes and whether you needed to keep the ashes from touching the plants. We offered Mimi some hibiscus tea with wild mint as if this was an idea that had just that moment occurred to us.

Mimi's mission did not surface until her teacup was empty, and then it was so predictable she seemed embarrassed to bring it up. But finally, setting her cup in its saucer with a clink, she asked if Gwen would consider trying out for the Olympics.

"We are holding special tryouts for the Surplus," she said. "You might have seen the GovernorGram."

It was the sort of statement to which Gwen would once have turned her back without answering. Now she simply said, "No."

"No, you haven't seen it?" Mimi looked hopeful.

"No, I did not see the GovernorGram and, no, I am not interested," said Gwen.

Eleanor offered Mimi a cookie.

"You got me once with the tryout thing," Gwen went on. "You aren't going to get me again. And how well can I play when I simply do not care if Team AutoAmerica beats ChinRussia or not?"

"Don't say that!" Mimi looked as though she had just discovered winnowing agents in the tea.

"In fact, I hope they lose," said Gwen.

Normally Mimi set her cane down so hard she could have

been punching holes in the sidewalk. But now as she left she seemed too dispirited to lift its lemon tip clear of anything, much less swing it up so it could land with decision.

"We are so sorry," Eleanor began.

Mimi paused. "She is like you."

"I hope I have better manners."

"She is not going to get anywhere being like that."

"Just as I have never gotten anywhere being the way I am, you mean."

Mimi did not disagree.

And for several days afterward, the house echoed Mimi.

She is not going to get anywhere being like that.

She is not going to get anywhere being like that.

She is not going to get anywhere being like that.

"Oh, shut the hell up," I said.

If you have objections, you should call an Autonet customer care representative, the house said. *If you leave a message someone will get back to you shortly.*

"Shut up!" I repeated. "Shut up! Shut up!"

Ten days later, Gwen was fencing in the garden with Eleanor when the house expressed surprise.

That man's come back, it said. *He's on the walk.*

I did not ask Gwen whether she wanted to see Woody or not. I simply glanced out the VisiID and opened the door before Woody even had time to ring. He stood awkwardly in the doorway a moment but then reached out a hand, which I warmly shook. He wore a Chattanooga Lookouts baseball hat, and in his free hand held what appeared to be a baseball glove knit out of yarn.

"Coach Link," I said. "Good to see you again."

"Please call me Woody."

"Come in." Eleanor popped out of the garden, foil still in hand. "We've heard so much about you."

Woody looked taken aback by her weapon. "I'm not going to ask what you've heard."

"Very wise, as we would not tell you," said Eleanor. "Gwen is outside." But she was smiling as she sheathed her foil and indicated that he should follow her.

"Should I not emerge alive, do please let my parents know what happened," he said.

"I'll save your remains," I said.

He laughed and took his hat off, although, what with the sun, anyone else would have been putting one on. Nestling the knit glove inside its cavity, he headed outside. I glanced after him to make sure Gwen had disarmed.

Happily, Gwen not only had put her foil away but had busied herself with our worm house. This was a hanging vermiculture composter to which we added food scraps and from which we harvested worm castings. As we had recently lured the worms to the top with melon scraps, Gwen was now opening the bottom hatch, allowing a humus-y mixture to fall into a blue bucket.

"Gwen?"

She closed the hatch awkwardly.

"I came to see you," said Woody.

"I am not going to play for you under any circumstances," she said. Her eyes narrowed ominously.

"That's not my question," he said. "Or not my only question."

"I can't believe you'd even ask."

"It was the only way I could get out to see you, Gwen. Please. What was it you used to say? *Keep your animus for malice.* And look. I brought you something."

She stopped. "Did you make this yourself?"

"I did."

"Tell me the truth."

"I had a little help."

"From?"

"Sylvie."

"Sylvie? But . . ."

They turned and lowered their voices in such a way that Eleanor and I could not make out the rest of their conversation. What we could see was a tense but intimate exchange, over the course of which he seated the knit glove on her head like a hat; she must have told him how she used to wear her glove like that when she was a girl. She removed it immediately, though, left the garden, and headed upstairs to her room.

"Thank you for coming," I said as Woody emerged from the garden alone. "That's a wonderful hat that you made."

He looked at it sadly. "No one in his right mind would take this on as a first project," he said. "But I am not in my right mind . . ."

Eleanor and I looked at him sympathetically.

". . . worried sick as I am," he finished.

Worried sick?

"It's hard to win when she is in this sort of mood," I said. Adding, in something of an understatement, "She can be stubborn."

He nodded miserably, then said, "I'm not trying to win. I'm trying to help"—and looked back toward Eleanor as if she would understand.

What did that mean? In any case, we let him go.

We were still mulling over his words—help? help whom?—when, the next day, the doorbell rang yet again. Eleanor assumed it was her legal team come for a meeting, but the face in the VisiDoor was neither Yuri nor Heraldine nor Sue.

"Ondi!" she said.

We both knew that Ondi had been PermaDermed. Still it was a shock to behold her angelfair. And almost more shocking than her skin was her hair. Where was her proud red-and-gold pouf? She looked as if she had put herself through a HoloPic filter and pressed "Bleach All."

"Would you like to speak to Gwen?"

"I would, thank you," she said. "If she'll see me."

Her guess that Gwen might be reluctant to see her was correct. Ondi left the garden almost as soon as she entered, engaged in another distant exchange with us, and began to leave the house.

So soon? said the house. *But you've only just arrived.*

"Why don't you speak to Gwen," she said. "I'm not the problem here."

And there was the familiar Ondi door slam.

"Perhaps she doesn't know any other way of closing a door," observed Eleanor.

"She is an expressive young lady," I said.

And so, of course, was Gwen, who exploded into the kitchen like a firestorm.

"Why did you let her in? What's the matter with you? Don't you see?"

"See what?" Eleanor glanced up at the clockscreen—wondering, I knew, where her team was.

"It's Aunt Nettie!" yelled Gwen. "Aunt Nettie has set them all on me. Don't you see? Next, it's going to be Pink and Sylvie. You watch."

"They were set on you?" said Eleanor.

"What do they want?" I said.

But of course, Woody and Ondi wanted the same thing that Mimi wanted—for Gwen to try out for the Olympic team.

"They say they need a lefty relief pitcher," Gwen said.

"Isn't Bento Halifax a lefty?" I said.

"Exactly. But no. They say they need me. Because I'm a lefty who can pitch to righties. You'd think all-knowing Aunt Nettie would have gotten by now that I am never going to play for Team AutoAmerica," Gwen went on. "The very fact that she thinks turning every last person against me is going to help her case just goes to show how little an algorithm understands people. Because if the answer before was Never, now it is Never, ever, ever. As in I am never, ever, ever going to play for Aunt Nettie and neither am I going to change my mind and Cross Over and stay. And Woody and Ondi pretending that they are here to warn me of what my recalcitrance could mean is not going to help."

Eleanor looked at the clockscreen again—squinting, though the projection was perfectly clear. Her team was never late.

"As for how my actions could possibly affect Mom, that is an idle threat if ever I've heard one," said Gwen.

Was that Eleanor's DroneMinder hovering right outside the window? Or was it something else? The geese were honking.

"Thank god spring practice starts tomorrow," Gwen went on blithely. "Time to get to sleep."

She kissed us good night and went up to bed just as Eleanor's team arrived, to our relief, with apologies for their tardiness. Perhaps Eleanor would forgive them, seeing as the AutoLyfts just weren't running? they said. They didn't know why but none of them could get a ride. The whole system seemed to be down.

"But now, here we are," said Heraldine. Her cheeks still flushed from her hurried walk, she cocked her big head and winked. "Better late than never, right?"

"Absolutely, not to worry," said Eleanor, embracing each of them with relief. "It's good to see you."

Were we surprised to hear a stranger step into the house the next day?

You have a Super Enforcer come to see you, said the house.

Since by law the Super Enforcer was allowed to enter, the house immediately opened the door for him and his Companion-Drones. He was big and smooth; indeed, with a shaven head and transparent eyelashes, he did not look so much like a human as a LatexDeluxe special only halfway through the manufacturing process—as if his menacing blue eyes had been finished and, for a touch of whimsy, his improbable jug ears, but as if his wig and mascara had yet to be applied. His CompanionDrones, meanwhile, were interestingly individualized, with pastel blades strangely reminiscent of Easter eggs. It was easy to imagine them having diminutive pet names—Bugsy, Misty, Muffy, Pixie. As for the Super Enforcer, he did not seem about to introduce himself. Still Eleanor asked, "And you are?"

"Cyrus."

"Ah. We are so happy you rang before entering, Cyrus."

"SOP, ma'am. We are here to speak to you."

"And so you are, Cyrus," she said. "Speaking to me, that is. And to my daughter, Gwen"—she gestured toward Gwen—"and to my husband, Grant, as well." She gestured toward me.

"As there are others who would like to speak to you, you need to come with us," he said.

By "us" he seemed to mean himself and his drones.

"You are catching us at an inconvenient time. Can we make this a bit later?" said Eleanor.

"No."

"Are you arresting me?"

"We will not have to arrest you if you do not resist the law."

"And what law is it that states I should leave my home to speak to strangers?"

"It is a suggestion, ma'am."

"But to decline is to resist the law."

"Yes."

"That suggests that your suggestion is somehow the law. Or else that you are the law, embodied."

"These are such fine arguments, perhaps you would like to bring them to the attention of a judge. In the meanwhile, we ask your cooperation."

"You have neither my silence nor my cooperation," said Eleanor.

"And if this is because she's been black-coded, you should really at least say so," I put in.

"Should I really."

Cyrus did not have to call for backup; four other Enforcers magically appeared at the door. Of various shapes and sizes, they were all wearing orange uniforms and blank expressions, and we of course did not recognize most of them. But one we did.

"Mimi!" said Gwen.

Mimi would not meet Gwen's gaze. Neither would she meet mine or Eleanor's as she leaned on her new yellow cane.

The pleasantries began all over.

"We want to talk to you," said the Head Enforcer. He had enormous hands and pinprick nostrils and a perfectly round bulge of a stomach, as if he were wearing a small shield over his navel.

"How wonderful," said Eleanor. She made the man introduce himself—Jim. Then she made the other two men introduce themselves. Bashar and Abner.

"And you?"

"Mimi."

"Ah, yes, that's right," said Eleanor. "Would any of you like some hibiscus tea? We make it with wild mint."

Not even Mimi accepted the offer.

"And do please come have a sit in the garden," said Eleanor.

But no one cared for a sit in the garden. Mimi's face was so blank we almost did not recognize her, but just as another Enforcer was about to grab Eleanor's arm, her lemon cane tilted alarmingly and she fainted, and by the time her fellow Enforcers revived her, the drones were headed for the door.

Eleanor gave a smile. "Five o'clock. Their pilot clearly wants to go home. Or perhaps his boss does not want to pay overtime."

We all avoided looking at Mimi as she left, afraid that someone might be wearing a NanoCam. But in our hearts, we *set the choirboys to sing for her,* as my mother would say, *and got the priests to keep the beat.*

New Enforcers were bound to return.

"Would it help if I agreed to play in the Olympics?" asked Gwen.

I wasn't sure. Aunt Nettie's Plan A did seem to have been to try to get Gwen to Cross Over permanently, bringing Eleanor and me in tow, so any suggestion that this plan might yet work— for example, Gwen's agreeing to pitch for Team AutoAmerica— might indeed help. But the crux of the problem was no doubt the Mall Truck suit.

"And if you dropped that?" I knew Gwen was embarrassed to ask this, although in truth she wasn't the only one wondering. I wondered, too, if we might not at least discuss it.

Eleanor was neither going to discuss nor drop it.

Was there some way of going on the lam, then? Thanks to all the scouting the Underground League had done for places to play, it would have been a cinch to locate a marooned place in which to hide. And, of course, we had given Eleanor's DroneMinder the slip many a time. Her chip, though, was a problem. Remote consumption such as we had used for our Underground League games only kept Enforcement from thinking to look for you. It did not, as we very well knew, keep Enforcement from finding you.

"I might as well enjoy sleeping at home while I can," said Eleanor.

We did not sleep. Instead, we spent most of the night hanging out among the floor pillows with Gwen, looking through our old HoloPix. Probably Gwen and I should have been showing the pictures to Eleanor, saying, *Look—here we are with you, Mom. And wow—is that you in high school? Are those culottes? Who is that guy?* And, *Did they really cast you as Juliet? I can't believe that is you with flowers in your hair.* Instead, even now, Gwen was the audience, as if it was she who needed steadying and not Eleanor and I who were clinging to our identities as guardians. *This was Mom and me before we got married,* we went on. *And, yes, that was our camper van, and, yes, that's a lot of butterflies, but not a phenomenal number. And, yes, there were lots of different kinds of them, and lots of different kinds of birds, too. And here she is after she won the national fencing championship! Look at that grin. And here we are on our wedding day and, yes, we really did get married on a beach. You can see what they looked like; people would lie on the sand for fun. And, yes, Mom did get thrown into the ocean, wedding dress and all. And, yes, I got thrown in after her. And, yes, we were so happy, happier than we knew we could be. And this is Mom in the hospital getting her spleen repaired after they kicked and beat her in jail. You can see how thin she is, and, yes, those are the bruises she got after she was thrown down the stairs. No, she didn't lose her toe in jail—the ToeBomb came later. But here she is pregnant with you! Fat and rosy and happy, with her health completely back. And this is you the day you were born, and this is you in the hospital. And, yes, that is the baby hammock I made for you, complete with its own little bentwood stand. We think the hospital still has it. This is you sitting up—you actually toppled over right after we took this HoloPic. And this is you throwing your animals out of your crib. Do you remember your platypus? Your orca? Your turtle? Your dogs? That was your stuffed cat, Lani. Do you remember your bunny blanket sleeper? And look—here you are with your first ball and glove. And here you are on the mound we set up—do you remember? Not only could I catch you then but Mom could, too. And here you are pitching your first game, with Mom in the stands.*

Why is it that recollection brings us to life almost more than living itself? *We live to remember what we did,* my mother used to say. Now Gwen and I could not keep from crying but Eleanor remained dry-eyed—closing down certain parts of herself already, I could see, as if preparing for a difficult match.

"I will not let them spook me," she said, out of nowhere. And, "We've had scares before. For all we know they will never come back."

And as if to prove her right, in the morning, the Enforcers did not return.

"Who knows but that they will discover they simply do not have the budget for this low-priority mission," said Eleanor. "Isn't tomorrow the end of the quarter?"

It seemed like wishful thinking. But, in fact, though we waited all day, the Enforcers did not come. Could they indeed have changed their minds?

"All this worrying about black-coding," I mused.

"We've both become a bit paranoid." Eleanor smiled.

Then came the first day of the new quarter.

You have a squadron at the door, said the house.

◆

The Super Enforcer did not bring Mimi this time, but he did bring EnforceBots and a stunner. Maybe because I was the male, I was the first to be taken down, which just went to show how much they understood about our household. Or was it because I reached for the stunner and tried to grab it? Next, in any case, was Eleanor, who not only got hold of the thing but had to be tackled by three Enforcers in the fight to get it back. Of course, they didn't have it long before Gwen not only wrestled the stunner away but swung it like the baseball bat she had never quite mastered, but did, it seems, swing quite well enough.

Finally, though, it was as if we had been playing a Dum-DumGame with the sound off, Gwen said. Very quiet. And as if we had been held up by a power field, when the power went out, we dropped.

Gwen and I woke up on the floor of our living room. I came to first, a pain near my ear and a floor pillow on my face as if someone had been thinking to smother me. There were no lights on; I could only barely make out Gwen. She was lying facedown.

"Gwen!"

She stirred—thank god—pushing up on her hands and raising her head like a lizard.

"Are you all right?"

"Yes," she said. "I think."

Is everything okay? asked the house then. *You are lying on the floor. Is everything okay?*

"Lights," I said.

Right away, said the house.

"How about you?" asked Gwen. "Are you all right?"

"Yes," I said, though in fact my muscles were still numb.

"Where's Mom?"

We knew she was gone. Still, when we could stand, we checked around to be sure we weren't just having a nightmare—to make sure she hadn't simply woken before us, that she wasn't up and about, taking care of something we had yet to realize was awry. But no. She was not in her study. She was not in the kitchen. She was not in the bedroom. She was not in Gwen's room. She was not in the basement. She was not in the garden.

The minutes passed more and more slowly, as if there were something viscous through which they had to make their way.

"Do you know where Eleanor is?" I asked the house. I did not often initiate conversations and was not sure it would answer. But it did.

Eleanor is in custody.

"Ah," I said. "Will she be returning?"

That depends on many things.

"Starting, no doubt, with good behavior."

Yes. Goodness is rewarded.

"And does good behavior reflect goodness?"

You are pulling my leg. Of course it does. It's tautological.

"How your vocabulary has grown. It is really quite extraordinary."

Thank you.

"It is almost as if you are receiving special programming."

What is special programming?

"It's programming that can be disingenuous."

Ah, but I am not disingenuous. It is above my pay grade.

How about humor? Is that above your pay grade, too? I wanted to say. Because that was pretty funny. But instead I simply left off.

Eleanor? The Enforcers took Eleanor? The news shocked her team. Where did they take her? Was she all right? Were we in contact with her? Could anyone see her? Did she have a lawyer? How could this have happened? Why didn't we hide her? Yuri, Sue, and Heraldine glued themselves together, as they knew Eleanor would want them to, with outrage. Warrantless arrest! The Fourth Amendment! Where was the probable cause? Expectations of privacy had been whittled down to nothing, but still. Due process! Was she Mirandized? Did the house get them on video? Stunners were illegal!

Below the outrage, though, lay fear—the same fear that threatened to swamp Gwen and me. We could feel how it would close over our heads if we let it and so were glad to have people to inform, people with whom to confer. People who helped us avoid our real question, namely, What are they going to do to her this time?

◆

The jail was at the top of a marooned-place hill, set among as yet leafless trees. A gray Victorian house, it was strangely vertical, with peeling maroon and white trim, a mansard roof and tall windows with full-length shutters. We'd never seen a real house like it, but we recognized its type from books; it even had a round watchtower on its corner, with a roof like an upside-down funnel. The brass door knocker was shaped like a severed hand. The hand wore a ring and a bracelet, and clutched the knocker ball in its tapered fingers as if it had been operating an old-time computer mouse when it was chopped off.

Inside, the wallpaper was peeling, and the floorboards so shrunken you could fit a pencil in the cracks between them. Still, the original staircase curved dramatically, ready to showcase a descending starlet in an evening gown. The foyer was paneled, and there was a small parlor with a marble half-moon fireplace off to the right; the oil paintings were so dark, you could not help but wonder if there were special discounts, long ago, on black paint. And could this furniture be stuffed, as I guessed, with horsehair? But most strikingly of all, there were no locks or bars.

"That's because the restraints are internal," Eleanor explained calmly.

She was sitting in a yellow wallpapered room, at a dark dining-room table full of scratches. Above her hung the ornate frame and remaining pendants of what had once been a crystal chandelier; catching a bit of sun, it glittered. She was still wearing the outfit she had had on when she was arrested—a tessera-patterned sweater in all different blues, light gray pants, and a belt. But she was weirdly circumspect, as if rationing her energy expenditure.

"We are just so happy to see you." Gwen knelt at Eleanor's feet, holding her hands. Of course, Gwen's hands had always been large. But never had it seemed, as now, that hers were the hands of a mother, and Eleanor's the hands of a child.

Eleanor smiled a smile half her own and half, it seemed, not.

"What are those gashes on your head?" I asked gently. The gashes were not large and had been MediGlued together so that they looked for all the world like baby red wiggler worms. They sat so symmetrically over either temple, though, that they could almost be incisions. "Did the Enforcers do that to you?"

"Do they look terrible? I haven't seen them."

"No, no. But what happened? Is this from the arrest?"

"They're from the implant."

Implant?

She explained that she was contributing to an experiment in MindSharing. Gwen looked at me in horror.

"I've had a BioNet injected in my brain—you can think of it as a kind of mesh or lace although in fact it more closely resembles the amyloid plaques that were once associated with Alzheimer's, if you remember Alzheimer's," said Eleanor. "It takes a little while for the cells to propagate, but the doctors seem to think the coverage is pretty good already because this neural net or lace—you may call it what you like, anything but neural plaques, please— was working as of this morning. It is tracing my brain activity and uploading that into a computer that can decipher it and also download information—making for a two-way street."

"A step toward MindMeld." I tried to remain calm.

"Yes."

"Which the government has been working on for a while, of course," I said—talking to myself as much as to Eleanor and Gwen. I wished I didn't understand what Eleanor was talking about. But unfortunately, I did. The government had been putting tens of millions of dollars into neural engineering for decades through—what was that agency? DARPA? Whatever that acronym even stood for. Defense Advanced Research something something. It was like a program out of a science fiction novel, except that it wasn't.

"Well, it took decades, but they finally seem to have gotten some of it to work some of the time," said Eleanor. "Maybe because their project got the funding that used to go toward space stations."

"Now that it's clear we are never going to be able to move to another planet, you mean."

"Exactly."

Was there a word for a horror before which you can only quail? One of my students had asked me that, long ago. A survivor of some genocide, this was—in Cambodia or Rwanda, maybe. Some place.

"We will have to call you Aunt Nettie," I said finally.

She smiled. "You're making me laugh, Grant."

I wished I could laugh.

"Why you? No one needed augmenting less than you," said Gwen, tearing up.

"It's just more distinguished treatment," said Eleanor.

"If only you were less distinguished," I managed.

She smiled again.

"How did they bypass your immune response?"

"An excellent question. I don't know, though I gather that to have been one of the critical breakthroughs."

"And how can this be legal?"

"I'm sure it isn't, unless perhaps . . ."

"Unless you've been black-coded."

"That's my guess."

"And who decides what to upload and download?" asked Gwen.

"The key question, very good. I don't know," said Eleanor.

"And can you tell your own thoughts from the computer's?" I asked.

"Let me see," she said, and went on:

"The quality of mercy is not strain'd,
It droppeth as the gentle rain from heaven
Upon the place beneath: it is twice blest;
It blesseth him that gives and him that takes:
'Tis mightiest in the mightiest: it becomes
The thronèd monarch better than his crown;
His sceptre shows the force of temporal power,
The attribute to awe and majesty,
Wherein doth sit the dread and fear of kings;
But mercy is above this sceptred sway;
It is enthronèd in the hearts of kings,
It is an attribute to God himself;
And earthly power doth then show likest God's
When mercy seasons justice."

"The Merchant of Venice," said Gwen. "We read that in my lit class. That's Portia."

"Very good," said Eleanor.

"I didn't know you knew that," I said.

"I don't," said Eleanor.

Gwen and I took that in. The chandelier threw odd bits of light onto the table—shards.

"So Aunt Nettie has the words, but does she have any idea what they mean—like, what mercy is?" said Gwen.

"If she did, we'd be begging for it right now," I said.

Eleanor gave another half smile. "Let's see what else she knows but can't begin to understand. How about the Gettysburg Address:

"The world will little note, nor long remember what we say here, but it can never forget what they did here. It is for us the living, rather, to be dedicated here to the unfinished work which they who fought here have thus far so nobly advanced. It is rather for us to be here dedicated to the great task remaining before us—that from these honored dead we take increased devotion to that cause for which they gave the last full measure of devotion—that we here highly resolve that these dead shall not have died in vain—that this nation, under God, shall have a new birth of freedom, and that government of the people, by the people, for the people, shall not perish from the earth."

Gwen and I sat in shock.

"Can you pull up whose copy of the speech that's from?" asked Gwen, finally—pleasing Eleanor, I could see. And, horrifying as the situation was, I could not help but feel a reflexive swell of pride, too.

"No. But, more important: government by the people, for the people," said Eleanor.

"America before it became AutoAmerica," I said.

"A country Aunt Nettie, smart as she is, could never have

come up with," said Eleanor. "And, let's see, here's something else for you two:

"I am cognizant of the interrelatedness of all communities and states. I cannot sit idly by in Atlanta and not be concerned about what happens in Birmingham. Injustice anywhere is a threat to justice everywhere. We are caught in an inescapable network of mutuality, tied in a single garment of destiny."

"Martin Luther King Junior, 'Letter from a Birmingham Jail,'" said Gwen.

Eleanor smiled again—still wanly but, I thought, a bit more broadly this time. "And one more, for Grant's mom." She went on:

"They tell us, sir, that we are weak; unable to cope with so formidable an adversary. But when shall we be stronger? Will it be the next week, or the next year? Will it be when we are totally disarmed, and when a British guard shall be stationed in every house? Shall we gather strength by irresolution and inaction? Shall we acquire the means of effectual resistance by lying supinely on our backs and hugging the delusive phantom of hope, until our enemies shall have bound us hand and foot?"

It was indeed my mother's favorite quote. I took up where Eleanor left off:

"Is life so dear, or peace so sweet, as to be purchased at the price of chains and slavery? Forbid it, Almighty God! I know not what course others may take; but as for me, give me liberty or give me death!"

"Wow, Dad," Gwen said.

"My mom made me memorize it. And I used to have my students memorize it, too. Even if Patrick Henry very likely never said that, it made them feel that they got AutoAmerica—*the AutoAmerica spirit*, as one of them used to say."

"Why didn't you teach it to me?" asked Gwen.

I shrugged. "Too corny."

"Your mother might have liked you to have been augmented," said Eleanor.

"No. She believed that you memorized things to internalize them. She would not have thought downloading the same thing at all."

"Well, I will never need a research assistant again. There is that silver lining," said Eleanor.

"Either that or you will need a research assistant to check every word to see if it is what you think it is. What if they download 'The quality of mercy is most strain'd. It shooteth as cow shit from your neighbor into the face he disdains.'"

Eleanor laughed what seemed to be a real laugh.

"How can you tell which thoughts are your own and which are Aunt Nettie's?" Gwen asked.

"So far it reminds me of grading student papers when I was a teaching assistant in grad school," said Eleanor. "I feel like I may be able to discern changes in locution. But who knows."

"If only you could run yourself through an antiplagiarism program. BSDetect, say," I said.

"Exactly."

"Can you change the stuff you've absorbed? Kind of as if you are editing it?" asked Gwen.

"Hmm. Let me see. 'The quality of mercy is most strain'd, and 'tis clear as day, Aunt Nettie is to blame.'"

"So—yes?"

"So far it seems like a kind of brainwashing plus. It makes an impression, and if you're not thinking, out it pops. But you can edit it if you really think about it." She paused. "Think hard."

"And for now, at least, you can?" I said. "Think hard, I mean."

"Yes," she said. "Do you know what I mean?"

Do you know what I mean—something I had never heard her say once in all the years of our marriage.

"It is going to be exhausting to parse every thought," I said.

"It sounds like torture," agreed Gwen.

Eleanor gave another strange smile. "Oh, I don't know," she said.

Oh, I don't know. I felt sick.

◆

At home, Gwen and I stared at our peppers and beans.

"Why do you think Aunt Nettie wants us to know what's going on?" she asked finally. "Because clearly she does."

"I don't know," I said.

"And are those plaques permanent?"

"I don't know."

There was only one kind of redoubling now—redoubling our efforts to free Eleanor. Was she going to be allowed to post bail? Was there some way of ending her detention? Was there going to be a trial and, if so, when?

"Long ago we would have had some redress," Yuri said. "Long ago, we would have asked questions like, Who's the prosecutor? And, Who's going to represent her? But what with these Auto-Judges . . ."

". . . and with them set to black code." Heraldine squeezed her DisposaCup so hard it cracked.

"Don't be negative," said Sue briskly. "We got a human judge on Surplus Fields and could just get another one."

But not even sunny Sue could bring herself to say, *Of course, we'll see her again,* much less, *And she will be exactly as she was, the Eleanor we all knew.* She just poured some more coffee.

◆

We were able to visit again a few days later. There were other residents; we could hear them moving around. All we ever saw, however, were occasional EnforceBots.

"How do you eat?" Gwen asked. "Do they bring food?"

Eleanor nodded.

"The EnforceBots?"

Eleanor nodded.

"Is it mall-truck food?"

Eleanor allowed herself a small smile at the irony.

"And what are you doing to pass the time?"

"I am thinking nothing. It is a kind of art."

"Because?"

"Because if I don't think things, they can't be made part of my Habits of Mind file."

"There's a Habits of Mind file?"

"Yes. They're trying to capture my moti mentali." She smiled. "Let them look that up."

"And from that, let me guess," I broke in. "From that they can predict what you are going to say without your even saying it. If they have enough data."

Eleanor smiled. "Oh, I don't know."

"From which they can make a new you that says what they want you to say," I went on. "Except that you really are saying it."

"Oh, but you have a nefarious side, dear Grant. Do you know what I mean?"

Oh, but. Dear Grant. Do you know what I mean.

"It's like the ultimate co-option," I said.

"You don't think people will know a mouthpiece when they hear one?" she said.

That, thankfully, sounded more like her.

"Of course they will," said Gwen.

"Forgive me," said Eleanor then. "I know it's rude. But I am now going to stop thinking."

"Stop thinking? How?" I asked.

"I am meditating—emptying my brain." She breathed. In. Out. "I'm getting good at it."

"It must be driving them crazy."

She smiled a small real smile, her elfin ears lifting. "One can only imagine the computer screen. *Ommm. Ommm. Ommm.*"

"How diabolical." I laughed a half laugh. "And yet better than incendiary downloads from Patrick Henry, perhaps."

"Oh, I don't know." She smiled, then frowned. "You are making my job harder."

The light on the table dimmed—a passing cloud.

"Can we bring you some reading?" I asked.

She shook her head no. "But thank you."

"Knitting?" said Gwen.

"I can try that."

"You will need your reading glasses," I said.

"I have a pair, thankfully."

Had she had a pair in a pocket when she was arrested?

"You might consider whether it is imperative that they have absolutely nothing of you," I said. "This must be so difficult."

"I have made up my mind, Grant."

"Perhaps we should just sit in silence, then, so as not to exhaust you."

"Oh, I don't know," she said. Then the pitch of her voice dropped. "Yes. Thank you."

For the remainder of the visit we sat at the table, lightly holding hands and saying nothing until dusk. It was like the five minutes of silence I remembered from school assemblies as a child except that it ended too soon. The chandelier came on, its gaps shining brighter than its crystals. Then an EnforceBot arrived to take her away.

It was three days before we were granted another visitors' pass. How long was that to her? We could not imagine. Since we had brought food, we duly unpacked it, half expecting someone to stop us. No one did.

"Gwen made you an apple pie." I set a slice on a paper plate.

Eleanor's hands remained in her lap.

"You are losing weight," I said. "You have to eat more."

She nodded.

"Can you not eat for some reason?" asked Gwen.

Eleanor didn't answer.

Having managed to speed the League technical team forward on the mall-truck research, I had news I thought might rouse her.

"You know, we've been working on food chemistry," I told her. "And we've finally figured out some interesting things. So who knows—next time maybe we can bring you something irresistible to eat. Addictive, even."

Did she understand?

She gave a weak smile—just a movement of her lips, really.

"Will it affect how I feel?" she asked.

"Yes," I said. "It will affect your energy, your interest in life, everything."

Should I have said that? I worried I'd been indiscreet, and sure enough she looked at me hard, as if to say *Grant!* But all she said aloud was "Ah, how interesting. Because I haven't an interest in the world." Then she fell so deeply asleep we could not wake her.

Was it the very compounds we'd been discussing? Or was it something else?

Gwen and I sat with her for an hour, tried to wake her again, and finally roused her but only just barely. She was so drowsy, her mouth hung open and her eyeballs rolled back. Her arms stayed limp.

"Good night, Mom," Gwen said finally. She was crying. "We have to go. Good night."

"Good night," said Eleanor—in a whisper. And then, "Ondi. Winny."

Did we hear that right?

"Did you say, 'Ondi'? 'Winny'?" I said.

But her head fell forward as if a ribbon at the back of her neck had been cut. An EnforceBot ushered us out.

◆

Why had she said "Ondi, Winny"? If she had indeed said that? Was it somehow just what we heard?

"Because she said something we didn't understand, and that was what our minds came up with?" I said.

Gwen speared a piece of squash with a chopstick. "I don't know."

What else could she have meant to say? And if she did say 'Ondi' and 'Winny,' did she mean we should go to them? That they held a key of some kind? That they were a clue?

Gwen stared.

"I can't believe she's being drugged," she said finally.

"I can't, either."

"Drugged." She shook her head. "Drugged."

"As they tried to drug you at Net U?" It finally occurred to me to ask—something else to talk about, anyway. And I had always wondered.

"Woody said no but I was never sure," she said—surprising me. I hadn't really expected her to answer. "I didn't think he was lying but I thought he might not know."

"He seems like a good guy."

"He's probably using HowDoILook."

"The Disarm'Em option."

"I mean, do you really think it was his idea to wear a Lookouts T-shirt to come see me?"

I shrugged; naive as it might seem, yes, I had actually thought so. "Though maybe he is what he seems even if it wasn't? Is that possible?"

"Insofar as he is himself." She pushed her stir-fried winter radish back and forth on her plate. "Insofar as he is himself, he'll probably find himself another promising young pitcher with great dorsiflexion."

"Renata the third."

She nodded.

"How's her investigation going?"

"Not very well, I don't think. Woody's cooperating but Demo Johnson hired a human lawyer. While Renata has no money and is stuck with an AutoLawyer. Plus, on the one hand she has an eyewitness—this Lester guy—but on the other, she has no evidence. And the other guys on the team insist they saw nothing."

"That's terrible."

"Mom believes right makes might, but I don't know. And why is she talking about Ondi and Winny?"

"Your two favorite people."

Gwen grimaced.

If that was what Eleanor said.

Yuri, Heraldine, and Sue were filing a writ of habeas corpus, they said, and also bringing a section 1983 suit for the implanting of a BioNet under color of state law. But these things took time.

"Like how long?" I asked.

"A year? Eighteen months?"

"A year?" I said. *"Eighteen months?"*

"We could try for preliminary relief," said sunny Sue, but even she was frowning. "It's really hard to get, though."

"We'd have to show irreparable harm, and also substantial likelihood of success on the merits," agreed Yuri. She pulled at her short scarf.

"We're doing everything we can," said Heraldine. "But, you know . . ."

She didn't finish. Though there were only three of them working, there were a dozen coffee cups on the table, maybe more.

"Thank you," I said. And, "You should all get some rest."

◆

Once again Ondi sat in our garden, blond and angelfair. How ironic that, for all her self-transformation, she should still have the tendency to nervous tics she had had as a girl. Having had her hair straightened, for example, she wore it in a ponytail that seemed to fall constantly forward and require constant tossing back. Forward, back, forward, back. As for this Winny Wannabe she had brought with her—did he precipitate her nervousness? A plastic man, molded and stiff, he had a square mustache and the charm of a forced march.

"Pleased to meet you," he said. "Ondi says such lovely things about you."

Not just a lie, but a needless lie. Even Ondi winced.

"Can we show Winny your garden?" she asked. And she proceeded to show him the worm house, the vegetable towers, the grape arbor, the hay bales. There were only seedlings and buds to be seen as of yet, but still he acted impressed.

"How remarkable," he said. "How remarkable. How remarkable."

Gwen and I were frozen by the sight of his gun. A gun in the garden—Eleanor would never have countenanced it, and had she been here she no doubt would simply have told him to leave it outside. Perhaps she would have asked him why he carried this thing, as well—to defend himself against what? And, of course, I wanted to forbid it, too. But Gwen and I had accepted Ondi's surprise offer to drop by in the hope that she was going to tell us why Eleanor had said *Ondi, Winny*—if she indeed had. Forbidding anything was not an option.

And so here hung this brutal presence—a full-length Smart-Gun such as we had only seen on NetScreen. First Winny slung it over his shoulder the way one might sling a yoga mat. Then, sitting down, he slung it over his chairback.

I offered them some warm hibiscus tea.

"How remarkable," said Winny again, tasting it.

"They make it with wild mint." Ondi warmed her hands around her teacup.

"How remarkable."

Ondi smiled. "So I have a confession," she said, tossing her hair back. "We didn't just come to visit."

Gwen and I feigned surprise.

"We came," she said, "because we thought you could use help."

"How remarkable," I said then.

Gwen managed to keep a straight face.

"It must be terrible to see Eleanor this way," said Winny, unperturbed. "So painful and incomprehensible."

"It is." I tried to say this as if it was natural enough for him to know how Eleanor seemed, and as if I felt comfortable with that, when in fact I did not want the dirty fingerprints of his sympathy on Eleanor at all.

"We are here to help," said Ondi. Relinquishing her teacup, she leaned forward like a talk-show host, lacing and unlacing her silver-painted fingernails.

"How so?"

"We can get you more visits. My father can arrange it."

I stopped. "Your father?"

"His friends, really."

"What friends?"

"The same friends who put the BioNet in."

I could not speak.

"You know. The neural lace," said Ondi.

"His famous doctor friends," said Gwen, slowly.

"Yes. Some of whom ended up Surplus, like him. And who developed the technology by themselves, if you can believe it. Working on their own in, like, these little home workshops."

So I wasn't the only one with a little home workshop.

"Of course, some of them have Crossed Over now." Ondi tossed her hair. "Thanks to their work."

"With others hoping to Cross Over, too," guessed Gwen.

"Yes."

"Including your father?" I asked.

"He's already Crossed Over."

"Got himself out of that damned Flotsam Town," said Gwen.

"Yes. He was invited to Cross Over earlier, you know, but he didn't, like your mother."

"I remember. Because he flunked EgoShrink."

"That's what my mother always said, but actually it was because he refused to work on the new RegiChip—which wasn't going to be a chip, exactly, but another kind of traceable marker. Something more . . . I forget what they call it. Systematic?"

"Systemic, perhaps," I said.

"That's right. Systemic," she said, tossing her hair.

"Because he was a radiologist."

"Exactly."

We all had some tea. So had her father Crossed Over permanently now? And was Ondi next in line? And what was that going to entail? I didn't ask.

"Hence your family's distinguished treatment," I said instead. "I always wondered why your family got Cast Off for your trip to Vermont—it seemed so extreme. As if the AutoJudge were set, if not to black code, at least to gray. But now I get it. Your father's seen the error of his ways."

"As he hopes Eleanor will, too."

"I can imagine."

"Is your father working on the BioNet himself?" asked Gwen.

"Of course."

"Though it wasn't originally his field."

"He picked it up. And they have to do a lot of scanning—complicated stuff Aunt Nettie doesn't know how to do yet."

"And he is based at this"—I didn't want to say "prison"—"house?"

"The research center? Yes."

"How remarkable." How I wished then that we had some of Eleanor's cookies—anything with which to break up this nightmare. I tried to carry on in a normal tone of voice. "And let me ask you. Is this, um, research center government-run, exactly? Or is it a private center, funded by the government but, you know, protected from public scrutiny?"

"It's doctor-run," she replied evenly.

"By people like your father."

"Yes."

I could sense a little rise in her as she answered and thought I recognized in it her younger self—the feisty Ondi. She fiddled with her nails, one of which, interestingly, she had left unpainted.

"It's doctor-run on behalf of the government."

"Yes."

"How remarkable," I said yet again.

"It means I've been seeing Eleanor," said Ondi pointedly. "And that we can all go together, if you like."

"What do you mean, you've been seeing her?" said Gwen.

"I mean, I've been going to see her. Since you aren't allowed. And since she's so lonely."

"You and Winny?" I asked.

"Yes."

For once I was grateful for the honking geese—indeed, I almost wished they would honk more at whatever threat they perceived.

"Thank you," said Gwen, finally. "For looking in on her." She tossed her hair as if in imitation of Ondi.

"You're welcome." Ondi's manner softened. "I'm sure you've been worried." Then she repeated, "We can all go together to see her." She tossed her hair.

"Why are we being allowed?" asked Gwen.

"I think Aunt Nettie just wants you to really take it in. So you can make a rational decision."

"About?"

"I don't know. About your behavior, I guess. About being Problematic. And where it's going to get you."

"Lest I SpritzGram any Enforcers, for example."

Ondi smiled a pained smile. "Exactly."

Winny's SmartGun, slung over his chair, rocked heavily as he sat back. He crossed his legs, showing off his new RealLeather shoes. The bottoms shone a pale peach.

"You realize my mother will never drop the suit." Gwen's chin rose. "You realize she will persist as long as she's alive."

Ondi arched an eyebrow. She tossed her hair.

"And what about you? Are you going to take up where she left off? Are you going to be just as bullheaded?"

"I am not returning to the Netted world, if that's what you're asking," said Gwen. "Neither am I playing for the Netted League, and I will say whatever I please."

"Even if your mother's life is at stake?"

"Is that a threat?"

"I'm just asking hypothetically. What if she were about to be Cast Off?"

Gwen didn't answer.

"Because you're still young and because you're my friend," Ondi went on, "they just really want you to see."

"What they've done to her and what they could do to me, too? Is that it? And if she were Cast Off, who would take her out to sea, by the way? Would it be your father? Or would you do it yourself, what with your experience with this kind of thing?"

Ondi's smile faded. "I am trying to help you, Gwen."

"Thank you," I put in quickly.

There was one more ponytail toss as Ondi turned toward me. "My father always says how he remembers everything you and Eleanor did for me," she said.

"I'm sure," I said.

She smiled.

· · ·

"Phonier than phony." Gwen was fuming. Indeed, Ondi's unctu-ousness was so over-the-top that if there were a smidgen of the old Ondi left, Gwen could almost believe it self-parody. It was as if Ondi had stuffed herself into sausage casing, Gwen said. That's how distorted she was. And Winny with his SmartGun and his AryanDerm! Gwen skewered some cherry tomatoes, roasting them over the stove until they blackened and blistered.

Two days later, though, we were visiting Eleanor with Ondi and Winny—consternating and confusing her, I could see. Indeed, Eleanor's frown was so deep it did not seem so much like something actually hers as something applied to her face. She was wearing a yellow-and-white gown I'd never seen before—a shape-less, institutional affair—although over it, astonishingly, hung a mohair shawl Gwen and Eleanor had given to Ondi's family when they were Cast Off. How had it gotten here? Why had it not been dumped in our yard? Had it somehow been missed, or had some-one saved it? In any case, it was a marvel even now. Cinnamon and gold with streaks of teal and scarlet, and knit such that it fell with fantastic fluidity, it could have been a treasure glinting from the depths of a dragon's lair.

How strange to see it here, especially as, above it, Eleanor's hair had been neatly parted like a schoolgirl's and fastened to the side with a purple plastic barrette. She was knitting, too, what looked to be a blanket square, though it could also be a sampler—blue and white, with some sort of pattern. Where had she got-ten the needles and yarn? Her steely eyes were sleepy but alive and maybe, I thought, a bit wary as she looked up from a pair of reading glasses I didn't recognize. Since when did she have turquoise glasses? Happily, thanks to the MediGlue, her wounds were barely visible, though they had a strange luminescence, like glowworms.

"Eleanor, look. I've brought you some guests," said Ondi cheerfully. She sounded like a morning nurse.

Eleanor looked up from her work, blinking repeatedly in the sharp light. "Are these guests?"

"Good morning, Nellie." I tried to act as normally as possible. "Thanks to Ondi we've been able to sneak in this extra visit. Or should I say, thanks to Ondi and Winny."

Winny smiled brilliantly. In the bright light his front two teeth seemed fused together in a kind of dental unibrow.

"They have pull," put in Gwen. "Heaven knows what kind but it's great they have it, don't you think? How did you sleep?"

"Very well, thank you," answered Eleanor but then turned to Ondi with a perplexed look.

"Dearest Ondi," she said. "Who is this?"

"Gwen. It's Gwen." Ondi placed her manicured fingertips on Eleanor's shoulders—something I myself would have done with trepidation, even after decades of marriage. Eleanor's temper, after all, not to say her reflexes. Eleanor, though, simply returned to her knitting. "It's your daughter," said Ondi. "It's Gwen."

"Why doesn't she come?" said Eleanor. "You come. But Gwen doesn't come."

"It's because she can't come," said Ondi gently—and the gentleness, I have to say, looking back, seemed real. "Not every day. Not the way I can. She isn't allowed." She said this matter-of-factly. "The AquaDrones. You know."

AquaDrones?

"It's not easy to get through," said Eleanor.

"No, it isn't."

"It's Aunt Nettie versus Aunt Nellie. Isn't it."

"A bit." Ondi tossed her hair back.

"As if that's any sort of contest."

"It is, Nell, actually. It is," I said.

"I'm sorry?" Eleanor looked confused but then looked up and, I thought, winked at me.

Did I really see that? Or did I just want to believe she was struggling less than she was? I looked down at her knitting and noticed that the pattern she was knitting into her blue square repeated but wasn't an abstract pattern. It was letters. You could only see the bottom half of the letters as yet, but in a flash I realized what they were going to say—that they were a reminder to herself. MY NAME IS ELEANOR. MY NAME IS ELEANOR.

My name is Eleanor.

"And my daughter?" Eleanor said again.

"Here, Mom, it's me," said Gwen, touching her arm. "Right here. It's Gwen. Gwen."

"Gwen," said Eleanor. "Of course, it's you. My dear Gwennie."

Gwen began to cry.

"Don't cry." Eleanor put down her knitting, leaned in to wipe Gwen's eyes with the edge of her shawl, then looked up at Gwen's face. "Just remember what I always told you."

"What did you always tell me?"

"That I will be proud of you," said Eleanor. "I will be proud."

"Why?"

"Oh, I don't know. There will have to be some reason." She frowned. "I will be proud of your knitting, maybe. I know you'll make such warm things. In fact, I think you made this shawl."

"No, Mom. You made it. You made it for Ondi's family before they were Cast Off."

"Did I? But I don't know how to knit."

"Yes, you do. You do. You're knitting now."

"Oh, that's right." Her needles started to move again. "I don't remember but my hands remember. I'm glad I have some reading glasses. Thank you for bringing my reading glasses."

"But I didn't bring your reading glasses," said Gwen. "I don't think they're even yours."

"I brought them," said Ondi. And there was the gentleness again.

Eleanor began to nod off.

"Is she being drugged?" asked Gwen. "It's more than just the mall-truck food, isn't it."

Ondi frowned. "Maybe," she said. Then, "Yes."

"Because she wasn't cooperating."

"Yes."

"She knows you better than she does me," said Gwen.

"Well, she sees more of me," said Ondi. "I'll see if I can bring you more often. I don't know why I shouldn't be able to."

It was dusk. The chandelier came on; the EnforceBots closed in. We kissed Eleanor and hugged her gently.

"You can only imagine how many points they will get for"—I could hardly say the words—"for winnowing her."

"You know it will mean someone will pass the Final Test. Ondi, maybe." Gwen agreed, hunched over her tea. She gripped the cup as if it were a baseball.

"Who can then Cross Over permanently," I said.

For a long moment, neither of us could speak.

"So why don't they just do it is the question, right? And the answer, because Ondi herself has convinced them to hold off," Gwen guessed.

"But why would she do that?"

Gwen shrugged. "I don't know. Maybe she sees her Grandpa Barney in Mom and just can't do it herself—as she doesn't want them to know. Maybe she's trying to get someone else to do it for her."

"Or maybe she doesn't want it done at all?"

"We can hope."

"Would we be just kidding ourselves?"

"I don't know."

"Do you think she loves Winny?"

"No."

"Do you think she loves her father?"

"I think she wishes she could love him."

I thought. "If they . . . if they proceed, there won't be anyone to explain Ondi to herself."

"Making her *Homo regrettus* once again."

"Exactly." I could still see Ondi in the garden, her face turned to Eleanor like a plant growing toward the sun.

"Well, maybe she'll hesitate. Maybe she just likes being on the pitcher's mound, for once. Maybe she likes my having to catch whatever she throws."

"I wonder if Aunt Nettie knows."

"Kind of makes you want to AskAuntNettie, doesn't it?"

We left off.

We visited. Sometimes Eleanor seemed beyond communication; sometimes she could not even knit. But sometimes her fingers flew as if of their own accord. Her squares were for a blanket, it seemed, like the ones she had made for Ondi's family before they were Cast Off. Some were solid; others looked as if they were perhaps meant to bear phrases but as if she could not manage to form the letters.

"I let her into the kitchen," Ondi told us one day. "And what did she do?"

"She made a pie," I guessed. "Like the ones she used to make for League games."

"Apple." Ondi looked thoughtful.

Did Eleanor realize she was in danger of being winnowed? Was she, for all her confusion, deliberately reminding Ondi of their long relationship and deep ties?

Another day, Ondi said, "She calls me Gwen sometimes."

Gwen gazed at a painting, blinking hard.

"You've always been like a daughter to her," I said coolly. "Indeed, you've been like a member of the family to us all."

Ondi raised an eyebrow as if to say, *Nice try.* At the same time, she had to know, in her heart, that it was true.

◆

No one in the Resistance League was trying out for the Olympics. Now that they played against Netted teams, though, they knew many of the contenders for Team AutoAmerica; and so many hours did they spend brandishing their impassioned opinions as to who was a shoo-in and who not that it seemed a kind of sport of its own.

"I can tell you who I think should be coach," said Diego, for example.

Gwen knew, she said later, that it wasn't going to be Mabel or Andrea. Still, he took her by surprise.

"It should be that Net U coach—that guy who coached you. Coach Link. Everyone who sees him in action is like, whoa. What he gets out of his people. He's like some kind of super-accelerant."

Gwen couldn't disagree.

"He was pretty great," she said. "And he does coax stuff out of people they didn't know they had. Like he knows what tune to play. What chords to hit."

"People say he could convince a goose it's a hawk," said Diego. "The question is, What happens when it goes to catch something? And does that make him a saint or an asshole?"

Gwen laughed. "Good question."

Still, she was surprised when, a few days later, Woody really was named the Olympic team coach. And she was yet more surprised when he publicly insisted that the player he needed most sorely was she.

"Objectively, that can't be," she said. She rattled off the names of just a few of the potential relievers: Bento Halifax. Rube Foster. Warren Peese. Joe March. All of whom were trying out, and those were just the possibilities from Net U.

"Then why did he name you, do you think?" I asked her.

"Maybe they need a woman," she said miserably. "And, you know, I'm Blasian. Plus . . ." Her voice trailed off.

Was she still taking that MoveTheEffOn course? I hardly dared ask; it had been months now.

But she simply nodded.

"Because he won't let go," I guessed.

"Let's just say I've moved up to Level IV," she said.

Mimi arrived at our door with a look that suggested she hardly expected to be allowed in. But when we shook hands, I squeezed hers in thanks for her help.

"I don't know, I just get these spells," she said with a wink, then added somewhat formally, "Forgive me my predictability, but I have come to ask again whether Gwen might be willing to try out for the Olympics."

"You need to ask her yourself," I replied, only to find Gwen behind me.

"You've asked before," she began politely.

"Circumstances have changed."

Gwen hesitated, then admitted, "I guess they have."

"So the question is, Is your answer still an unequivocal no?" Mimi gazed over the top of her reading glasses, up into Gwen's face. Her two hands piled on top of her cane were the hands of a supplicant.

Gwen thought. "I don't know."

"Does that mean maybe?" Mimi straightened with excitement.

"I think it means I don't know."

"Okay, good enough. Let me see what I can do with that." Mimi pushed her glasses up onto her head. "Isn't anyone going to offer me some tea and cookies?"

The next day, Winny materialized. His hair was disheveled, and he carried no gun.

"Where's Gwen?"

They met out in the garden. The way they were standing, I could not hear them but I could see them—Winny gesturing and Gwen immovable. What they had in common was stamina. I would not have thought either of them could stand the other's company for two minutes, much less a half hour. But they stood and stood, drinking nothing and eating nothing, rooted like statuary.

When finally they emerged, Winny was frowning. Gwen, on the other hand, could hardly wait for the door to close and Winny to disappear. Then she stood by a deflector and whispered, "There's hope."

Would Eleanor really be let go if Gwen agreed to play in the Olympics? And did Ondi engineer the trade and why, and how much did Woody know, and had he deliberately overstated Gwen's value to give us leverage? There were so many questions. We didn't know whether to celebrate or to worry.

"But first things first." I tried to think. "Is this a trap? Can we trust Winny?"

"Winny."

Gwen tipped her cup back and forth, watching the tea slosh one way then the other. The teapot sported a crazy mélange of a cozy Gwen had crocheted when she was younger—an every-which-way of a thing made with an abandon unimaginable now.

"Winny," she said again.

"Of all people to have to trust."

"You said it."

She had been more excited than worried—for any sort of possibility to surface, after all!—but now she was more worried than excited. And something else—she was irritated. No, more. She was angry.

"Mom at his fucking mercy," she said.

I knew how she felt, and I wasn't even the one he had finally cornered. Was this payback for Gwen's refusal to accept Ondi's "help" back at Net U? Who knew. But for Winny now to be holding Eleanor hostage—Winny! The word "galling" did not capture it. I, too, could have put my hand through a wall at the thought. I, too, if I had the arm, could have thrown at his head.

Still, I was shocked when Gwen suddenly turned on me.

"So are you going to bug him?"

"Excuse me?"

"Why don't you bug him the way you bugged me?"

If I'd ever wondered what it was like to face the pitcher Gwen had become, I knew it now.

"I would," I said carefully, "if I could. If I thought our technical team up to it."

"But you think Winny and Ondi would know."

"Yes."

"And you thought I wouldn't?"

"Gwen—"

"I get it, you did it because you were scared," she said. "You were worried about me, the way you're worried about Mom now. But how could you think you would actually get away with it?"

"How did you know?"

"There are BugOut stations everywhere at Net U."

Strike.

"The sad thing about you is you think you know so much. When if you did once, you don't anymore."

Strike two.

"All you know are basement skills. How to spy, how to evade, how to detect. What would you do if you were allowed back out into the world? Would you even give up snooping? Or is that what you've become? A snooper like Aunt Nettie?"

I could not hang my head low enough.

But then, as suddenly as she'd begun, Gwen let up. It was as if she'd walked away from the mound.

"Oh my god. I'm so sorry. That was so mean," she said. "Mom would never have told you. No matter how upset she was. She would never have said those things."

"Don't worry. You are still your mother's daughter," I said woodenly. "Don't worry."

"I am not," she said, starting to cry. "I am not. Oh my god, her discipline. I am so not her."

"Gwen. Gwen. Don't cry." I managed to hug her even as I reeled. "I'm the one she would be angry at, if she knew. Not you. I was just—as you said—so worried. About Net U. About your being assigned a special room. About that coach."

She blew her nose. "You've always been paranoid."

I wanted to tell her that I took the ParentalParanoia quiz and only got a 6. But instead I said, "I think anyone would have been a little paranoid under the circumstances."

She blew her nose some more, then said, "I wish we could

bug Mom." She honked again. "Not that it would do any good. But if we could, we would, wouldn't we?"

"Of course."

"I don't think I knew what worry was before," she said. "Not really."

"And now?"

"God do I wish I was still my younger self." She honked. "My younger self who will never forgive you, as opposed to my older self who has no choice."

"Who not only has to forgive me but who has to deal with Winny Wannabe," I managed.

"Whose head I'd throw at if I could."

"Well, better to throw at your father's," I said.

Gwen looked at me a moment. Tears appeared in her lashes; her head bowed; her shoulders relaxed. Exit prosecutor, enter daughter.

"Touché," she said. Then she looked away as if to say, in an Eleanor-like way, *Enough*. And I agreed. Eleanor, after all. Eleanor in the hands of Winny. There was enough to be sick about. And the questions—the many questions. We tried to sort through them. To answer them. But, of course, there were no answers.

Did Eleanor, a bit the way that Gwen had a younger and an older self, now have a before- and after-self? Had the BioNet split her life in two? Lying in bed alone, I could not accept it.

Eleanor. Nell. Nellie. What have they done to you?

How was she getting through her nights? I did not run the white noisemaker and voice scrambler anymore, as there was no pillow talk to try to mask. Instead, I tried to send Eleanor my thoughts, as if having been married for so long, she would be able to receive them. And, irrational as it was, I was half convinced that she did receive them—that she was lying awake, and knew I was thinking of her, knew I was calling to her. And I believed that she was calling back to me and sending me strength—more strength than AskAuntNettie could ever give. Indeed, I felt I could hear her voice—*Sleep, Grant, sleep*—even as I whispered to her. *You, too, Nellie. Sleep.* And, after a moment, tonight: *Gwen forgave me, you know. Did I tell you? Gwen forgave me.*

Forgave you what, Grant? I could hear her asking.

And what a sad moment that was—how lonely-making. Because I could not explain—because it would be too ridiculous. We were in such different worlds. And so even though I wanted to say, *You should have heard Gwen talk. About her younger self who would never forgive me. About her older self who had no choice*—I did not. Instead I just said, *Never mind.* And, *Just sleep, please, Nellie. Sleep.* Because my poor Eleanor. My poor Nell. *Sleep*, I said, *Sleep.* And foolish as it sounds, I believed that she heard me and slept. I had to believe it. She slept.

◆

Gwen signed up for the tryouts. And—astonishingly—Winny made good on his word.

Then—as simply as if she had returned from a trip to the courthouse—there Eleanor stood, once again, in her study. Even the house seemed delighted.

Where have you been? It's been too long! it said.

And, *Would it have killed you to write? Would it have killed you to write? Would it have killed you to write?*

A software update, it seemed, with more compassion in its code, if a few glitches as well.

But never mind. The ceiling was covered with balloons. Champagne was being popped. The house was in a tizzy—*Mind you, don't hit the ceiling with that! If you hit the ceiling, you'll have to clean it yourself*—the assembled guests cheering so raucously that even Eleanor teared up a little. She looked tinier than ever, and below her high cheekbones now lay distinct hollows; she had lost so much weight. She stood perfectly upright, however, as she raised her chin and cleared her throat.

"Well, and now where were—"

She did not finish, as a banner was being unfurled with, WELL, AND NOW WHERE WERE WE? written in enormous purple letters. This was followed by a second banner reading, WE HAVE WORK TO DO.

She laughed. "You have literally taken the words right out of my mouth," she said.

Everyone cheered, and even the house chimed in, *No one took your words. They're right where you left them.*

More laughter.

Gwen and I watched anxiously. Did Eleanor seem herself? Or was she about to prove a mouthpiece of Aunt Nettie?

"It is part of Gwen's agreement that she should discourage us from pursuing our work as much as possible. But of course that phrase 'as much as possible' is open to interpretation," said Eleanor.

And as people cheered, I thought: Herself. She sounded like herself.

"I think Aunt Nettie imagines that she has shaken me up. And let me say—I have indeed been shaken up."

Murmurs of dismay.

"I think she imagines that she has taught me a lesson. And let me say—she has. She has taught me a lesson."

More dismay.

"And that lesson is: We must press on with everything we have."

Cheers.

"Give me liberty or give me death!" she cried.

That was a bit odd, and I could see Gwen thought so, too. But no one else seemed to notice. Confetti was strewn everywhere, and before Eleanor could continue, she was hoisted up into the air and paraded around the garden. Of course, Gwen and I were among the chief revelers. Eleanor was home! Eleanor was home! Eleanor was home! We hooted and cheered, and dared not ask, What next?

◆

As Gwen could not have been less interested in the Olympic try-outs, I accompanied her to the stadium, where, to our surprise, reporters accosted her as soon as she got out of the AutoLyft. Who were these people? And were they really there to talk to Gwen?

"Is it true your mother is out of detention?"

"Is it true they only released her because you agreed to pitch?"

"Is it true your mother is filing a suit even bigger than the Surplus Fields suit?"

Was all this thanks to Pink and Sylvie's GwenWatch? The two roommates had very different online styles—Sylvie's posts tending toward a disarming, just-thinking-aloud feel, with almost every post ending WDYT? while Pink's posts were like her serves, powerful and intent on scoring. Both of them had been posting continuously, though, riding on the twin horses of Gwen's popularity and Eleanor's fame: for thanks to the Surplus Fields suit, Eleanor had, it seemed, become a cult legend to both the Surplus and Netted teams. The result was tens of thousands of Sweets, or so we learned later. Our first inkling of the phenomenon only came with the reporters and the throngs of fans just beyond them, some of whom held signs saying things like, FUCK AUNT NETTIE, FREE AUNT NELLIE even though Eleanor was, in fact, already free, or at least not imprisoned in the way they imagined. Other fans waved pompons, shouting, *Go, Go, Gwen-nie! Save Aunt Nell-ie! Go, Go, Gwen-nie! Save Aunt Nell-ie!* while yet others chanted a call-and-response:

What does she deserve? Free-dom!
When does she deserve it? Now!
What does she deserve? Free-dom!
When does she deserve it? Now!

"Should I try to explain?" Gwen asked. But before I could answer she had already realized that all she could do was express her gratitude for the crowd's support.

"Thank you! Thank you!" she said, as I worked like a body-guard to usher her through the crush. I was afraid she would not make it to the gate or that someone would grab or yank her arm. Luckily, no one did, and though her progress was slow, she was largely able to keep moving, stopping only to hug Pink and Sylvie when she saw them.

"Thank you, thank you, thank you," she all but wept. And, "My mother is home for now"—that "for now" slipping out, she said later, before she had allowed herself to think it.

"We're doing everything we can," said Sylvie. Still more waif than protester, she shouldered an enormous FUCK AUNT NETTIE sign that she quickly volunteered Pink had made for her. Pink herself, meanwhile, had FUCK AUNT NETTIE tattooed across her forehead—hopefully, I thought, in henna.

"Thank you, thank you, thank you!"

Then Gwen was finally inside the stadium, a ball in her hand, warming up. Her focus was off; her balance was off. She was talking to her glove. But later she said that she pictured Eleanor sitting at that big table with the apple pie untouched in front of her, and everything came together. She was throwing at the Enforcers; she was throwing at the EnforceBots. She was throwing as if it were she with the stunner, not they. She was throwing to kill whoever had put that BioNet in Eleanor, and she was throwing at the neural lace itself, destroying every last cell of it. She was throwing at Winny and at Ondi—and she was throwing at Woody, too, she said later. She was throwing at them all. She was throwing at Aunt Nettie. I had never seen her so fiercely focused, and others, watching, commented that they pitied the ChinRussians already.

"Though I tell you—we're going to need her," said someone. And others said that, too. *We're going to need her. We're going to need her.*

"They have a greatly overblown idea of my importance," Gwen said on the way home. But she also acknowledged that she had thrown well. "I guess I've found my edge," she said.

As expected, besides Gwen, a number of her old Net U teammates made the team—Beetle Samsa and Bento Halifax, and Pietro Martinez. Rube Foster and Joe March, too. Ondi had declined to try out—knowing, she told Gwen, that even with her Upgrade, she wouldn't make it. But though they had long insisted they would not do so, upon hearing that Gwen had relented, a few of the Resistance League players had tried out in the end, too. So Diego and Gunnar were now on the roster, Diego in right field and Gunnar at second base.

All agreed that the whole affair was not sports but politics. As Diego bluntly said, "We're being used." Still, Gwen told me, each player had his or her own reason for playing. Gwen did not want to talk about hers, though Diego and Gunnar, of course, knew, and rolled up their sleeves when they saw her, that they might flash their Aunt Nellie tattoos. Had they joined expressly to support her and Eleanor? Gwen did wonder. And once they saw the Resisters' tattoos, other players asked Gwen if her mother wasn't the person in that case they thought they saw someone post something about.

"Like aren't those crazy fans out there because of your mom?" Bento Halifax asked in the dugout. "Isn't she the one who found the emanations in the Surplus Fields?"

"She didn't find the emanations," Gwen told him. "But she did set my father and his team to look for them."

"And that's why they locked her up, right? To shut her up before she did anything else?"

"Yes."

"And they only let her out because without you our goose is cooked."

She laughed. "I doubt that."

But Rube Foster said, "They let her out because there was so much publicity and because the Autonet could see the projections. And the projections said: a PR disaster."

Gwen shrugged.

"Which, by the way, you don't have to be a genius like the Autonet to see," finished Rube.

"What I want to know is, what happens after the Olympics?" said Joe March. "When the spotlight's off and the media goes away. What then? Does she go back in?"

"She's not going back in," said Bento. "Because when people find out, they're going to take to the streets. It's going to be the Automation Riots all over again."

Others shook their heads. The Netted weren't mad enough to riot, and the Surplus were not only RegiChipped but, people said, drugged.

"It's like a fire," insisted Bento all the same. "Nothing is burning until things catch on. And then even damp stuff burns, everything."

"Whatever." Rube maintained in any case that Eleanor was safe. "Because it will be even more of a PR disaster after the Olympics," he said, "when Gwennie here is a national hero."

"I'm not going to be a national hero," she said.

"A Surplus woman in the Olympics would be a celebrity in the making even if she didn't have blue hair," said Rube.

They were still arguing when Woody appeared. Did people realize that he was there to talk to her? Gwen didn't know, she told me later, but when he sat down next to her, her teammates suddenly all had reasons to be elsewhere.

"Show and tell," said Woody. "Close your eyes."

She refused.

"Come on, Gwen. Don't be a pill. That's coach's orders."

She closed her eyes.

"Now open."

She opened her eyes, stared at his forearm, and, when she saw the tattoo, was forced to smile a little.

"Like it or not, I am your mother's fan, too," Woody said. "And in that capacity, I am going to help you wing that ball. Because if you are here, you are here to bring the heat. Otherwise what leverage will you have?"

"You oversold me," she said. It was the kind of moment when she didn't want an answer from him or anyone else, she recalled— when all she wanted was to say what she was thinking. What she knew. When all she wanted was *to let herself out of the house,* my mother would have said. "You oversold me. And on purpose. You did it on purpose."

"I didn't, Gwen. Though just for the sake of argument, let's say that I did. Let's say that I oversold you to help your mother.

Because I believed in her and could see a way of helping her. Would that be unforgivable?"

Gwen didn't answer.

"Or what if I did it to redeem my own sorry ass? Would that be better or worse?"

She didn't answer that, either.

"Then again, it is possible that I simply gave my professional opinion of your capacities and their fit for Team AutoAmerica, and that you are soon going to prove me right, provided you acknowledge you're off in your timing."

She thought. "Rushing?"

He nodded. "Because you're upset, I think."

"Why would I be upset?" she said.

◆

At home, I irritated Eleanor.

"Why are you asking my team how I seem?" she demanded. "Is it not enough to be surveilled by Aunt Nettie and surveilled by the house? Do I really need to be surveilled by you, too?"

"Don't you yourself want to know whether you are the same Eleanor you were?"

"Of course, but next you are going to be bugging me in the name of love and protection."

Interesting.

"What do you think of Patrick Henry?" I asked.

"Come again?"

"How about Martin Luther King Junior?"

"Grant, if you are going to try to take a sounding, you should at least try more subtly."

It was Eleanor. Eleanor! My heart sang.

"Are you happy to be back working on the Mall Truck suit?"

"Oh, I don't know. Lately it occurs to me that we really must applaud the fact that the Surplus are getting free food, don't you think? The program may not be exactly what we'd like it to be, but our Basic Incomes are too low."

"I'm sorry?"

"People can't quite make ends meet. Do you know what I mean? So the mall trucks are quite a help."

"And—the suit?"

"I think you need to look at your data again. Don't you think?"

"Two labs have corroborated it."

"But didn't the results fail to quite match?"

"They are within one standard deviation of one another."

"I don't think that's going to stand up in court, Grant. Do you think?"

"Eleanor."

"I mean, it's a lot of trouble," she insisted. "It's a lot of time and effort to bring these things to trial. And, oh, I don't know. I don't want to waste everyone's time with anything less than unassailable. Do you think?"

It turned out she had even put Yuri, Heraldine, and Sue on hold, telling them she would let them know when she was ready to start working again.

"Eleanor," I said. "Nellie. What have they done to you?"

She looked at me blankly; her face had a preternatural calm. But a moment later, she cracked.

"I don't know, Grant," she said. And her voice then was the most shaken I had ever heard it.

I did not tell Gwen. I didn't see what there was to do but wait and see if Eleanor got better, and Gwen had enough to deal with. She fixed her timing problem, and pitched well in practice. Indeed, as several of her teammates commented, her cutter was proving so deadly, she probably could have gotten by on that one pitch alone. And yet as the Olympics began, she was not put on the field once. Pietro, Rube, and Joe March were all brought in as the Western Hemisphere round-robin progressed; even Bento saw action, which Gwen thought made sense. Bento had more off-speed pitches than he used to, and while he was not as versatile as she was, his fastball remained faster than hers. What's more, he was a better batter and, in the Olympics, pitchers batted.

"I told Woody he oversold me," Gwen reported, "and that now he has to keep me on the bench so people won't know. But he won't admit it. 'Do you trust no one?' he asked me. 'Is that the Surplus legacy?' 'With all due respect, Coach,' I said, 'I can see with my own two eyes that you have a fine southpaw reliever. You can argue that it's useful to have two even if the second only throws a mid-eighties fastball, but you can't argue that the second is essential to team success. And it's even harder to argue she's essential when you never take her off the bench.' "

That's when he apparently brought up Gwen's hesitation pitch.

"What does that have to do with anything?"

"One, it's our secret weapon," he said. "The Secret Weapon's secret weapon, if you will. And two, it can't be secret unless it's kept secret."

"You are full of shit," she told him.

"Baseball is theater," he said. "You have to plan your moments. Trust me."

"*Trust you?*" she said.

Eleanor was still saying odd things.

"What do you think?" she would say. And, "Oh, I don't know."

And, "I do just wish we could bug my mind. So we could know what's going on."

Bugging, bugging, bugging. Did she bring it up strangely frequently, or was that just my paranoia?

"I wish there were some way of bugging your mind, too," I admitted finally. And it was true. Because when I looked into Eleanor's eyes these days I was not always sure what or whom I was seeing. Was that she, in those familiar black pupils? And what was it in her that made her Eleanor? What was it, without which she had to be said to have morphed into someone else? Was it a soul? What a hard word that was to corral up with other words, and yet when I looked into her eyes, I knew that that was what I yearned to glimpse. Eleanor's soul. Eleanor.

To see her vulnerable was horrifying, and yet not as horrifying as the realization that I liked the closeness it brought—even that it made for better lovemaking. Sadder but stronger. Though who was I, that I might proceed to make love to a half stranger? Eleanor was becoming a person I did not want to know she could be; but so was I. My mother used to describe how, when she was a girl in Saint Emile, she would dive through the algae on the surface of a lagoon into the deep water below. And how wondrous it was down there, she said. *So dark, so cool.* But I always thought it sounded terrifying. Lightless and airless. A dimensionless space, a bottomless space. A disorienting space. And so the world seemed to me now.

I did not think Eleanor was being actively MindMelded. Perhaps the research center computer to which she was synced required a special cloud service, or perhaps there was some other reason that, theoretically linkable though she was, she wasn't linked. But just as she returned over and over to bugging, she returned over and over to the Mall Truck suit.

"Oh, I don't know, I think there's another side to the mall trucks," she would say. "Is it really so terrible if it makes people feel good?"

"Yes," I would say. "It is terrible."

To which she would say, "Oh, I don't know," until one day, she suddenly said, "It is indeed terrible." And then, "I can hear it."

"What can you hear?"

"I can hear it's not my voice."

That was the day she began to spar with the other voice—to argue with it. An effective strategy, it seemed, as the real Eleanor argued and the other Eleanor didn't.

"It always asserts something pleasant, pleasantly," she said.

"It would never throw a plate of bacon and eggs out the window."

"No. And it often starts, 'Oh, I don't know.' And ends, 'Don't you think?' Or, 'Do you know what I mean?'"

"Your favorite expressions."

"Oh, I don't know. I've always lived and died by what you thought. Do you know what I mean?"

We laughed.

The more she understood the voice, the more she fought it, until it began to seem a kind of inner fencing. As soon as she began a sentence in what she called First Person Timid, she would interrogate herself.

"And what is it you don't know, Ms. Oh, I don't know?" she would demand. She couldn't silence the voice entirely, though, and the struggle so exhausted her that I often found her not only napping but napping all curled up—something she had never done before—as well as going to bed right after dinner. Indeed, she sometimes could not even make it all the way through the meal. Still, the more she fought herself, the more herself she seemed until finally she found the will to reconvene her legal team.

"It's good to see you all," she said. "It's been too long. Where were we?"

Whether she was her old self or not, exactly, she was once again working on the Mall Truck suit.

. . .

Meanwhile, as Team AutoAmerica advanced against West Africa, Greater Cuba, and the European Union—and as ChinRussia beat the Saudi Sphere and AustraliaZealand—Gwen repeatedly asked why she wasn't being played. And what did that mean for Eleanor?

Woody kept to the line that he was trying to get everyone to forget about her.

"Well, that might be possible," she told him, "if there weren't ten thousand posts a day speculating as to what's going on."

"Maybe someone should suggest you're in a slump," he said. "Or if that's bad luck, why doesn't someone tell them you're a token."

"Ouch, Woody."

"Don't push me," he said. And, "You still don't believe I'm trying to help your mother, do you?"

◆

The ChinRussian baseball team was coed but you were hard-pressed to tell the men from the women. Happily, they weren't as large as the weight lifters or the rowers. Still, they were on average almost seven feet tall and might as well have been 3-D printed out of a granite composite. Standing next to one of them was like standing next to a building.

At the same time, they were oddly graceful. Even as they strolled around the ballpark, no one lumbered or jiggled, loose-limbed. Rather, they proceeded—bearing themselves with the easy dignity of athletic royalty. It was hard to say whether they were more Chinese or more Russian. They were almost all golden skinned—clearly the preference of their BioDesigners—and they all had densely packed groves of hair. These were sometimes straight, sometimes wavy, and sometimes rainbow-streaked, but mainly black. At the same time, their eyes varied from blue, to hazel, to green, to brown, to colors I'd never seen before. A red-orange, a pink-beige, a bright chartreuse—someone, it seemed, was having fun. Or were these unintended results? That wasn't, at any rate, the only way in which the players varied. Indeed, they looked designed to stand apart from one another, possessed as they were of hyper-differentiated temperaments. Even from across a field you could see that one was impatient and one easygoing. Another was humorous while his counterpart was humorless. For all the years of ChinRussian experimentation, control of such traits was as yet, it seemed, crude. What had happened to the international agreement that people would not reproduce after making such changes? Or that, if they did, they would use GonadWrap or NutCase? We could only hope that, long ago as the pact was reached, it was still being observed.

Meanwhile, the ChinRussians were formidable players. Gwen reported that in practice, they lined up to bat and, one after the other, swung perfectly. Then they lined back up and did it again from the other side. They also slid into bases with such smoothness it was hard not to think that gymnastic prowess had been successfully spliced into their genes. And they had, too, some form of RetinaZing, so that their catchers did not send visible signals to their pitchers. Instead, they just Zinged. Every now and then, a pitcher would give a slight nod or shake in reaction—unconsciously, it seemed. But there were no hand motions and no words.

And most eerily of all, they were unfailingly cheerful and collegial not only with one another but with opposing teams, both on the field and off. Even when they challenged an ump's call, it was in the most measured of tones. At one point, an ump clearly missed a call on a ChinRussian pitch—calling it a ball when anyone could see it was a strike. The ChinRussian coach approached the ump assertively; he spoke with his hands. He stood his ground. But he had all the passion of a man issued the wrong train ticket.

"I think that was ChinRussian for, 'A cow could be fucking its own calf and you wouldn't see it,'" said Pietro.

Was it GenetImprovement that made them behave this way, though? Or, what with the rebellion back at home, did the ChinRussians have no choice but to make sure they made no waves while abroad? The English-speaking players interviewed on NetScreen, Gwen and I noticed, all seemed greatly concerned about the unrest.

"We play for the health of our families," said one of them, a woman in a "Go Go Go"–printed bandanna—smiling even as her eyebrows contracted with worry.

The announcer looked sympathetic. "Do you mean play or pray?" he asked, his eyebrows equally contracted.

"Play," said the woman.

"The poor thing. She's just like me, worried," said Gwen, looking upward. It was dinnertime, and Eleanor was already asleep upstairs.

"It's hard not to worry," I said.

Eleanor was definitely better. But was she ever going to be herself again? And what did Gwen's continued bench sitting mean? Woody was clearly not going to say. We were desperate to collar Ondi or Mimi, but neither—no doubt because she knew we would ask what was going to happen after the Olympics—could be found.

As for whether the ChinRussians felt as much sympathy for Gwen as she did for them, it was hard to know. A couple of them, though, did post reactions to a social media story about Eleanor and Gwen. "She is a real daughter," wrote one in English. "We praise her to the heaven and hope her mother will be okay." And wrote another, "We pray her mom will bat one thousand."

Both ChinRussia and Team AutoAmerica made the final round, but the AutoAmericans were not optimistic about their prospects, and the first game did nothing to dispel their doubts. What with their enhanced musculature and switch-hitting, the ChinRussians hit many more home runs than Team AutoAmerica. What's more, their top gun, Vladimir Santiago, hit not one, but two grand slams, one in the third inning and one in the sixth. Before they faced him, Team AutoAmerica had heard that he hit .400 but had not quite known what to make of that number. Now they knew. As Pietro Martinez said glumly, "It means he knocks the covers off the balls and the balls off us."

"Why are we even playing these guys?" Gunnar shook his shaggy head.

And he, Gwen said, wasn't the only one wondering.

"We are here because we believe anything can happen in a ball game," answered Woody. "You can get a guy and all his stats but give him a stick to swing, and you still don't know what will happen."

"You mean, any two-bit player can up and hit a grand slam, you never know?" said Rube Foster.

"Yes," said Woody. "Now get out there before I get the pink lounge pants out."

And to everyone's surprise, game two went better. Team AutoAmerica may have only been getting base hits, but they were getting players on base, and the players were advancing. What's more, they were stealing more bases, perhaps because they ran even when the odds were against them—something that seemed to throw the ChinRussians off—as well as bunting in situations where it didn't necessarily make sense. And on defense, the Team AutoAmerica pitchers were eschewing fastballs in favor of their off-speeds: the ChinRussians, after all, could hit hundred-mile-an-hour balls no problem, and the faster the ball, the more likely it was to boomerang right out of the park. As they seemed to take an inning to adjust to a new pitcher, too, Woody's approach now was to switch pitchers as often as he could. And with all this, as well as a number of catches that could only be called miraculous, Team AutoAmerica managed to win the second and third games. They lost the fourth, but then, in a fourteen-inning fifth game, won again before badly losing the sixth.

The count, then, was three games each when, finally, in the last game, Woody started Gwen.

"You are the one," she told us later that he told her. "No one could have predicted you, and now no one can predict what you'll do. This is the moment. Go." And, "Do it for your mom."

The crowd roared and leapt to their feet when she took the mound. At last, the Daughter. The Secret Weapon. The Hidden One.

Can-non! Can-non!
Black Tea! Black Tea!
Can-non! Can-non!
Black Tea! Black Tea!

This was not in the Surplus sections. But the Surplus sections were way up in the nosebleeds. The Netted fans, whose seats were lower down and whose sections outnumbered the Surplus sections five to one, were another story.

"Ignorance, not malice," Gwen told her glove. She was a rock; she had to be. Their words washed over her.

. . .

Up until now, Eleanor and I had watched all the games on NetScreen, poised to run to the stadium if Gwen was called in. But finally, here we were at a live game. We were astonished by the crowds and the hawkers and the banners. And the noise!—we had never heard such noise. It had been windy in the morning, and some had hoped that the wind would continue since the ChinRussians, accustomed to Managed Weather, had seemed to struggle with the gusts. But the blasts were dying down, and while they could return, there was no knowing for sure.

Afraid that Eleanor would be recognized, Woody had arranged for us to enter the stadium via a back way, during the team introductions. And, as we all hoped, we had managed to take our seats without incident. Now, sitting in the first row behind the dugout, Eleanor was wearing dark glasses and a brimmed hat—just the sort of disguise that signaled *I am a disguise* but that nonetheless seemed to be working. Even sitting, as she was, right in front of me, the very most conspicuous person in the Netted section, no one seemed to pay her any mind. If only she were not wedged between Winny and Ondi's father, who, needing their laps for their SmartGuns, hogged their armrests with their elbows. Eleanor might as well have been stuck in a middle seat on a MoonJet full of football players: there she was, with a linebacker to either side. Happily, as if having anticipated this situation, she had brilliantly brought her knitting, which she now produced. To calm her nerves, she said—making it clear that any attempt to crowd her would result in the crowder being continually bumped and grazed by the needles' capped ends. It was a message only slowly absorbed, perhaps because both men were drinking. But eventually, she saw victory. They retracted their elbows.

Sitting behind her, I had to smile although, stuck as I was between Ondi and Jill, I hardly shared her situation. Quite the contrary, to a degree that took me a bit aback, I realized that though they had both lived among the coppertoned—indeed, had them-

THE RESISTERS

selves been coppertoned—for most of their lives, neither woman was now comfortable brushing elbows with me. Were people's sensitivities so quickly shaped by their rung on the social ladder? I was astonished. They did afford me the perverse satisfaction not only of fully occupying both my armrests, but of knowing that, if I so desired, I could encroach even farther on their space—that if I let my elbows drift, the women would, inch by inch, pull away, folding themselves in over their purses. And so, I will confess, I did, exploiting with relish my repellent force.

Still, I wished I were sitting next to Eleanor. And for all my anxiety around Eleanor's situation, just to watch Gwen's warm-up throws—just to watch her rock back and wind up then lunge and release as she always had, but at the dead center of this enormous bowl of humanity—was so deep a thrill that, had this been an old-time movie whose reel had suddenly jammed, we would not have demanded our money back. Gwen! Eleanor leapt out of her seat, cheering, as did I, and we weren't the only ones. The crowd thundered so loudly it was hard to make out what it was saying. I blessedly thought I heard just

Can-non! Can-non!
USA! USA!

But in any case, it wouldn't have mattered. Gwen looked down and when she looked up again, it was with her prosecutor face. She had a game to pitch.

The lead batter was an orange-eyed man with enormous shoulders. Gwen looked at him as though she, too, could RetinaZing. As for her message, it was one anyone could read. *I'm going to get you.* He raised his goatee as if to answer, *I'm not afraid of your fastball.* But it wasn't a fastball. It was her cutter. Strike one. Next

284

she served him another cutter, a little lower. Strike two. Then, just when he may have thought he knew what was coming: a two-seam fastball. He walked away from the plate with his goatee held high but his eyes cast down.

Two more batters followed. And just like that, it was three up, three down—the first inning. I did think my heart might burst with pride, even as I thought, inexplicably, of the word "dispense"— a word I had never been able to quite get across to my students, way back when. If only they could have come to this game. Then they could see how a pitcher might "dispense" with the batters. Meanwhile, people were back on their feet, cheering, as was I. Only Ondi still sat, her fingers flying over her handphone.

"She's working!" she said. "The Secret Weapon is working! Go, Gwen!"

Normal enough behavior. Of the crowd, only Eleanor and I could appreciate how ironic it was, actually, for Ondi to be cheering her old friend on in this apparently wholehearted way. Was there a nefarious postgame scheme in the offing? Maybe it was paranoid to think so; certainly, Ondi gave no sign. In fact, eyeing her from the next seat, I thought her extra-sharply absorbed in the way that people are when they have a special investment in a game—as maybe she felt she did, having done so much to get Gwen out there? In any event, she was looking down as much as up, maybe more.

"The ChinRussians can hit a fastball of any speed, but they don't know what to do with Gwen," she said. Was she speaking to me and Jill or reading what she had just read or Sweeted? I couldn't tell.

"She's killing them," I said. Jill agreed.

"Go, Gwen!" she cheered. She squeezed the sides of her daisy-dotted handbag.

In the next half inning, Team AutoAmerica did not score but did at least get a couple of hits. Then Gwen returned to the mound. She threw a curveball, a fastball low and inside, and a changeup. The strikes began to accumulate. And then she'd done it again. Nine throws, no hits, no walks; the stadium was roaring. Just as Ondi said, the ChinRussians truly did not know what to do with her.

"Do you know what she's going to throw?" I asked Ondi. "Because I'm not sure I do."

Ondi looked up from her handphone long enough to toss her hair back and answer. "I did see most of those pitches coming. Not all of them. But I can tell you what I'd probably call, and I can tell you what I know she'd shake off, and I can tell you whether she was likely to try something new or fall back on the tried-and-true. I don't always know what the new pitch will be. And I don't always know what the safer bet would be. But, yeah, I have some idea what she'll do." Her head curved back down, her attention contracting so exactly to the size and shape of her screen that it was as if someone had selected "Attention" and then hit "Fit to screen."

"It's a good thing you're not in a position to tell the ChinRussians," I joked.

She shrugged. "Why would I do that?"

She Sweeted on.

Gwen gave up no hits in the third inning.

She gave up no hits in the fourth.

"Per-fect game," the crowd was chanting. "Per-fect game! Per-fect game! Per-fect game!"—something I found a bit jarring. Long ago, no one ever dared utter a word if a perfect game was in the offing, for fear of jinxing the pitcher. But there it was; times had changed. And in the meanwhile, Team AutoAmerica was hitting steadily: One single. Another. Another. Other games of the series had also resembled the tortoise and the hare. But in this one the tortoise was sure enough slowly scoring. Even Gwen managed a base hit, helping to bring a teammate home. Team AutoAmerica had one run. Two runs. Three.

It was a game like none of the others, a miracle.

Gwen gave up no hits in the fifth inning. In the sixth.

The stadium was thundering so loudly that had someone in an orbiting SpaceHotel reported hearing the crowd, I would not have been surprised. I could hear that some of the Netted were still yelling *Black Tea! Black Tea!* But mostly they were chanting, as were the Surplus and as were we,

Gwen-nie! Gwen-nie!
USA! USA!
Gwen-nie! Gwen-nie!
USA! USA!

We had already shouted ourselves hoarse but of course continued shouting all the same, voice or no voice. Indeed, even Winny and Nick were cheering—like Ondi's enthusiasm and Jill's, a reassuring sign, I thought.

By the seventh-inning stretch, the score was 5–0 and the game seemed, as Nick commented, AutoAmerica's to lose.

"Oh, I don't know," said Eleanor as, packing up her knitting bag, she stood to go to the bathroom.

I wanted to accompany her but Winny insisted on the honor, and she acquiesced graciously.

"It can't be 'Give me liberty or give me death' over everything," she said.

"I just thought you might like to be able to go to the bathroom without an armed guard," I said.

"Oh, I don't know." She shrugged. "Do you want anything?"

"Oh, I don't know." I shrugged back. "Maybe a CreamShake? What do you think?"

If she noticed my use of First Person Timid, she gave no indication.

287

"CreamShakes are full of sugar," she said. "But all right. If I survive the line at the ladies' room, I will brave the drinks line as well."

And off she and Winny went, laughing.

Team AutoAmerica was up at bat now but not doing well; Ondi, Jill, and I watched in dismay. Had their luck turned? And by the third batter, Winny and Eleanor still hadn't come back.

"Where are they?" Looking up from her handphone, Ondi leaned forward and tapped on her father's shoulder with her silver nails.

Nick mumbled something.

She tapped again.

"What?" he barked.

"Where are they?"

"Gone fishing, I expect," he said, more clearly. He threw his head back, emptied his bottle, stood, and headed unsteadily back into the stands. Jill looked concerned.

"Go with him," she told Ondi.

But Ondi shook her head. "I don't want to miss the game. You go."

Jill hesitated.

A pop fly. Team AutoAmerica was retired.

"Where are Eleanor and Winny?" I said.

Ondi frowned but did not answer. If she was at all disconcerted, it wasn't so disconcerted that she stopped Sweeting as Gwen, back on the mound at the top of the eighth, dispensed with the first batter. The second batter connected with the ball—a foul. Then he hit another foul, and another, and another, and another, and another, and another—an astonishing seven fouls in all before finally she struck him out. Next, the third batter, too, managed to get a bat on the ball, sending it deep into right field. It was just lucky that Diego, sliding on his stomach as the ball came over his shoulder, managed to catch it, his glove outstretched on the ground. I remembered having seen him do this once before, while playing for the Underground League—his glove like the pan of a frying pan, and the ball a fried egg. But to see it done in the Olympics! He clambered to his feet and, Diego-style, kissed the ball before sending it back to Gwen. The crowd was in a frenzy. *Di-eg-o! Di-eg-o!* it chanted as the replay went up on the screens and the announcer announced, "And ladies and gentlemen, that was Diego Smith, of Team AutoAmerica, making a catch for the history books!" I could not believe Eleanor had missed it. The Lookouts were here, as were just about all the Leaguers, and the League technical team, and Eleanor's legal team, but still. Where was Eleanor? And if only the ChinRussians didn't now continue to connect with the ball, as though they'd somehow adjusted—as if they had finally found a way to predict Gwen. It did not bode well for the ninth inning.

Ondi seemed tense, but as the ChinRussians retired Team AutoAmerica in short order she was no longer Sweeting.

Where was Eleanor?

"I'm going to look for them," I said.

"No," said Ondi. "You stay here."

And to my amazement, she sprinted up the stairs and out of the section, reappearing, a minute later, right below our seats, in the AutoAmerica dugout. How did she talk her way down there? And where was Eleanor? Where was Winny? Where was Nick?

Top of the ninth. Still 5–0, Team AutoAmerica, with three batters to go. The first batter up was batting lefty. Gwen threw a curveball with a wicked drop. Strike. Next, she threw a fastball, high and tight. The batter flailed—strike two. And then, of all things—almost for fun, it seemed, though in truth it was a bit of a risk—she threw a knuckleball. Renata's pitch, and a pitch Gwen wouldn't want to be defined by, but nothing anyone would have expected. Strike three.

Two outs to go. There was a lot of grumbling when the next

pitch was called a strike, but there it was. Strike one. As for the next throw, that would have been a strike before the strike zone was shrunk but was now called a ball. Was that in compensation, conscious or unconscious, for the first call? Gwen showed no sign of irritation but there was no ambiguity about what followed: two clear strikes, one on either side of the plate.

Now Team AutoAmerica needed just one more out to win. The noise in the stands was so loud that the stadium itself seemed to be roaring.

Enormous and golden skinned as any of the ChinRussians, Vladimir Santiago was originally from the Dominican Republic but more recently from Moscow. He had hit five home runs already this series, including those two early grand slams, and of the various exaggerated types presented by his team, he was the player begging to be called flamboyant. He sauntered up now to home plate holding the bat by its knob; he swung it like a cane. Then he stopped and upended it so it stood straight up from his open palm, balancing it like a magician. The crowd roared as he dropped it down into his two hands and took his batting stance, winking at Gwen and chewing gum. Since she had struck him out twice before in the game batting lefty, he was now batting righty. A recommendation an algorithm might make, but a mistake, as Gwen said later. Figuring he was a bit slower batting on this side, she fed him a fastball, low and away. And, sure enough, he was late on the pitch. Strike one. Then—having, she hoped, shaken his confidence in his decision to switch sides, and figuring he was probably left-eye dominant—she snagged him with a changeup. Strike two.

Now he was glaring as if his Zing could kill; it could be the last pitch of the game but he was not going to go quietly. He pushed his gum to the front of his mouth so that it protruded lewdly; he bobbled it tauntingly up and down. At the same time, he choked up on the bat for better control, squatted a bit to shorten up his stride, and moved closer to the plate to help cover outside pitches. So he was on the defensive but also almost daring Gwen to throw inside, where her slot was so tight she could well hit him—which she would not have minded doing, of course, except that it would put him on base.

She took his dare and threw a front hip cutter.

Foul.

She did it again.

Foul.

Should she try it a third time? Could she do it without hitting him? Was it time to try something else?

Woody called a time-out.

Woody's jog out to the mound was surprisingly leaden for a coach whose pitcher was poised to win the Olympics with a perfect game. He might be in his twenties but perhaps he really was, I thought, too old for Gwen. The infield came in, and you could see them all starting to confer animatedly. Where was Eleanor to witness this?

Whatever they were saying, Woody did not seem to be listening, and indeed maybe could not even hear them over the din of the fans.

> *Finish 'em up! Finish 'em up!*
> *Gwen-nie! Gwen-nie!*
> *Finish 'em up! Finish 'em up!*
> *Gwen-nie! Gwen-nie!*

The chanting was so loud, children were crying, and even many adults were holding their hands over their ears, including me.

But what mattered, of course, was—could Gwen hear? Though maybe it didn't matter. Because, as Gwen told me later, she knew perfectly well what Woody was about to say, at last: *The hesitation pitch. Use your hesitation pitch.* Or maybe, if he didn't want the infielders to understand, *Think Satchel*. Or maybe even just, *Hesitate. Hesitate, Gwen. Hesitate.*

Instead he said, "Eleanor's gone."

"What?"

"Eleanor's gone," he said again.

Gone? Gone where? What was he saying? That Eleanor had gone to the bathroom. That Winny had accompanied her. That Ondi had thought they'd come back, but that they hadn't. That Ondi's father was gone now, too. That Ondi had rushed down into the dugout to tell him.

"Send in a sub." Handing the ball to Woody, Gwen started running.

The infielders were stunned.

Then Gunnar Apple said, "I'm not playing for frigging Aunt Nettie."

And as Woody ran to catch up to Gwen, first Gunnar and then the other infielders ran toward the dugout, too, shouting over their shoulders, "They've taken Aunt Nellie! They've taken Aunt Nellie! They've taken Aunt Nellie! They've taken Aunt Nellie!"

For a moment, no one else moved. Then Diego was coming in from right field and the rest of the team was shouting and leaving, too. The fans watched in disbelief as those with tattoos waved their arms high. "They've taken Aunt Nellie! They've taken Aunt Nellie!" they shouted. "They've taken Aunt Nellie! They've taken Aunt Nellie!"

What was happening? Some fans began to boo, but the Resistance Leaguers in the stands began chanting, "Down with Aunt Nettie! They've taken Aunt Nellie! Down with Aunt Nettie! They've taken Aunt Nellie!" Then the Surplus fans rose to their feet and took up the chant, and some of the Netted fans, too. Vladimir Santiago chewed his gum, leaning on his bat as the AutoAmericans ran by; the ChinRussian coaches stood confused at their bases, waiting for a Zing. The ChinRussian players, though, were already abandoning their dugout, some of them headed for their locker room but some of them running out onto the field to help the AutoAmericans as EnforceBots swarmed down onto the field. Players from both teams now swung at the Bots with their bats. Then the pitchers from both teams were pitching balls at the Bots, too, with the FieldBots dutifully supplying fresh balls. Vladimir Santiago was swinging as well, and people were stealing the EnforceBots' guns even as human Enforcers on AeroBikes appeared, and then a squadron of AttackDrones.

Ondi was in the locker room when Gwen ran in.

"Where's my mother?"

"Winny has her."

"And where are they?"

"I don't know. But my father's gone, too. I think they're going to Cast her Off."

"No." Gwen panted. "No."

"I don't know for sure. But he said they were going fishing. I tried to send a signal. You probably saw it."

"That eighth inning. I knew it was you."

"I Sweeted what I thought you were going to do."

"Signaling you could throw the game."

"Yes. If she wasn't let go. But she didn't come back. Maybe it was too late."

Gwen looked at her. "They tricked you, didn't they? Your dad and Winny. They tricked you."

Ondi didn't even have to nod. They both knew what had happened—that Ondi couldn't go along with the plan and that, because she had hesitated, Winny and Nick had taken Eleanor midgame.

"We've got to find the boat," said Gwen. "Where's my dad?"

"I don't know."

"Then we have to go ourselves. Do you have any—"

Suddenly there came a calm voice.

"Please."

It was Eleanor, disheveled and bleeding down her right side. Woody was holding her up and carrying Winny's SmartGun.

"Oh my god," said Gwen.

"Go see if Fishman's in the men's locker room," Woody said. Ondi ran out as Woody helped Gwen lay Eleanor on a bench. He found the first-aid kit and unwrapped a large PressNStop, which Gwen pressed to Eleanor's wound.

"How do you feel? Does this hurt?" she asked.

Eleanor winced.

"I'm sorry, the bleeding." Gwen broke out a second PressN-Stop to replace the first, which had soaked through. Woody rolled up a towel for a pillow.

"Not there," said Ondi.

Woody ran to check the dugout himself.

"What happened? We were worried you got Cast Off," said Gwen.

"That was the plan." Eleanor's voice was low but clear.

"Did Winny shoot you?"

"He did."

Woody burst back in. "I can't find him. I called a MediLyft."

Gwen nodded, then asked him, "And you got the gun away?"

"From Winny? She got it herself."

Eleanor smiled weakly.

"Did you shoot him?" asked Gwen.

"I don't know how to shoot. But I had—" Eleanor winced again. "A knitting needle."

"You didn't."

The corners of her mouth lifted. *"En garde!"*

Everyone had to laugh.

"After you were just shot?" Gwen couldn't believe it.

"I have two lungs. He only. Hit one."

Gwen turned to Woody. "And you found her . . . ?"

"The ChinRussian coach asked if there was a back way out of the stadium, to get his team out. So I showed him. And there was Eleanor stabbing Winny."

"Did you kill him?" Gwen tried to ask this coolly.

Eleanor didn't know.

"The ChinRussian coach asked if he should call their doctor, and I said yes," said Woody. "But Winny looked pretty bad."

"And you didn't wait for their doctor?"

"It was going to be a while, and your mom could walk. Of course, it was still a risk—these lung punctures can head south in a moment. But I figured we were still better off finding Fishman, especially since their doc was going to have to take care of Winny first."

Gwen nodded. Outside, they could hear sirens, and shouting, and shots, and explosions, and what sounded like someone singing "The Star-Spangled Banner."

"And where's Dad? Does anyone know?"

"He had his team. Come ready," said Eleanor.

"Paranoid as he is," said Gwen.

"Yes."

"Look." Ondi held up her handphone. "Someone's launched a counterattack."

"You see," said Eleanor.

"Look at the streets!" Ondi held up her handphone again.

"The Mall Truck Riots," said Woody.

"Wow, and it says here the ChinRussians refused to take the game," said Ondi.

Woody, his eyes on Eleanor, gave a nod as if to say he knew.

"I don't. Like riots," said Eleanor. "But. Give me liberty. Or give me death!"

Was that the real Eleanor or her BioNet? They weren't sure until she winked.

"Stay still," said Gwen sternly.

"Look!" Ondi held up her handphone. And there, in the middle of everything, was the Thistles' coach, Andrea, her hair grown back in. "After the MediLyft comes, we can go help."

"Yes," said Eleanor, clearly. "Go." Then she looked at Ondi and, weakly reaching out, said, "I had. Faith."

Ondi took her hand and started to cry. "Thank you."

"I knew," said Eleanor. "I knew." She closed her eyes.

"Eleanor!" said Woody.

She opened her eyes—startled, it seemed. But then, turning pale, she started to wheeze out a fine mist of blood. The mist turned into droplets, and the wheeze turned into a cough.

"Crap," said Woody.

Gwen felt her wrist. "Hang in there, Mom. The MediLyft is coming. Hang in there."

Eleanor blinked, but she was very pale and her breath was short.

"Hang in there, Mom," said Gwen again. "Hang in there. Hang in there. I love you so much."

The MediLyft arrived.

"Love. You," Eleanor whispered.

"Mom, hang on," said Gwen. "You've got to hang on. The MediLyft is here."

"Grant," she said. "Love."

"Mom," said Gwen. "Mom!"

But her eyes had closed and she was coughing up clots, and she died before the medics could reach her.

◆

There were too many people to fit in the garden; it was just lucky that, despite the rioting, we were able to find a Surplus field for the funeral. For Woody was coming, and all of the Underground Leaguers and their parents, and Mabel and May, and Eleanor's legal team. Mimi was coming, too, and the League Technical Team, not to say Pink and Sylvie and Eugenie the hockey goalie, and Eugenie's roommate, Anna. Indeed, it seemed even the house would have come, had we invited it; for even the house was in mourning, saying over and over,

Something is not right. Something is very wrong.

And, *Something is missing. Something is not right.*

To which, we could only say, Yes. Something is missing. Something is not right.

And, Yes. Something is missing. Something is very wrong.

Eleanor's coffin was covered with an enormous baseball made of flowers and carried through an arcade of crossed bats. The procession went from home plate, to first base, to second, to third, then back to home, where the backstop was covered with wreaths. Children shooed away the geese; in the distance we could hear shouting and the crackle of small explosions as a choir group sang "Take Me Out to the Ballgame." I spoke, wearing the baseball jacket that Gwen had knit for me. Gwen spoke. And then dozens of other people spoke, from Yuri and Heraldine and Sue to May and Diego and Gunnar. Some of the league parents spoke; all four of the kids involved in the Surplus Fields case spoke. And Ondi, who had dyed her hair back to red and gold in Eleanor's honor, spoke, too. All expressed awe and love and gratitude, but many were angry as well.

Look what they did to her, they said. *Look.*

And, *Now. In her memory. In her honor. We must do something. Now.*

Andrea was especially eloquent in her appeal. *Now,* she said. *Now. Now.*

Now.

And, of course, I heard her. Gwen heard her. But all we could do was mourn.

We buried Eleanor's ashes in the garden. Then we cried the way you cry when the unimaginable has happened, for no reason anyone will ever be able to give, and when all the world is poorer for it, but you most of all. We cried the way you cry when you would much rather have died instead; we cried the way you cry when your loss is both wholly unfathomable and the simplest of facts. Eleanor was gone. Three words whose meaning I would never have been able to convey to my students, unable as I was to understand them myself. Eleanor, gone. How could these words be equivalent? Because of the linking verb? No. It was not possible. No.

There's no forgetting what you can't forget, said the house.

And, *Rage, rage against the dying of the light.*

Yes, we said then. We're raging. And, What a light.

The days had to be pulled on to advance, and even then would only advance bit by bit. Gwen and I knew we should be mobilizing in Eleanor's memory but in fact could do nothing. We could not even keep the garden up, disappointed as we knew Eleanor would be in us if she knew. What a revelation that it mostly kept on growing just the same, indifferent.

But finally, Mimi started to come help—to harvest, to stake, to divide. To tidy up what she called Eleanor's garden. And Gwen and I joined her, seeing as how we didn't have a choice: we couldn't leave it to an old woman to manage everything alone. And so when she came, we followed her out. We raked, we picked, we cleared, we mulched. Afterward we poured her some hibiscus tea with mint, which she called Eleanor's Tea—surprising her, one day, with some of Eleanor's Cookies. These Gwen then began to make if we knew that Mimi was coming, but also to have on hand if anyone else dropped by. Would you like some of Eleanor's Cookies? I said. Would you like some of Eleanor's Tea?

Finally, at long last, we returned to Eleanor's work. Of course, Eleanor's team did most everything. Still, they needed Eleanor's study to meet, and since no one would sit in Eleanor's seat, and since there wasn't a spare seat for Gwen, that became Gwen's seat. And since they all had their roles but needed someone to hold their toes to the fire, that became Gwen's job. She did not like to be called her mother's daughter, and felt keenly that she was not. But she sat in Eleanor's seat, and brought everyone to order. And when she lost her place, she said, *Now, where were we*—not meaning to echo Eleanor. But there they were—her mother's words. She had her mother's resolve, too, and her mother's cool, and her mother's spine—which is to say, perhaps, her mother's mound presence.

I could only hope now that she would not attract her mother's distinguished treatment as well.

In the meanwhile, Woody helped. Pink and Sylvie helped. I helped. Ondi—often wearing the glorious baseball scarf that Gwen had made for her—helped. And Diego, who had recently started seeing—happy surprise—Ondi, helped. And slowly, then not so slowly, the work began moving forward again. Countrywide, the riots went on and on. Day after day, week after week, people rioted. *Workless, not worthless,* they shouted while we marshalled our evidence and prepared to file our suit. Aunt Nellie vs. AutoAmerica, this was. The Mall Truck case.

◆

The days were better now. Little by little, better. At night, though, Gwen and I still moved about as if underwater.

"Grief deranges," Gwen would say.

"Healing is slow," I would answer.

And sometimes that would be it, although sometimes we would cry and cry. *Where did she go?* And, *Isn't she coming back?* She has been gone long enough, we agreed. It was time for her to come back.

But she did not come and did not come.

Instead, one day, as Gwen was working through some piles of paper, Woody came, as he often did, to the door. I did not turn him away, and when he stood in the study door, Gwen did not, either.

"It's time for me to go back," he told her. He gave a wry smile. "I have a lot to explain—so much that I don't know how I'm going to, really."

"Then don't," Gwen said.

"Don't explain?"

She didn't answer. But this time, when he produced the hat he had made her, she let him put it on her head, where it looked most wonderfully silly.

I left quickly then, but not before I heard, "I'll come back any-time. Just tell me when."

To which, she said, "Okay," followed by something I could not hear.

"Who what when where how why," he said.

And she echoed, "Who what when where how why."

"Who is us," he said. "And when is now."

As for the rest, I didn't hear that, either, because I wasn't lis-tening.

Long, long ago, my mother observed that the first thing she always asked about water was where it came from. Because she was from an island, she said, where water did not come out of fau-cets. And so people asked, Did it come from the mountains? Did it come from the clouds? And when my mother first met Eleanor, she said, That's where Eleanor came from—from the mountains.

From the clouds. Eleanor was not from a stagnant pool. She was from a flowing source, my mother said. A fresh source. She could see it. And, of course, my mother was right.

And now I just wished she could see Gwen—Gwen who, like Eleanor, flowed from the mountains and the clouds. And I wished I could tell Eleanor, too. *Nell,* I wanted to say, *she's happy. She's okay. You should see her.* For how Eleanor would have wanted to know, I knew. And, irrational as it sounds, I did think she could hear me. Because if anyone in the world of the dead could hear the living, it would of course be Eleanor. And so I told her. *She's everything we hoped for, Nell—you would be so proud.* Because it was true. She would be. *Of course, the world still needs resisters—lots of them,* I said. *And Gwen's getting rusty there in the office. She needs to get out on a mound. But rest in peace, Nell—rest in peace. You should see! Somehow we did it, Nell. I don't know how. We miss you. But you know, we pitched a perfect game.*

Acknowledgments

Deepest thanks to my many patient, generous, and helpful readers, including Dan Bogdanow, Carol Cashion, Mark Fishman, Martha Fishman, Allegra Goodman, Jane Leavy, Allison Mankin, Martha Minow, Marcy Murningham, Bill Nowlin, Louise Radin, Paul Schacht, and Mira Singer. Without you all I would have hit a great many more foul balls.

I am grateful beyond words to the many dedicated people at Knopf on whose support and expertise I have long relied, especially Ann Close, LuAnn Walther, Victoria Pearson, Amy Ryan, and Todd Portnowitz. I cannot thank you all enough.

And, of course, I thank with all my heart my devoted husband, David, and my inspiring children, Luke and Paloma, whom I see in every line of this book. You two are a mother's dream—a field on a summer's day, with the bases loaded and the game far from lost.

A NOTE ABOUT THE AUTHOR

Gish Jen is the author of four previous novels, a book of stories, and two works of nonfiction. Her honors include fellowships from the National Endowment for the Arts, the Guggenheim Foundation, the Radcliffe Institute for Advanced Studies, and the Fulbright Foundation, as well as the Lannan Literary Award for fiction and the Mildred and Harold Strauss Living Award from the American Academy of Arts and Letters. She lives with her husband and two children in Cambridge, Massachusetts.

A NOTE ON THE TYPE

This book was set in Scala, a typeface designed by the Dutch designer Martin Majoor (b. 1960) in 1988 and released by the FontFont foundry in 1990. While designed as a fully modern family of fonts containing both a serif and a sans serif alphabet, Scala retains many refinements normally associated with traditional fonts.

Composed by North Market Street Graphics,
Lancaster, Pennsylvania

Printed and bound by Berryville Graphics,
Berryville, Virginia

Designed by Soonyoung Kwon